BIRTHRIGHT

VOLUME ONE
HOMECOMING

IMAGE COMICS, INC.
Robert Kirkman *Chief Operating Officer*
Erik Larsen *Chief Financial Officer*
Todd McFarlane *President*
Marc Silvestri *Chief Executive Officer*
Jim Valentino *Vice-President*

Eric Stephenson *Publisher*
Ron Richards *Director of Business Development*
Jennifer de Guzman *Director of Trade Book Sales*
Kat Salazar *Director of PR & Marketing*
Corey Murphy *Director of Retail Sales*
Jeremy Sullivan *Director of Digital Sales*

www.imagecomics.com

Emilio Bautista *Sales Assistant*
Branwyn Bigglestone *Senior Accounts Manager*
Emily Miller *Accounts Manager*
Jessica Ambriz *Administrative Assistant*
David Brothers *Content Manager*
Jonathan Chan *Production Manager*
Drew Gill *Art Director*
Meredith Wallace *Print Manager*
Addison Duke *Production Artist*
Vincent Kukua *Production Artist*
Tricia Ramos *Production Assistant*

SKYBOUND
www.skybound.com

Robert Kirkman *CEO*
Sean Mackiewicz *Editorial Director*
Shawn Kirkham *Director of Business Development*
Brian Huntington *Online Editorial Director*
June Alian *Publicity Director*
Rachel Skidmore *Director of Media Development*
Helen Leigh *Assistant Editor*
Michael Williamson *Assistant Editor*
Dan Petersen *Operations Manager*
Sarah Effinger *Office Manager*
Nick Palmer *Operations Coordinator*
Lizzy Iverson *Administrative Assistant*
Stephan Murillo *Administrative Assistant*

International inquiries: *foreign@skybound.com*
Licensing inquiries: *contact@skybound.com*

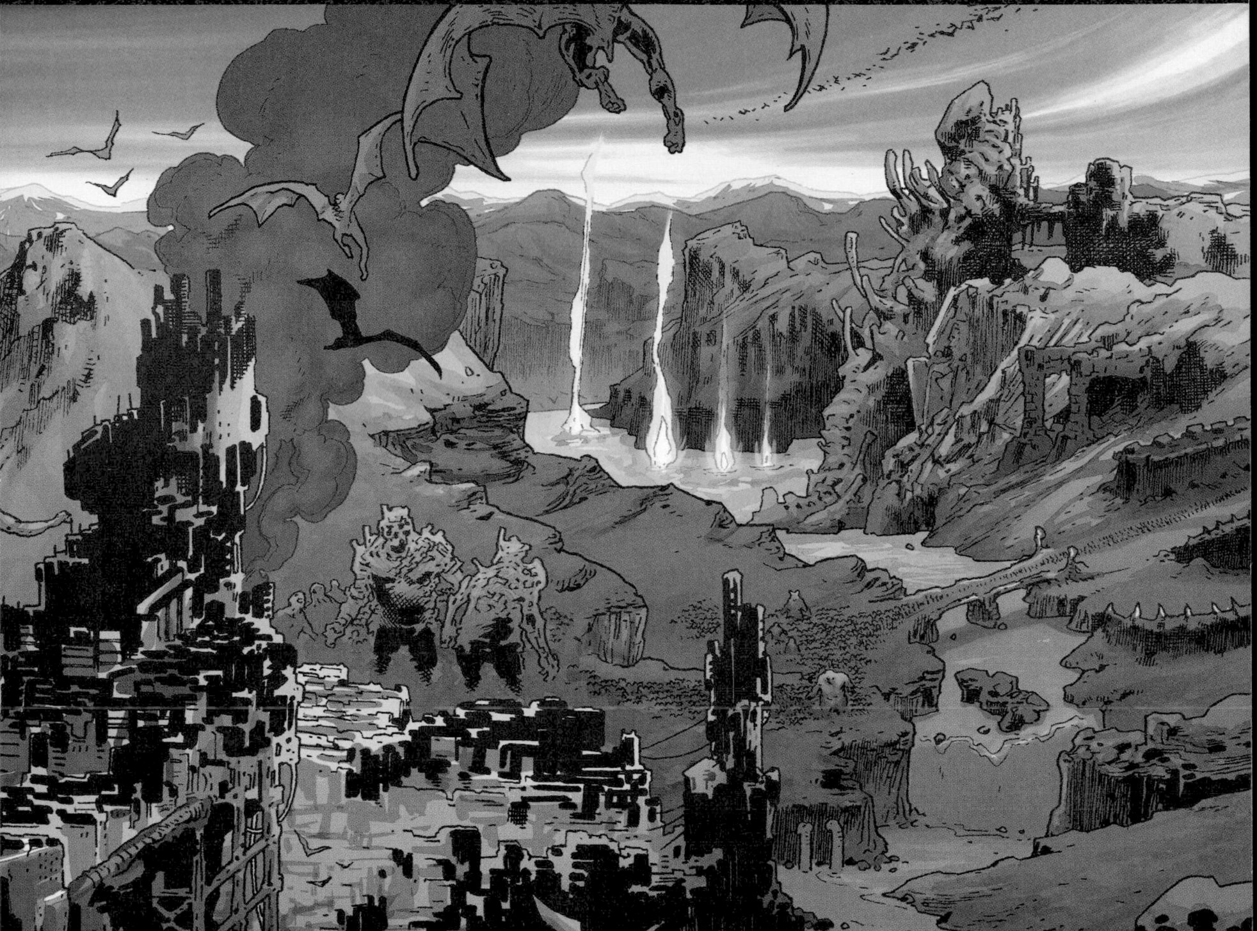

Joshua Williamson
creator, writer

Andrei Bressan
creator, artist

Adriano Lucas
colorist

Pat Brosseau
letterer

Helen Leigh
assistant editor

Sean Mackiewicz
editor

logo design by **Rian Hughes**

cover by **Andrei Bressan** *and* **Adriano Lucas**

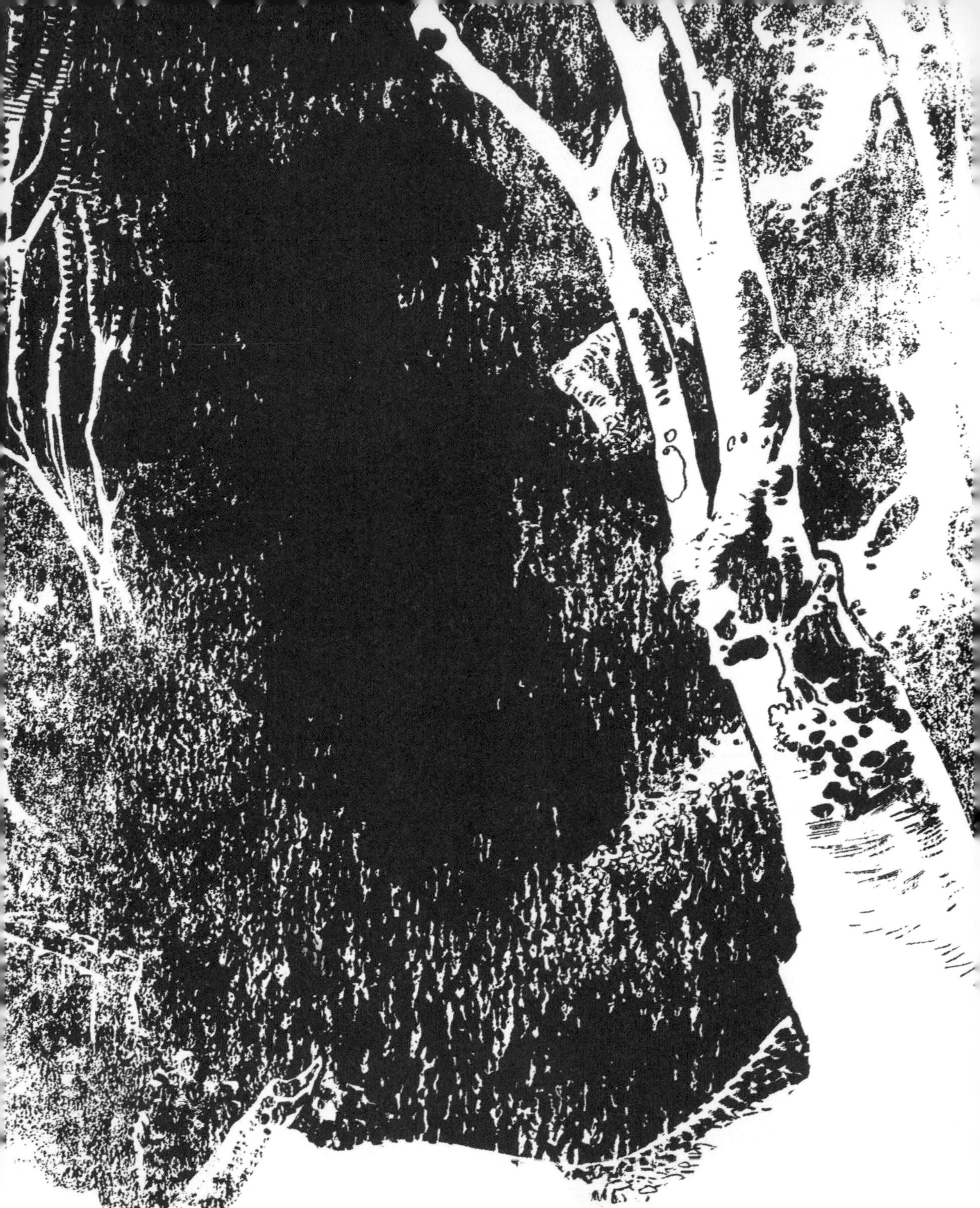

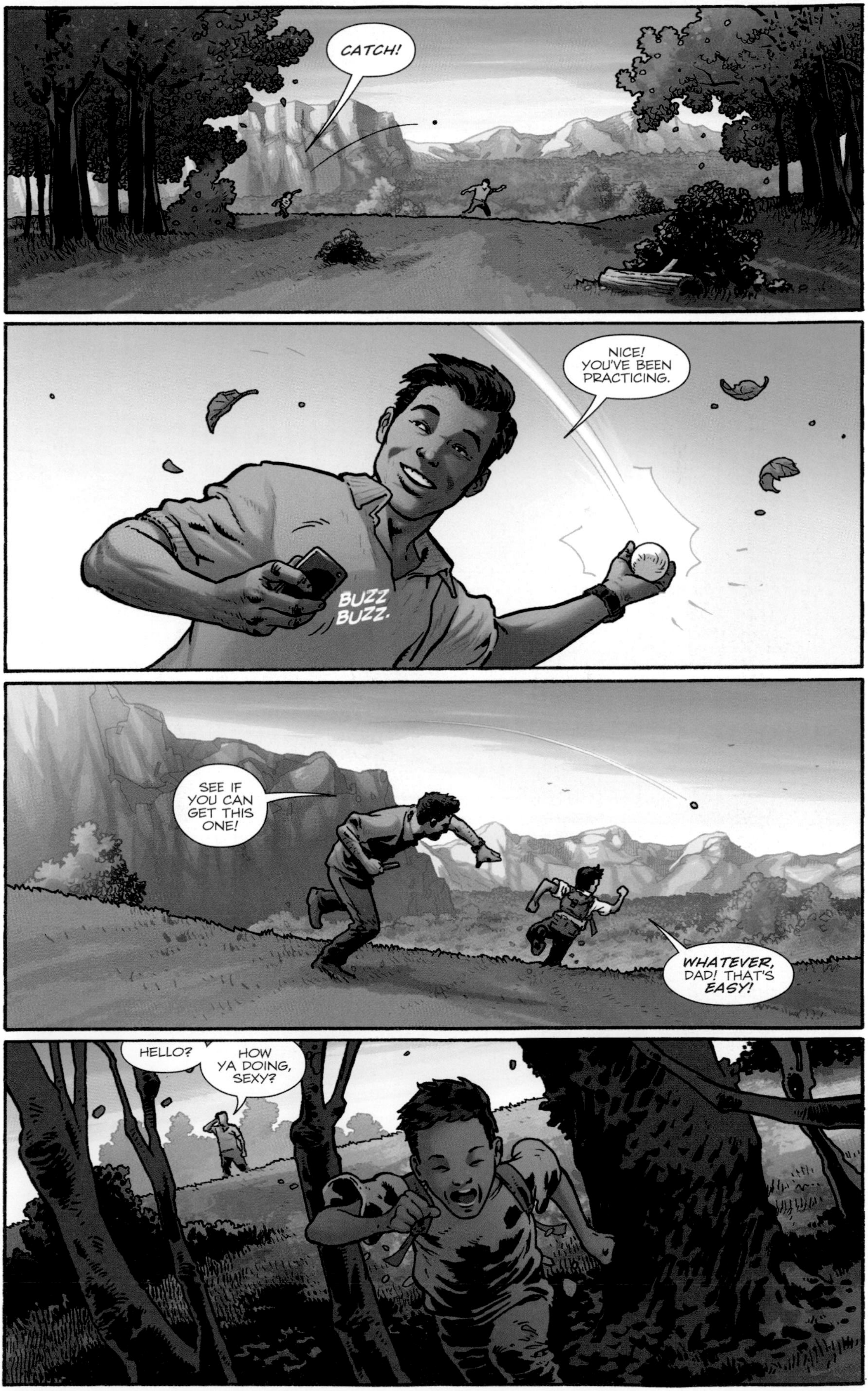
CATCH!
NICE! YOU'VE BEEN PRACTICING.
BUZZ BUZZ.
SEE IF YOU CAN GET THIS ONE!
WHATEVER, DAD! THAT'S EASY!
HELLO?
HOW YA DOING, SEXY?

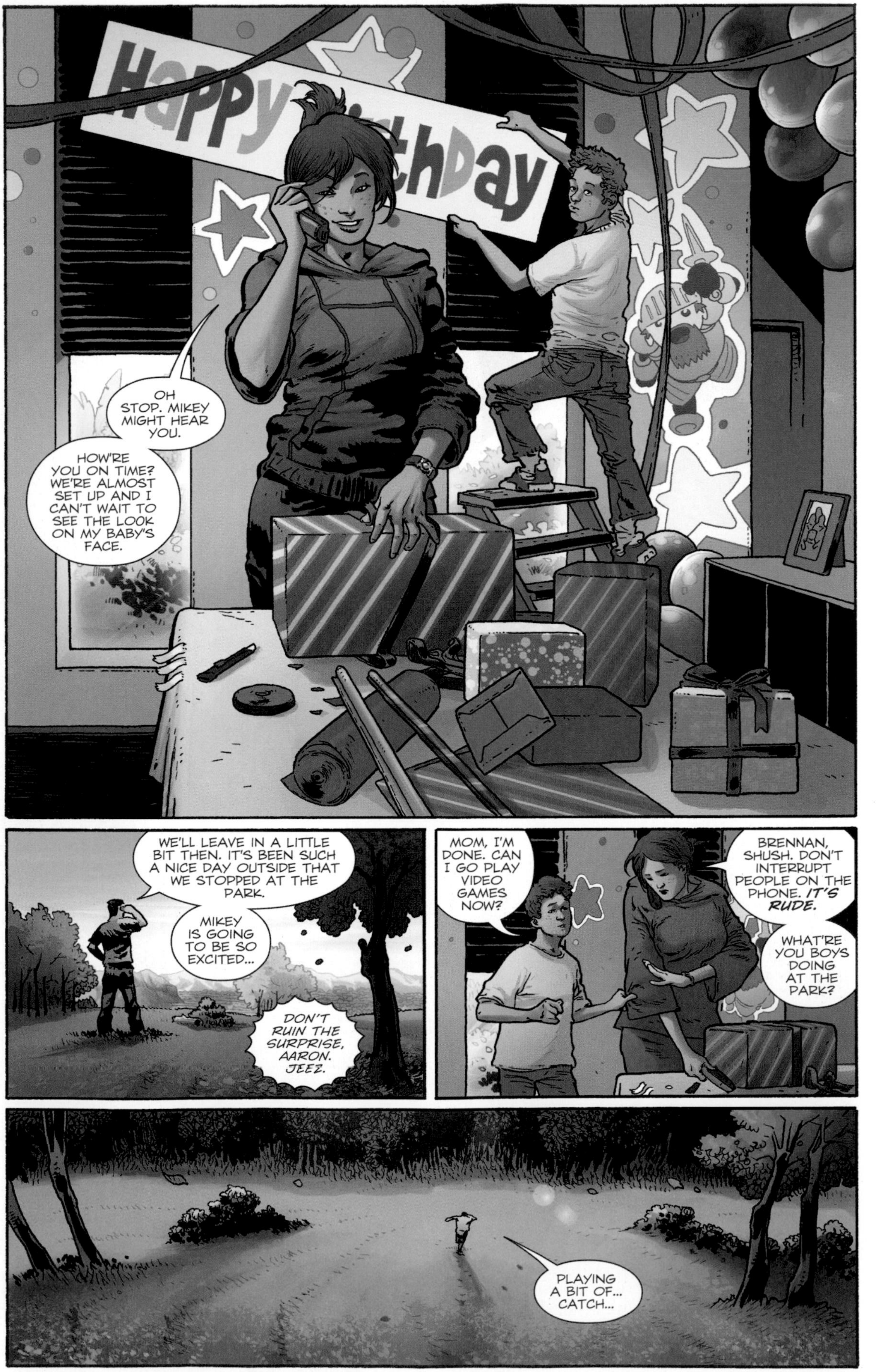
HAPPY
OH STOP. MIKEY MIGHT HEAR YOU.
HOW'RE YOU ON TIME? WE'RE ALMOST SET UP AND I CAN'T WAIT TO SEE THE LOOK ON MY BABY'S FACE.
WE'LL LEAVE IN A LITTLE BIT THEN. IT'S BEEN SUCH A NICE DAY OUTSIDE THAT WE STOPPED AT THE PARK.
MIKEY IS GOING TO BE SO EXCITED...
DON'T RUIN THE SURPRISE, AARON. JEEZ.
MOM, I'M DONE. CAN I GO PLAY VIDEO GAMES NOW?
BRENNAN, SHUSH. DON'T INTERRUPT PEOPLE ON THE PHONE. *IT'S RUDE.*
WHAT'RE YOU BOYS DOING AT THE PARK?
PLAYING A BIT OF... CATCH...

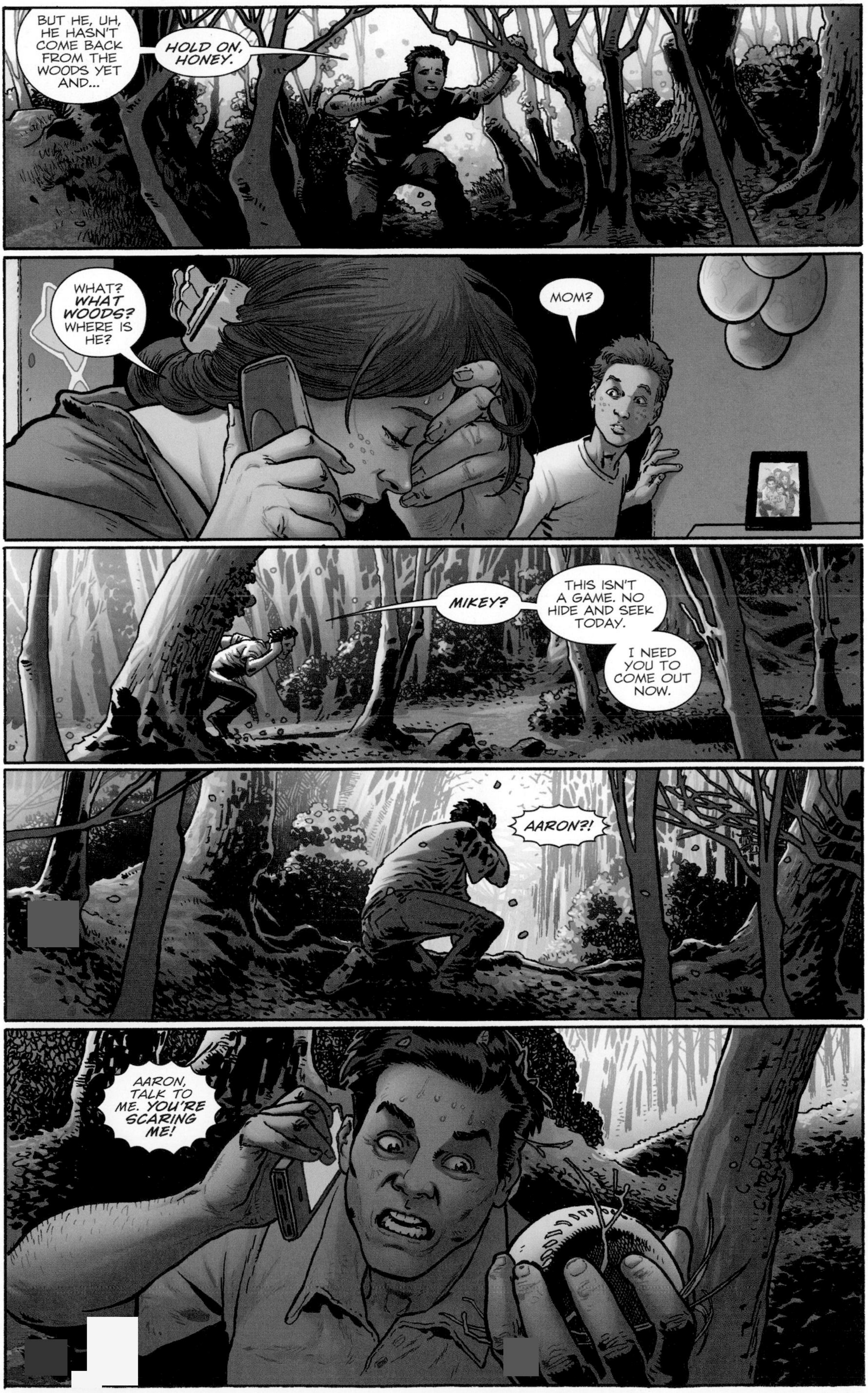
BUT HE, UH, HE HASN'T COME BACK FROM THE WOODS YET AND...
HOLD ON, HONEY.
WHAT? WHAT WOODS? WHERE IS HE?
MOM?
MIKEY?
THIS ISN'T A GAME. NO HIDE AND SEEK TODAY.
I NEED YOU TO COME OUT NOW.
AARON?!
AARON, TALK TO ME. YOU'RE SCARING ME!

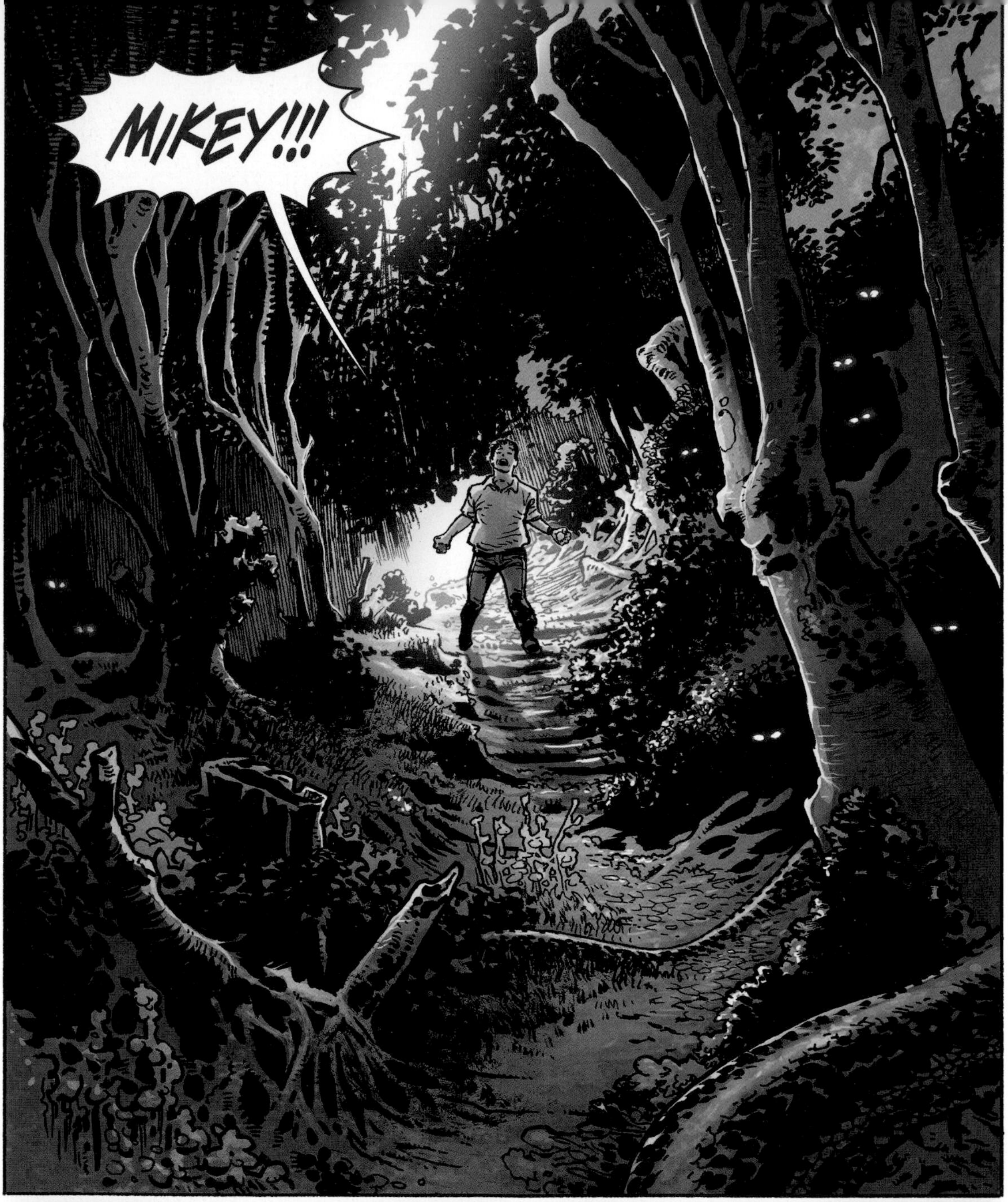
MIKEY!!!

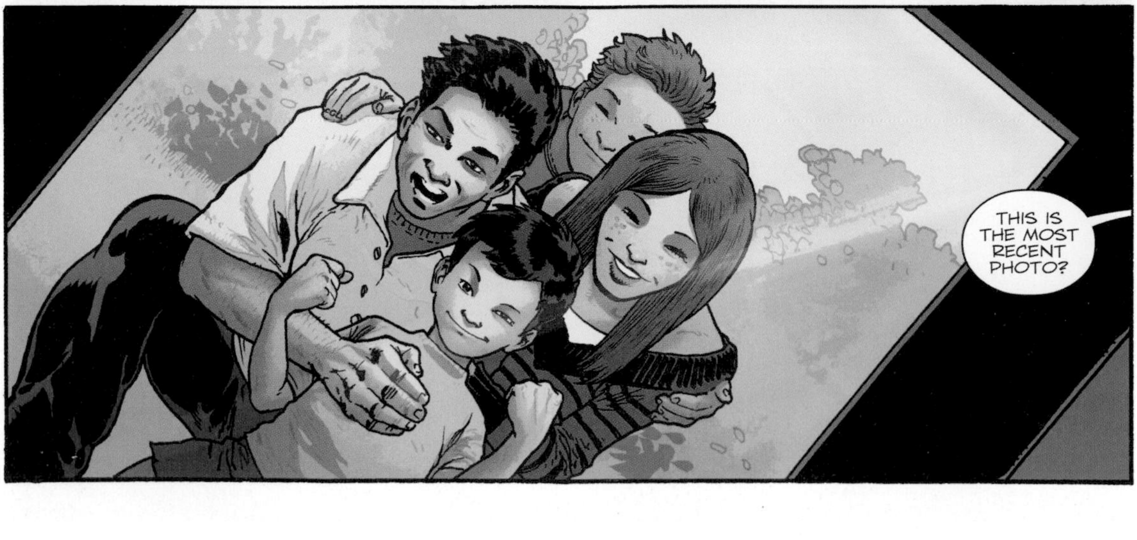
THIS IS THE MOST RECENT PHOTO?

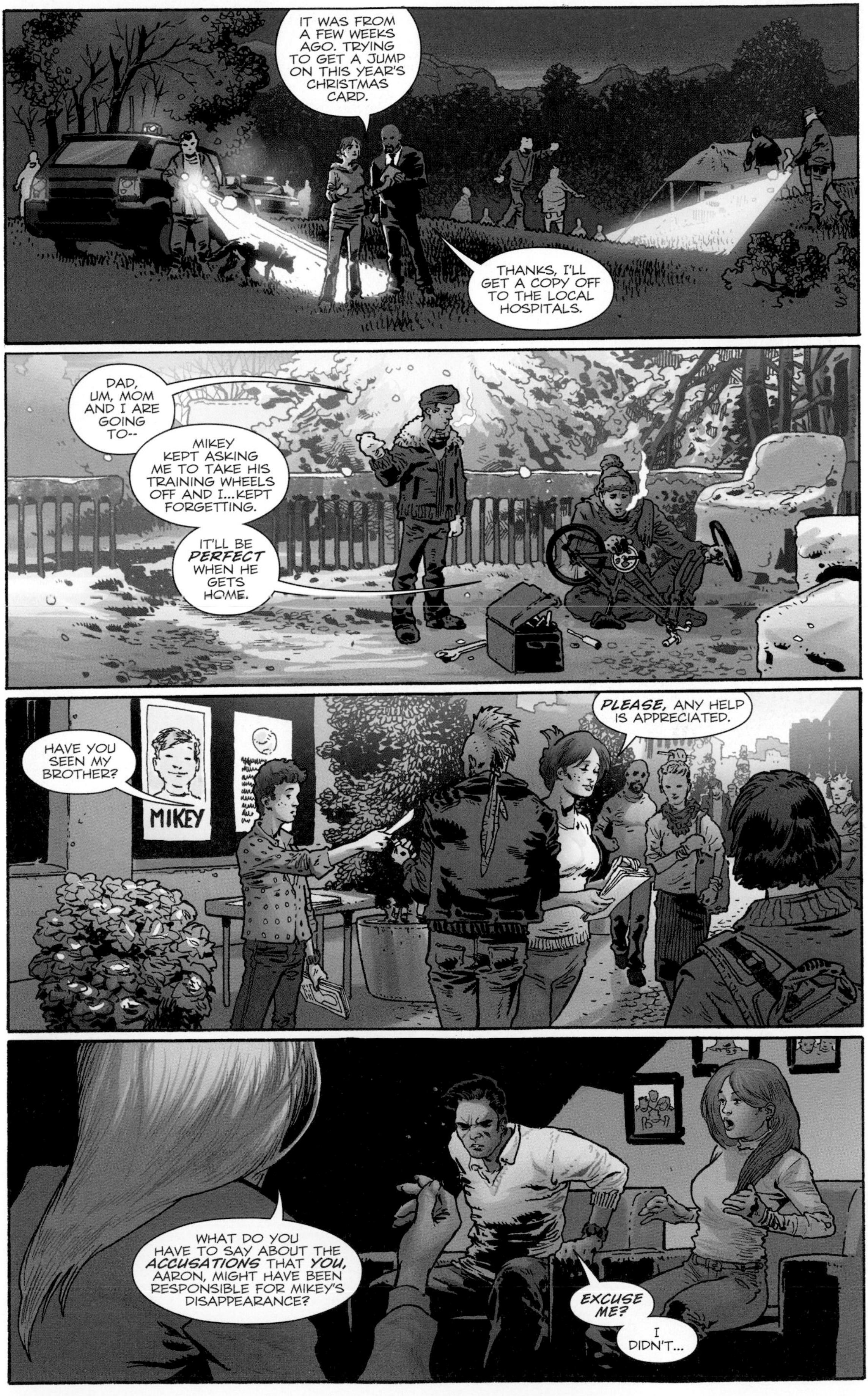
IT WAS FROM A FEW WEEKS AGO. TRYING TO GET A JUMP ON THIS YEAR'S CHRISTMAS CARD.
THANKS, I'LL GET A COPY OFF TO THE LOCAL HOSPITALS.
DAD, UM, MOM AND I ARE GOING TO--
MIKEY KEPT ASKING ME TO TAKE HIS TRAINING WHEELS OFF AND I...KEPT FORGETTING.
IT'LL BE PERFECT WHEN HE GETS HOME.
MIKEY
HAVE YOU SEEN MY BROTHER?
PLEASE, ANY HELP IS APPRECIATED.
WHAT DO YOU HAVE TO SAY ABOUT THE ACCUSATIONS THAT YOU, AARON, MIGHT HAVE BEEN RESPONSIBLE FOR MIKEY'S DISAPPEARANCE?
EXCUSE ME?
I DIDN'T...

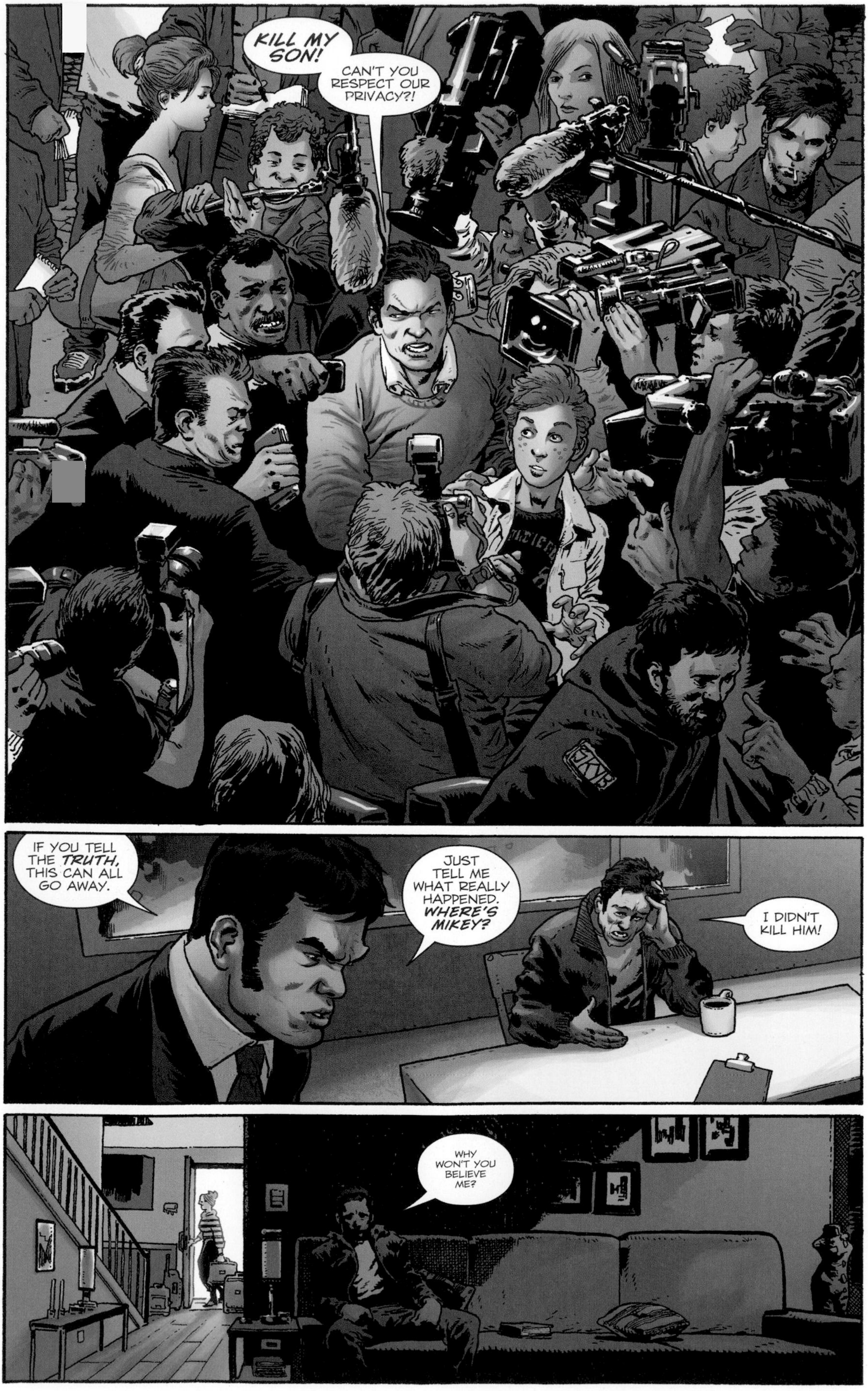
KILL MY SON!
CAN'T YOU RESPECT OUR PRIVACY?!
IF YOU TELL THE TRUTH, THIS CAN ALL GO AWAY.
JUST TELL ME WHAT REALLY HAPPENED. WHERE'S MIKEY?
I DIDN'T KILL HIM!
WHY WON'T YOU BELIEVE ME?

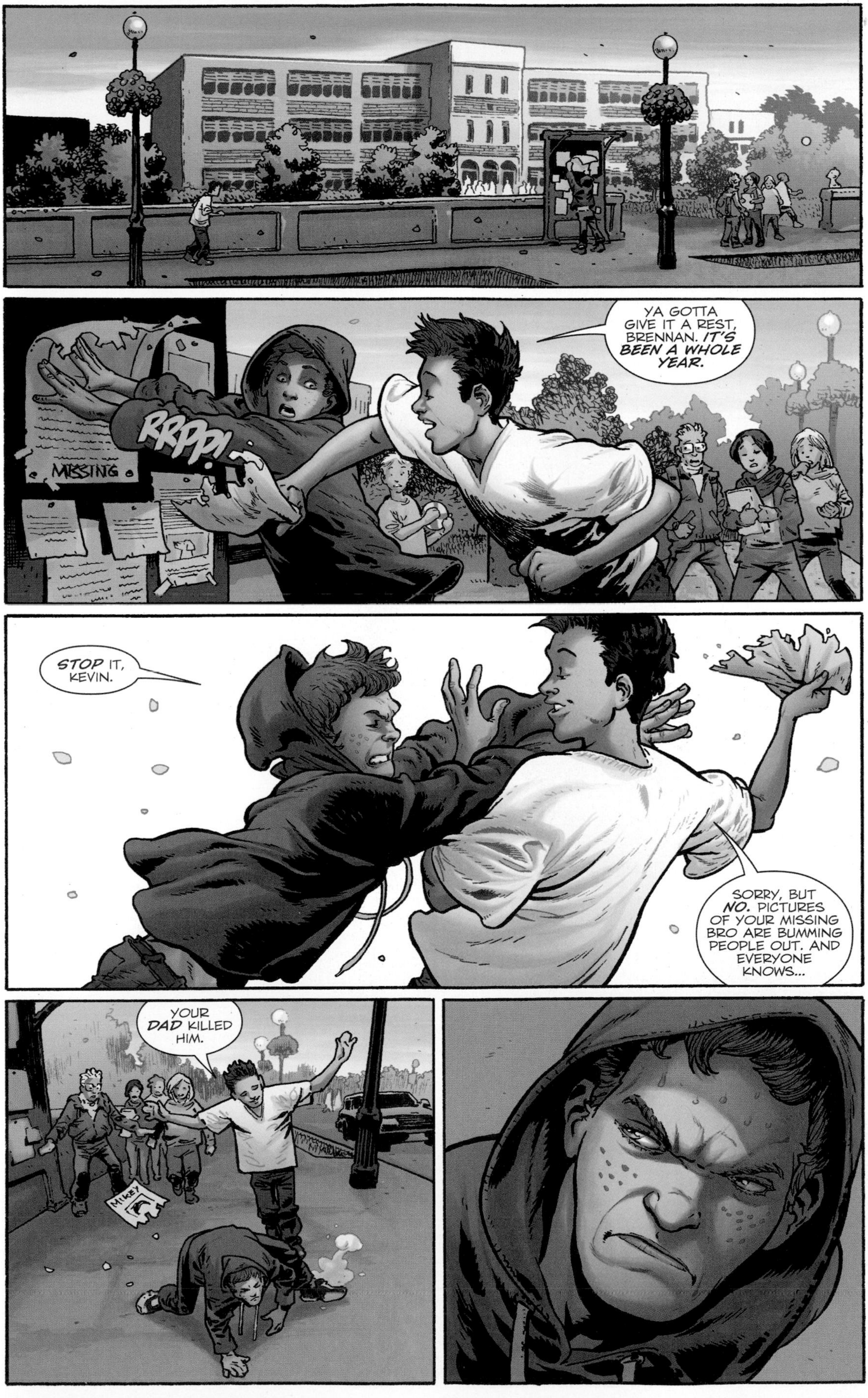
YA GOTTA GIVE IT A REST, BRENNAN. IT'S BEEN A WHOLE YEAR.
RRPP!
MISSING
STOP IT, KEVIN.
SORRY, BUT NO. PICTURES OF YOUR MISSING BRO ARE BUMMING PEOPLE OUT. AND EVERYONE KNOWS...
YOUR DAD KILLED HIM.
MIKEY

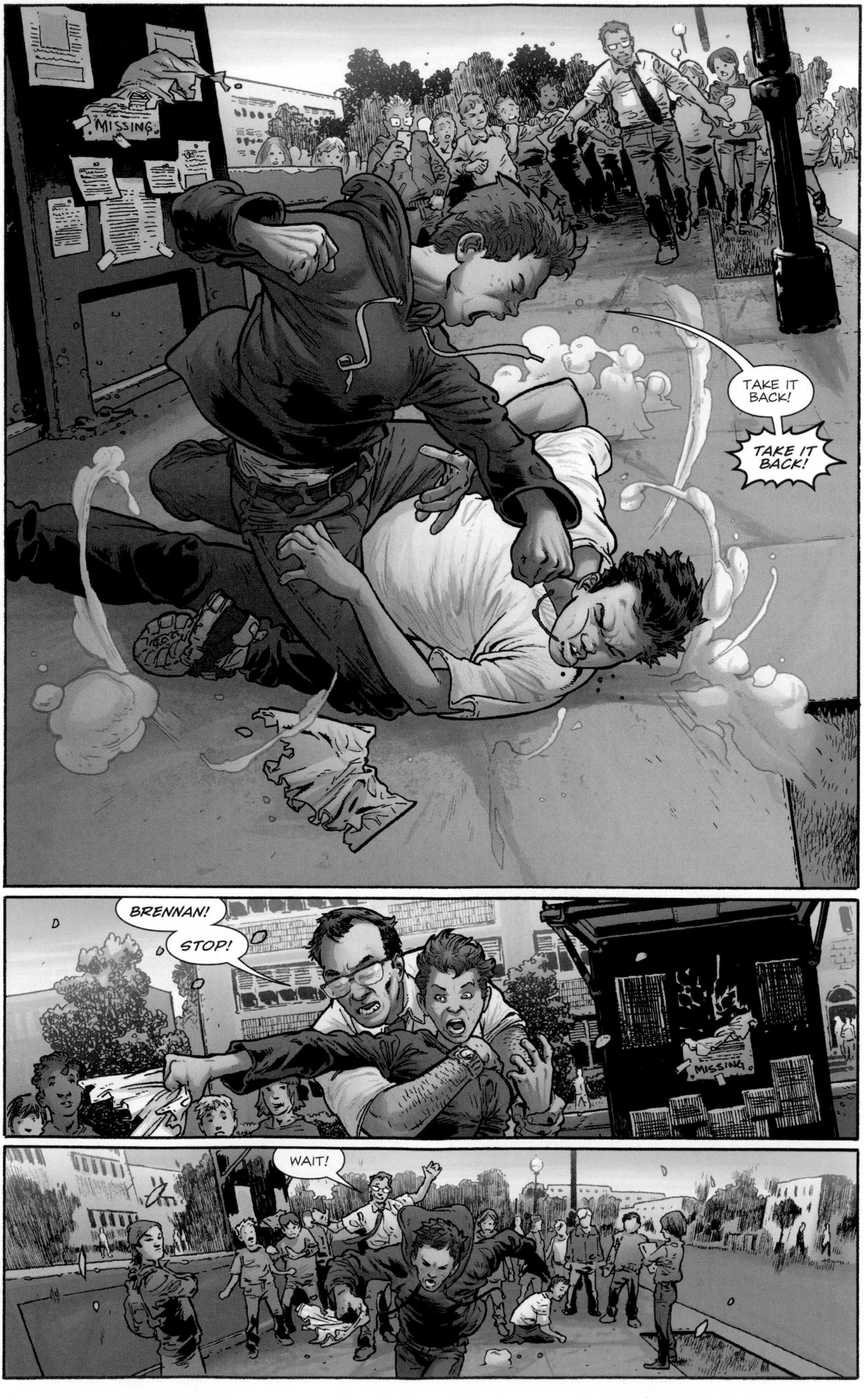
MISSING
TAKE IT BACK!
TAKE IT BACK!
BRENNAN!
STOP!
MISSING
WAIT!

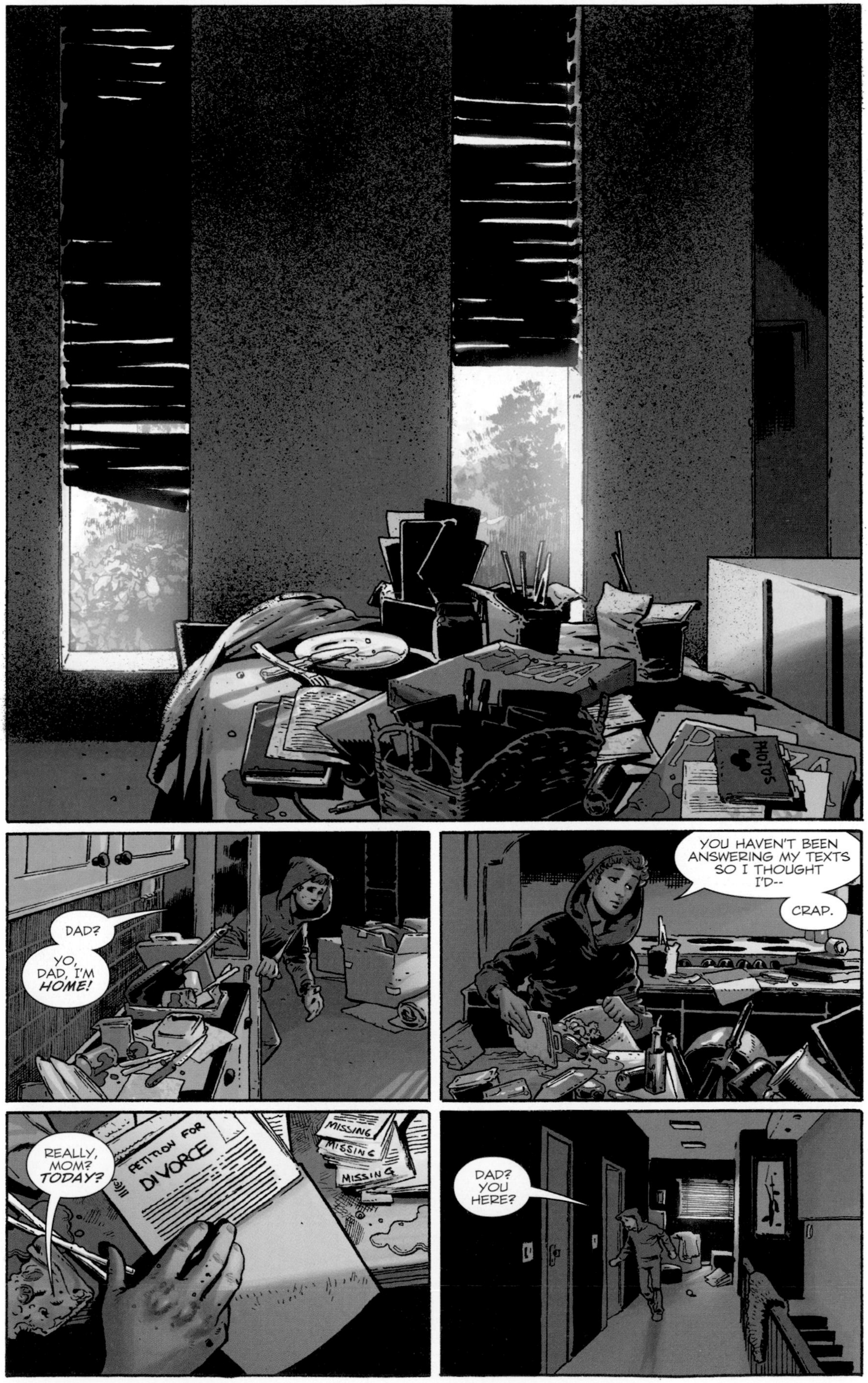
PHOTOS
DAD?
YO, DAD, I'M HOME!
YOU HAVEN'T BEEN ANSWERING MY TEXTS SO I THOUGHT I'D--
CRAP.
REALLY, MOM? TODAY?
PETITION FOR DIVORCE
MISSING
MISSING
MISSING
DAD? YOU HERE?

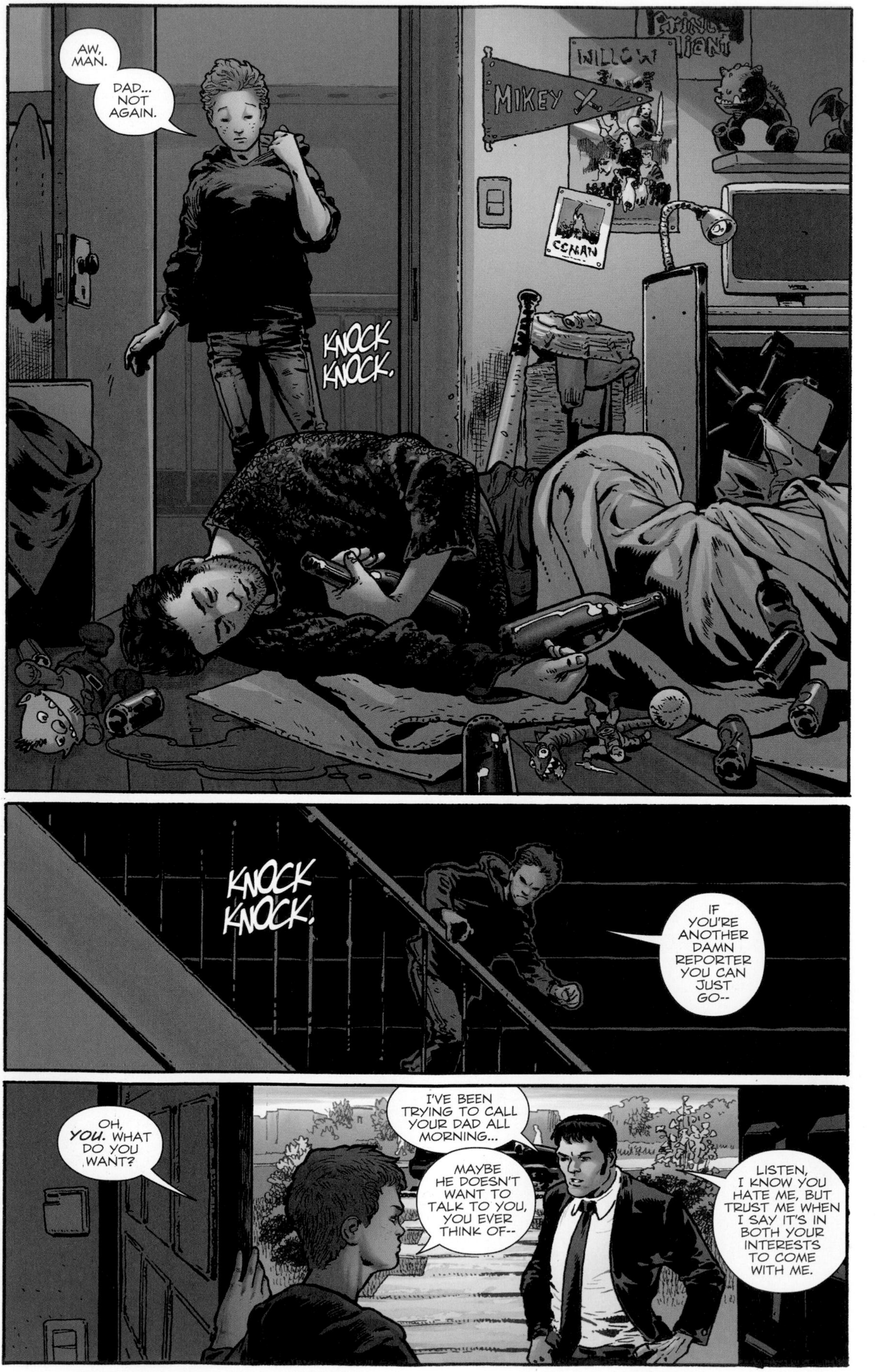
AW, MAN.
DAD... NOT AGAIN.
KNOCK KNOCK.
MIKEY
WILLOW
CONAN
KNOCK KNOCK.
IF YOU'RE ANOTHER DAMN REPORTER YOU CAN JUST GO--
OH, YOU. WHAT DO YOU WANT?
I'VE BEEN TRYING TO CALL YOUR DAD ALL MORNING...
MAYBE HE DOESN'T WANT TO TALK TO YOU, YOU EVER THINK OF--
LISTEN, I KNOW YOU HATE ME, BUT TRUST ME WHEN I SAY IT'S IN BOTH YOUR INTERESTS TO COME WITH ME.

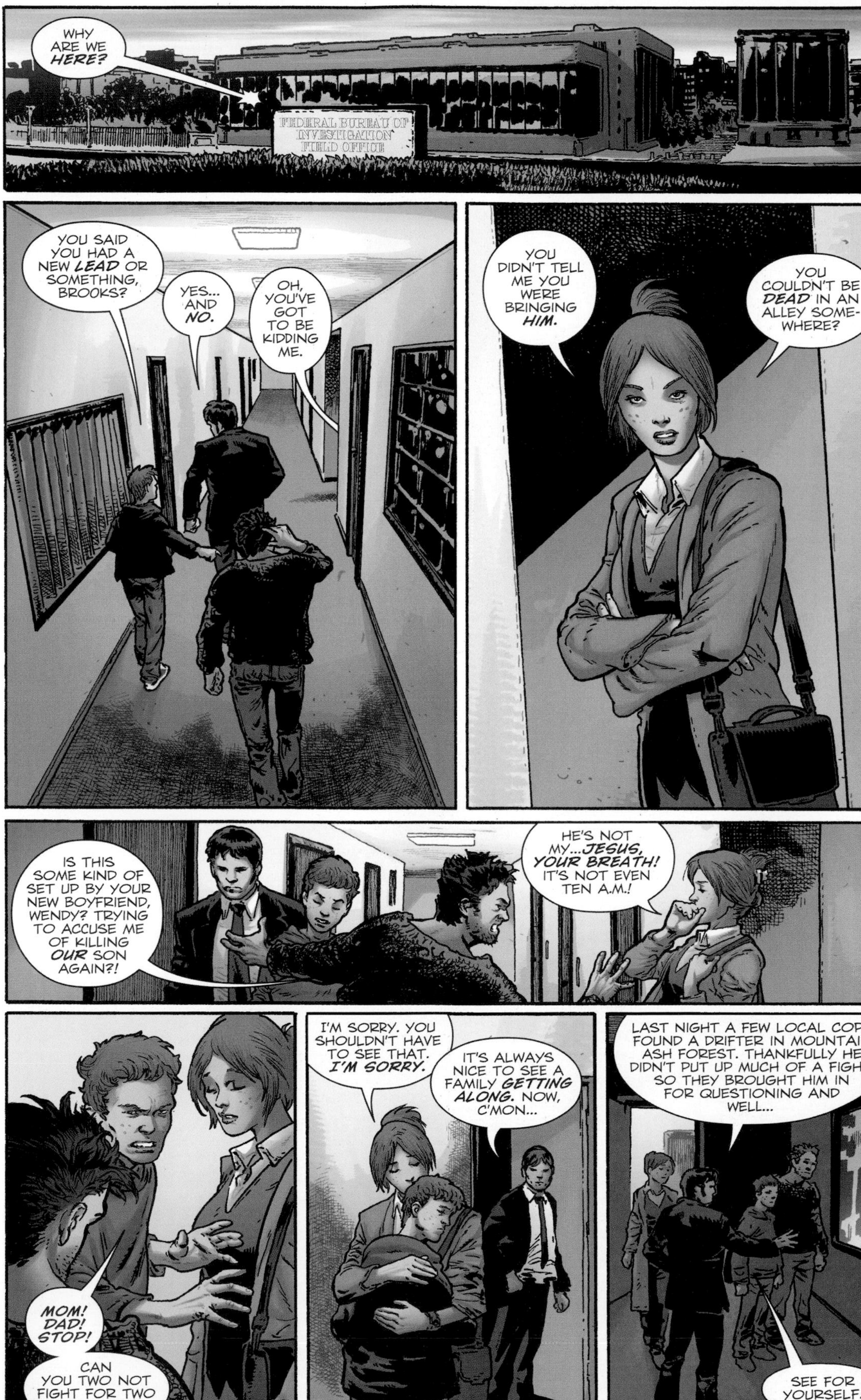
WHY ARE WE HERE?
FEDERAL BUREAU OF INVESTIGATION FIELD OFFICE
YOU SAID YOU HAD A NEW LEAD OR SOMETHING, BROOKS?
YES... AND NO.
OH, YOU'VE GOT TO BE KIDDING ME.
YOU DIDN'T TELL ME YOU WERE BRINGING HIM.
YOU COULDN'T BE DEAD IN AN ALLEY SOMEWHERE?
IS THIS SOME KIND OF SET UP BY YOUR NEW BOYFRIEND, WENDY? TRYING TO ACCUSE ME OF KILLING OUR SON AGAIN?!
HE'S NOT MY...JESUS, YOUR BREATH! IT'S NOT EVEN TEN A.M.!
MOM! DAD! STOP!
CAN YOU TWO NOT FIGHT FOR TWO SECONDS?!
I'M SORRY. YOU SHOULDN'T HAVE TO SEE THAT. I'M SORRY.
IT'S ALWAYS NICE TO SEE A FAMILY GETTING ALONG. NOW, C'MON...
LAST NIGHT A FEW LOCAL COPS FOUND A DRIFTER IN MOUNTAIN ASH FOREST. THANKFULLY HE DIDN'T PUT UP MUCH OF A FIGHT, SO THEY BROUGHT HIM IN FOR QUESTIONING AND WELL...
SEE FOR YOURSELF.

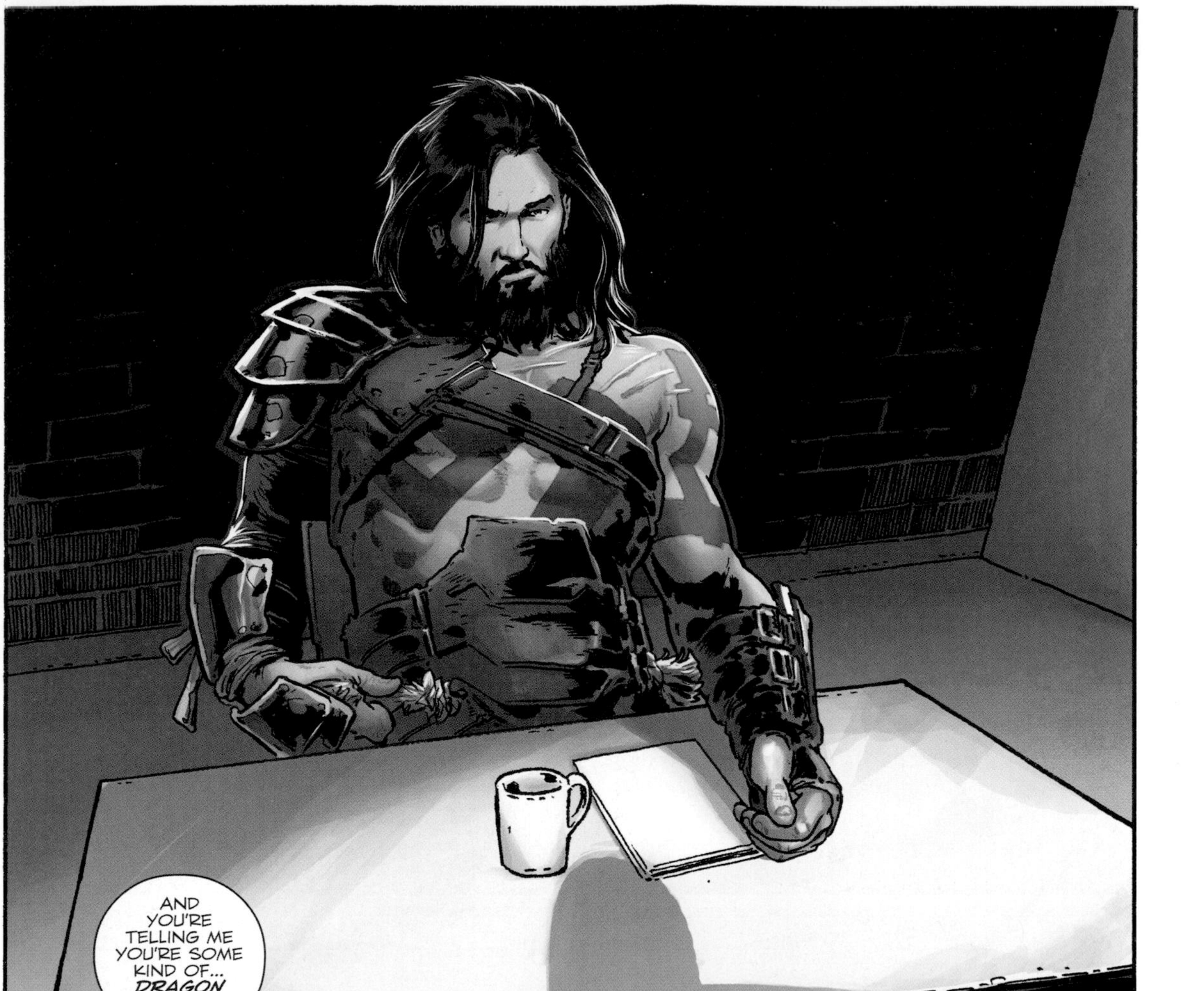
AND YOU'RE TELLING ME YOU'RE SOME KIND OF... *DRAGON SLAYER?*
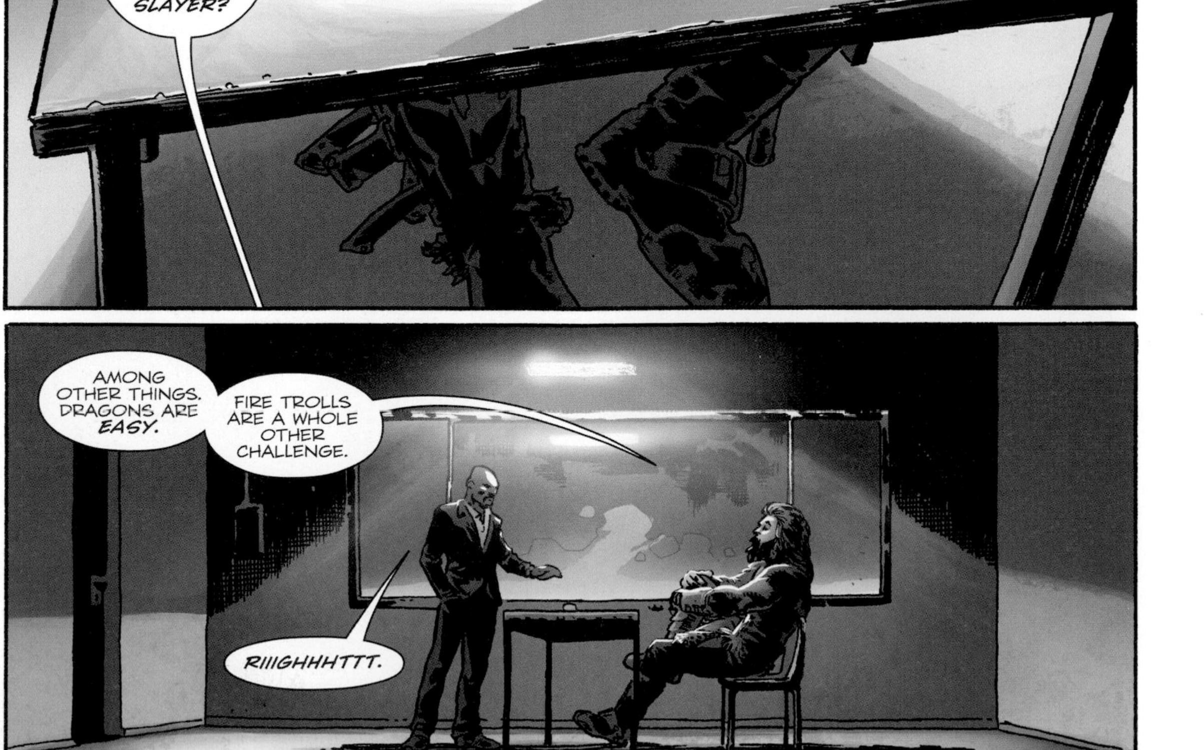
AMONG OTHER THINGS. DRAGONS ARE *EASY.*
FIRE TROLLS ARE A WHOLE OTHER CHALLENGE.
RIIIGHHHTTT.

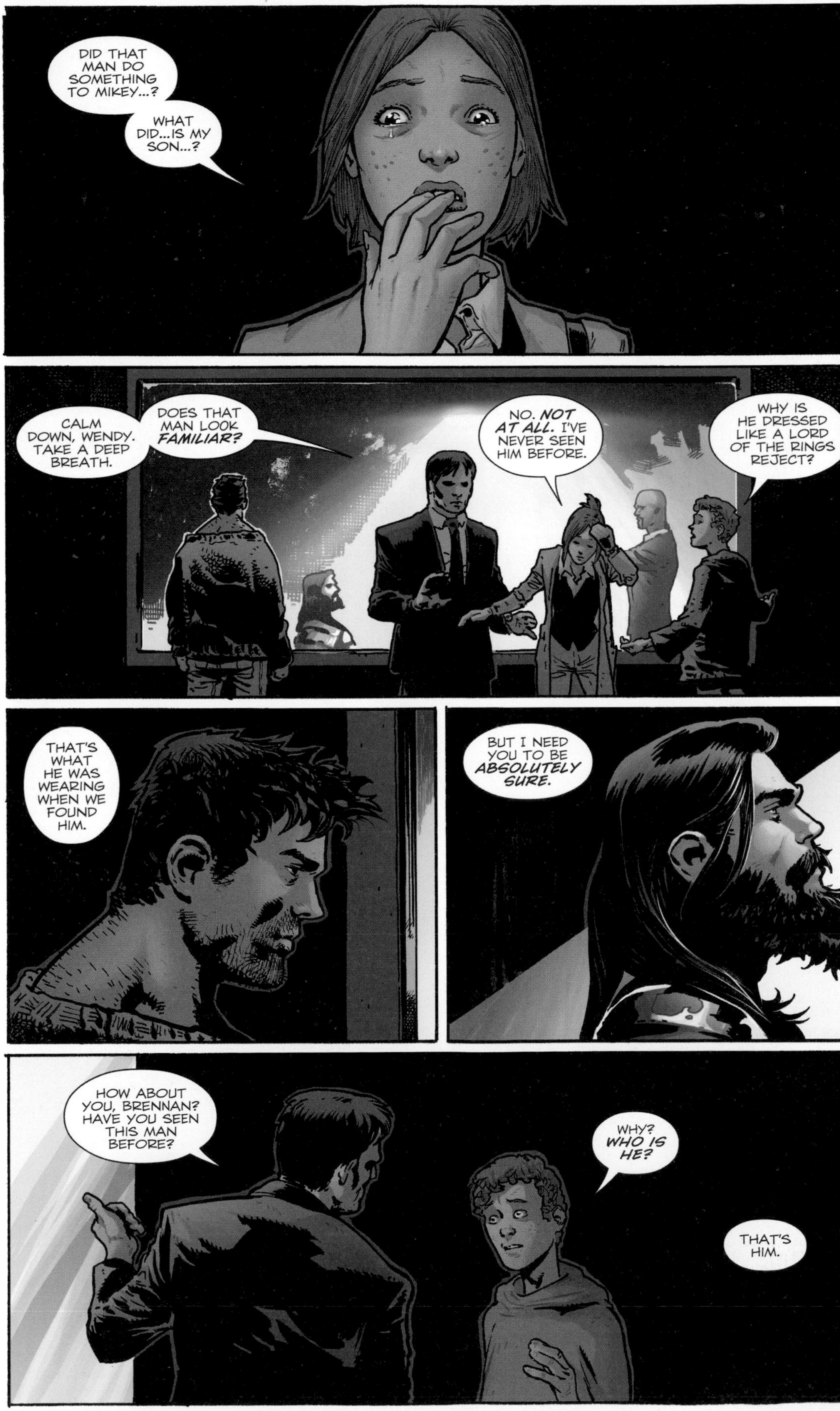
DID THAT MAN DO SOMETHING TO MIKEY...?
WHAT DID...IS MY SON...?
CALM DOWN, WENDY. TAKE A DEEP BREATH.
DOES THAT MAN LOOK FAMILIAR?
NO. NOT AT ALL. I'VE NEVER SEEN HIM BEFORE.
WHY IS HE DRESSED LIKE A LORD OF THE RINGS REJECT?
THAT'S WHAT HE WAS WEARING WHEN WE FOUND HIM.
BUT I NEED YOU TO BE ABSOLUTELY SURE.
HOW ABOUT YOU, BRENNAN? HAVE YOU SEEN THIS MAN BEFORE?
WHY? WHO IS HE?
THAT'S HIM.

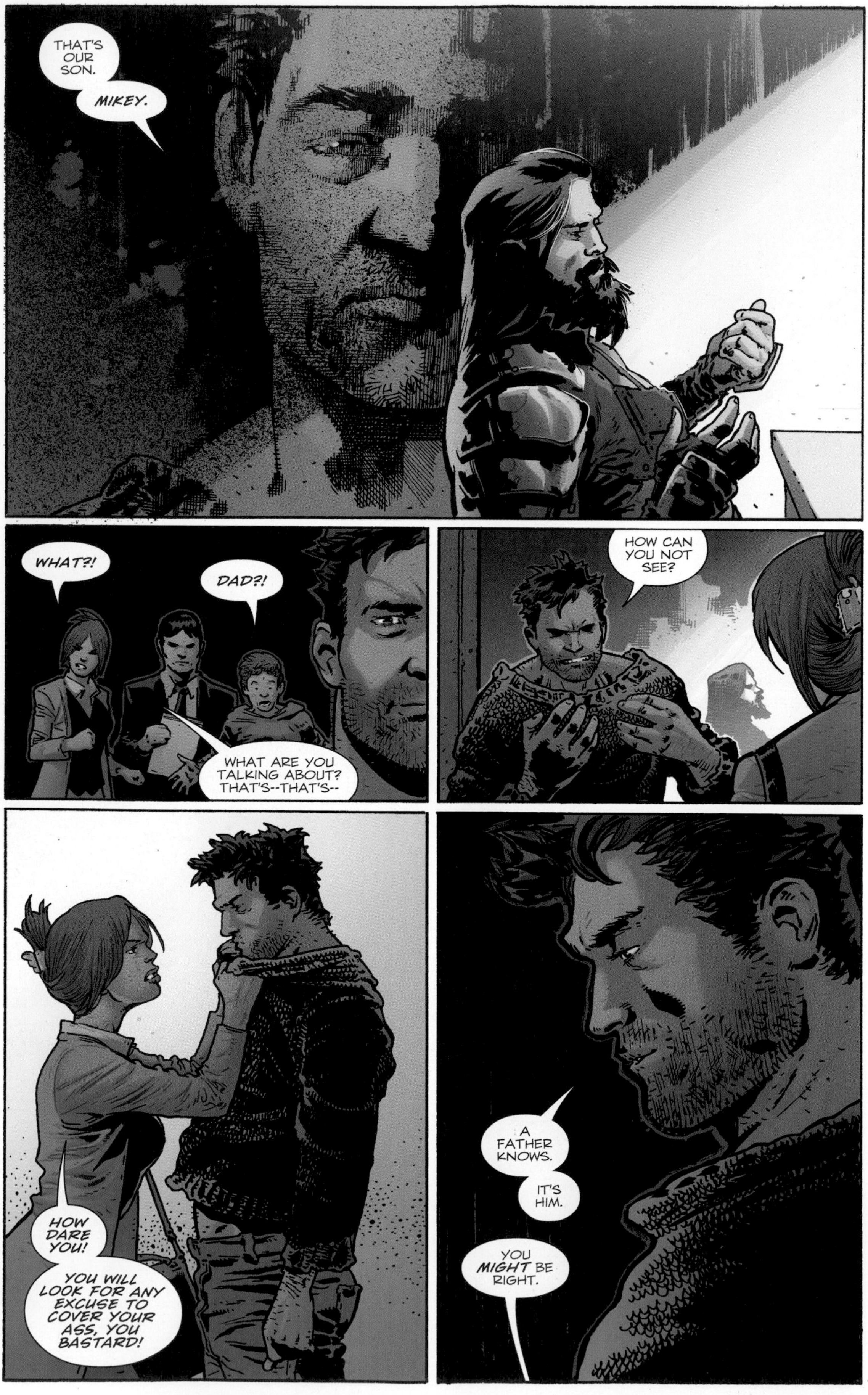
THAT'S OUR SON.
MIKEY.
WHAT?!
DAD?!
WHAT ARE YOU TALKING ABOUT? THAT'S--THAT'S--
HOW CAN YOU NOT SEE?
HOW DARE YOU!
YOU WILL LOOK FOR ANY EXCUSE TO COVER YOUR ASS, YOU BASTARD!
A FATHER KNOWS.
IT'S HIM.
YOU MIGHT BE RIGHT.

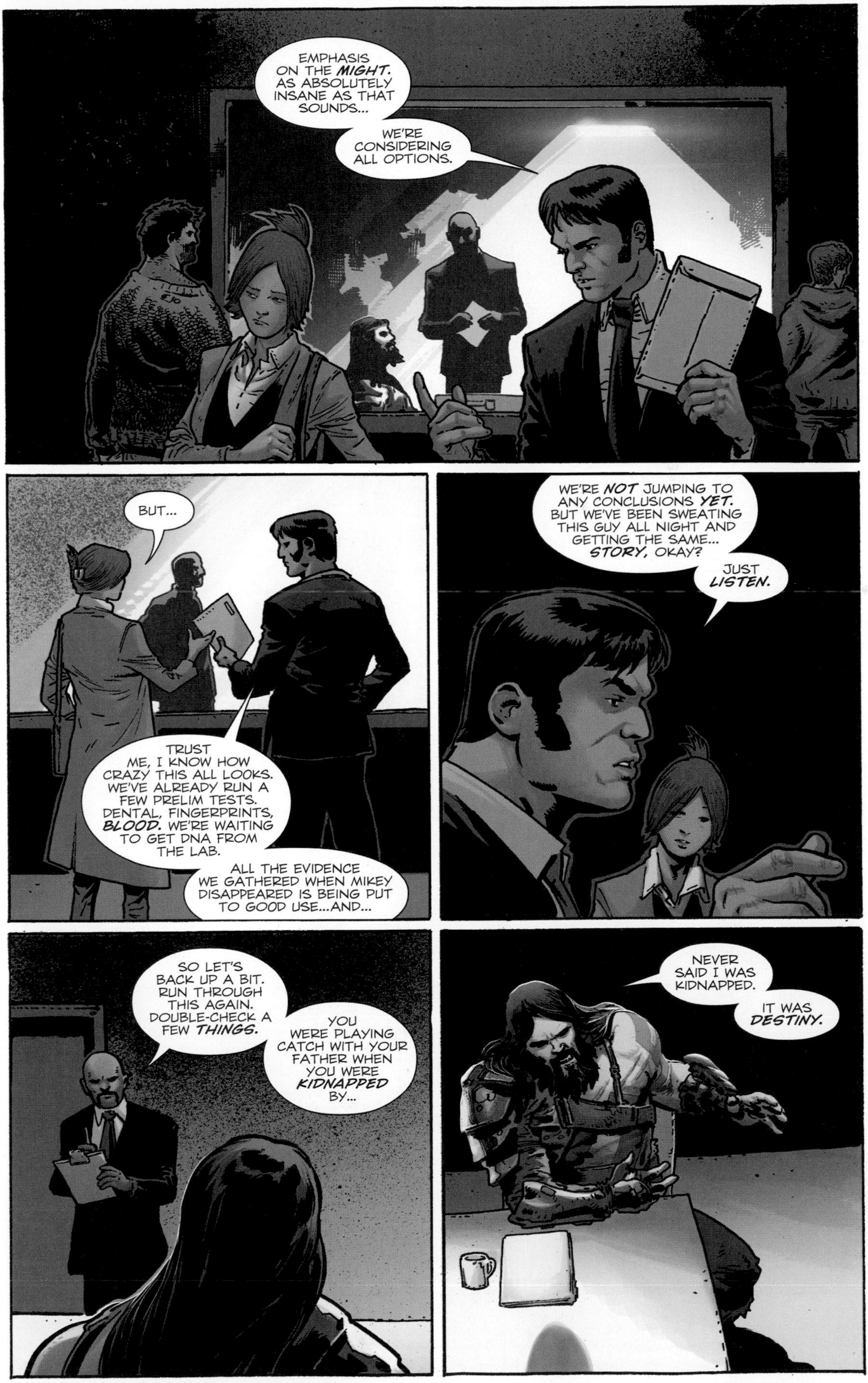
EMPHASIS ON THE *MIGHT.* AS ABSOLUTELY INSANE AS THAT SOUNDS...
WE'RE CONSIDERING ALL OPTIONS.
BUT...
TRUST ME, I KNOW HOW CRAZY THIS ALL LOOKS. WE'VE ALREADY RUN A FEW PRELIM TESTS. DENTAL, FINGERPRINTS, *BLOOD.* WE'RE WAITING TO GET DNA FROM THE LAB.
ALL THE EVIDENCE WE GATHERED WHEN MIKEY DISAPPEARED IS BEING PUT TO GOOD USE...AND...
WE'RE *NOT* JUMPING TO ANY CONCLUSIONS *YET.* BUT WE'VE BEEN SWEATING THIS GUY ALL NIGHT AND GETTING THE SAME... *STORY,* OKAY?
JUST *LISTEN.*
SO LET'S BACK UP A BIT. RUN THROUGH THIS AGAIN. DOUBLE-CHECK A FEW *THINGS.*
YOU WERE PLAYING CATCH WITH YOUR FATHER WHEN YOU WERE *KIDNAPPED* BY...
NEVER SAID I WAS KIDNAPPED.
IT WAS *DESTINY.*

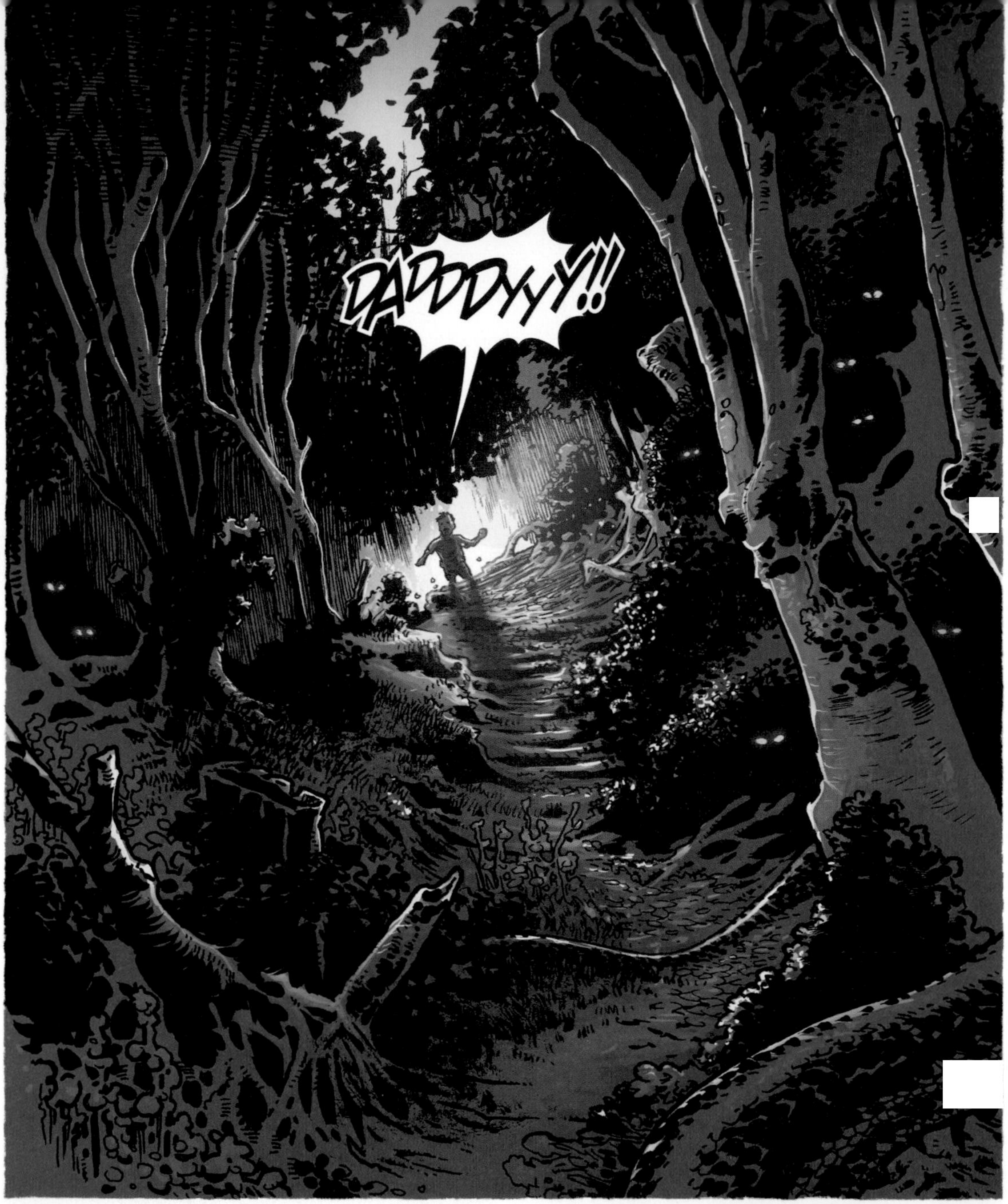
DADDDYYY!!

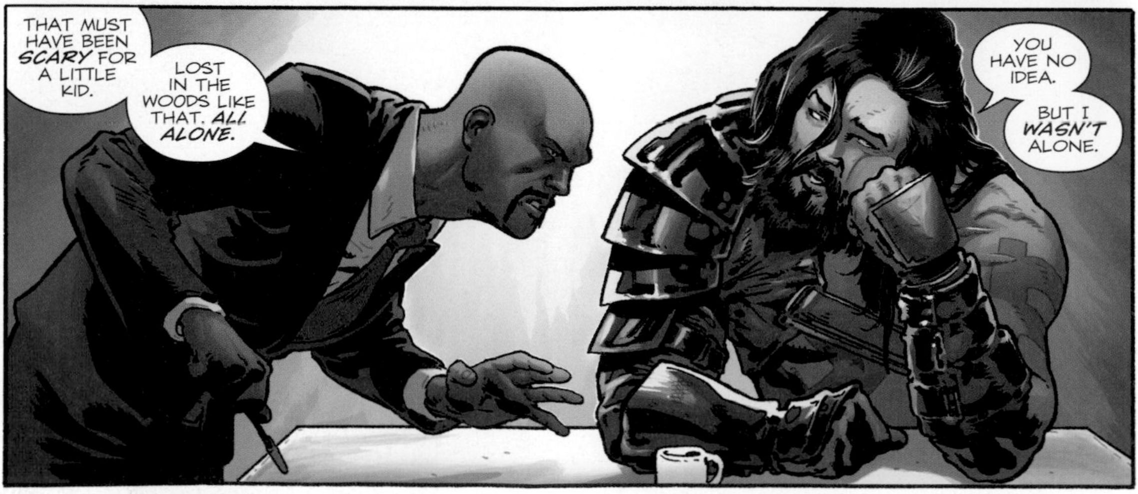
THAT MUST HAVE BEEN SCARY FOR A LITTLE KID.
LOST IN THE WOODS LIKE THAT. ALL ALONE.
YOU HAVE NO IDEA.
BUT I WASN'T ALONE.

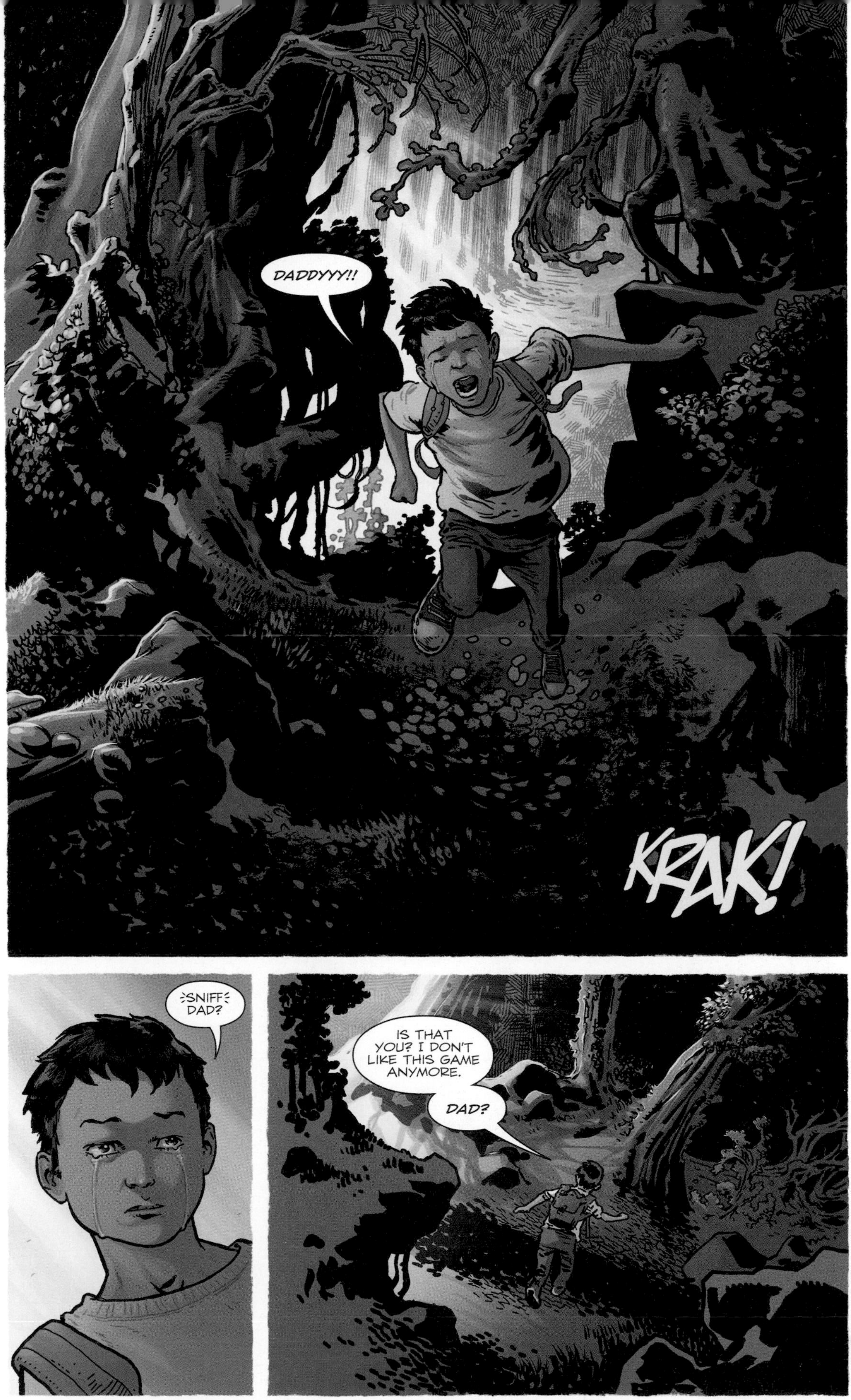
DADDYYY!!
KRAK!
SNIFF
DAD?
IS THAT YOU? I DON'T LIKE THIS GAME ANYMORE.
DAD?

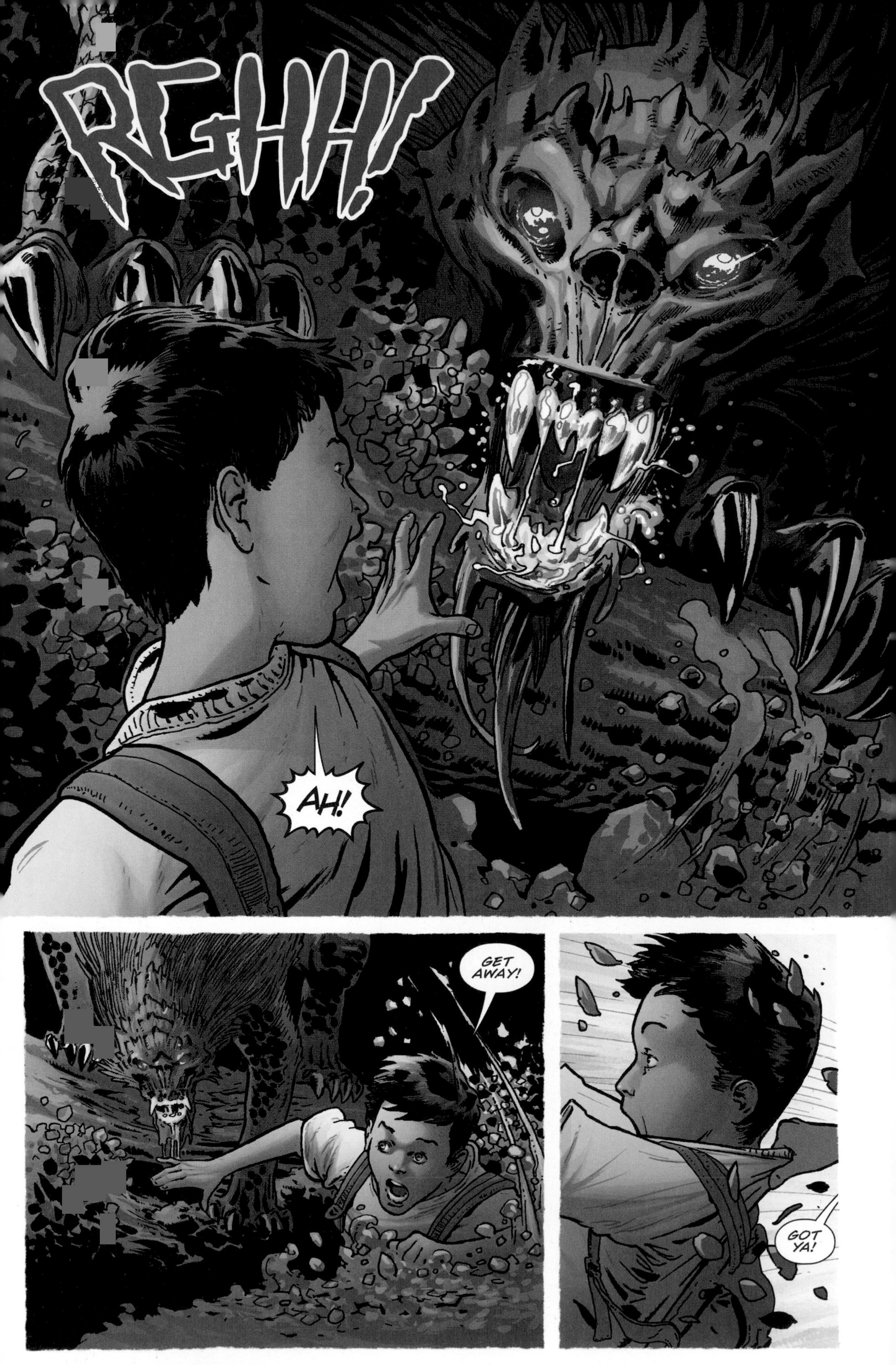
RGHH!
AH!
GET AWAY!
GOT YA!

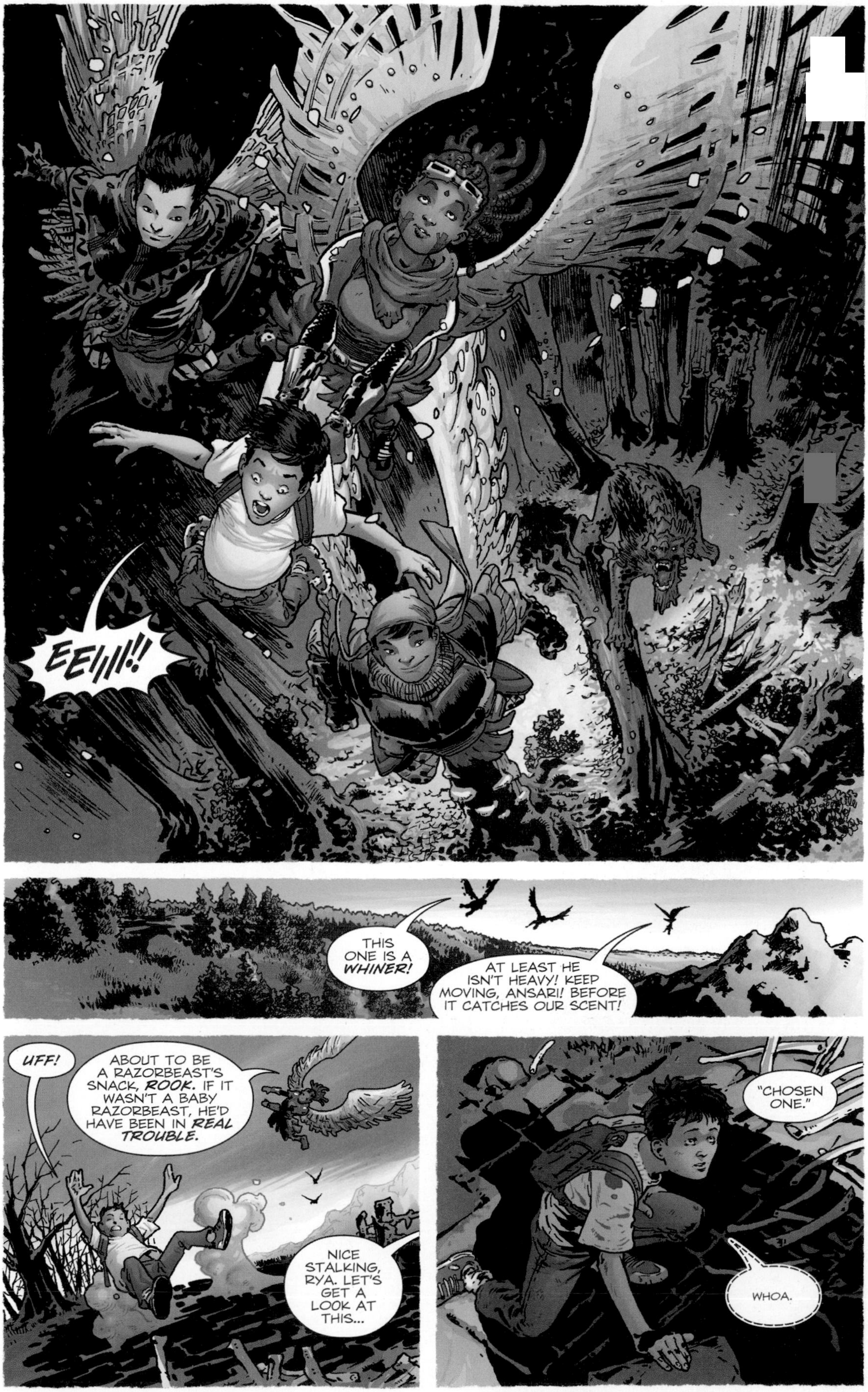
EEIIII!!
THIS ONE IS A WHINER!
AT LEAST HE ISN'T HEAVY! KEEP MOVING, ANSARI! BEFORE IT CATCHES OUR SCENT!
UFF!
ABOUT TO BE A RAZORBEAST'S SNACK, ROOK. IF IT WASN'T A BABY RAZORBEAST, HE'D HAVE BEEN IN REAL TROUBLE.
NICE STALKING, RYA. LET'S GET A LOOK AT THIS...
"CHOSEN ONE."
WHOA.

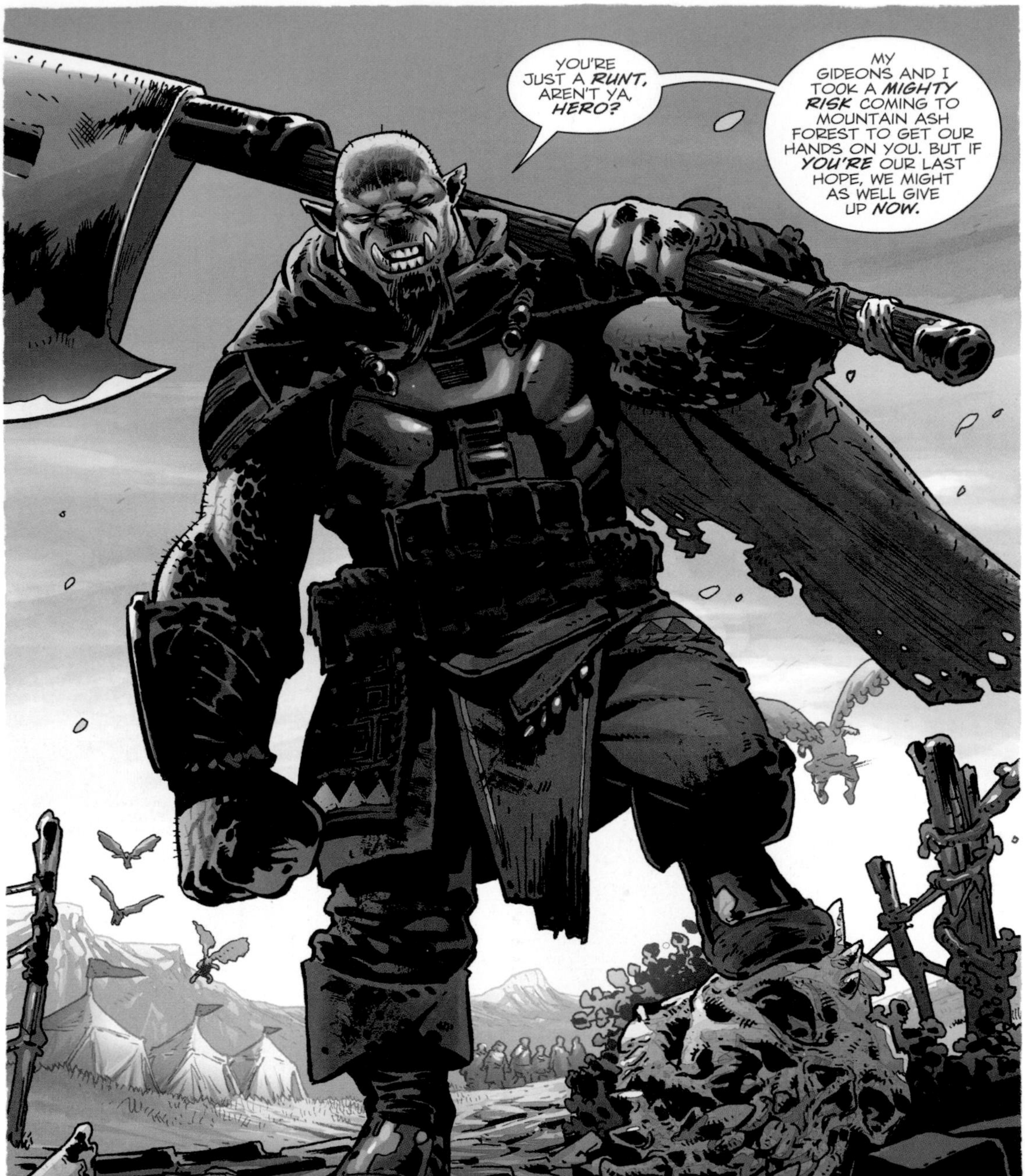
YOU'RE JUST A *RUNT*, AREN'T YA, *HERO?*
MY GIDEONS AND I TOOK A *MIGHTY RISK* COMING TO MOUNTAIN ASH FOREST TO GET OUR HANDS ON YOU. BUT IF *YOU'RE* OUR LAST HOPE, WE MIGHT AS WELL GIVE UP *NOW.*

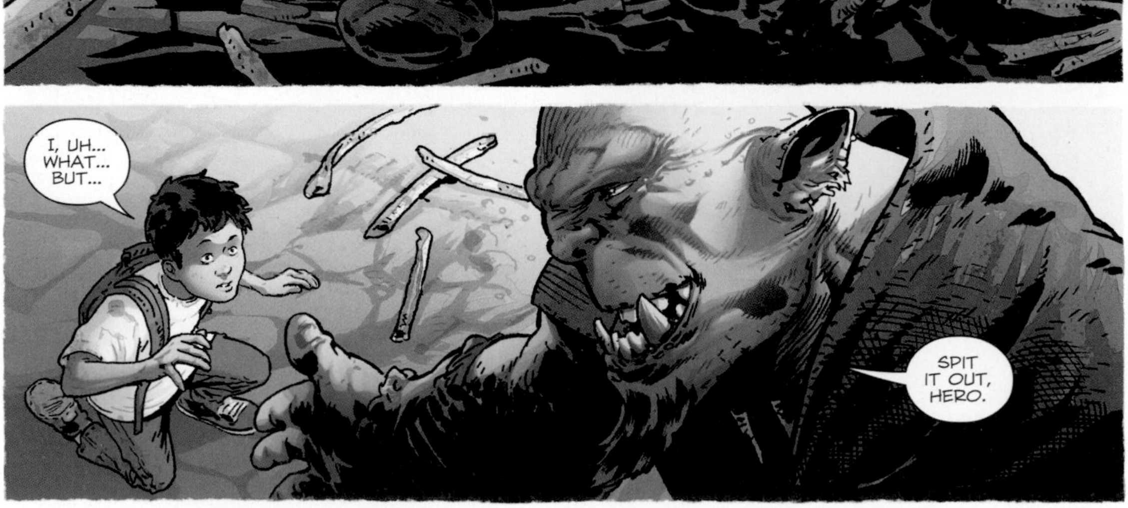
I, UH... WHAT... BUT...
SPIT IT OUT, HERO.

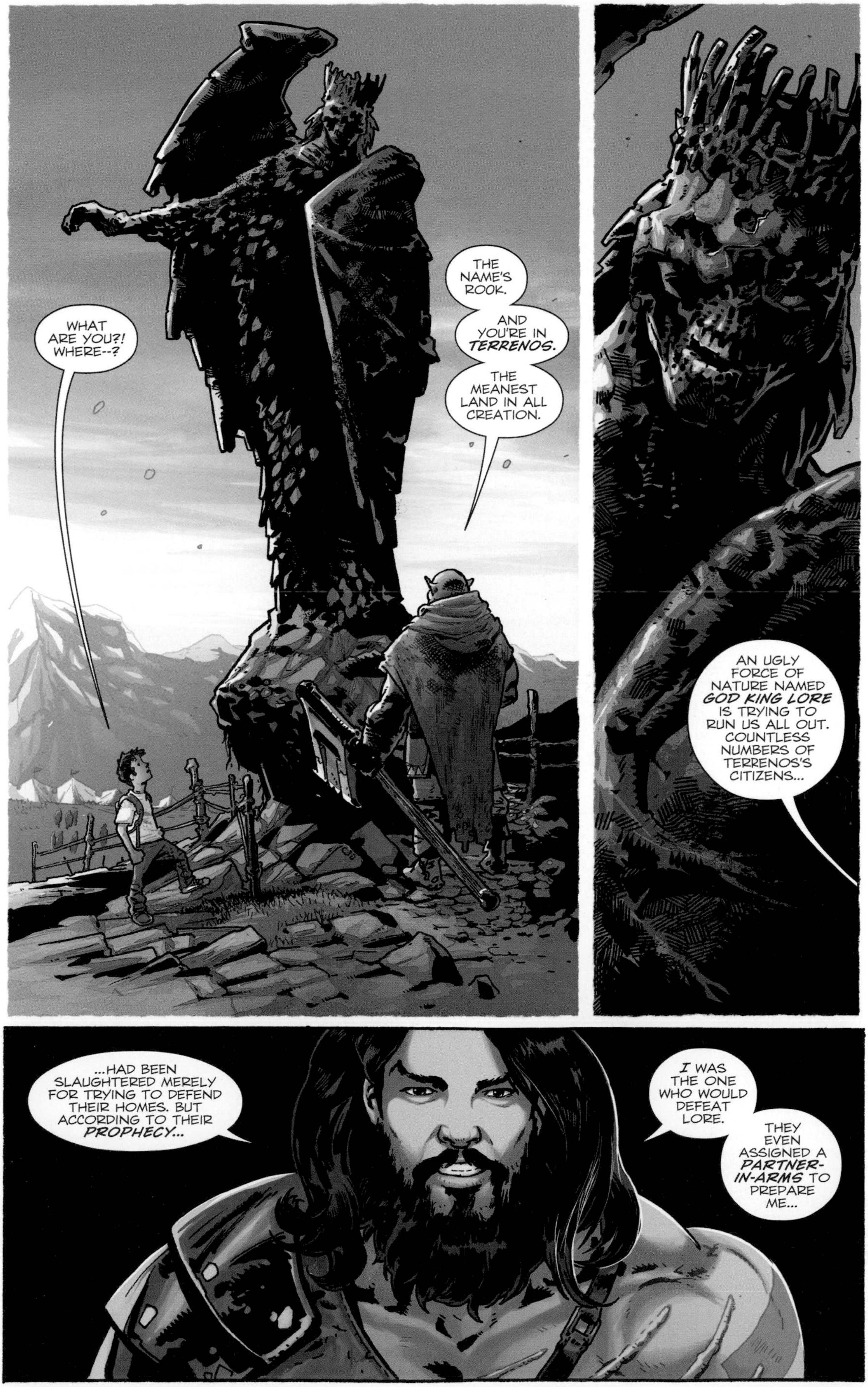
WHAT ARE YOU?! WHERE--?
THE NAME'S ROOK.
AND YOU'RE IN TERRENOS.
THE MEANEST LAND IN ALL CREATION.
AN UGLY FORCE OF NATURE NAMED GOD KING LORE IS TRYING TO RUN US ALL OUT. COUNTLESS NUMBERS OF TERRENOS'S CITIZENS...
...HAD BEEN SLAUGHTERED MERELY FOR TRYING TO DEFEND THEIR HOMES. BUT ACCORDING TO THEIR PROPHECY...
I WAS THE ONE WHO WOULD DEFEAT LORE.
THEY EVEN ASSIGNED A PARTNER-IN-ARMS TO PREPARE ME...

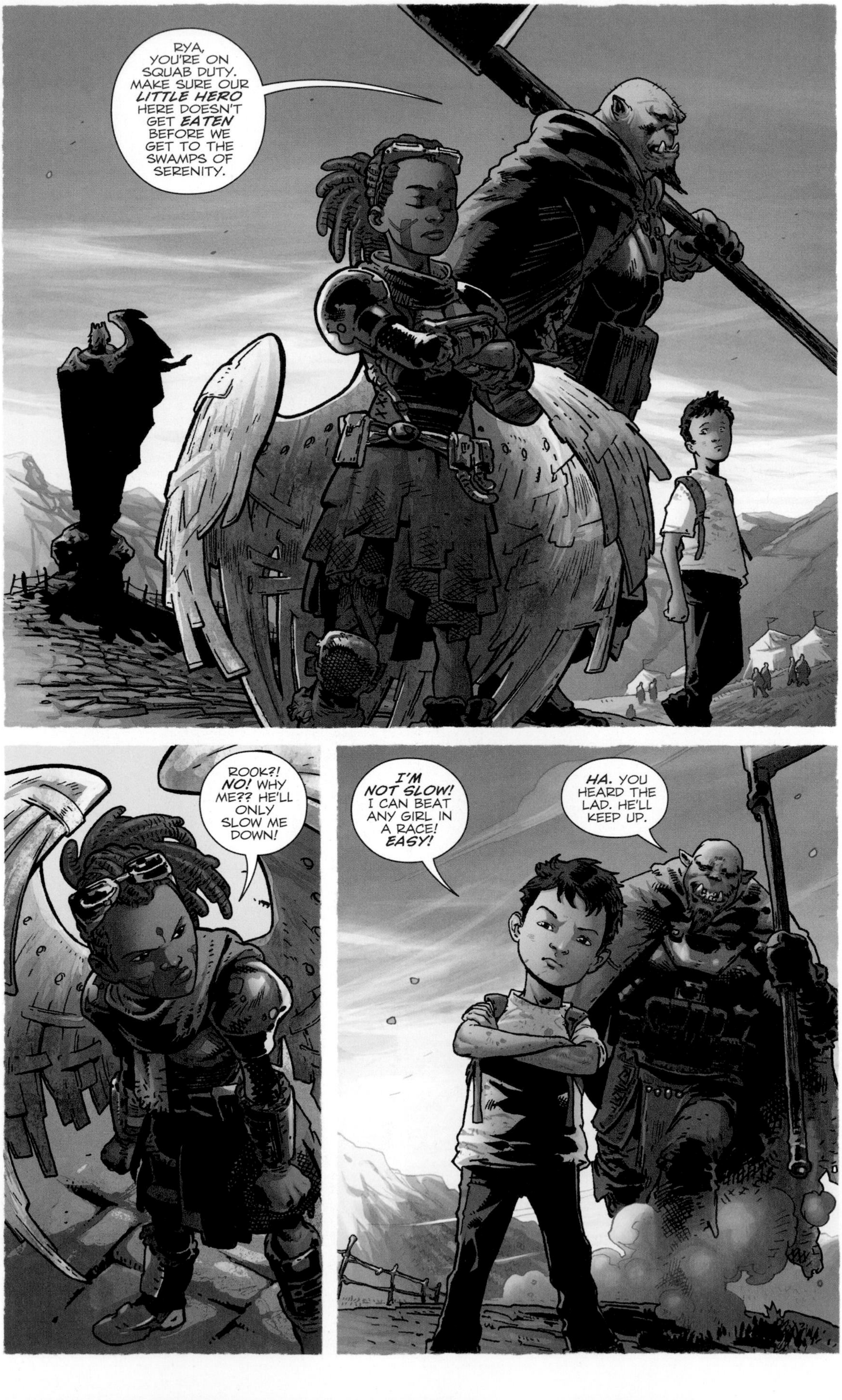
RYA, YOU'RE ON SQUAB DUTY. MAKE SURE OUR LITTLE HERO HERE DOESN'T GET EATEN BEFORE WE GET TO THE SWAMPS OF SERENITY.
ROOK?! NO! WHY ME?? HE'LL ONLY SLOW ME DOWN!
I'M NOT SLOW! I CAN BEAT ANY GIRL IN A RACE! EASY!
HA. YOU HEARD THE LAD. HE'LL KEEP UP.

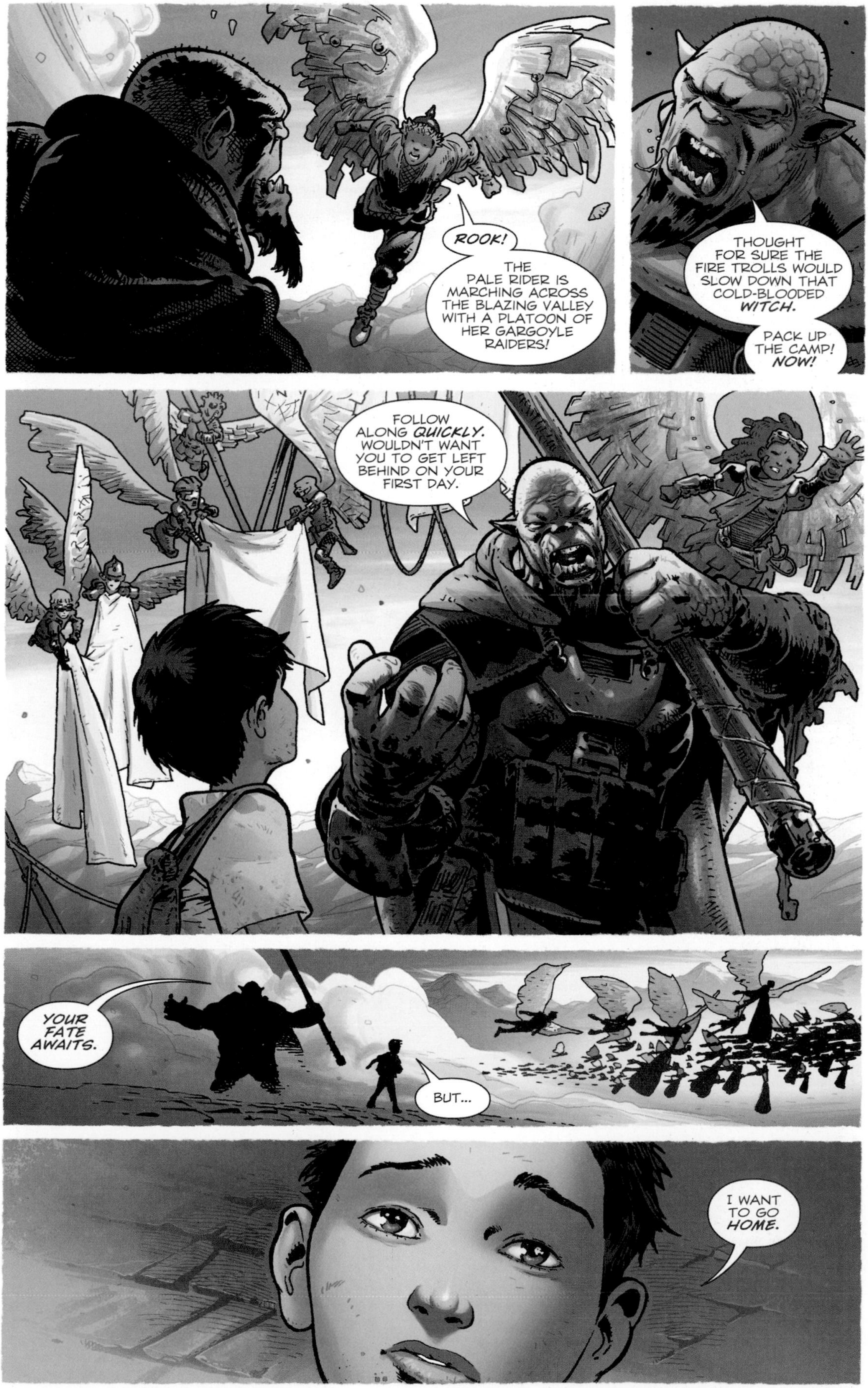
ROOK!
THE PALE RIDER IS MARCHING ACROSS THE BLAZING VALLEY WITH A PLATOON OF HER GARGOYLE RAIDERS!
THOUGHT FOR SURE THE FIRE TROLLS WOULD SLOW DOWN THAT COLD-BLOODED WITCH.
PACK UP THE CAMP! NOW!
FOLLOW ALONG QUICKLY. WOULDN'T WANT YOU TO GET LEFT BEHIND ON YOUR FIRST DAY.
YOUR FATE AWAITS.
BUT...
I WANT TO GO HOME.

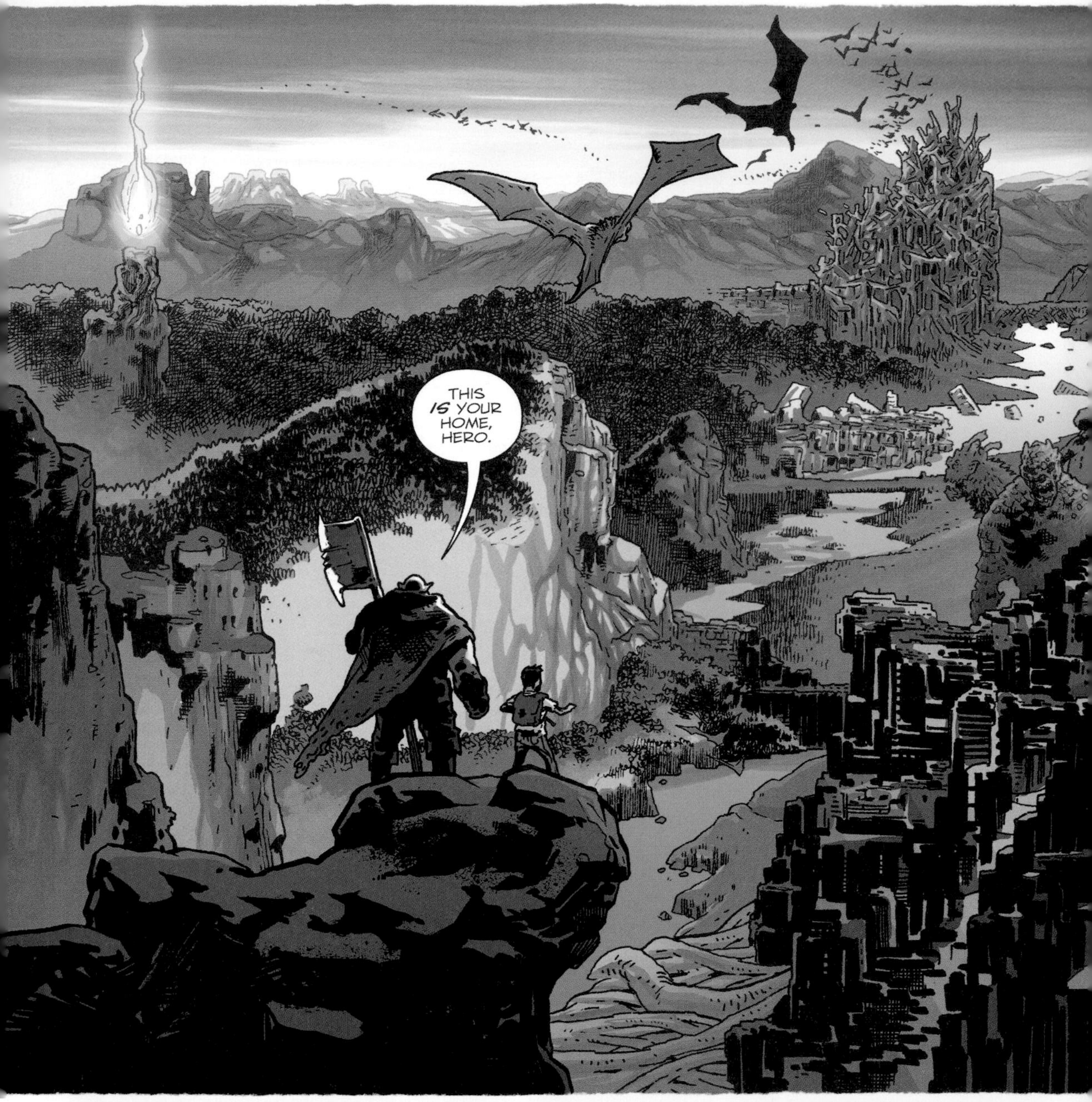
THIS *IS* YOUR HOME, HERO.

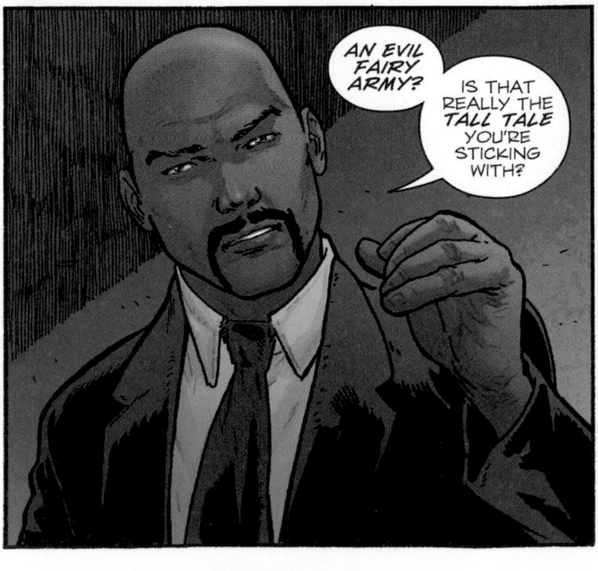
AN EVIL FAIRY ARMY?
IS THAT REALLY THE *TALL TALE* YOU'RE STICKING WITH?

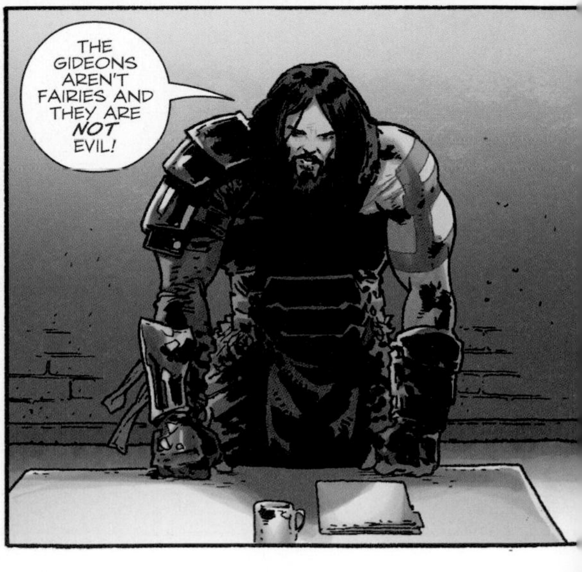
THE GIDEONS AREN'T FAIRIES AND THEY ARE *NOT* EVIL!

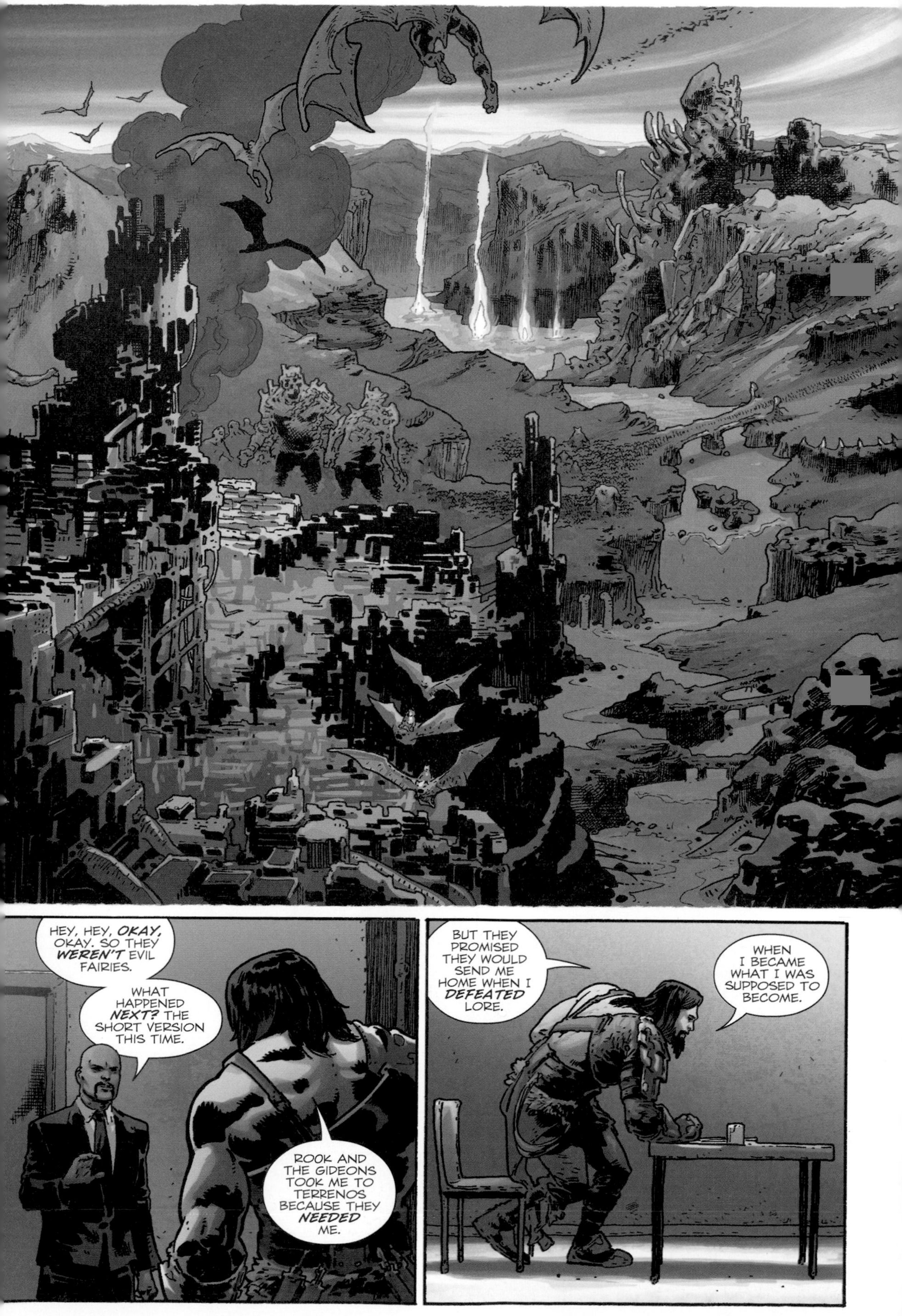
HEY, HEY, OKAY, OKAY. SO THEY WEREN'T EVIL FAIRIES.
WHAT HAPPENED NEXT? THE SHORT VERSION THIS TIME.
ROOK AND THE GIDEONS TOOK ME TO TERRENOS BECAUSE THEY NEEDED ME.
BUT THEY PROMISED THEY WOULD SEND ME HOME WHEN I DEFEATED LORE.
WHEN I BECAME WHAT I WAS SUPPOSED TO BECOME.

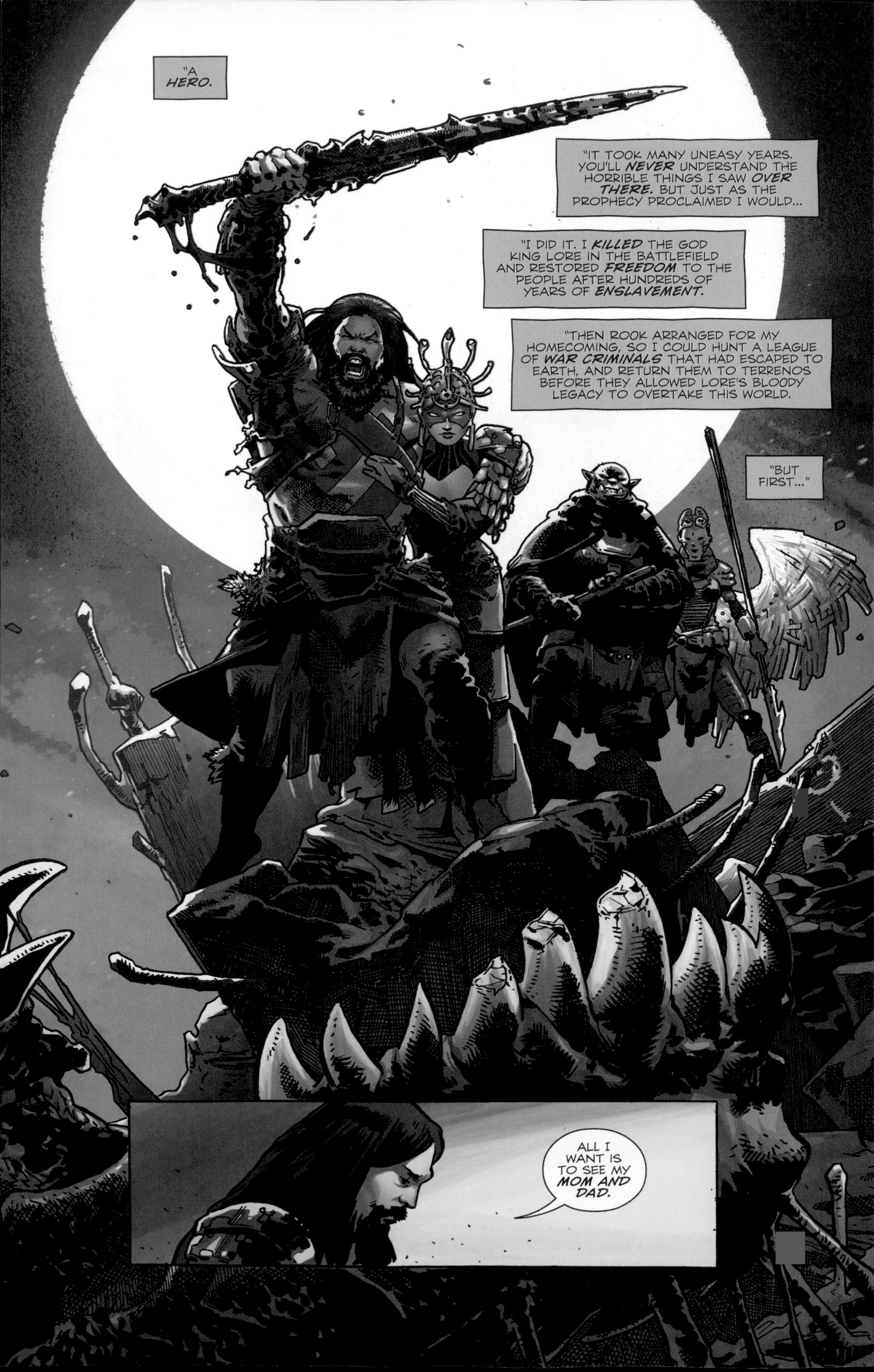

"A *HERO*.
"IT TOOK MANY UNEASY YEARS. YOU'LL ***NEVER*** UNDERSTAND THE HORRIBLE THINGS I SAW ***OVER THERE***. BUT JUST AS THE PROPHECY PROCLAIMED I WOULD...
"I DID IT. I ***KILLED*** THE GOD KING LORE IN THE BATTLEFIELD AND RESTORED ***FREEDOM*** TO THE PEOPLE AFTER HUNDREDS OF YEARS OF ***ENSLAVEMENT***.
"THEN ROOK ARRANGED FOR MY HOMECOMING, SO I COULD HUNT A LEAGUE OF ***WAR CRIMINALS*** THAT HAD ESCAPED TO EARTH, AND RETURN THEM TO TERRENOS BEFORE THEY ALLOWED LORE'S BLOODY LEGACY TO OVERTAKE THIS WORLD.
"BUT FIRST..."
ALL I WANT IS TO SEE MY ***MOM AND DAD***.

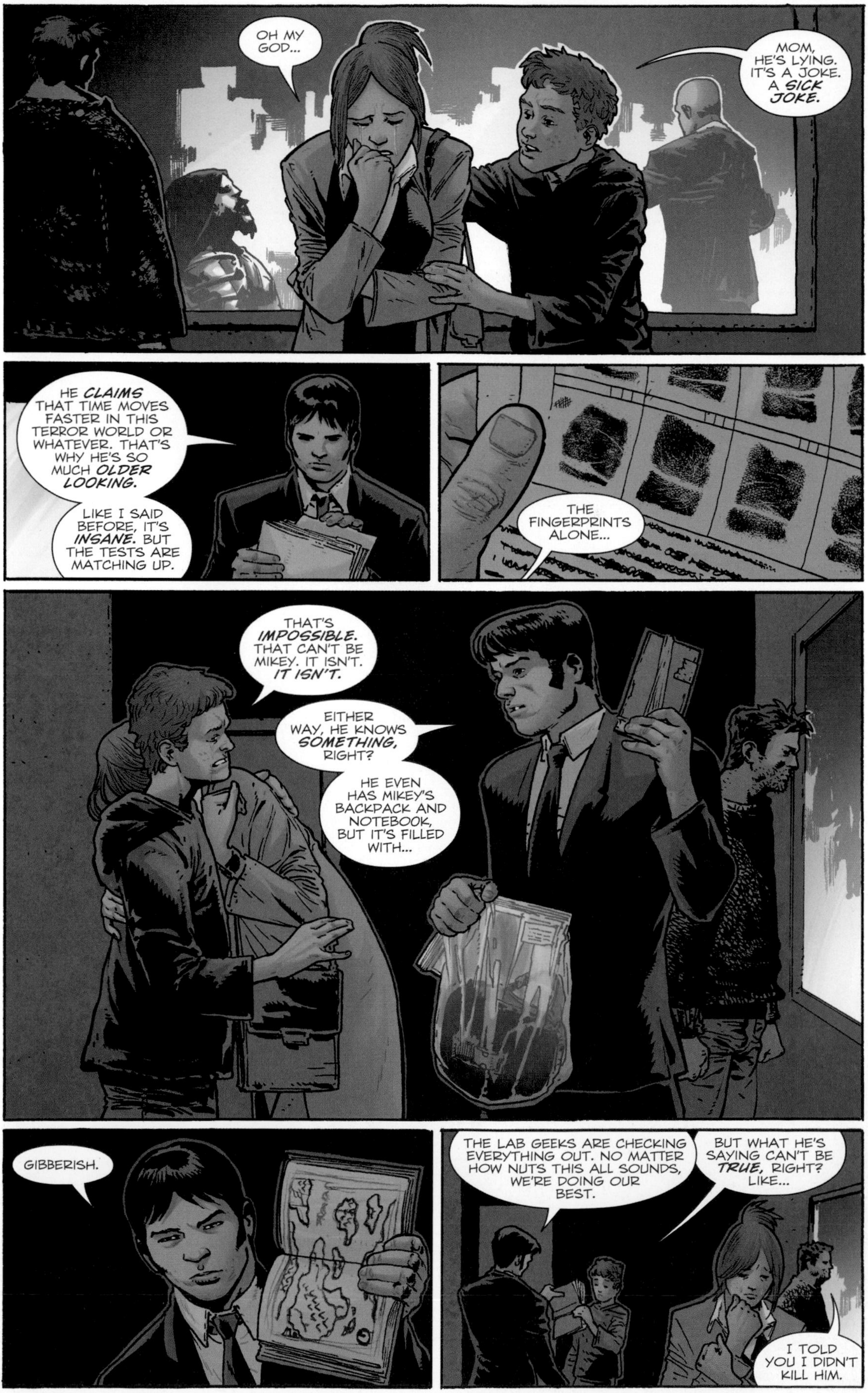
OH MY GOD...
MOM, HE'S LYING. IT'S A JOKE. A SICK JOKE.
HE CLAIMS THAT TIME MOVES FASTER IN THIS TERROR WORLD OR WHATEVER. THAT'S WHY HE'S SO MUCH OLDER LOOKING.
LIKE I SAID BEFORE, IT'S INSANE. BUT THE TESTS ARE MATCHING UP.
THE FINGERPRINTS ALONE...
THAT'S IMPOSSIBLE. THAT CAN'T BE MIKEY. IT ISN'T. IT ISN'T.
EITHER WAY, HE KNOWS SOMETHING, RIGHT?
HE EVEN HAS MIKEY'S BACKPACK AND NOTEBOOK, BUT IT'S FILLED WITH...
GIBBERISH.
THE LAB GEEKS ARE CHECKING EVERYTHING OUT. NO MATTER HOW NUTS THIS ALL SOUNDS, WE'RE DOING OUR BEST.
BUT WHAT HE'S SAYING CAN'T BE TRUE, RIGHT? LIKE...
I TOLD YOU I DIDN'T KILL HIM.

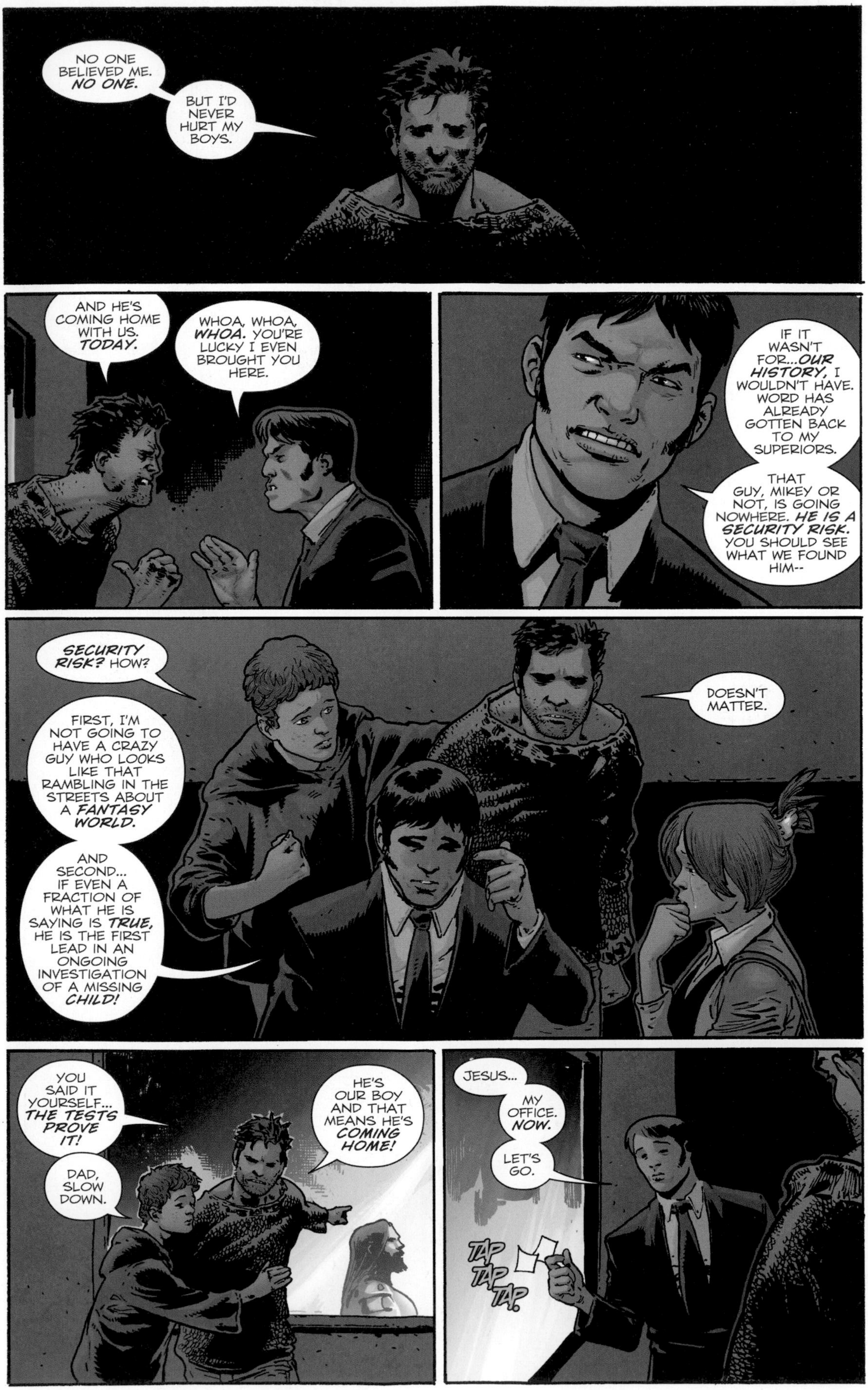
NO ONE BELIEVED ME. NO ONE.
BUT I'D NEVER HURT MY BOYS.
AND HE'S COMING HOME WITH US. TODAY.
WHOA, WHOA, WHOA. YOU'RE LUCKY I EVEN BROUGHT YOU HERE.
IF IT WASN'T FOR...OUR HISTORY, I WOULDN'T HAVE. WORD HAS ALREADY GOTTEN BACK TO MY SUPERIORS.
THAT GUY, MIKEY OR NOT, IS GOING NOWHERE. HE IS A SECURITY RISK. YOU SHOULD SEE WHAT WE FOUND HIM--
SECURITY RISK? HOW?
DOESN'T MATTER.
FIRST, I'M NOT GOING TO HAVE A CRAZY GUY WHO LOOKS LIKE THAT RAMBLING IN THE STREETS ABOUT A FANTASY WORLD.
AND SECOND... IF EVEN A FRACTION OF WHAT HE IS SAYING IS TRUE, HE IS THE FIRST LEAD IN AN ONGOING INVESTIGATION OF A MISSING CHILD!
YOU SAID IT YOURSELF... THE TESTS PROVE IT!
DAD, SLOW DOWN.
HE'S OUR BOY AND THAT MEANS HE'S COMING HOME!
JESUS...
MY OFFICE. NOW.
LET'S GO.
TAP TAP TAP.

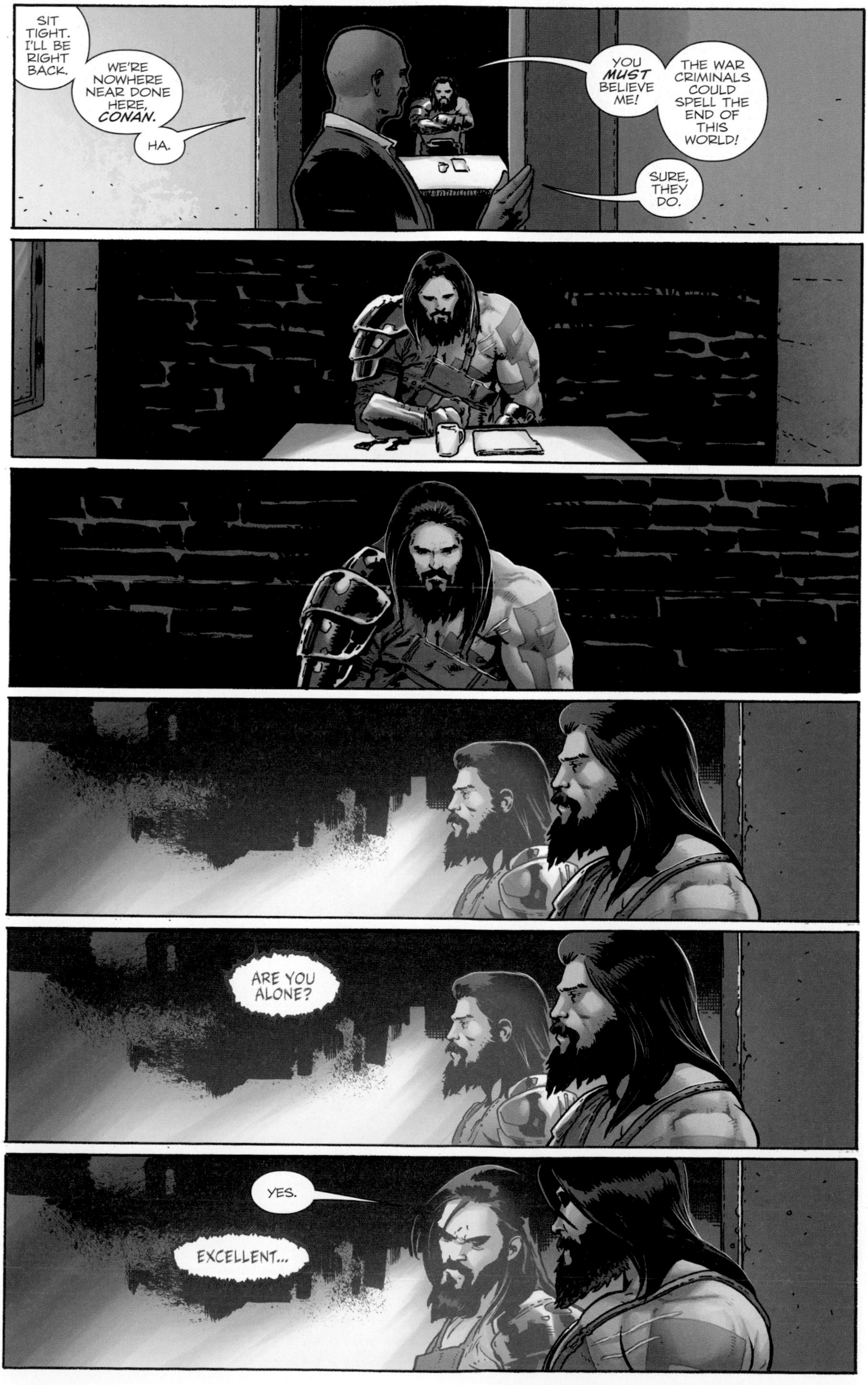
SIT TIGHT. I'LL BE RIGHT BACK.
WE'RE NOWHERE NEAR DONE HERE, CONAN.
HA.
YOU MUST BELIEVE ME!
THE WAR CRIMINALS COULD SPELL THE END OF THIS WORLD!
SURE, THEY DO.
ARE YOU ALONE?
YES.
EXCELLENT...

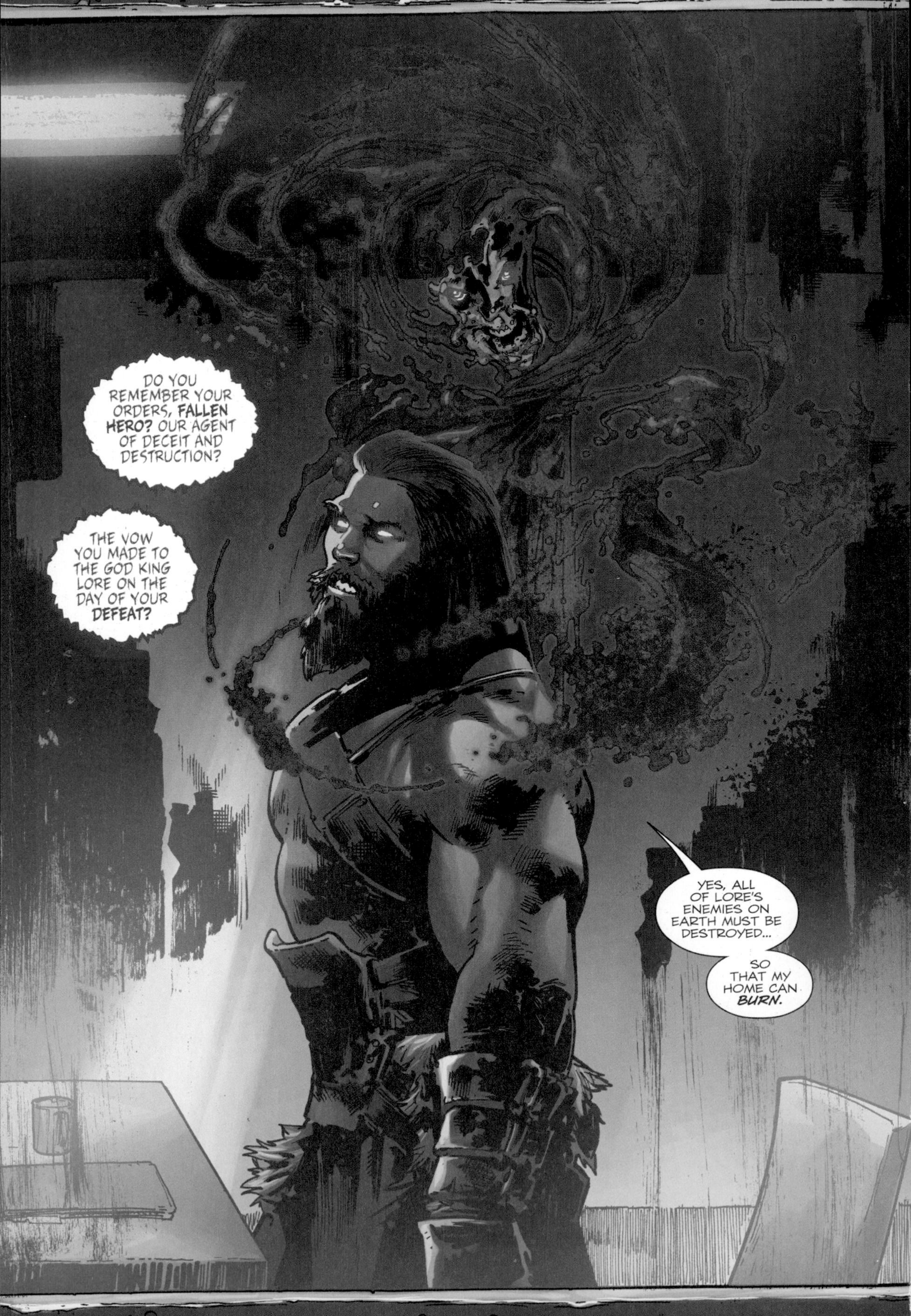
DO YOU REMEMBER YOUR ORDERS, FALLEN HERO? OUR AGENT OF DECEIT AND DESTRUCTION?
THE VOW YOU MADE TO THE GOD KING LORE ON THE DAY OF YOUR DEFEAT?
YES, ALL OF LORE'S ENEMIES ON EARTH MUST BE DESTROYED...
SO THAT MY HOME CAN BURN.

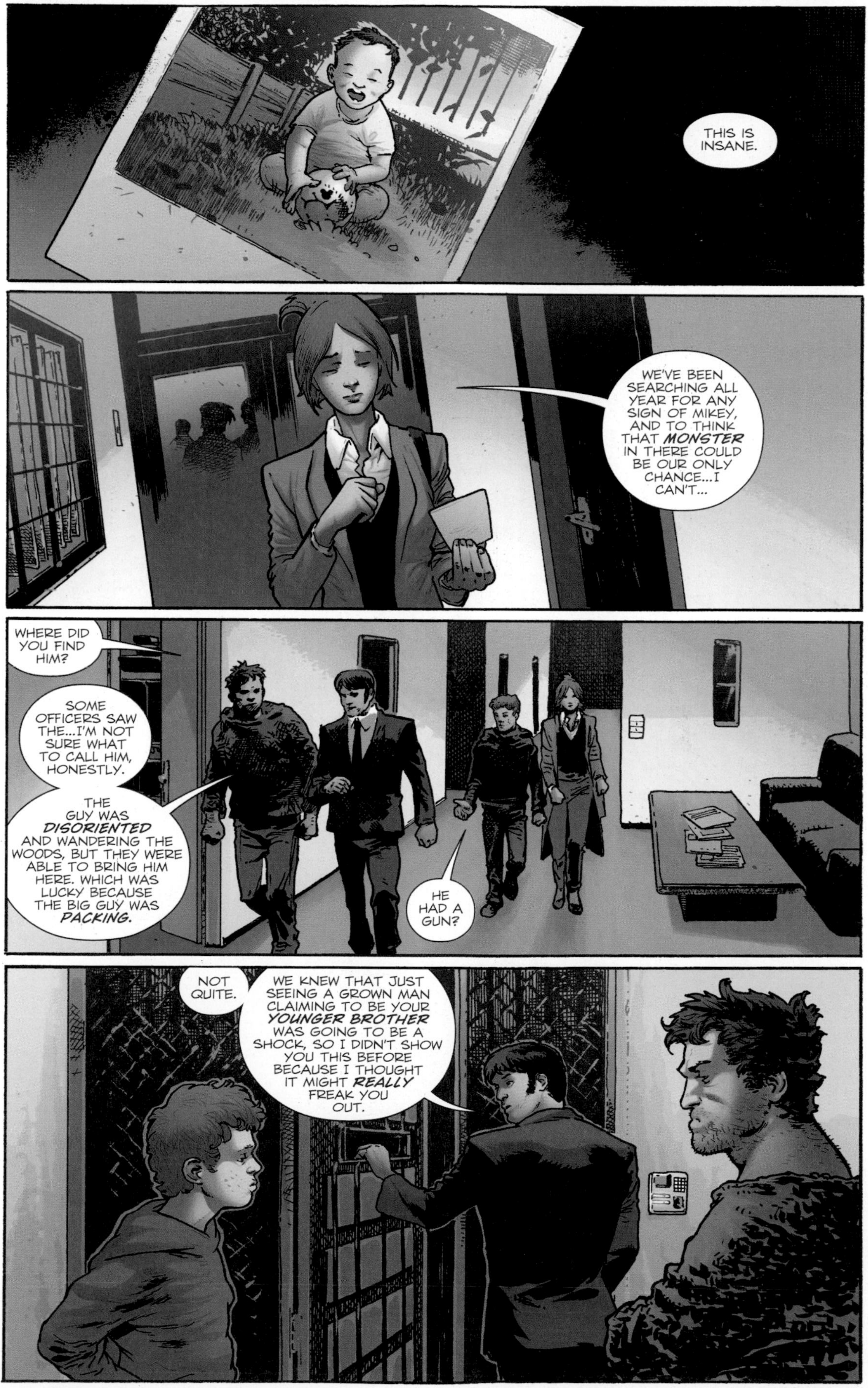
THIS IS INSANE.
WE'VE BEEN SEARCHING ALL YEAR FOR ANY SIGN OF MIKEY, AND TO THINK THAT MONSTER IN THERE COULD BE OUR ONLY CHANCE...I CAN'T...
WHERE DID YOU FIND HIM?
SOME OFFICERS SAW THE...I'M NOT SURE WHAT TO CALL HIM, HONESTLY.
THE GUY WAS DISORIENTED AND WANDERING THE WOODS, BUT THEY WERE ABLE TO BRING HIM HERE. WHICH WAS LUCKY BECAUSE THE BIG GUY WAS PACKING.
HE HAD A GUN?
NOT QUITE.
WE KNEW THAT JUST SEEING A GROWN MAN CLAIMING TO BE YOUR YOUNGER BROTHER WAS GOING TO BE A SHOCK, SO I DIDN'T SHOW YOU THIS BEFORE BECAUSE I THOUGHT IT MIGHT REALLY FREAK YOU OUT.

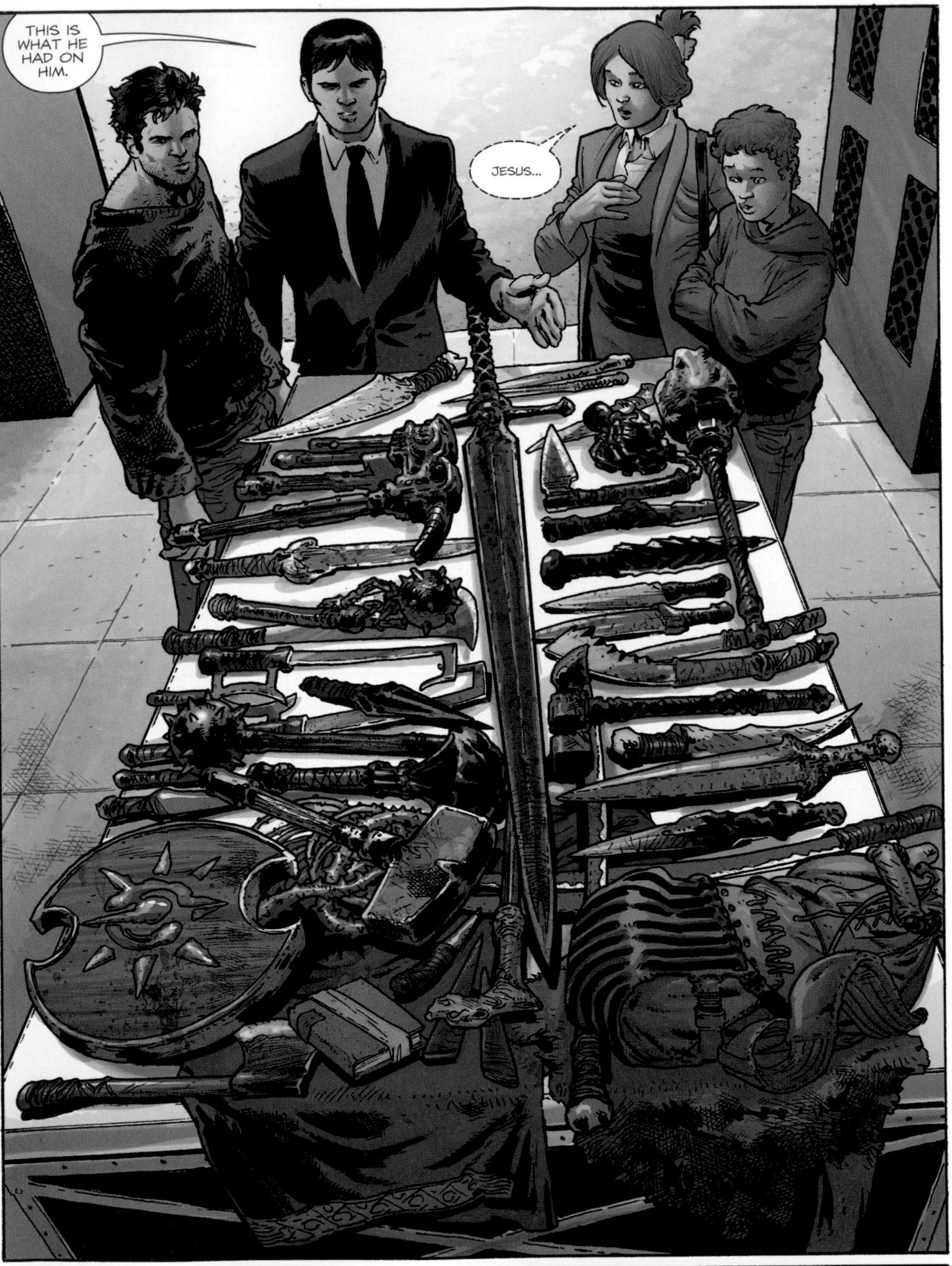
THIS IS WHAT HE HAD ON HIM.
JESUS...
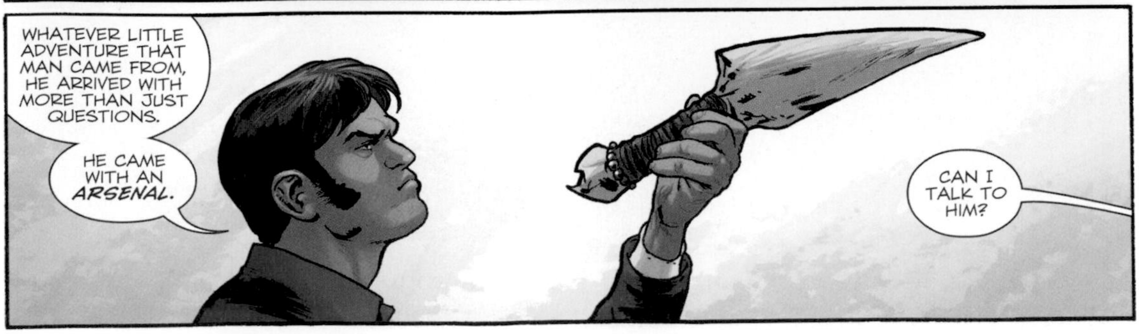
WHATEVER LITTLE ADVENTURE THAT MAN CAME FROM, HE ARRIVED WITH MORE THAN JUST QUESTIONS.
HE CAME WITH AN ***ARSENAL.***
CAN I TALK TO HIM?

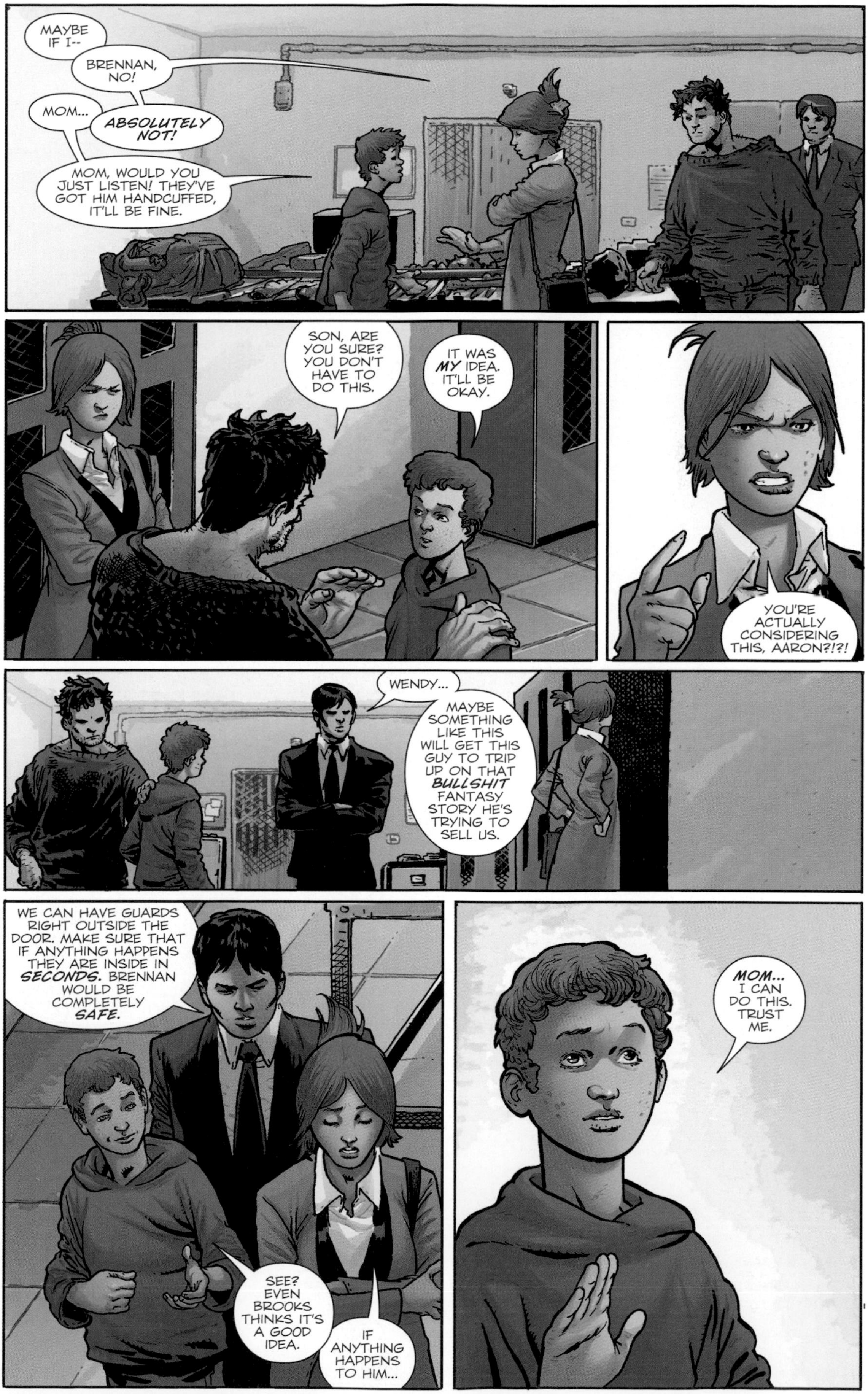
MAYBE IF I--
BRENNAN, NO!
MOM...
ABSOLUTELY NOT!
MOM, WOULD YOU JUST LISTEN! THEY'VE GOT HIM HANDCUFFED, IT'LL BE FINE.
SON, ARE YOU SURE? YOU DON'T HAVE TO DO THIS.
IT WAS MY IDEA. IT'LL BE OKAY.
YOU'RE ACTUALLY CONSIDERING THIS, AARON?!?!
WENDY...
MAYBE SOMETHING LIKE THIS WILL GET THIS GUY TO TRIP UP ON THAT BULLSHIT FANTASY STORY HE'S TRYING TO SELL US.
WE CAN HAVE GUARDS RIGHT OUTSIDE THE DOOR. MAKE SURE THAT IF ANYTHING HAPPENS THEY ARE INSIDE IN SECONDS. BRENNAN WOULD BE COMPLETELY SAFE.
SEE? EVEN BROOKS THINKS IT'S A GOOD IDEA.
IF ANYTHING HAPPENS TO HIM...
MOM... I CAN DO THIS. TRUST ME.

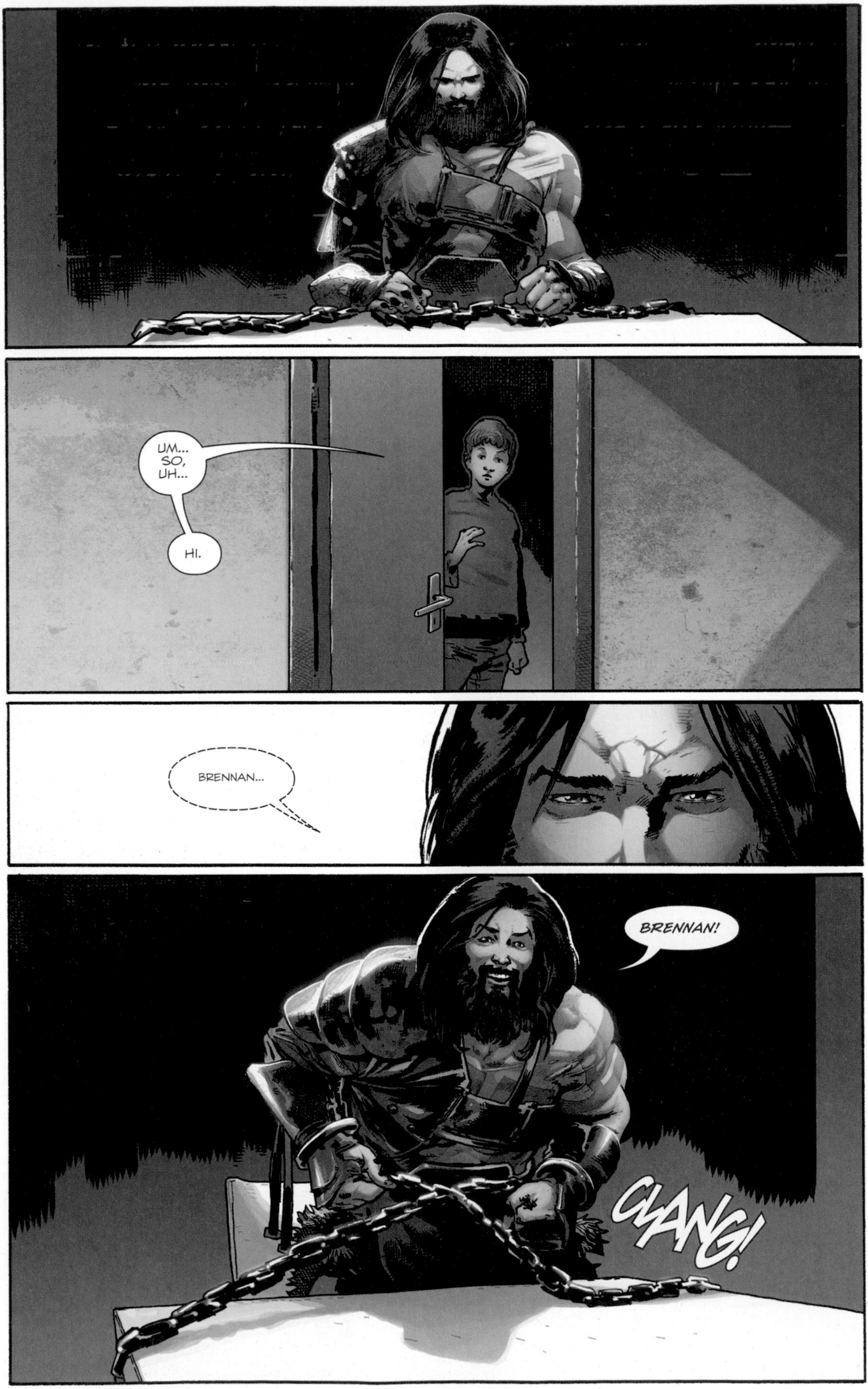
UM... SO, UH...
HI.
BRENNAN...
BRENNAN!
CLANG!

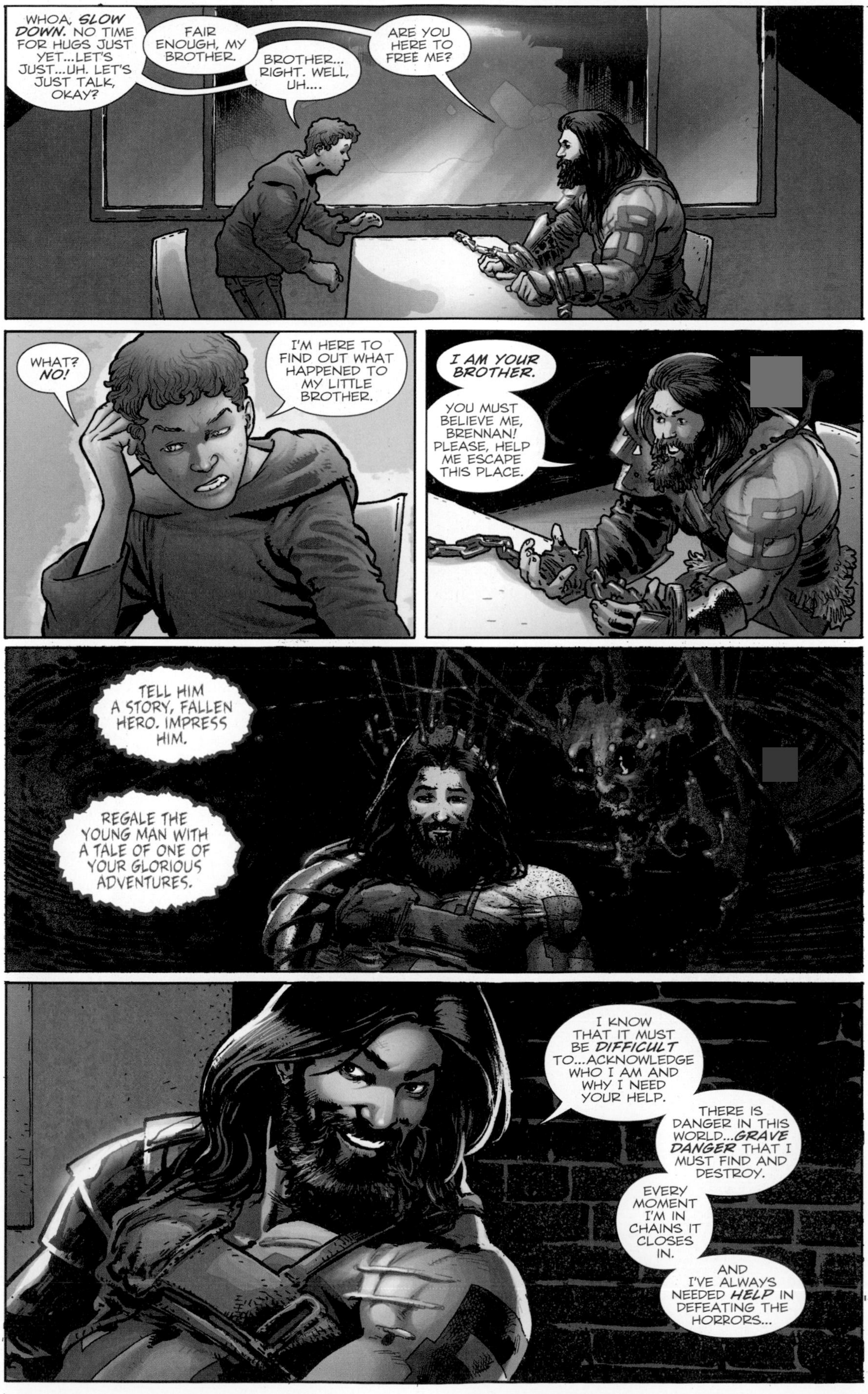
WHOA, SLOW DOWN. NO TIME FOR HUGS JUST YET...LET'S JUST...UH. LET'S JUST TALK, OKAY?
FAIR ENOUGH, MY BROTHER.
BROTHER... RIGHT. WELL, UH....
ARE YOU HERE TO FREE ME?
WHAT? NO!
I'M HERE TO FIND OUT WHAT HAPPENED TO MY LITTLE BROTHER.
I AM YOUR BROTHER.
YOU MUST BELIEVE ME, BRENNAN! PLEASE, HELP ME ESCAPE THIS PLACE.
TELL HIM A STORY, FALLEN HERO. IMPRESS HIM.
REGALE THE YOUNG MAN WITH A TALE OF ONE OF YOUR GLORIOUS ADVENTURES.
I KNOW THAT IT MUST BE DIFFICULT TO...ACKNOWLEDGE WHO I AM AND WHY I NEED YOUR HELP.
THERE IS DANGER IN THIS WORLD...GRAVE DANGER THAT I MUST FIND AND DESTROY.
EVERY MOMENT I'M IN CHAINS IT CLOSES IN.
AND I'VE ALWAYS NEEDED HELP IN DEFEATING THE HORRORS...

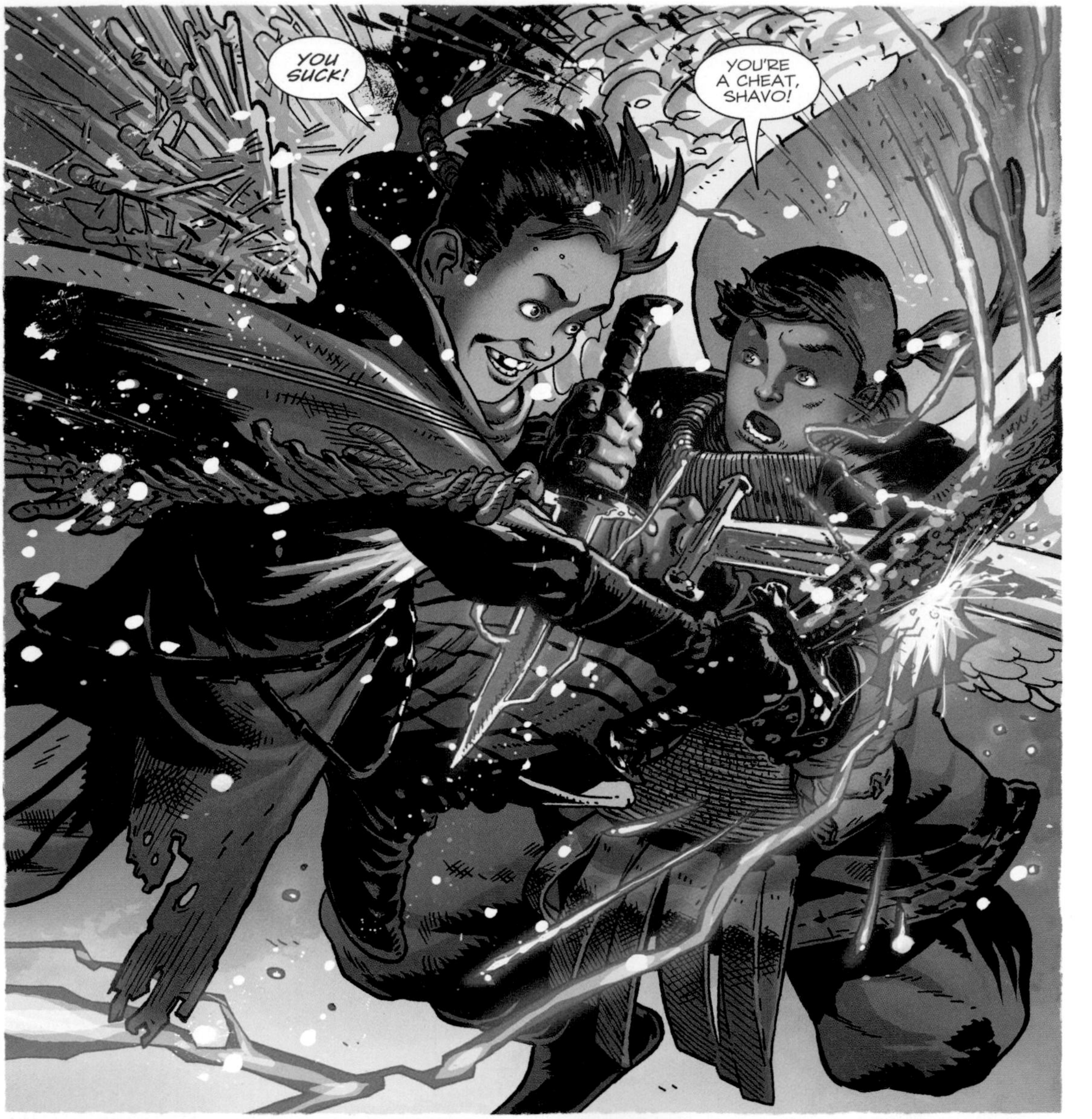
YOU SUCK!
YOU'RE A CHEAT, SHAVO!
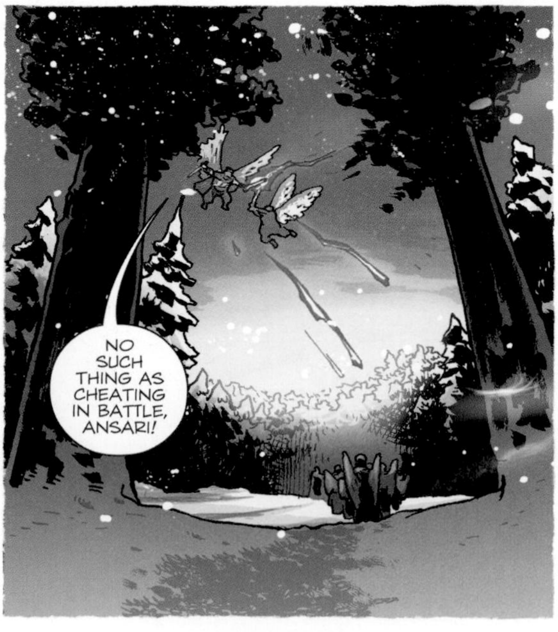
NO SUCH THING AS CHEATING IN BATTLE, ANSARI!
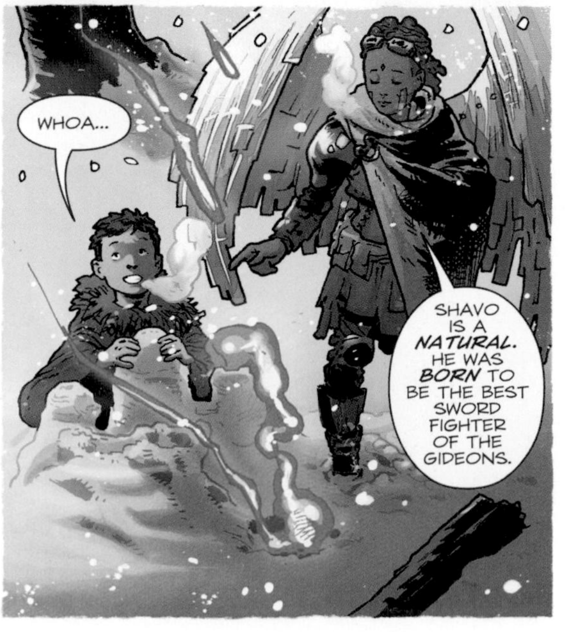
WHOA...
SHAVO IS A **NATURAL.** HE WAS **BORN** TO BE THE BEST SWORD FIGHTER OF THE GIDEONS.

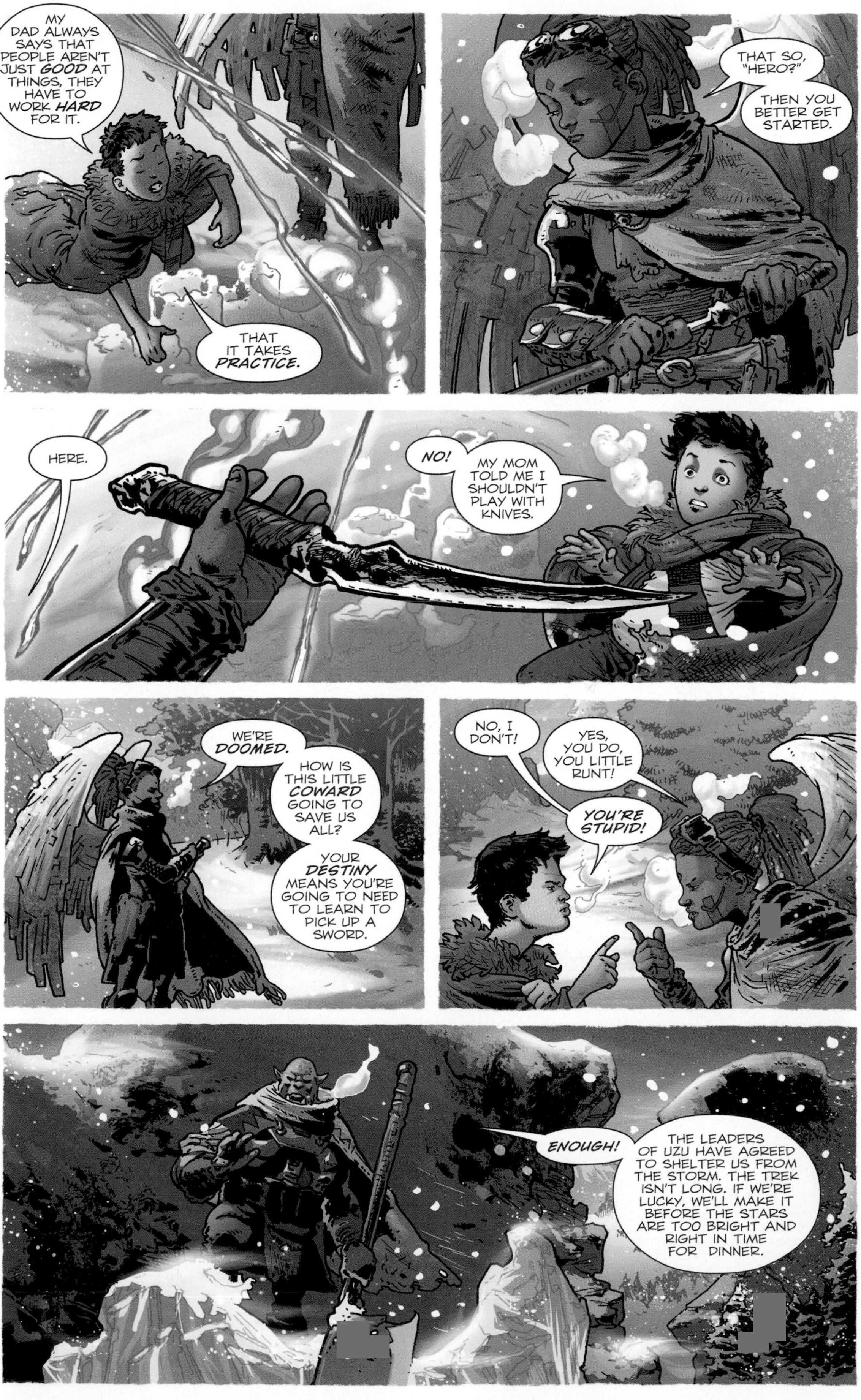
MY DAD ALWAYS SAYS THAT PEOPLE AREN'T JUST *GOOD* AT THINGS, THEY HAVE TO WORK *HARD* FOR IT.
THAT IT TAKES *PRACTICE.*
THAT SO, "HERO?"
THEN YOU BETTER GET STARTED.
HERE.
NO!
MY MOM TOLD ME I SHOULDN'T PLAY WITH KNIVES.
WE'RE *DOOMED.*
HOW IS THIS LITTLE *COWARD* GOING TO SAVE US ALL?
YOUR *DESTINY* MEANS YOU'RE GOING TO NEED TO LEARN TO PICK UP A SWORD.
NO, I DON'T!
YES, YOU DO, YOU LITTLE RUNT!
YOU'RE STUPID!
ENOUGH!
THE LEADERS OF UZU HAVE AGREED TO SHELTER US FROM THE STORM. THE TREK ISN'T LONG. IF WE'RE LUCKY, WE'LL MAKE IT BEFORE THE STARS ARE TOO BRIGHT AND RIGHT IN TIME FOR DINNER.

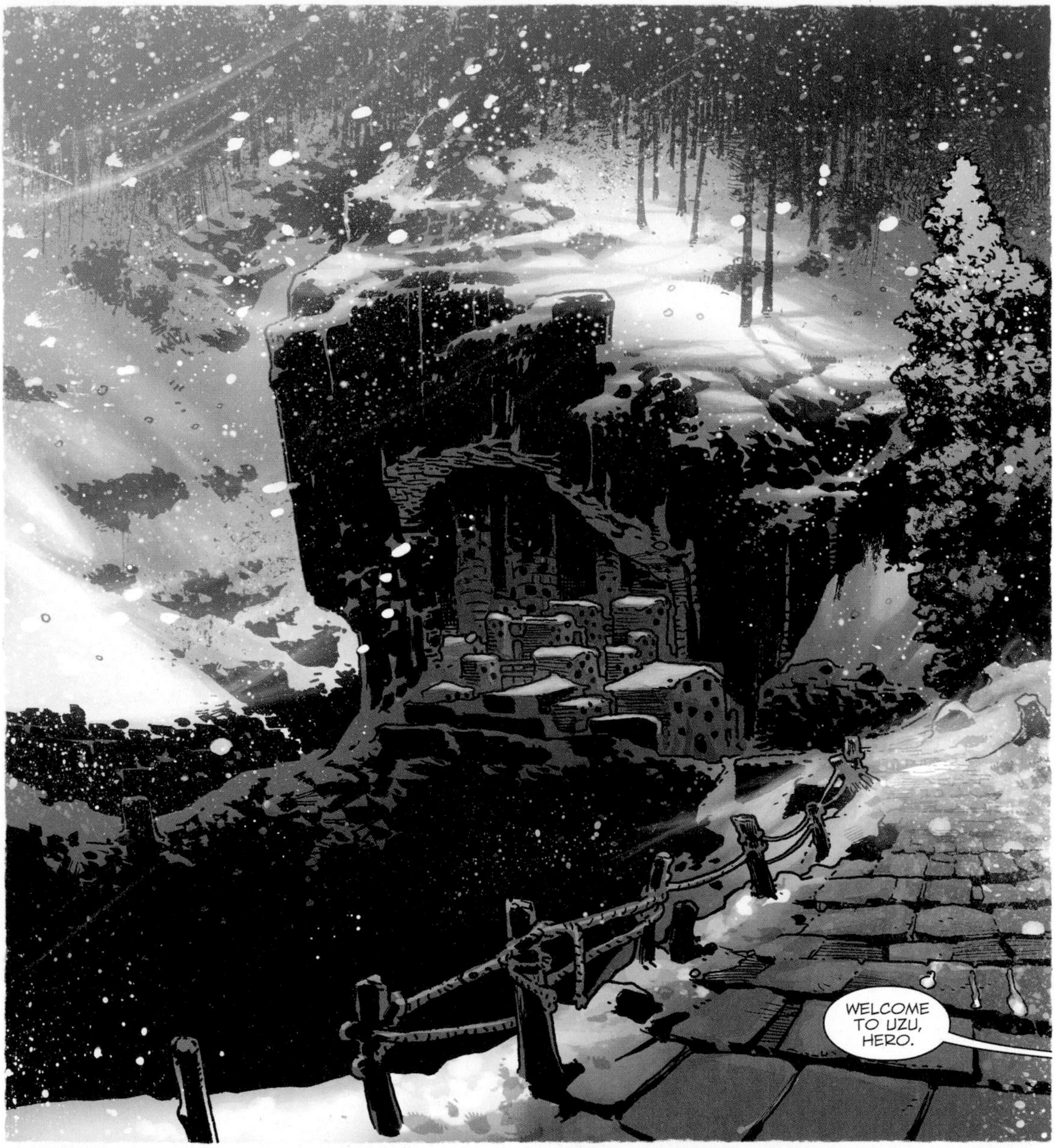
WELCOME TO UZU, HERO.

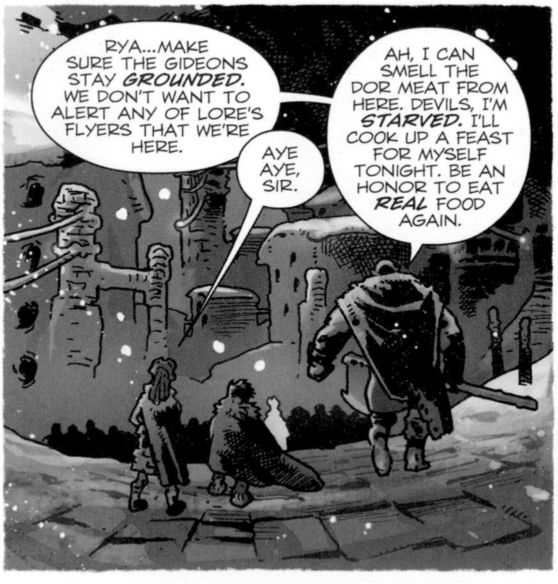
RYA...MAKE SURE THE GIDEONS STAY GROUNDED. WE DON'T WANT TO ALERT ANY OF LORE'S FLYERS THAT WE'RE HERE.
AYE AYE, SIR.
AH, I CAN SMELL THE DOR MEAT FROM HERE. DEVILS, I'M STARVED. I'LL COOK UP A FEAST FOR MYSELF TONIGHT. BE AN HONOR TO EAT REAL FOOD AGAIN.

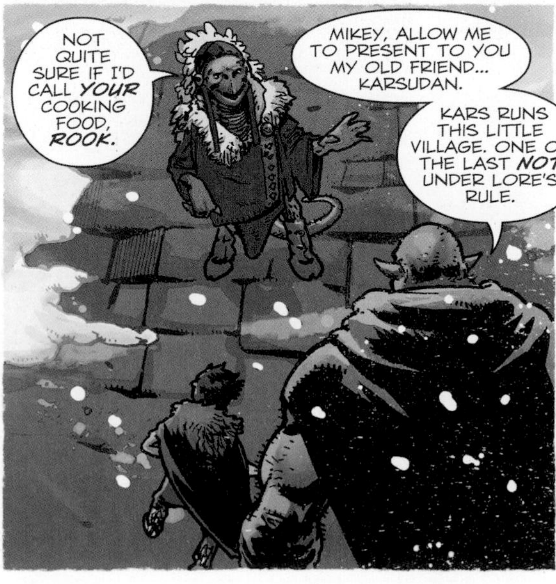
MIKEY, ALLOW ME TO PRESENT TO YOU MY OLD FRIEND... KARSUDAN.
KARS RUNS THIS LITTLE VILLAGE. ONE OF THE LAST NOT UNDER LORE'S RULE.
NOT QUITE SURE IF I'D CALL YOUR COOKING FOOD, ROOK.

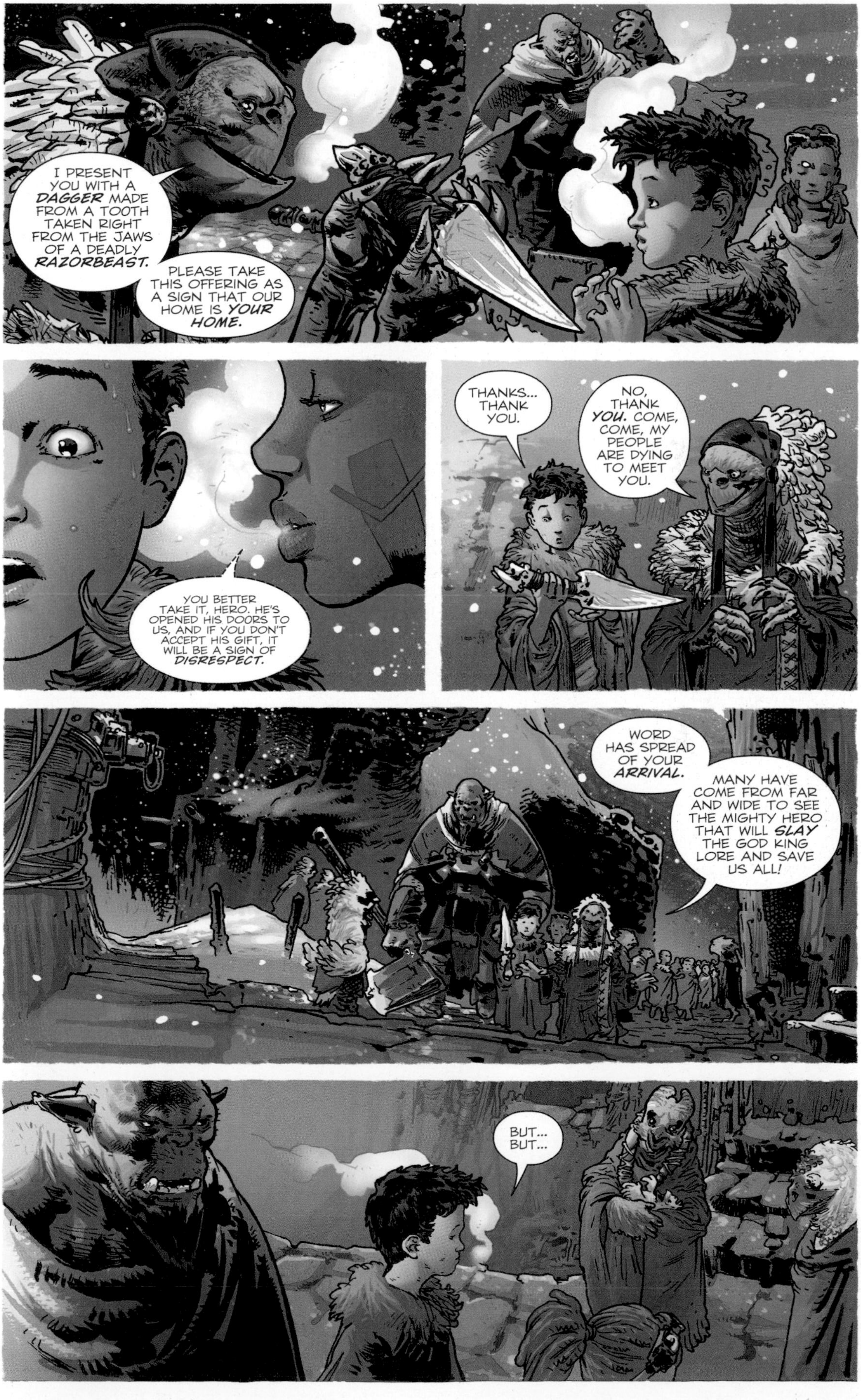
I PRESENT YOU WITH A DAGGER MADE FROM A TOOTH TAKEN RIGHT FROM THE JAWS OF A DEADLY RAZORBEAST.
PLEASE TAKE THIS OFFERING AS A SIGN THAT OUR HOME IS YOUR HOME.
YOU BETTER TAKE IT, HERO. HE'S OPENED HIS DOORS TO US, AND IF YOU DON'T ACCEPT HIS GIFT, IT WILL BE A SIGN OF DISRESPECT.
THANKS... THANK YOU.
NO, THANK YOU. COME, COME, MY PEOPLE ARE DYING TO MEET YOU.
WORD HAS SPREAD OF YOUR ARRIVAL.
MANY HAVE COME FROM FAR AND WIDE TO SEE THE MIGHTY HERO THAT WILL SLAY THE GOD KING LORE AND SAVE US ALL!
BUT... BUT...

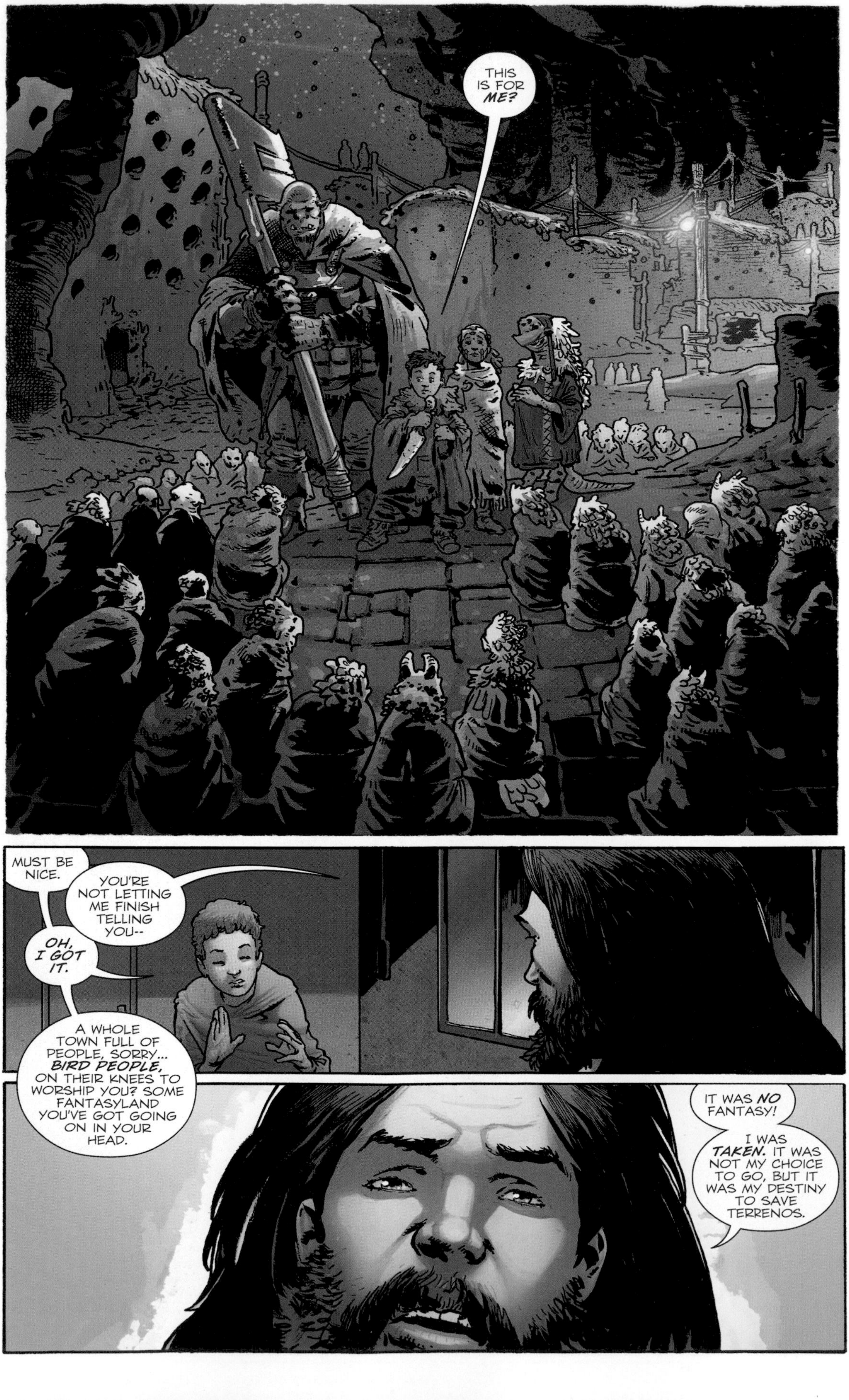

THIS IS FOR ME?
MUST BE NICE.
YOU'RE NOT LETTING ME FINISH TELLING YOU--
OH, I GOT IT.
A WHOLE TOWN FULL OF PEOPLE, SORRY... BIRD PEOPLE, ON THEIR KNEES TO WORSHIP YOU? SOME FANTASYLAND YOU'VE GOT GOING ON IN YOUR HEAD.
IT WAS NO FANTASY!
I WAS TAKEN. IT WAS NOT MY CHOICE TO GO, BUT IT WAS MY DESTINY TO SAVE TERRENOS.

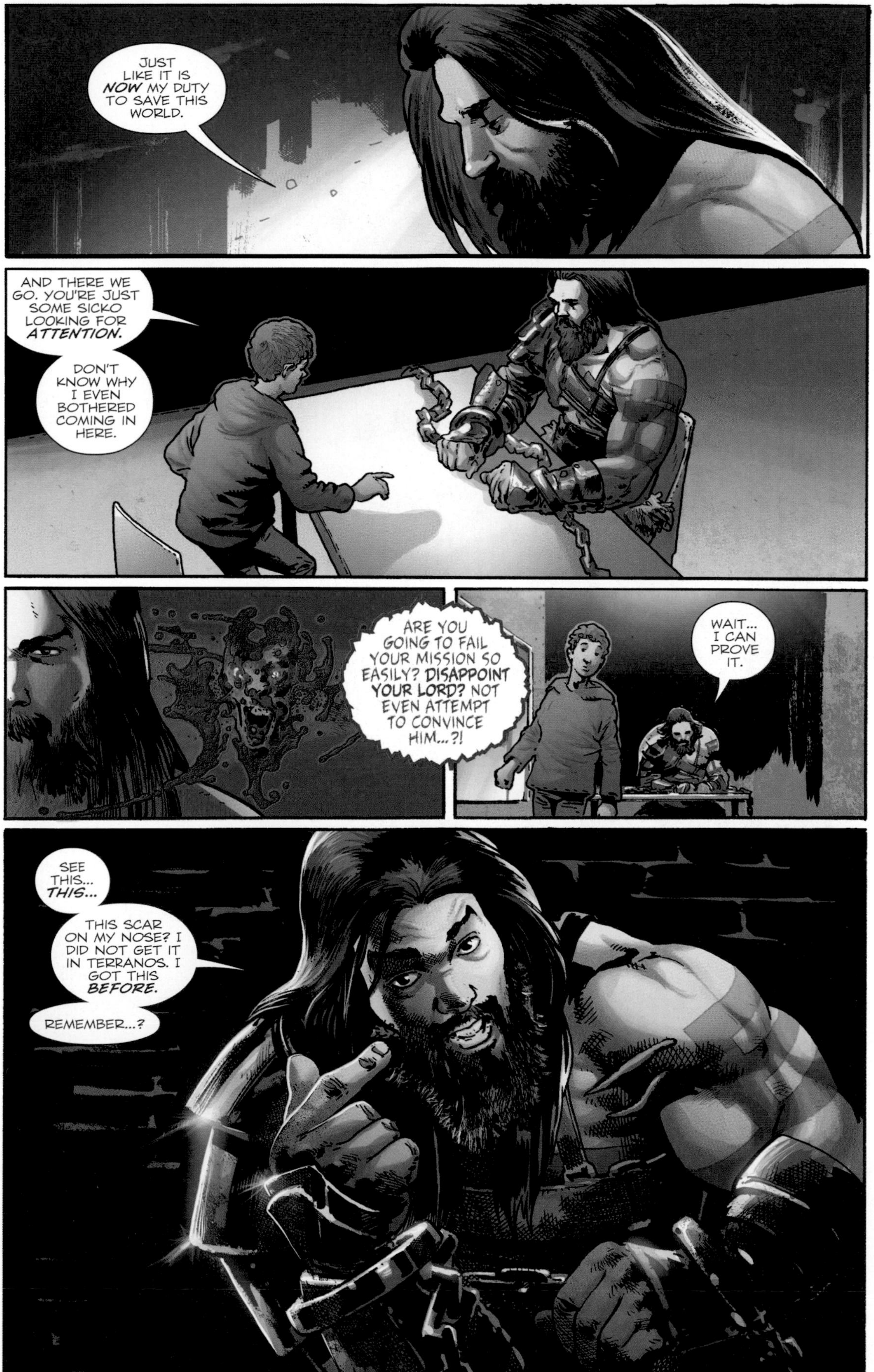
JUST LIKE IT IS NOW MY DUTY TO SAVE THIS WORLD.
AND THERE WE GO. YOU'RE JUST SOME SICKO LOOKING FOR ATTENTION.
DON'T KNOW WHY I EVEN BOTHERED COMING IN HERE.
ARE YOU GOING TO FAIL YOUR MISSION SO EASILY? DISAPPOINT YOUR LORD? NOT EVEN ATTEMPT TO CONVINCE HIM...?!
WAIT... I CAN PROVE IT.
SEE THIS... THIS...
THIS SCAR ON MY NOSE? I DID NOT GET IT IN TERRANOS. I GOT THIS BEFORE.
REMEMBER...?

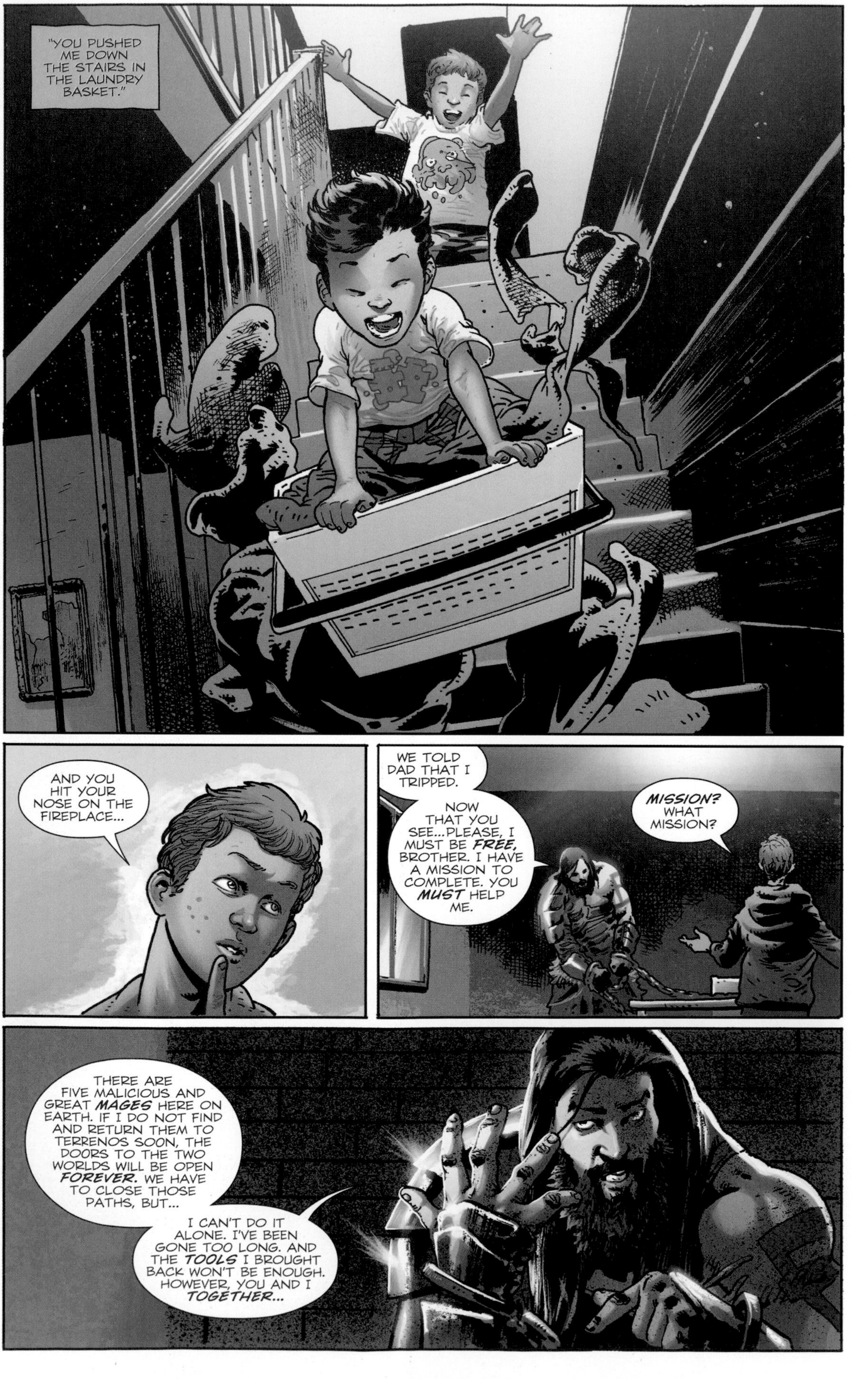
"YOU PUSHED ME DOWN THE STAIRS IN THE LAUNDRY BASKET."
AND YOU HIT YOUR NOSE ON THE FIREPLACE...
WE TOLD DAD THAT I TRIPPED.
NOW THAT YOU SEE...PLEASE, I MUST BE FREE, BROTHER. I HAVE A MISSION TO COMPLETE. YOU MUST HELP ME.
MISSION? WHAT MISSION?
THERE ARE FIVE MALICIOUS AND GREAT MAGES HERE ON EARTH. IF I DO NOT FIND AND RETURN THEM TO TERRENOS SOON, THE DOORS TO THE TWO WORLDS WILL BE OPEN FOREVER. WE HAVE TO CLOSE THOSE PATHS, BUT...
I CAN'T DO IT ALONE. I'VE BEEN GONE TOO LONG. AND THE TOOLS I BROUGHT BACK WON'T BE ENOUGH. HOWEVER, YOU AND I TOGETHER...

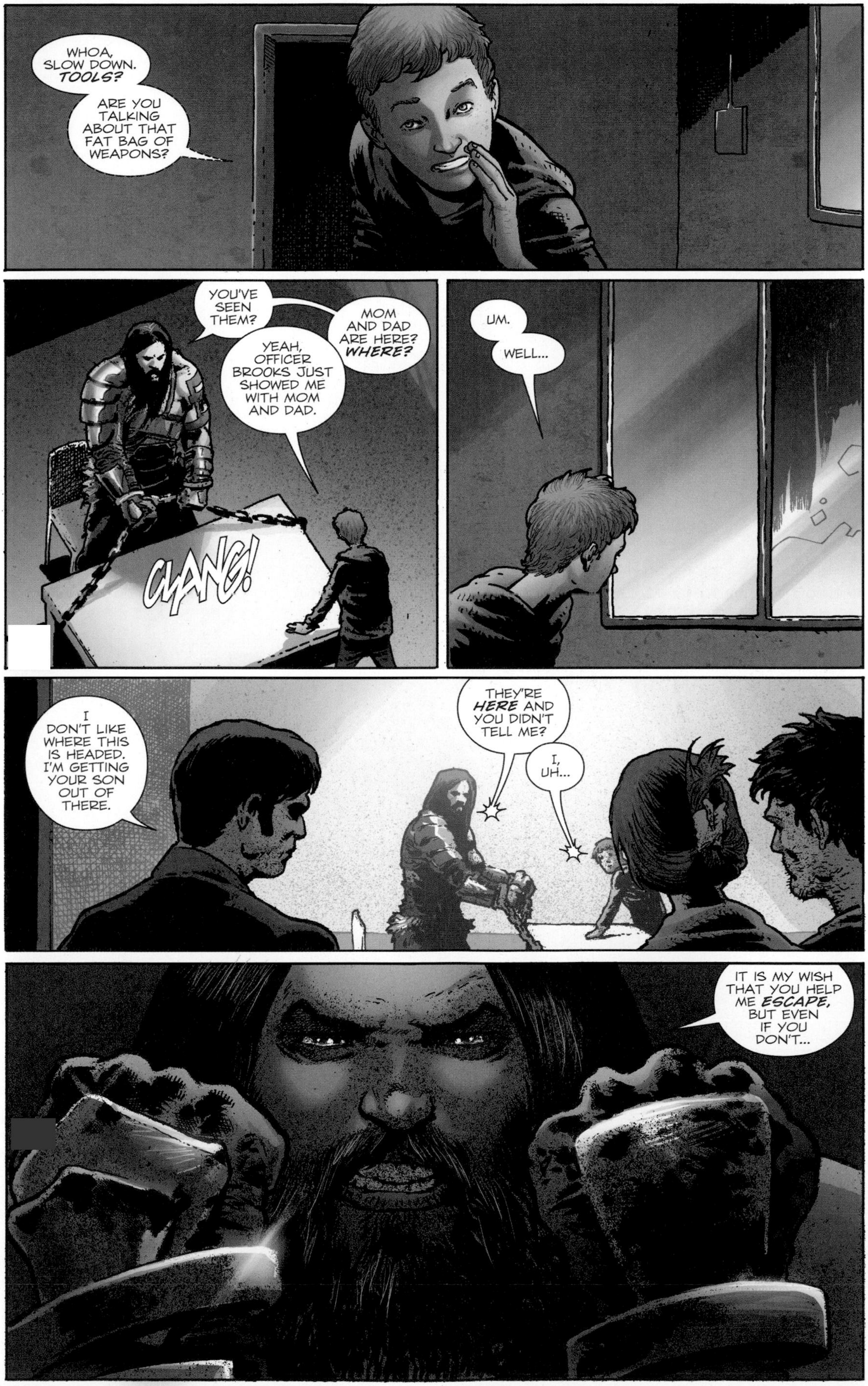
WHOA, SLOW DOWN. TOOLS?
ARE YOU TALKING ABOUT THAT FAT BAG OF WEAPONS?
YOU'VE SEEN THEM?
YEAH, OFFICER BROOKS JUST SHOWED ME WITH MOM AND DAD.
MOM AND DAD ARE HERE? WHERE?
CLANG!
UM.
WELL...
I DON'T LIKE WHERE THIS IS HEADED. I'M GETTING YOUR SON OUT OF THERE.
THEY'RE HERE AND YOU DIDN'T TELL ME?
I, UH...
IT IS MY WISH THAT YOU HELP ME ESCAPE, BUT EVEN IF YOU DON'T...

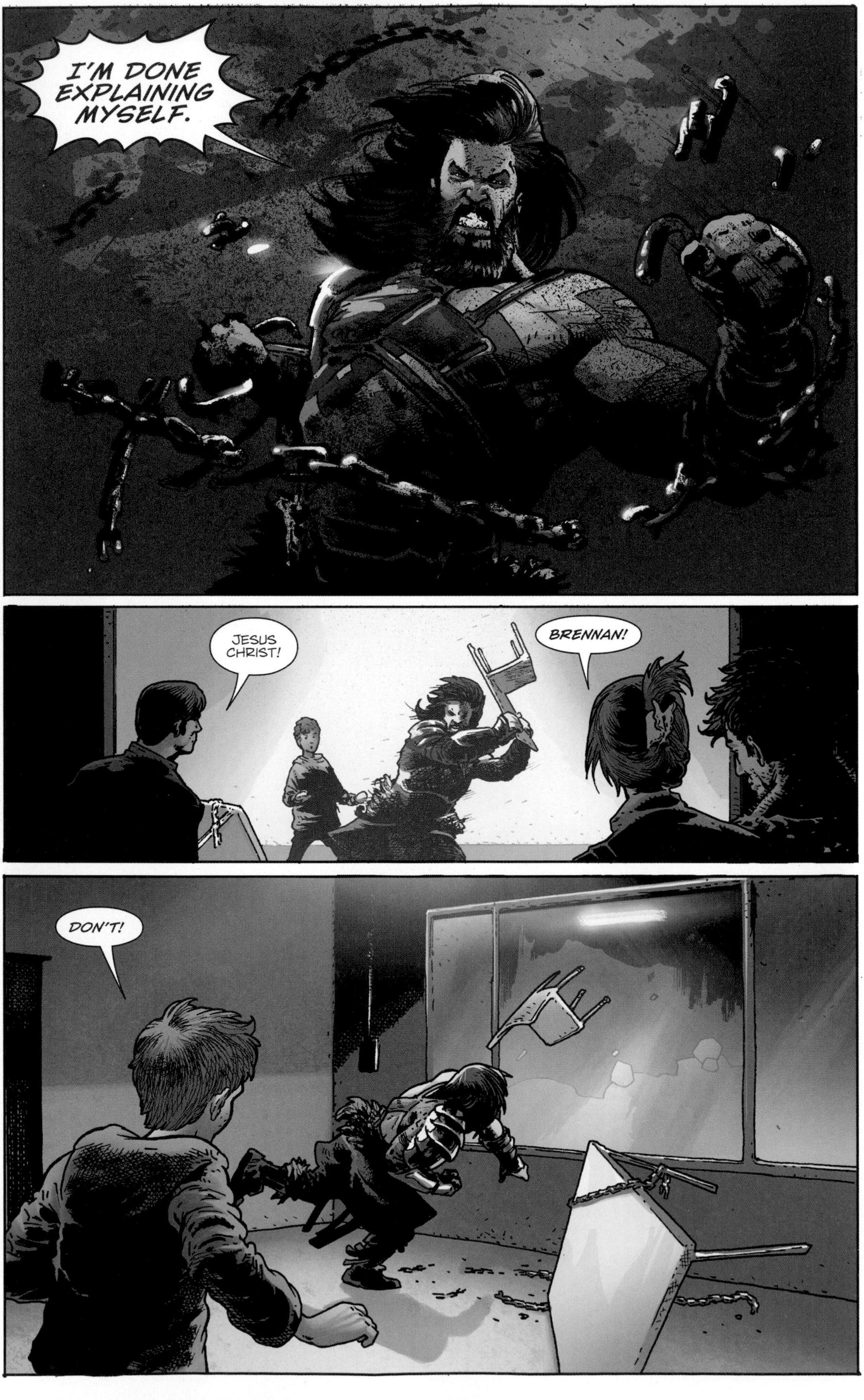
I'M DONE EXPLAINING MYSELF.
JESUS CHRIST!
BRENNAN!
DON'T!

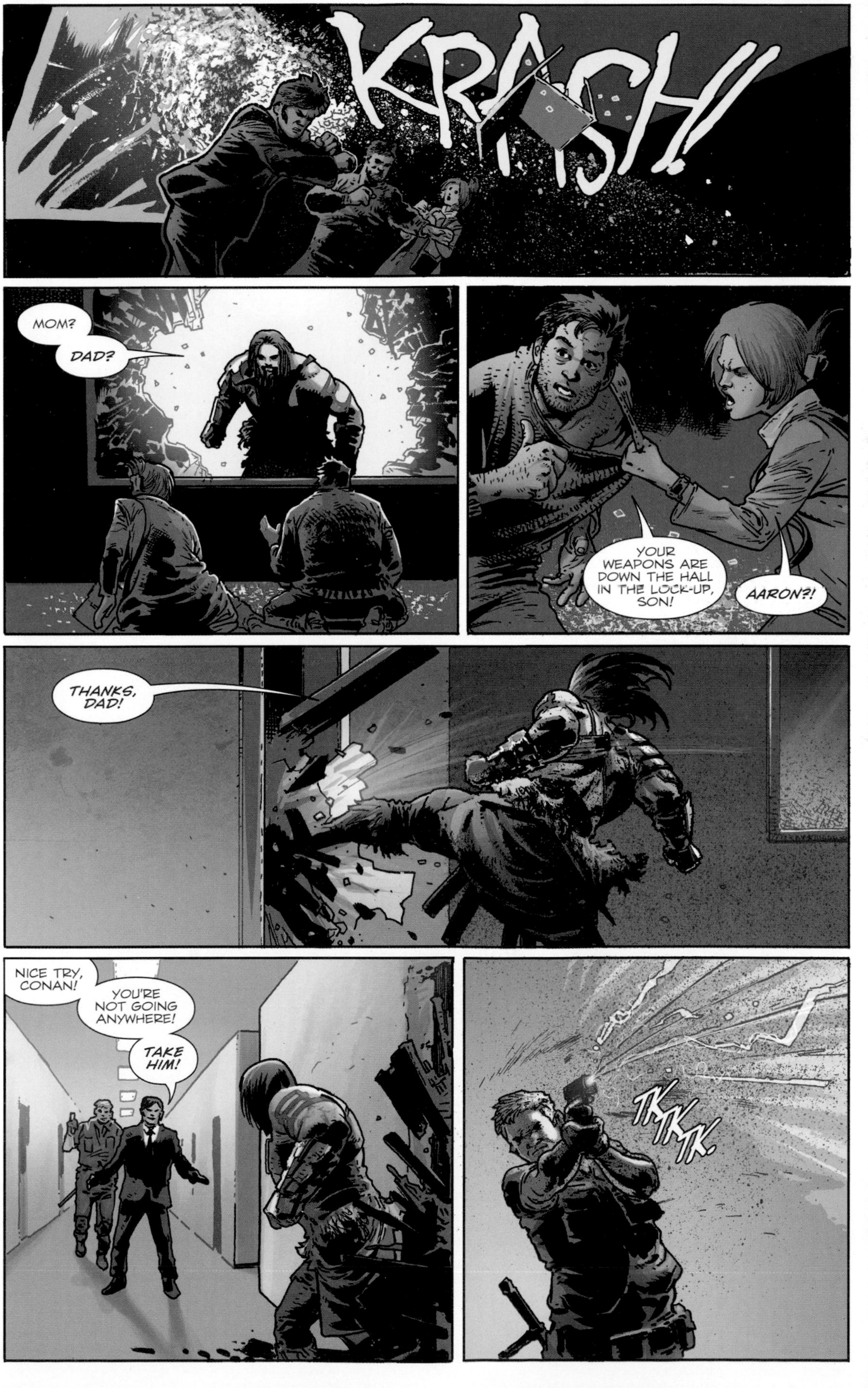
KRASH!
MOM?
DAD?
YOUR WEAPONS ARE DOWN THE HALL IN THE LOCK-UP, SON!
AARON?!
THANKS, DAD!
NICE TRY, CONAN!
YOU'RE NOT GOING ANYWHERE!
TAKE HIM!
TK TK TK.

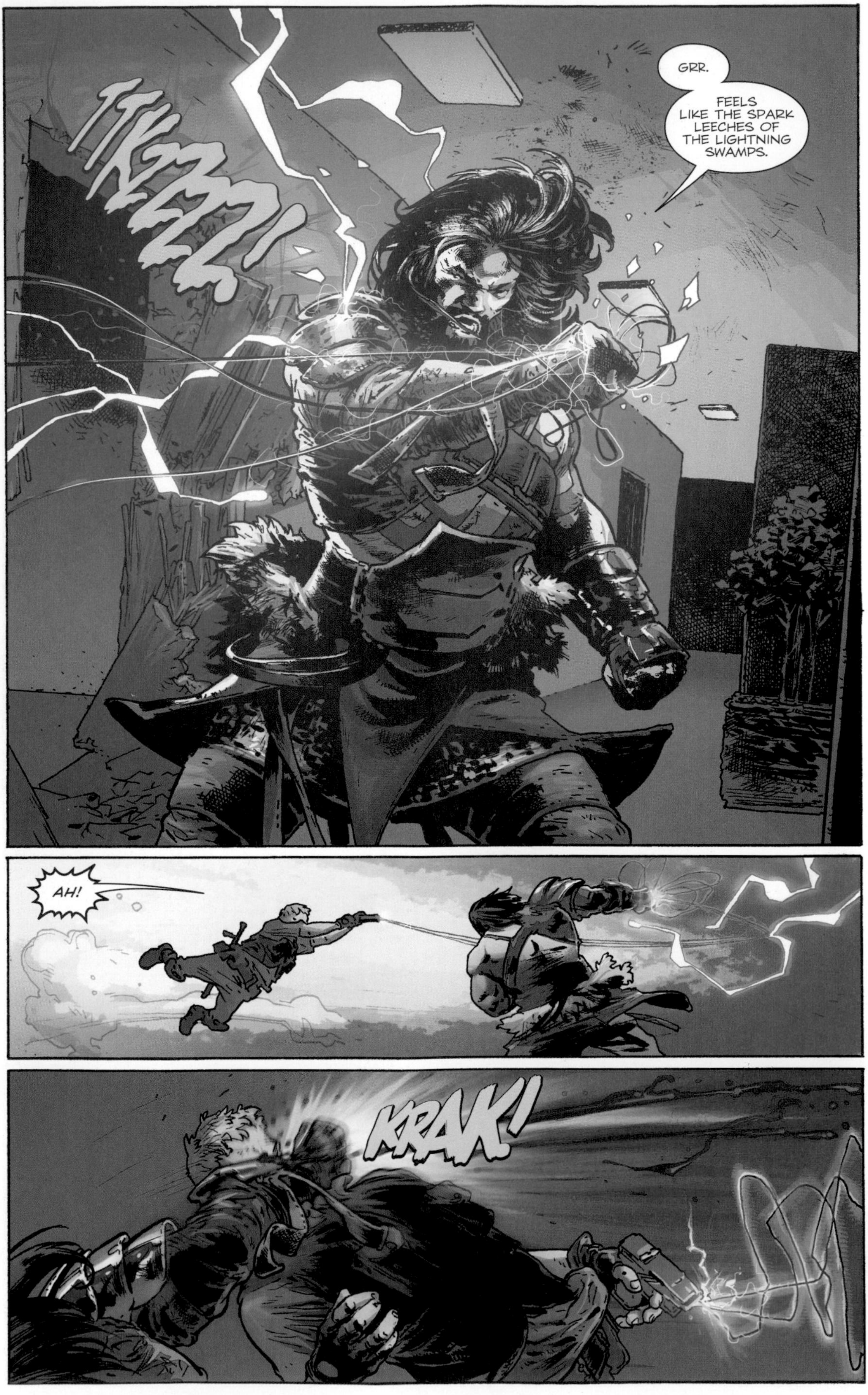
TTKZZZZ!
GRR.
FEELS LIKE THE SPARK LEECHES OF THE LIGHTNING SWAMPS.
AH!
KRAK!

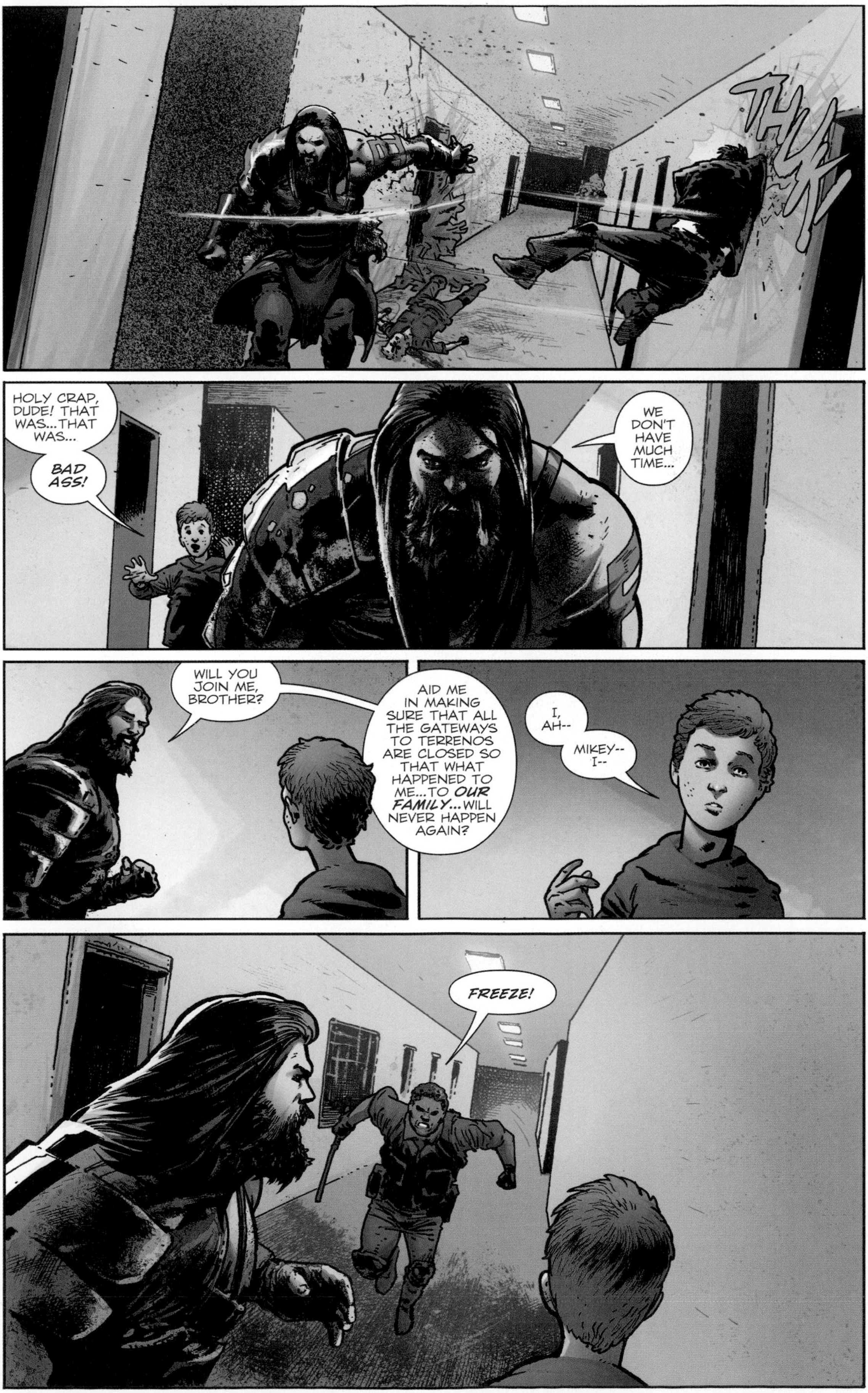
THUK!
HOLY CRAP, DUDE! THAT WAS...THAT WAS...
BAD ASS!
WE DON'T HAVE MUCH TIME...
WILL YOU JOIN ME, BROTHER?
AID ME IN MAKING SURE THAT ALL THE GATEWAYS TO TERRENOS ARE CLOSED SO THAT WHAT HAPPENED TO ME...TO OUR FAMILY...WILL NEVER HAPPEN AGAIN?
I, AH--
MIKEY-- I--
FREEZE!

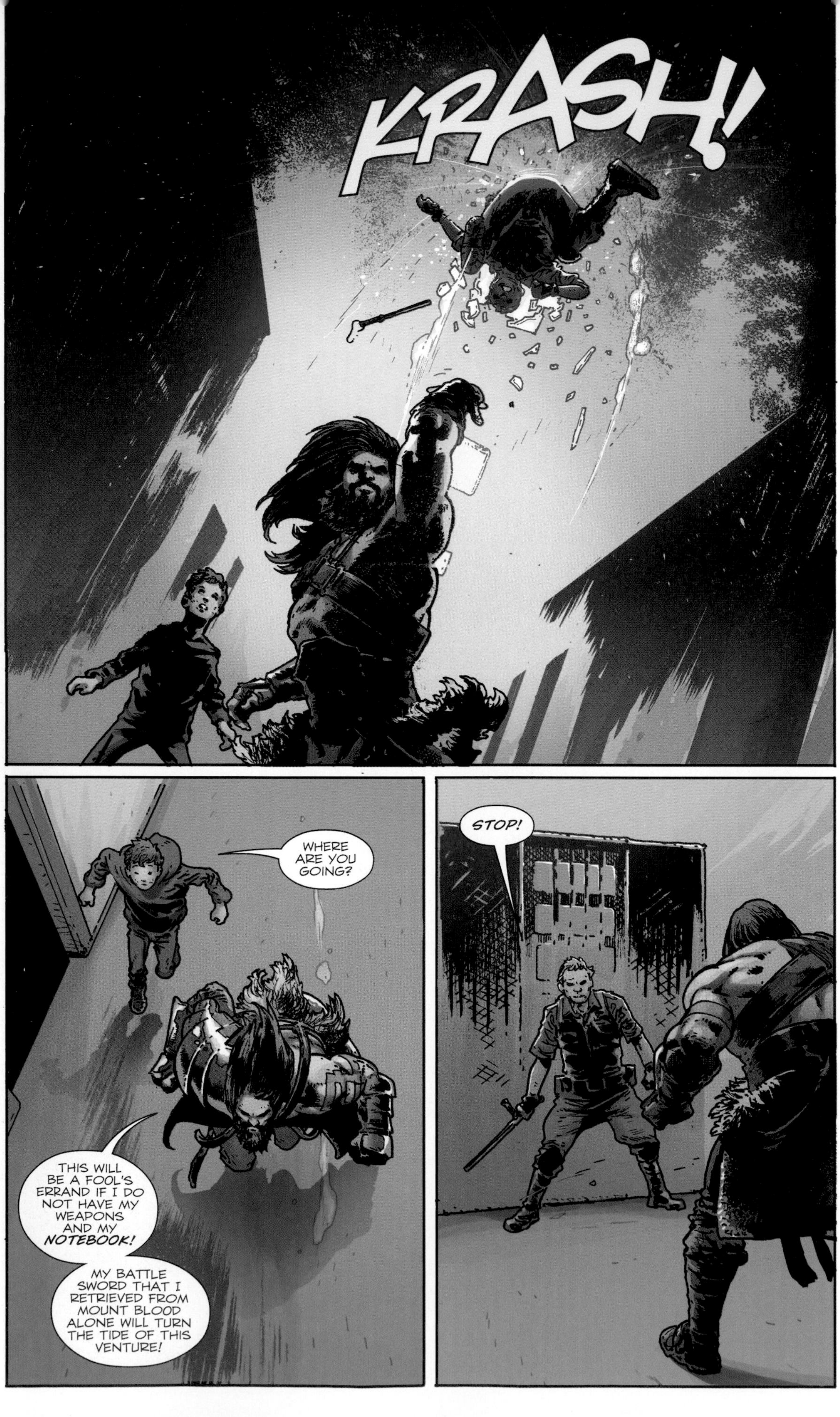
KRASH!
WHERE ARE YOU GOING?
THIS WILL BE A FOOL'S ERRAND IF I DO NOT HAVE MY WEAPONS AND MY NOTEBOOK!
MY BATTLE SWORD THAT I RETRIEVED FROM MOUNT BLOOD ALONE WILL TURN THE TIDE OF THIS VENTURE!
STOP!

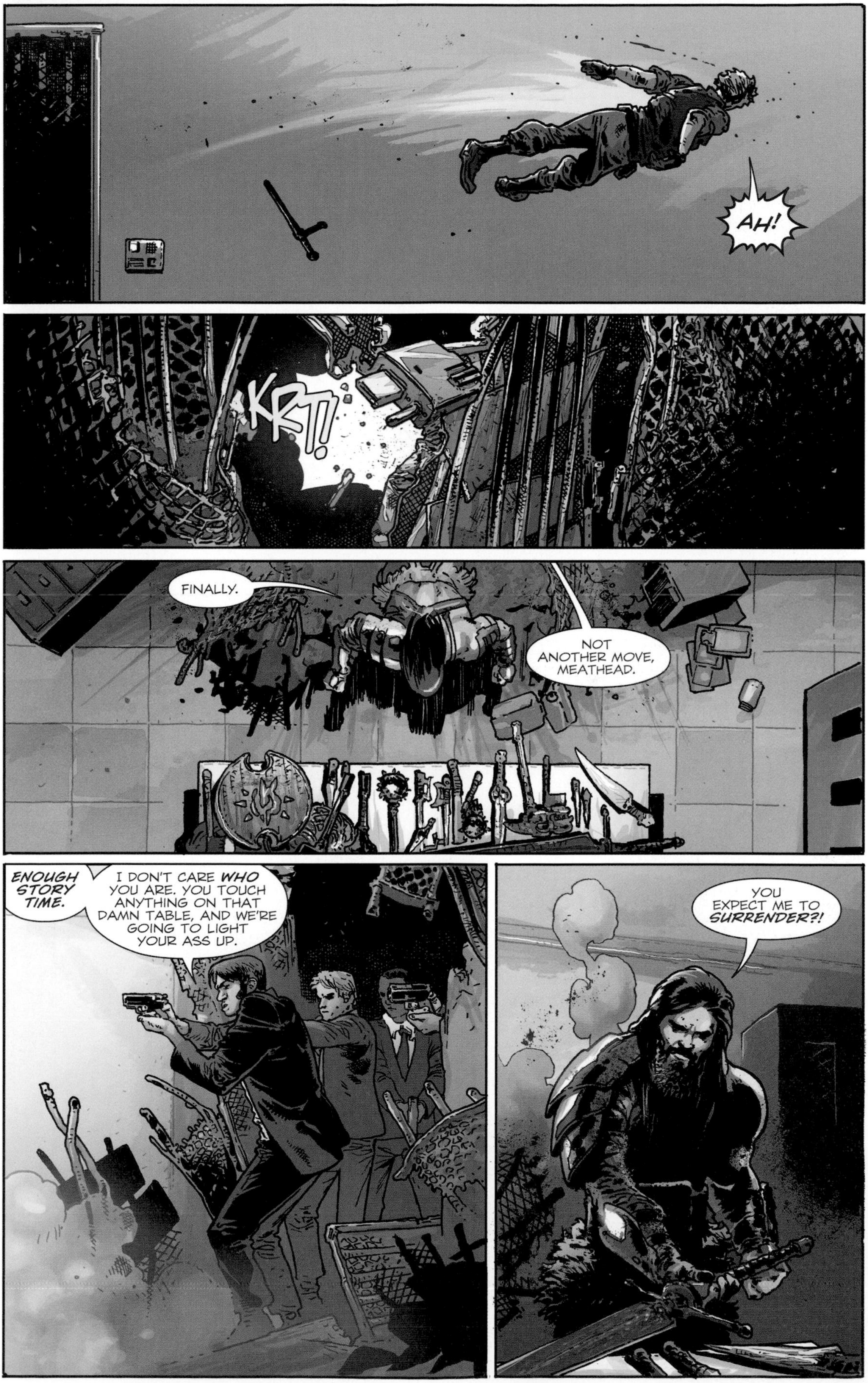
AH!
KRT!
FINALLY.
NOT ANOTHER MOVE, MEATHEAD.
ENOUGH STORY TIME.
I DON'T CARE WHO YOU ARE. YOU TOUCH ANYTHING ON THAT DAMN TABLE, AND WE'RE GOING TO LIGHT YOUR ASS UP.
YOU EXPECT ME TO SURRENDER?!

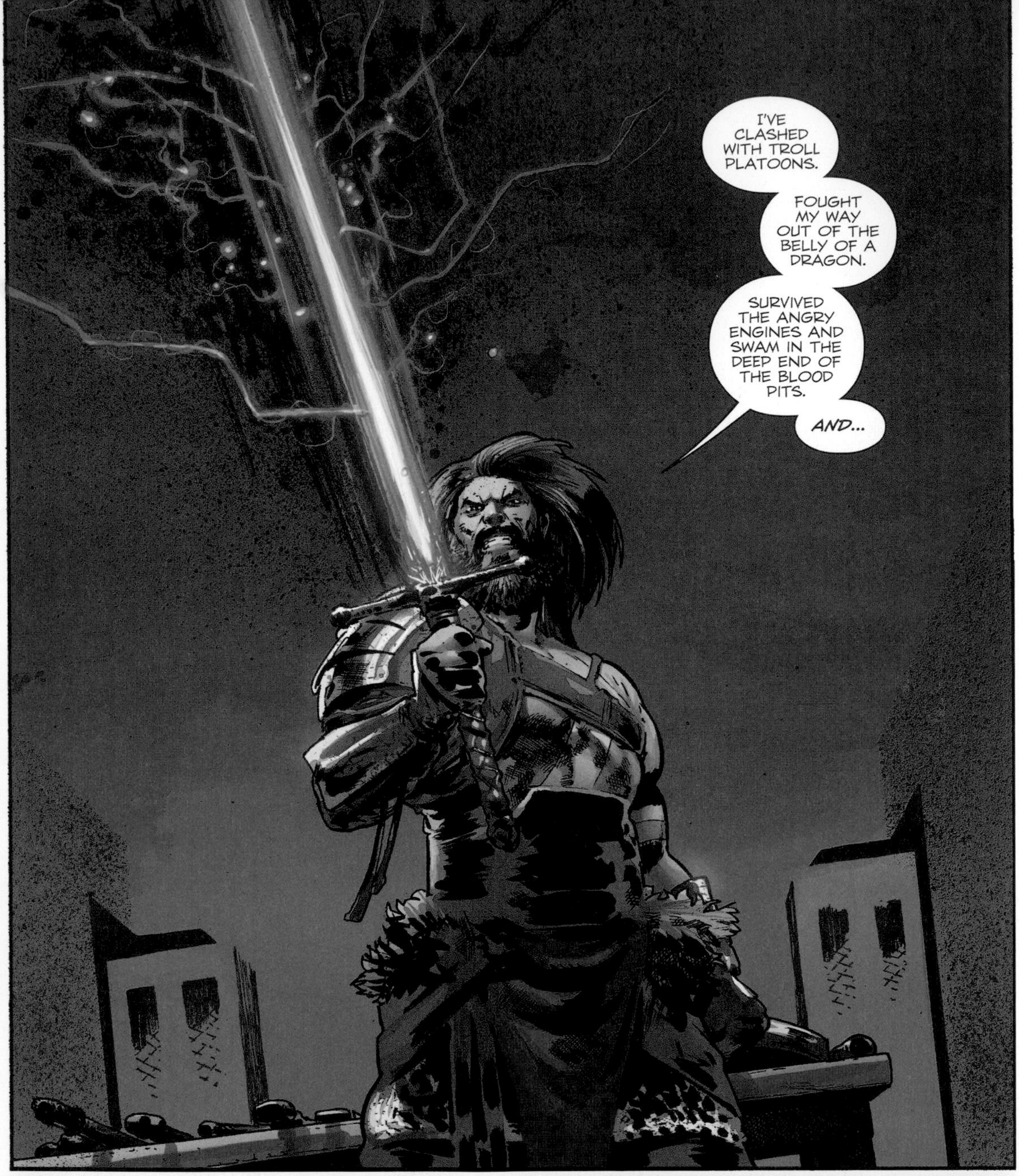
I'VE CLASHED WITH TROLL PLATOONS.
FOUGHT MY WAY OUT OF THE BELLY OF A DRAGON.
SURVIVED THE ANGRY ENGINES AND SWAM IN THE DEEP END OF THE BLOOD PITS.
AND...

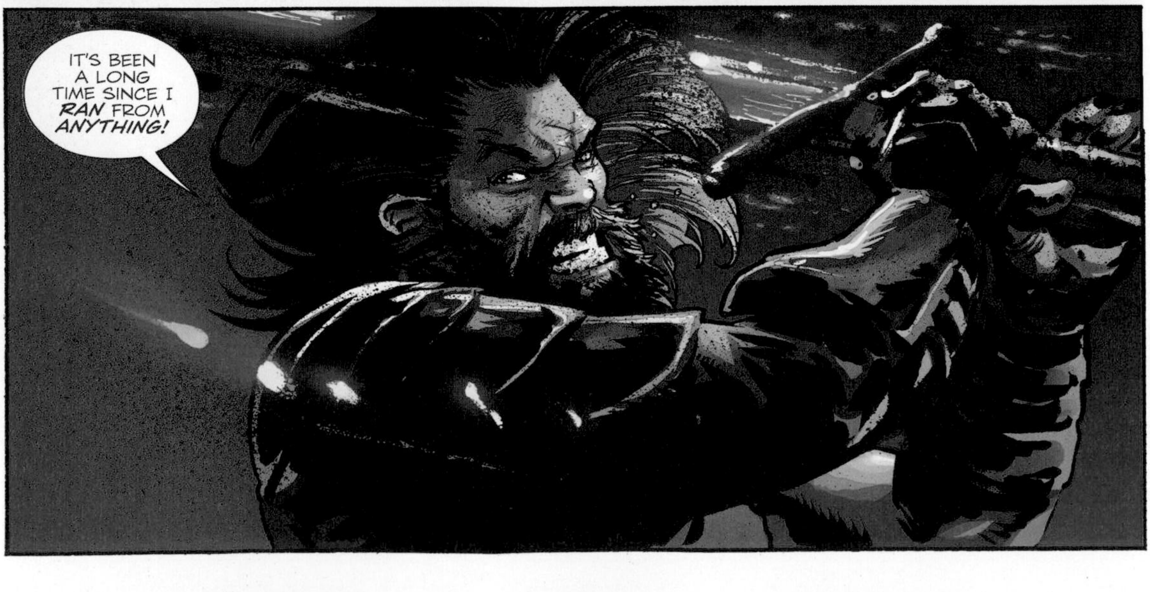
IT'S BEEN A LONG TIME SINCE I *RAN* FROM *ANYTHING!*

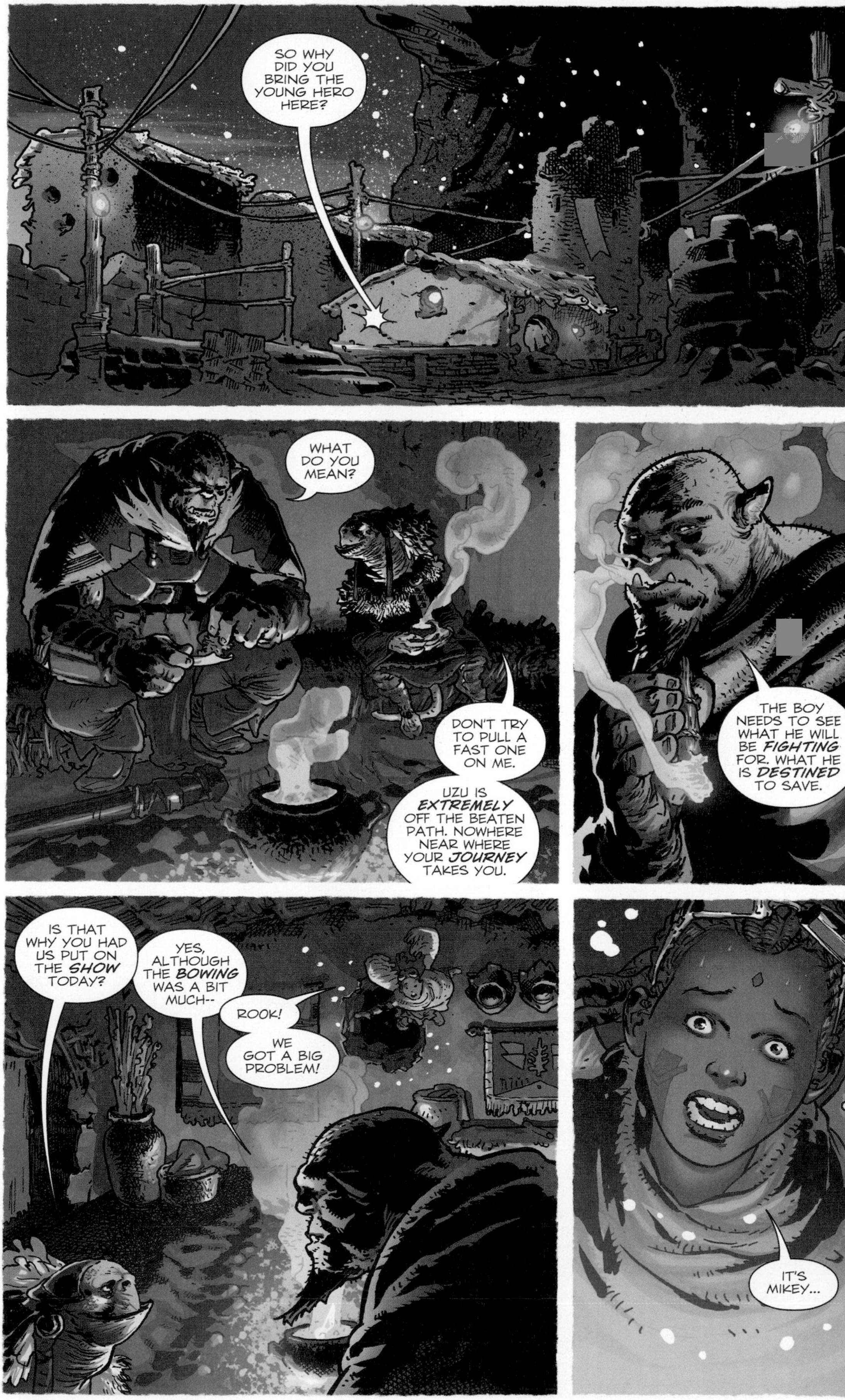
SO WHY DID YOU BRING THE YOUNG HERO HERE?
WHAT DO YOU MEAN?
DON'T TRY TO PULL A FAST ONE ON ME.
UZU IS EXTREMELY OFF THE BEATEN PATH. NOWHERE NEAR WHERE YOUR JOURNEY TAKES YOU.
THE BOY NEEDS TO SEE WHAT HE WILL BE FIGHTING FOR. WHAT HE IS DESTINED TO SAVE.
IS THAT WHY YOU HAD US PUT ON THE SHOW TODAY?
YES, ALTHOUGH THE BOWING WAS A BIT MUCH--
ROOK!
WE GOT A BIG PROBLEM!
IT'S MIKEY...

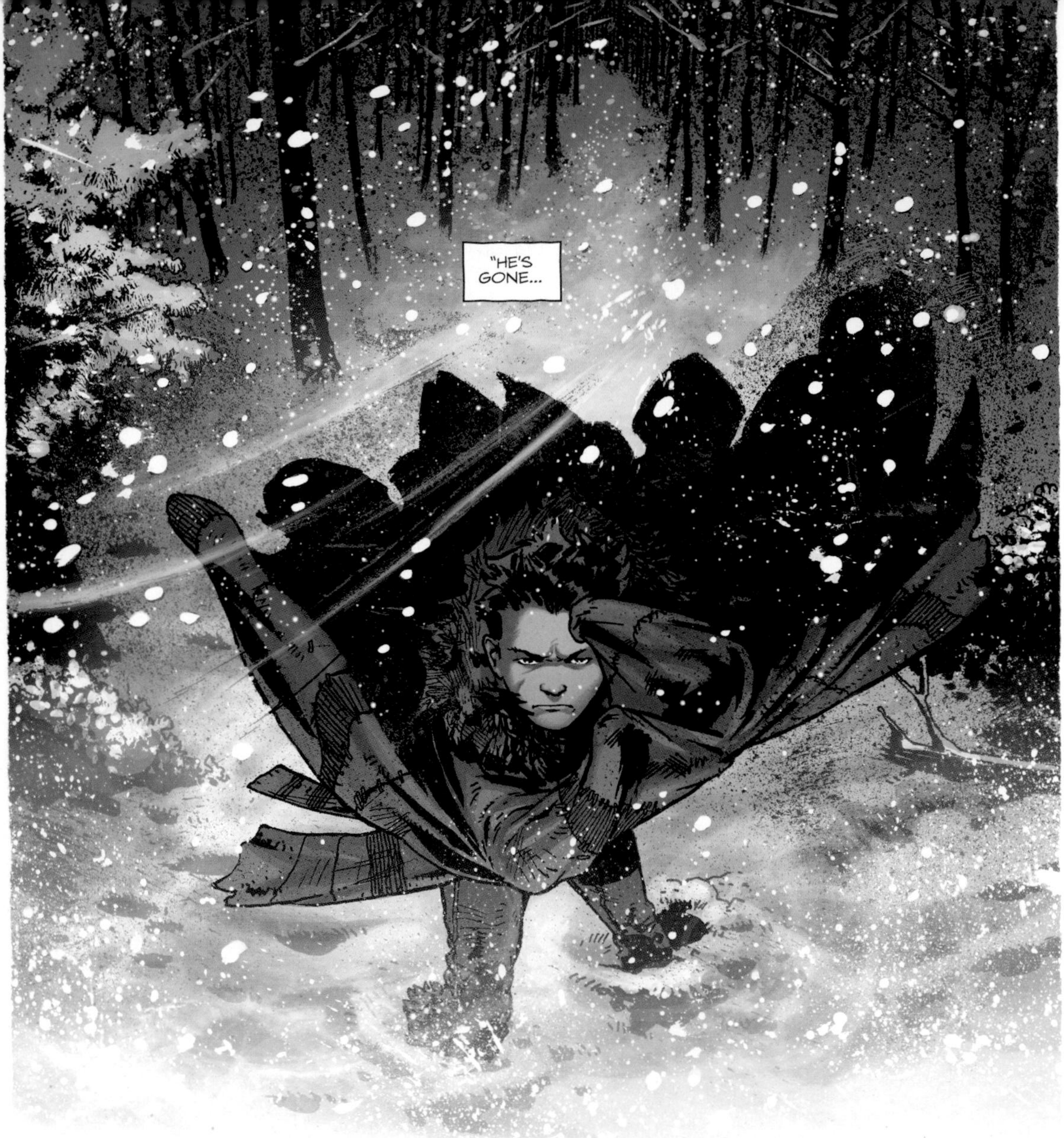
"HE'S
GONE...

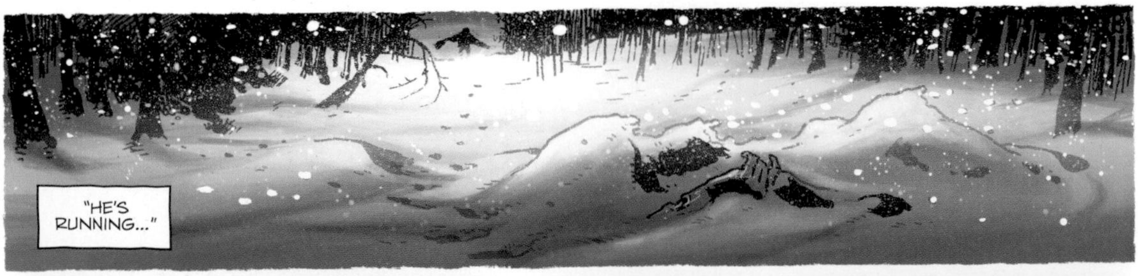
"HE'S
RUNNING..."

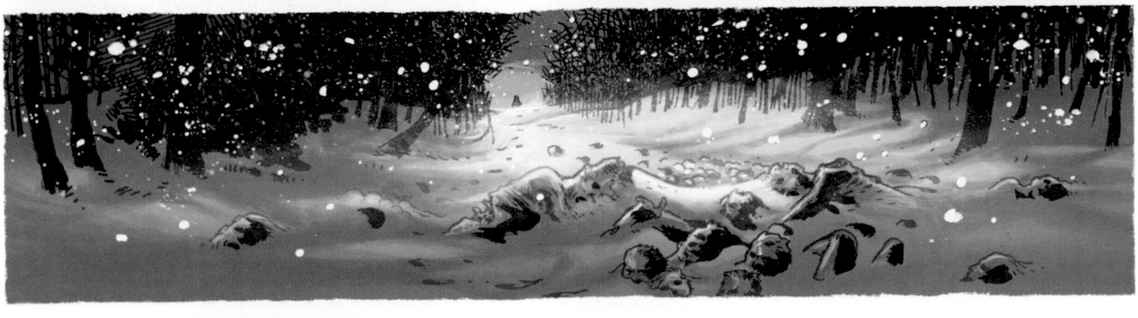

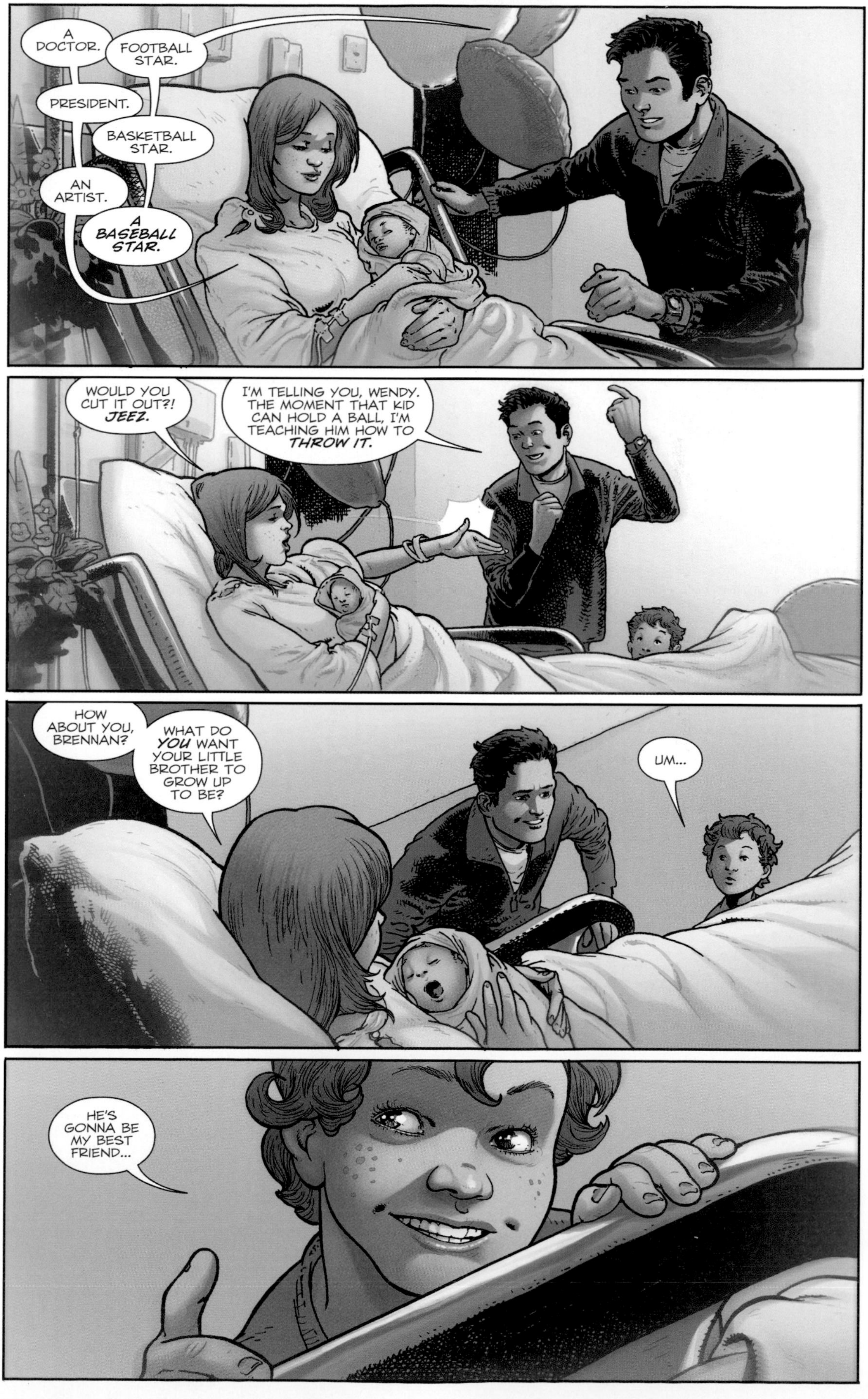
A DOCTOR.
FOOTBALL STAR.
PRESIDENT.
BASKETBALL STAR.
AN ARTIST.
A *BASEBALL STAR.*
WOULD YOU CUT IT OUT?! *JEEZ.*
I'M TELLING YOU, WENDY. THE MOMENT THAT KID CAN HOLD A BALL, I'M TEACHING HIM HOW TO *THROW IT.*
HOW ABOUT YOU, BRENNAN?
WHAT DO *YOU* WANT YOUR LITTLE BROTHER TO GROW UP TO BE?
UM...
HE'S GONNA BE MY BEST FRIEND...

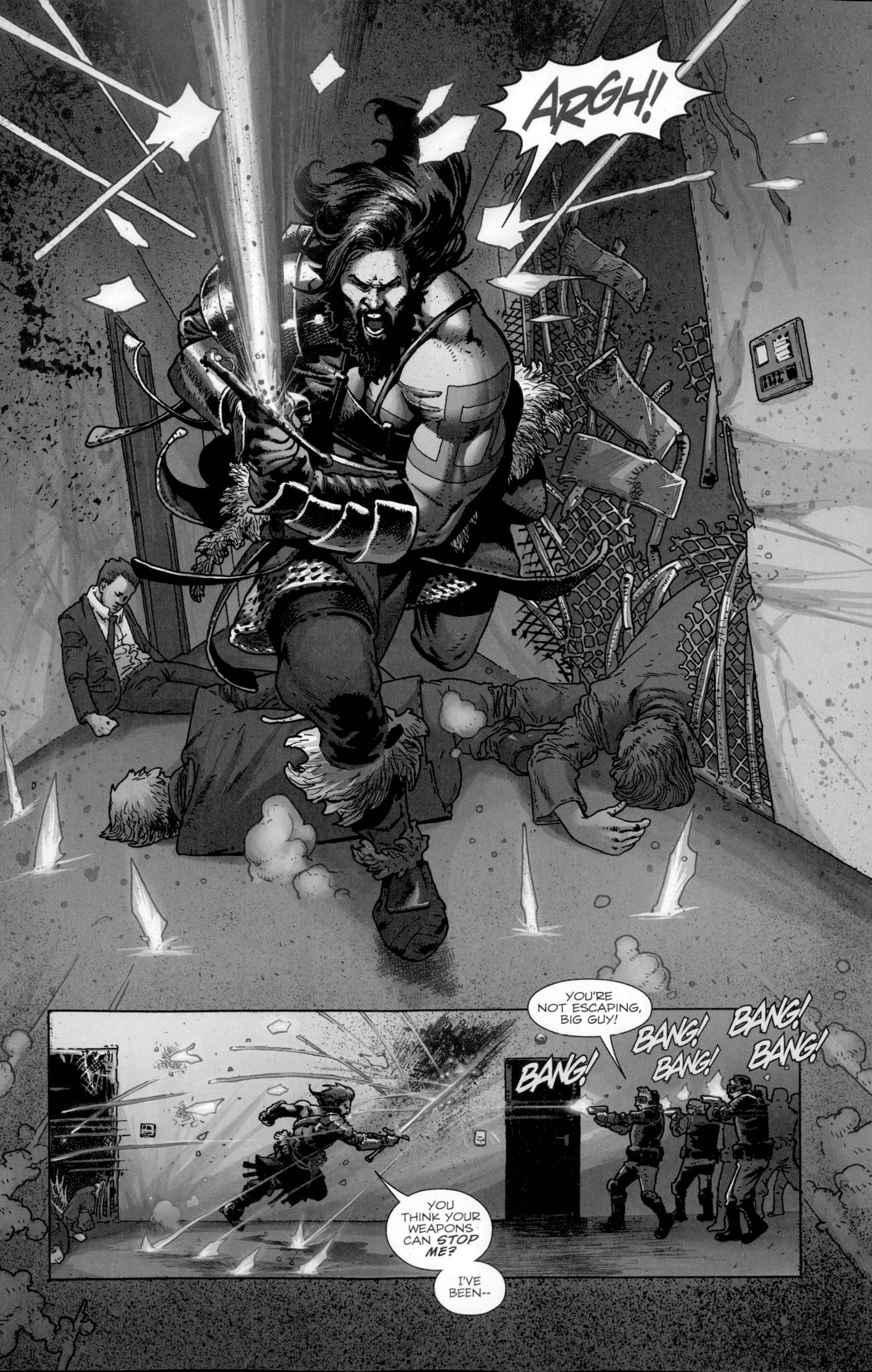
ARGH!
YOU'RE NOT ESCAPING, BIG GUY!
BANG!
BANG!
BANG!
BANG!
BANG!
YOU THINK YOUR WEAPONS CAN STOP ME?
I'VE BEEN--

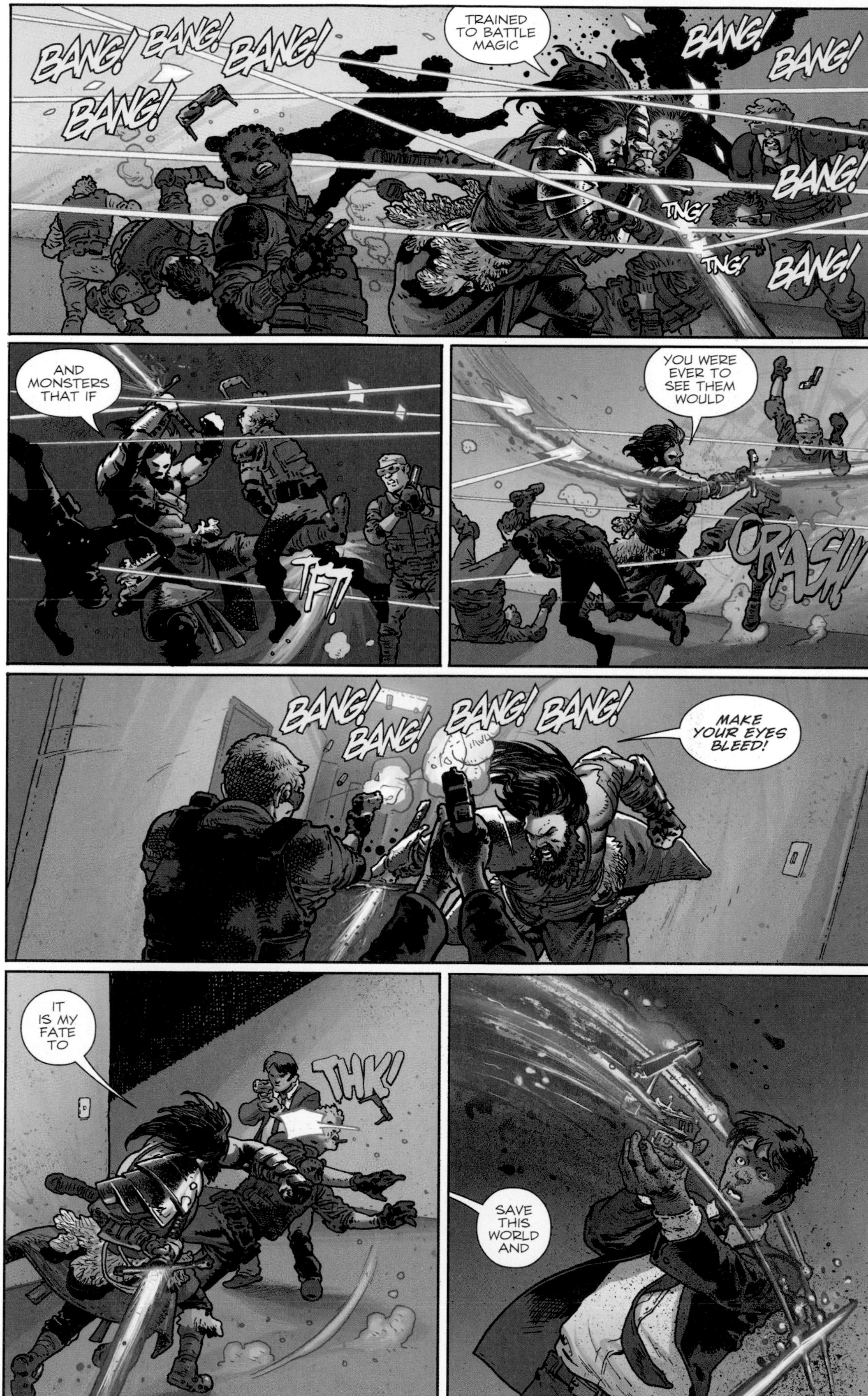
BANG! BANG! BANG!
BANG!
TRAINED TO BATTLE MAGIC
BANG!
BANG!
BANG!
TNG!
TNG!
BANG!
AND MONSTERS THAT IF
TFT!
YOU WERE EVER TO SEE THEM WOULD
CRASH!
BANG! BANG!
BANG! BANG!
MAKE YOUR EYES BLEED!
IT IS MY FATE TO
THK!
SAVE THIS WORLD AND

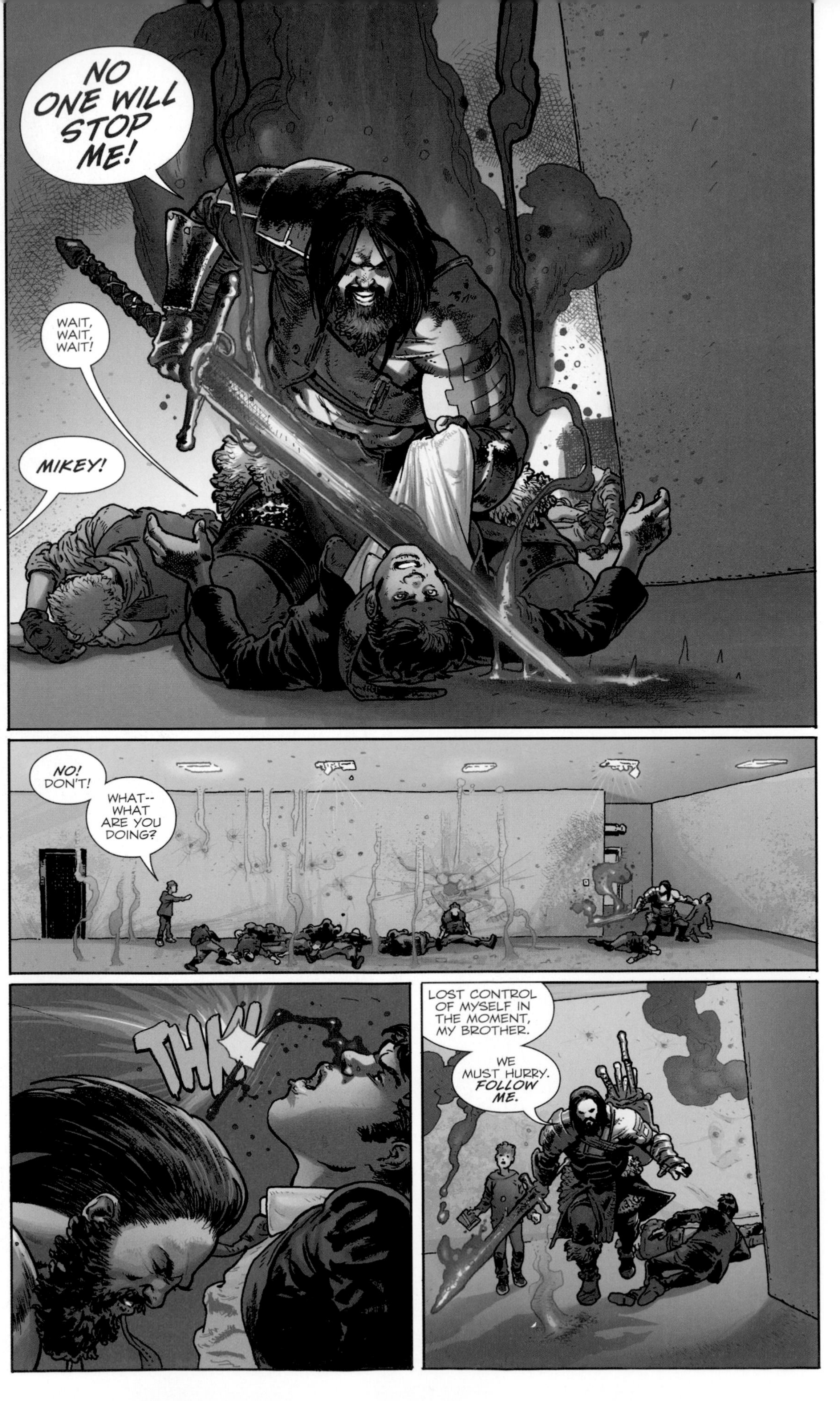
NO ONE WILL STOP ME!
WAIT, WAIT, WAIT!
MIKEY!
NO! DON'T!
WHAT-- WHAT ARE YOU DOING?
THK
LOST CONTROL OF MYSELF IN THE MOMENT, MY BROTHER.
WE MUST HURRY. FOLLOW ME.

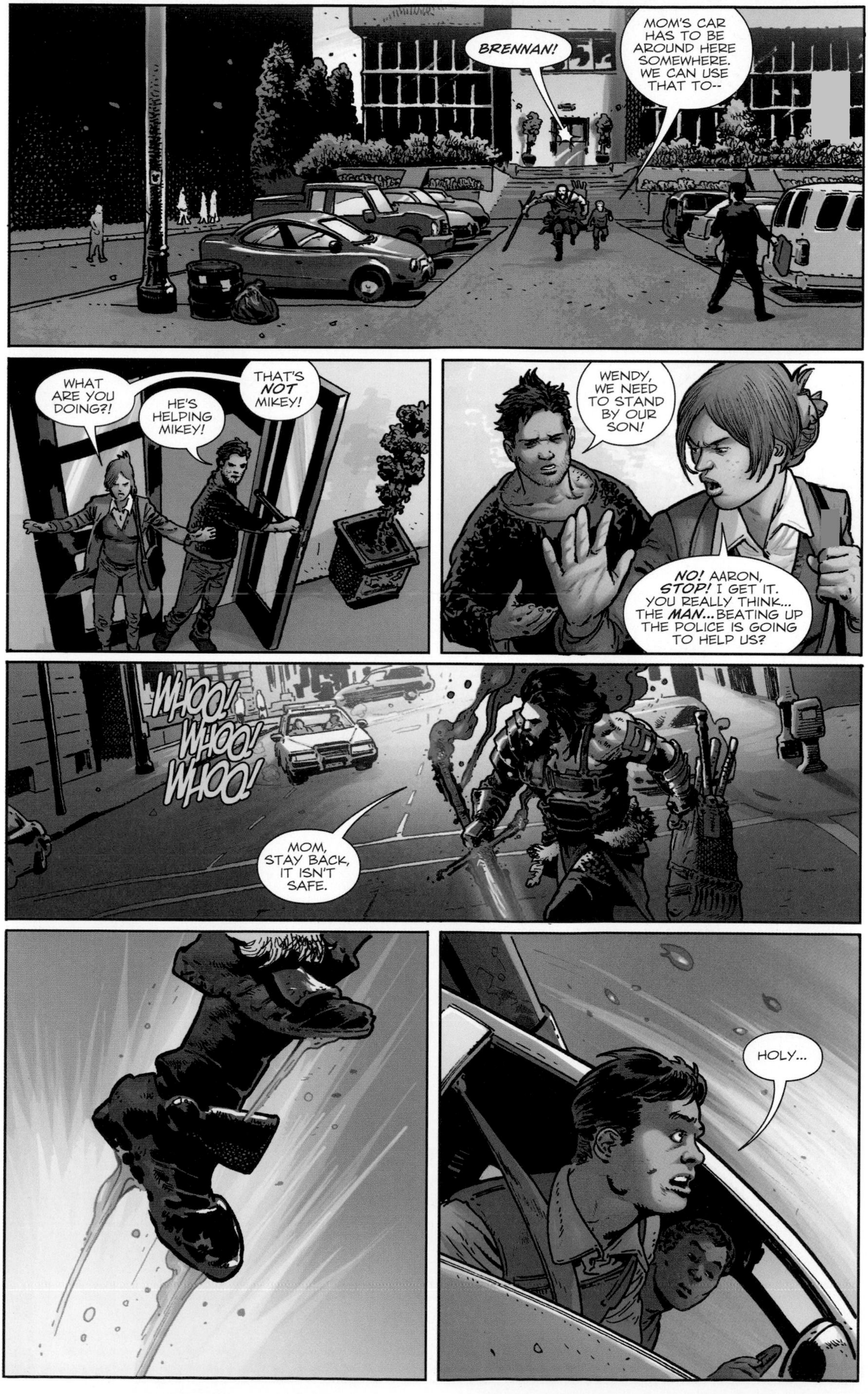
BRENNAN!
MOM'S CAR HAS TO BE AROUND HERE SOMEWHERE. WE CAN USE THAT TO--
WHAT ARE YOU DOING?!
HE'S HELPING MIKEY!
THAT'S NOT MIKEY!
WENDY, WE NEED TO STAND BY OUR SON!
NO! AARON, STOP! I GET IT. YOU REALLY THINK... THE MAN... BEATING UP THE POLICE IS GOING TO HELP US?
WHOO! WHOO! WHOO!
MOM, STAY BACK, IT ISN'T SAFE.
HOLY...

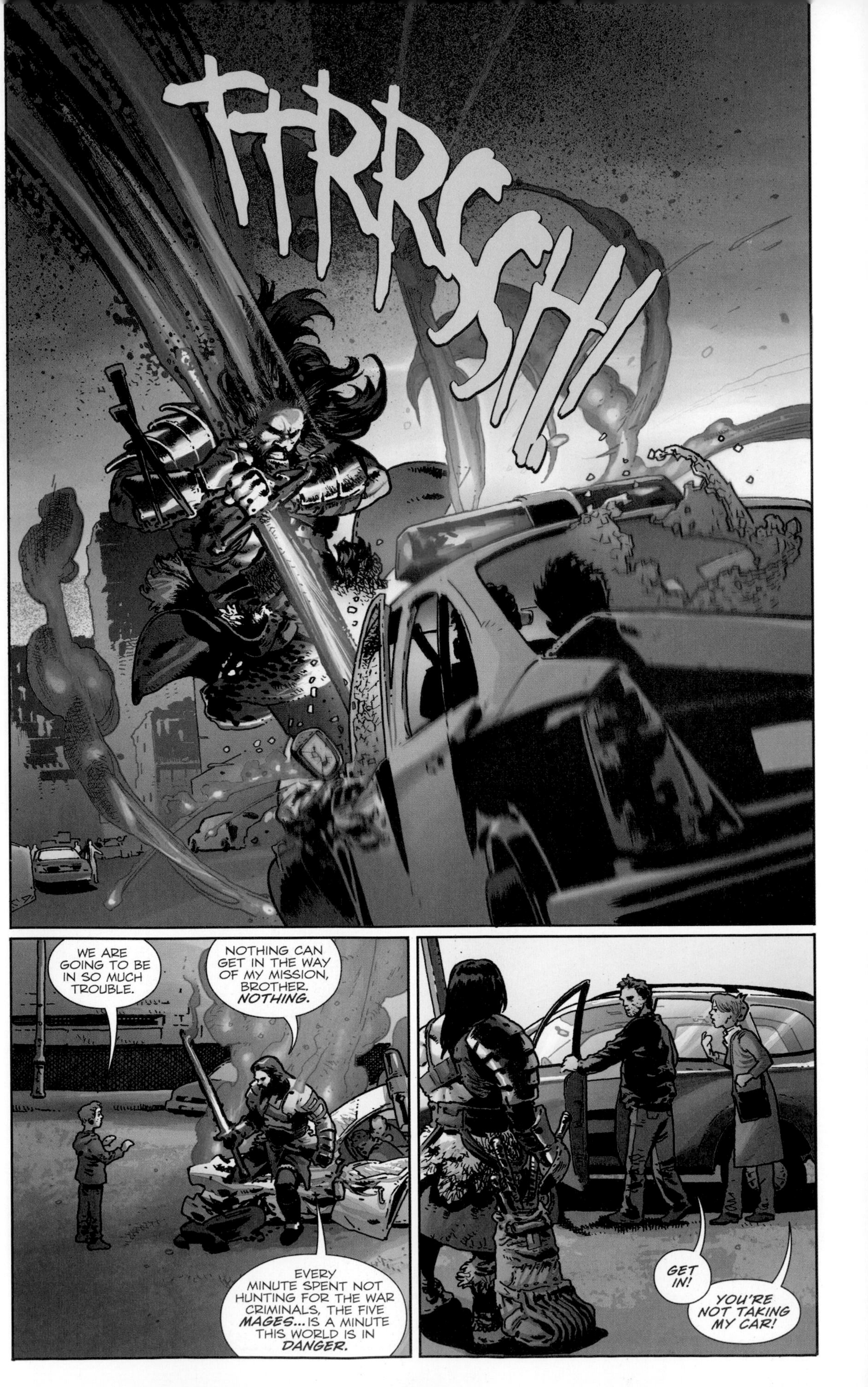
FTRRSSH!
WE ARE GOING TO BE IN SO MUCH TROUBLE.
NOTHING CAN GET IN THE WAY OF MY MISSION, BROTHER. NOTHING.
EVERY MINUTE SPENT NOT HUNTING FOR THE WAR CRIMINALS, THE FIVE MAGES... IS A MINUTE THIS WORLD IS IN DANGER.
GET IN!
YOU'RE NOT TAKING MY CAR!

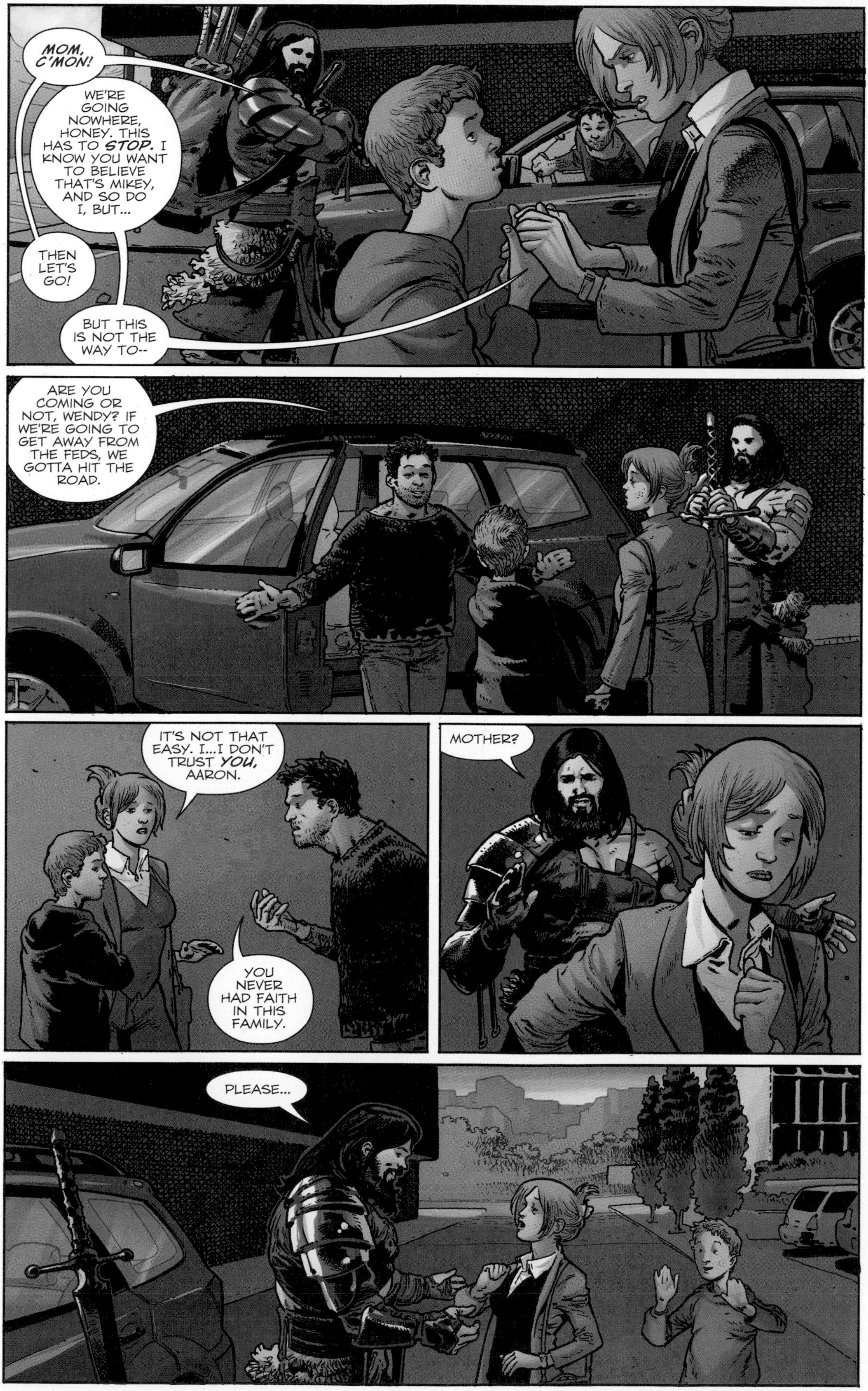
MOM, C'MON!
WE'RE GOING NOWHERE, HONEY. THIS HAS TO STOP. I KNOW YOU WANT TO BELIEVE THAT'S MIKEY, AND SO DO I, BUT...
THEN LET'S GO!
BUT THIS IS NOT THE WAY TO--
ARE YOU COMING OR NOT, WENDY? IF WE'RE GOING TO GET AWAY FROM THE FEDS, WE GOTTA HIT THE ROAD.
IT'S NOT THAT EASY. I...I DON'T TRUST YOU, AARON.
YOU NEVER HAD FAITH IN THIS FAMILY.
MOTHER?
PLEASE...

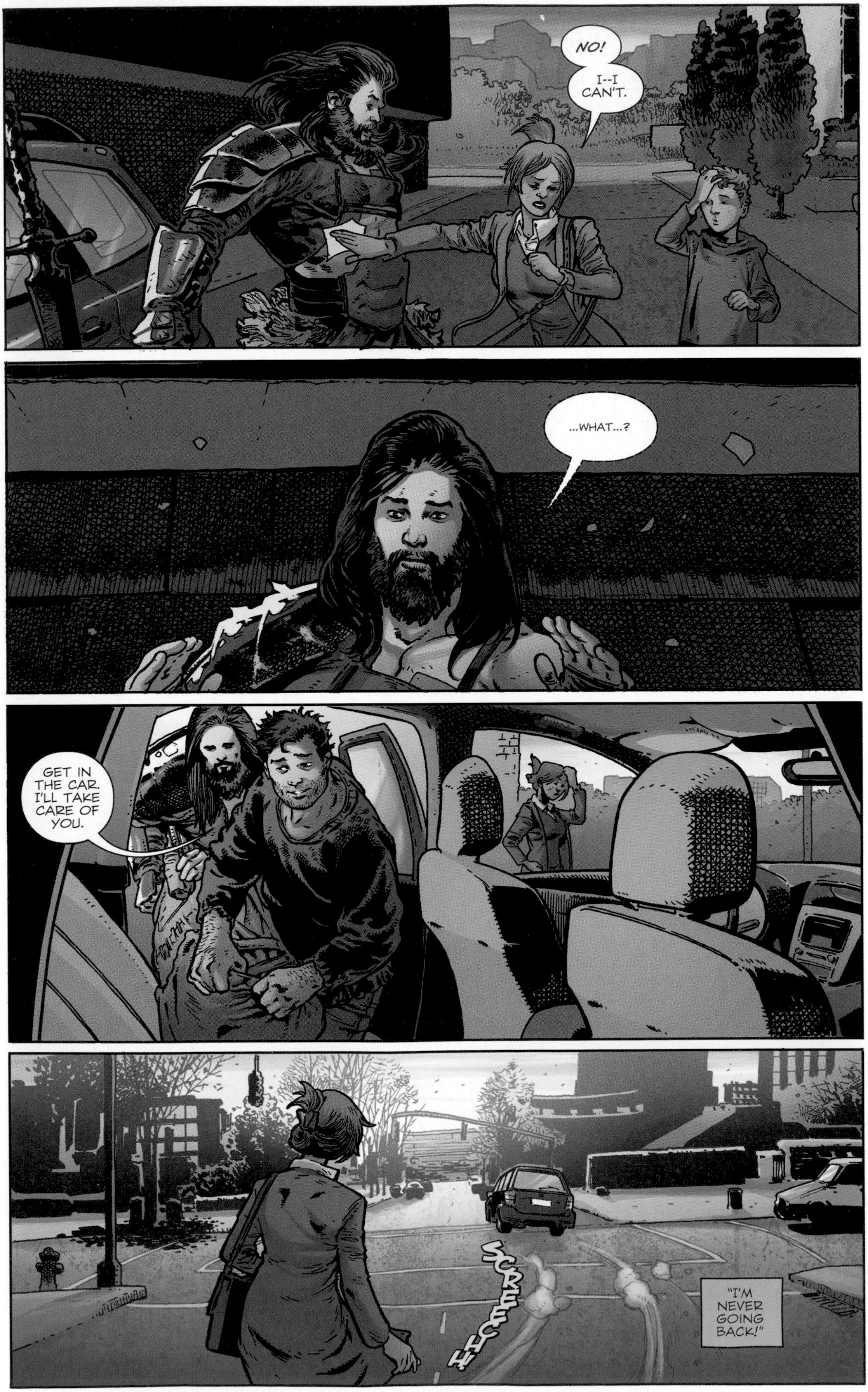
NO!
I--I CAN'T.
...WHAT...?
GET IN THE CAR. I'LL TAKE CARE OF YOU.
SCREEECH!
"I'M NEVER GOING BACK!"

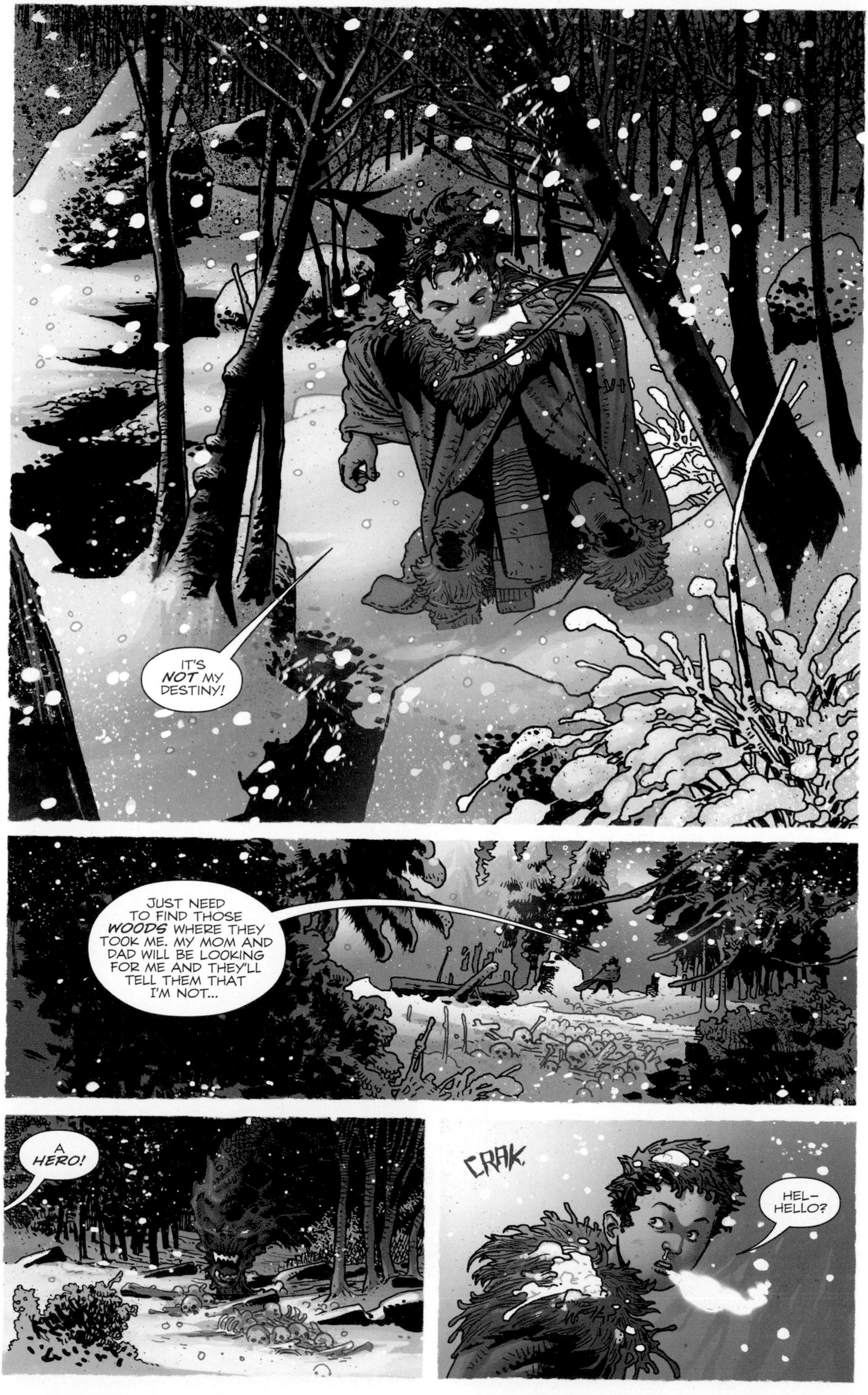
IT'S NOT MY DESTINY!
JUST NEED TO FIND THOSE WOODS WHERE THEY TOOK ME. MY MOM AND DAD WILL BE LOOKING FOR ME AND THEY'LL TELL THEM THAT I'M NOT...
A HERO!
CRAK.
HEL— HELLO?

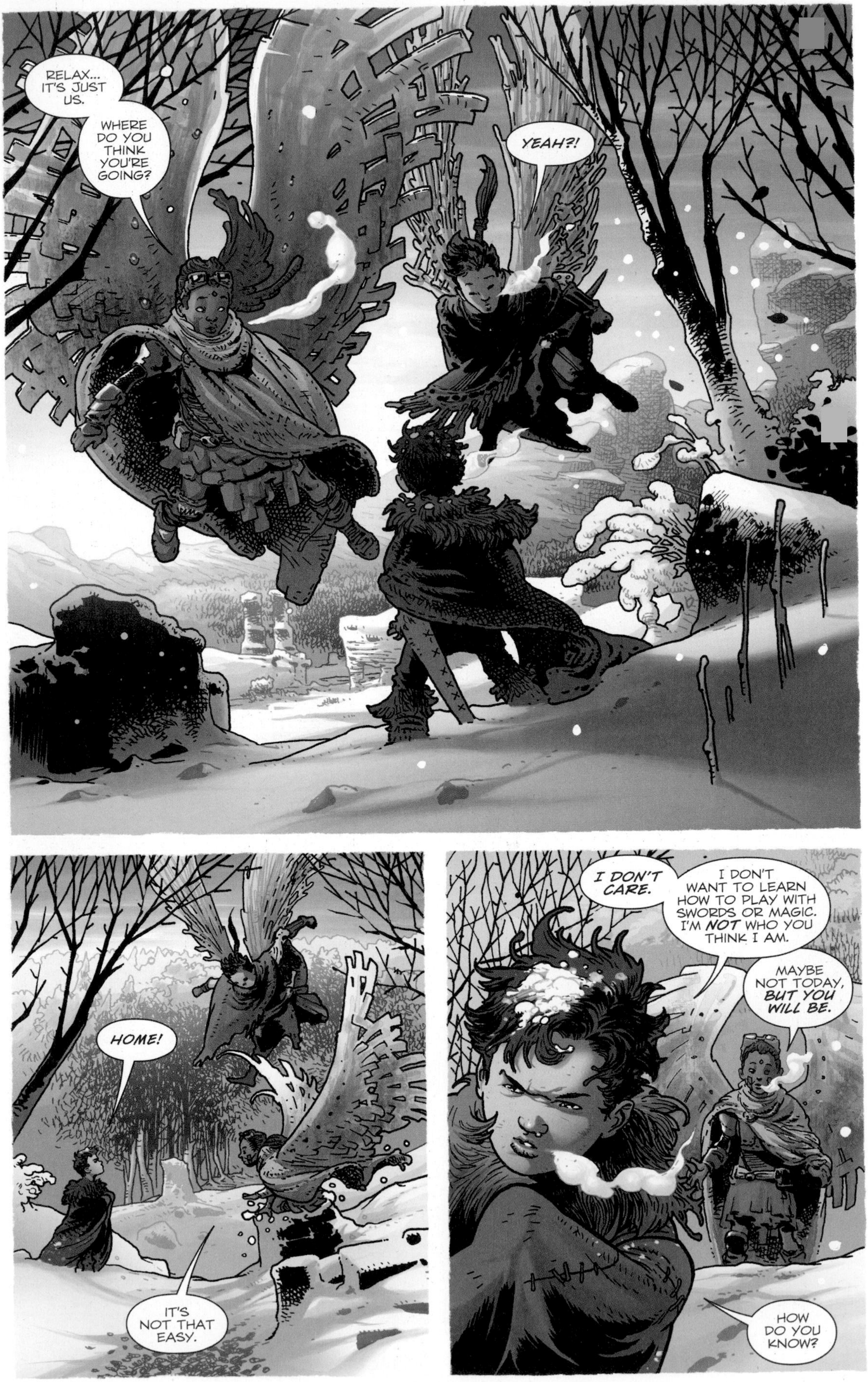

RELAX... IT'S JUST US.
WHERE DO YOU THINK YOU'RE GOING?
YEAH?!
HOME!
IT'S NOT THAT EASY.
I DON'T CARE.
I DON'T WANT TO LEARN HOW TO PLAY WITH SWORDS OR MAGIC. I'M NOT WHO YOU THINK I AM.
MAYBE NOT TODAY, BUT YOU WILL BE.
HOW DO YOU KNOW?

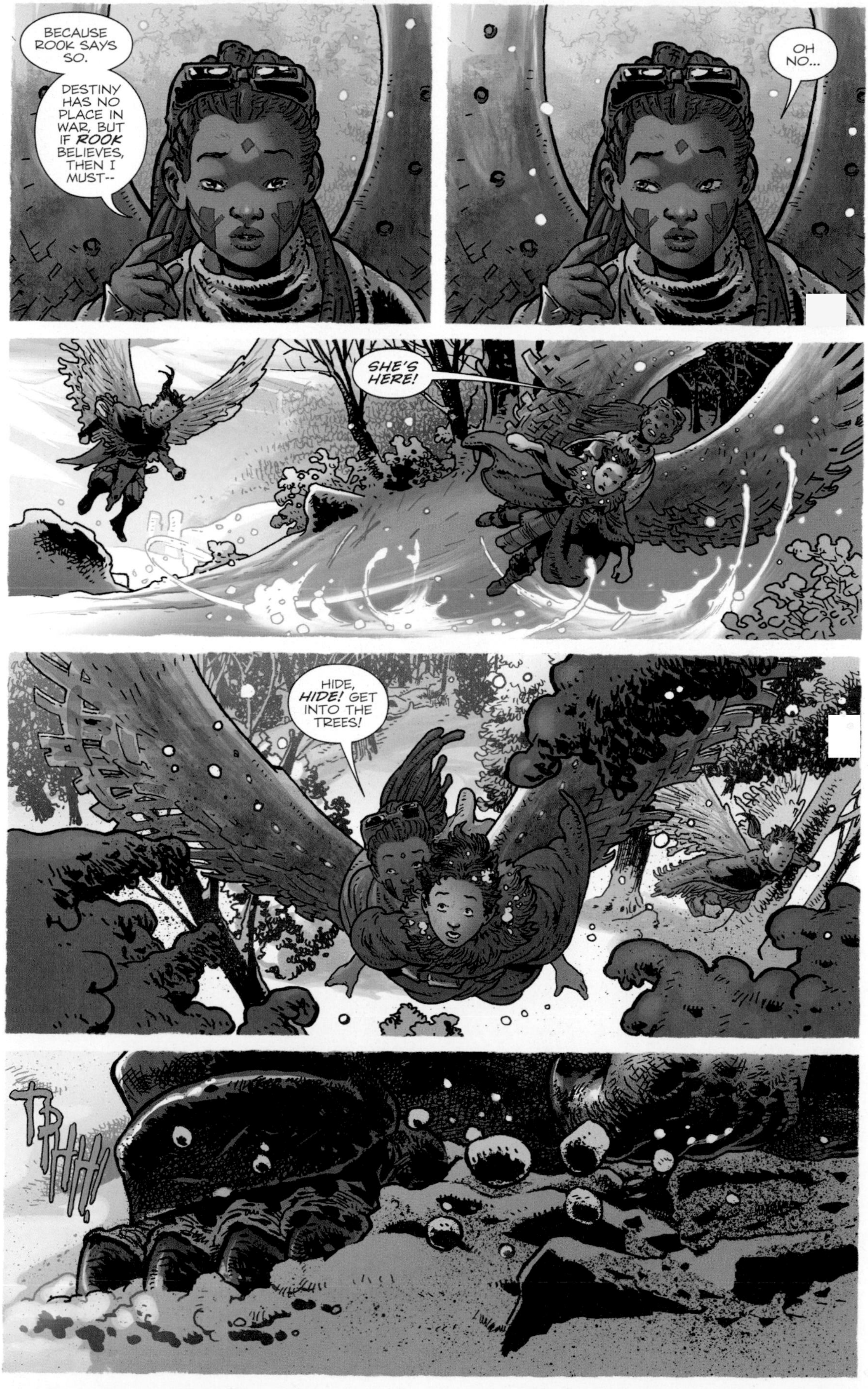

BECAUSE ROOK SAYS SO.
DESTINY HAS NO PLACE IN WAR, BUT IF ROOK BELIEVES, THEN I MUST--
OH NO...
SHE'S HERE!
HIDE, HIDE! GET INTO THE TREES!

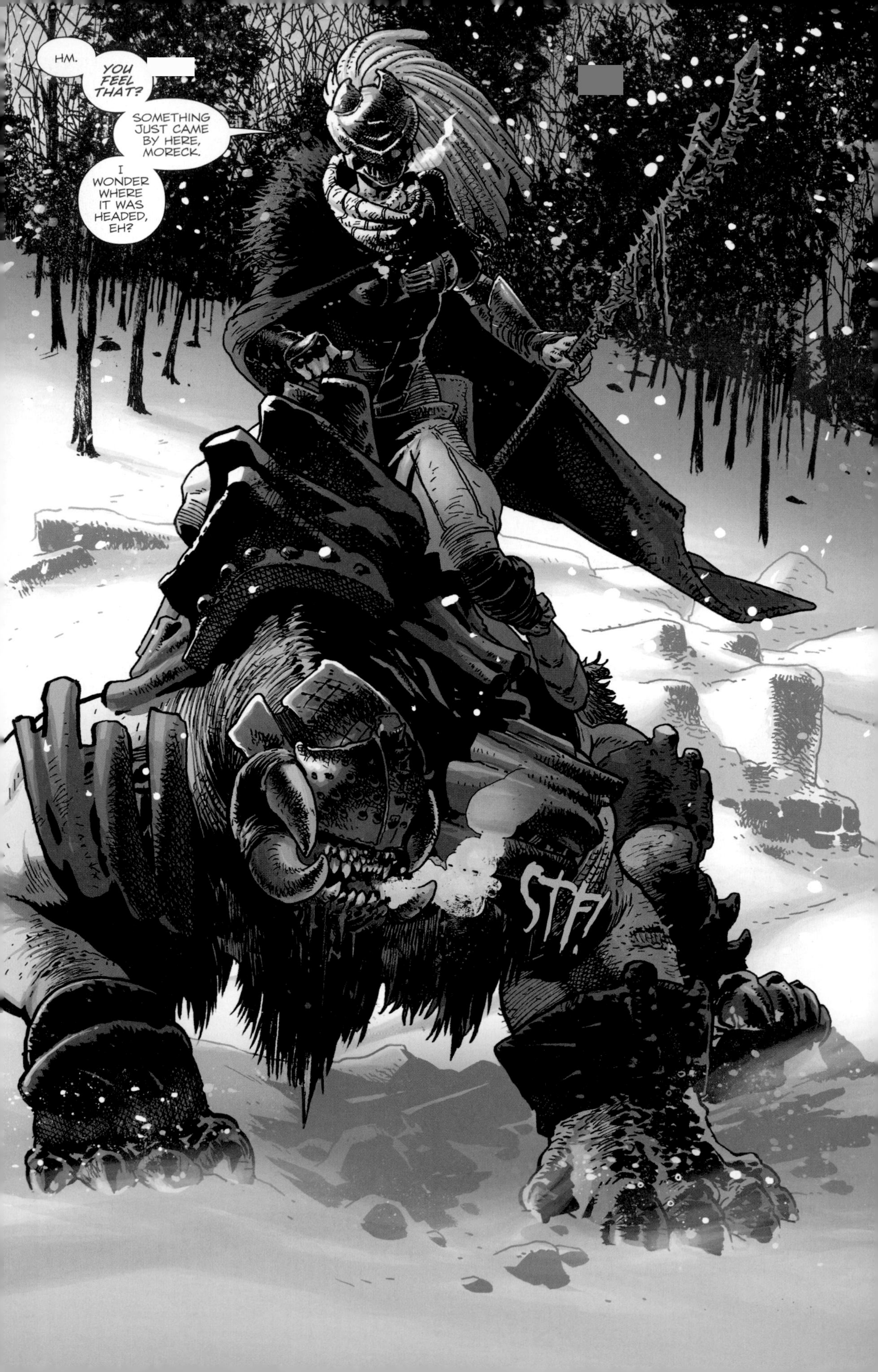
HM.
YOU FEEL THAT?
SOMETHING JUST CAME BY HERE, MORECK.
I WONDER WHERE IT WAS HEADED, EH?
STF!

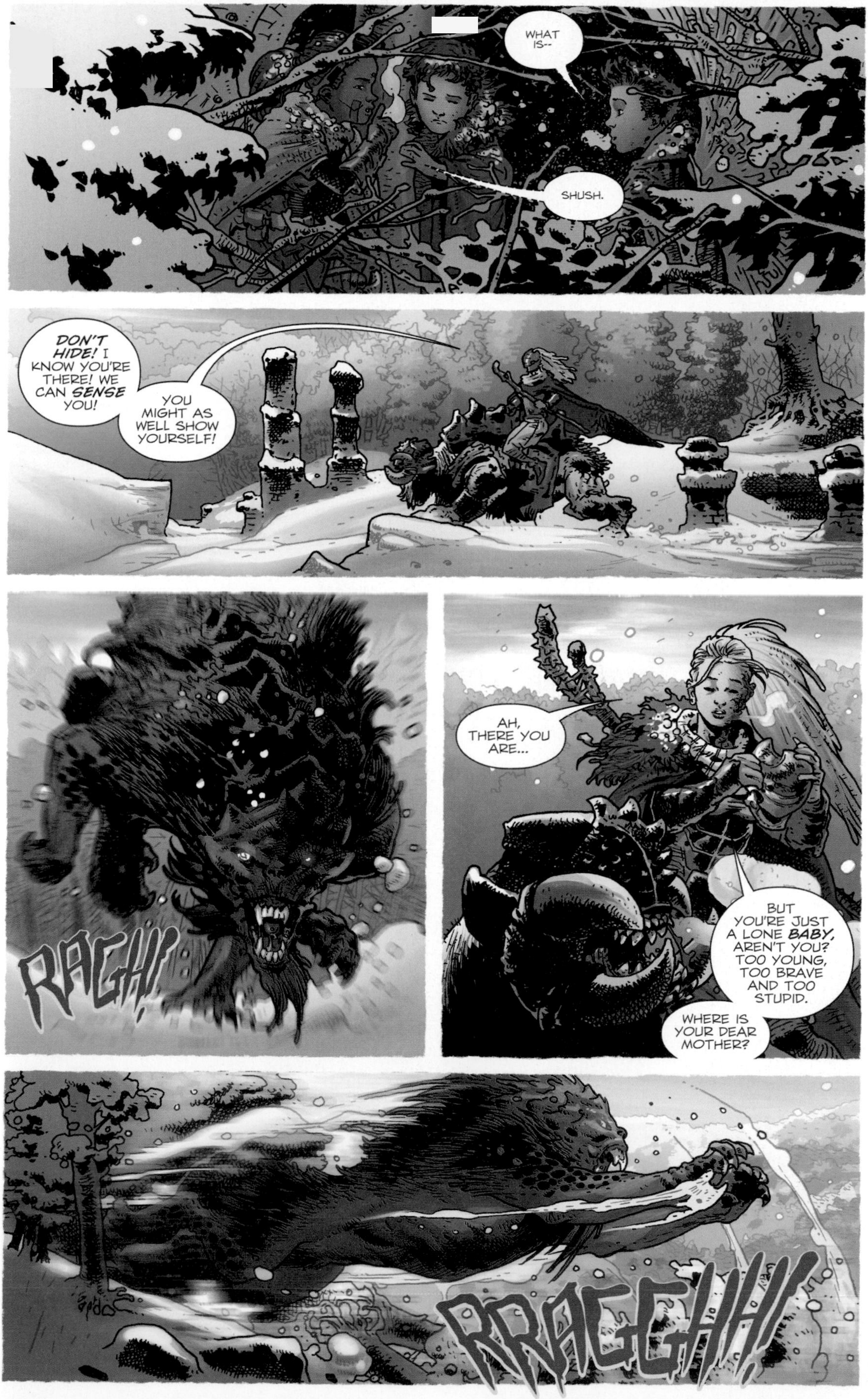
WHAT IS--
SHUSH.
DON'T HIDE! I KNOW YOU'RE THERE! WE CAN SENSE YOU!
YOU MIGHT AS WELL SHOW YOURSELF!
RAGH!
AH, THERE YOU ARE...
BUT YOU'RE JUST A LONE BABY, AREN'T YOU? TOO YOUNG, TOO BRAVE AND TOO STUPID.
WHERE IS YOUR DEAR MOTHER?
RRAGGHH!

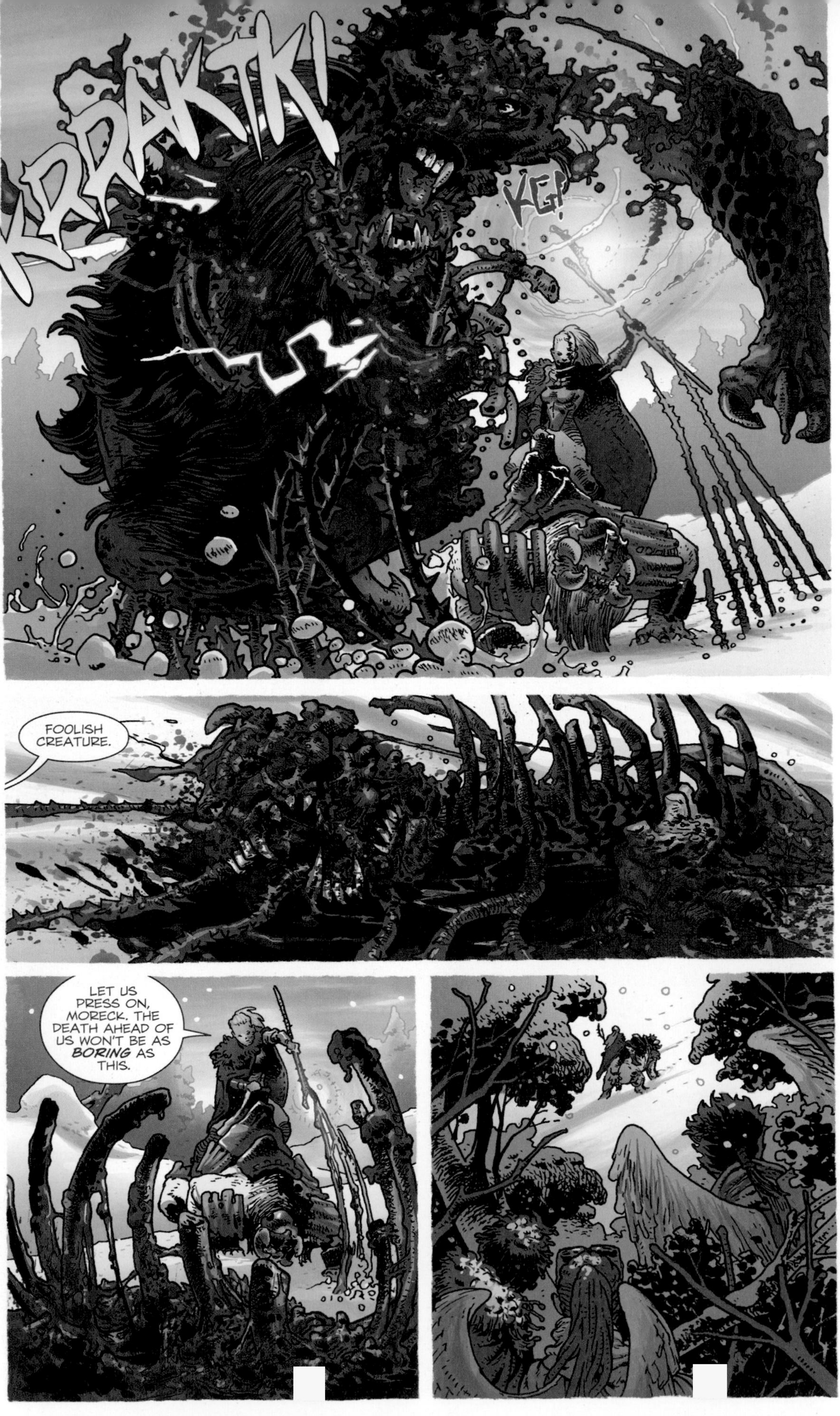
KRRAKTK!
KGP!
FOOLISH CREATURE.
LET US PRESS ON, MORECK. THE DEATH AHEAD OF US WON'T BE AS *BORING* AS THIS.

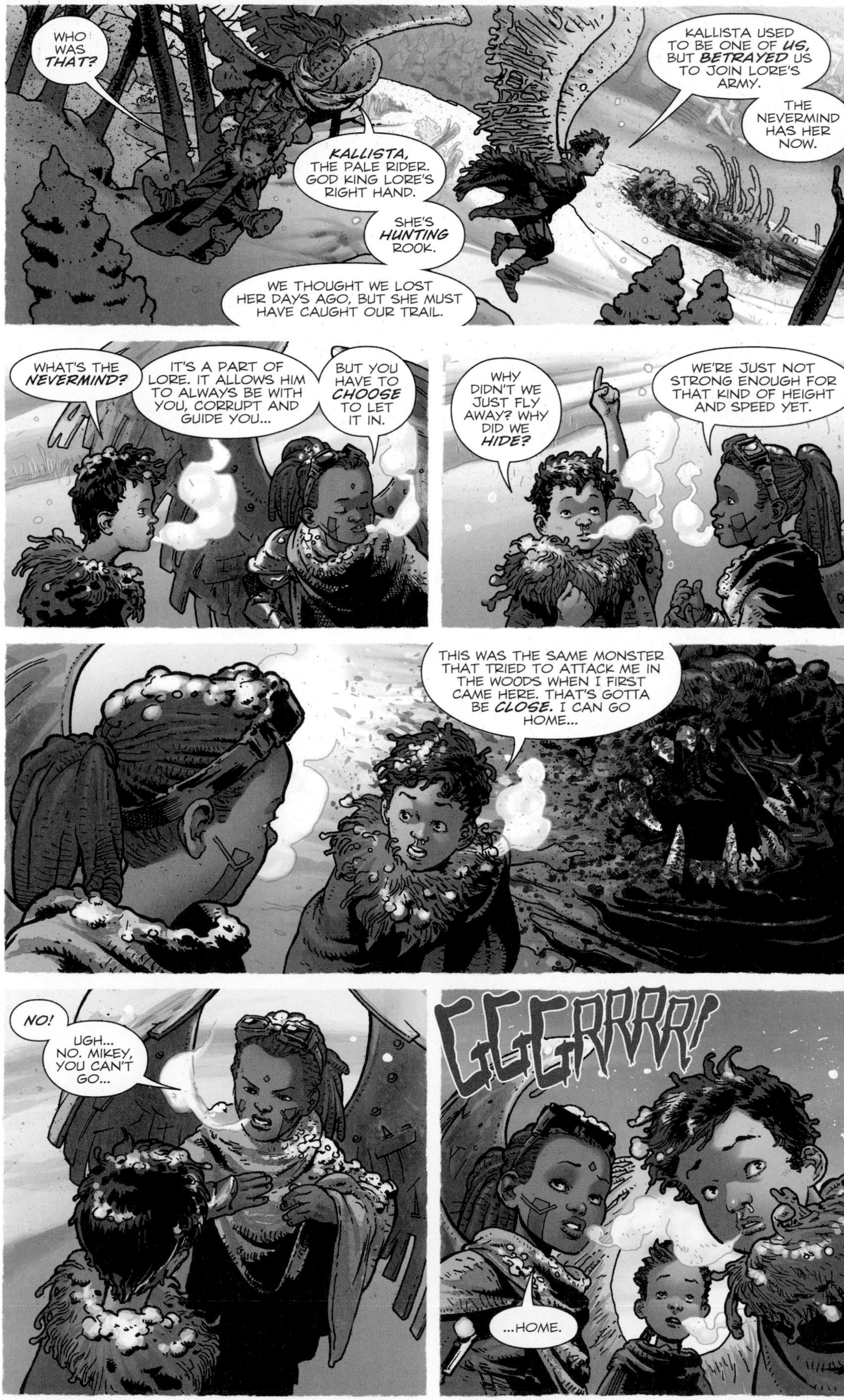
WHO WAS THAT?
KALLISTA, THE PALE RIDER. GOD KING LORE'S RIGHT HAND.
SHE'S HUNTING ROOK.
WE THOUGHT WE LOST HER DAYS AGO, BUT SHE MUST HAVE CAUGHT OUR TRAIL.
KALLISTA USED TO BE ONE OF US, BUT BETRAYED US TO JOIN LORE'S ARMY.
THE NEVERMIND HAS HER NOW.
WHAT'S THE NEVERMIND?
IT'S A PART OF LORE. IT ALLOWS HIM TO ALWAYS BE WITH YOU, CORRUPT AND GUIDE YOU...
BUT YOU HAVE TO CHOOSE TO LET IT IN.
WHY DIDN'T WE JUST FLY AWAY? WHY DID WE HIDE?
WE'RE JUST NOT STRONG ENOUGH FOR THAT KIND OF HEIGHT AND SPEED YET.
THIS WAS THE SAME MONSTER THAT TRIED TO ATTACK ME IN THE WOODS WHEN I FIRST CAME HERE. THAT'S GOTTA BE CLOSE. I CAN GO HOME...
NO!
UGH... NO. MIKEY, YOU CAN'T GO...
GGGRRRR!
...HOME.

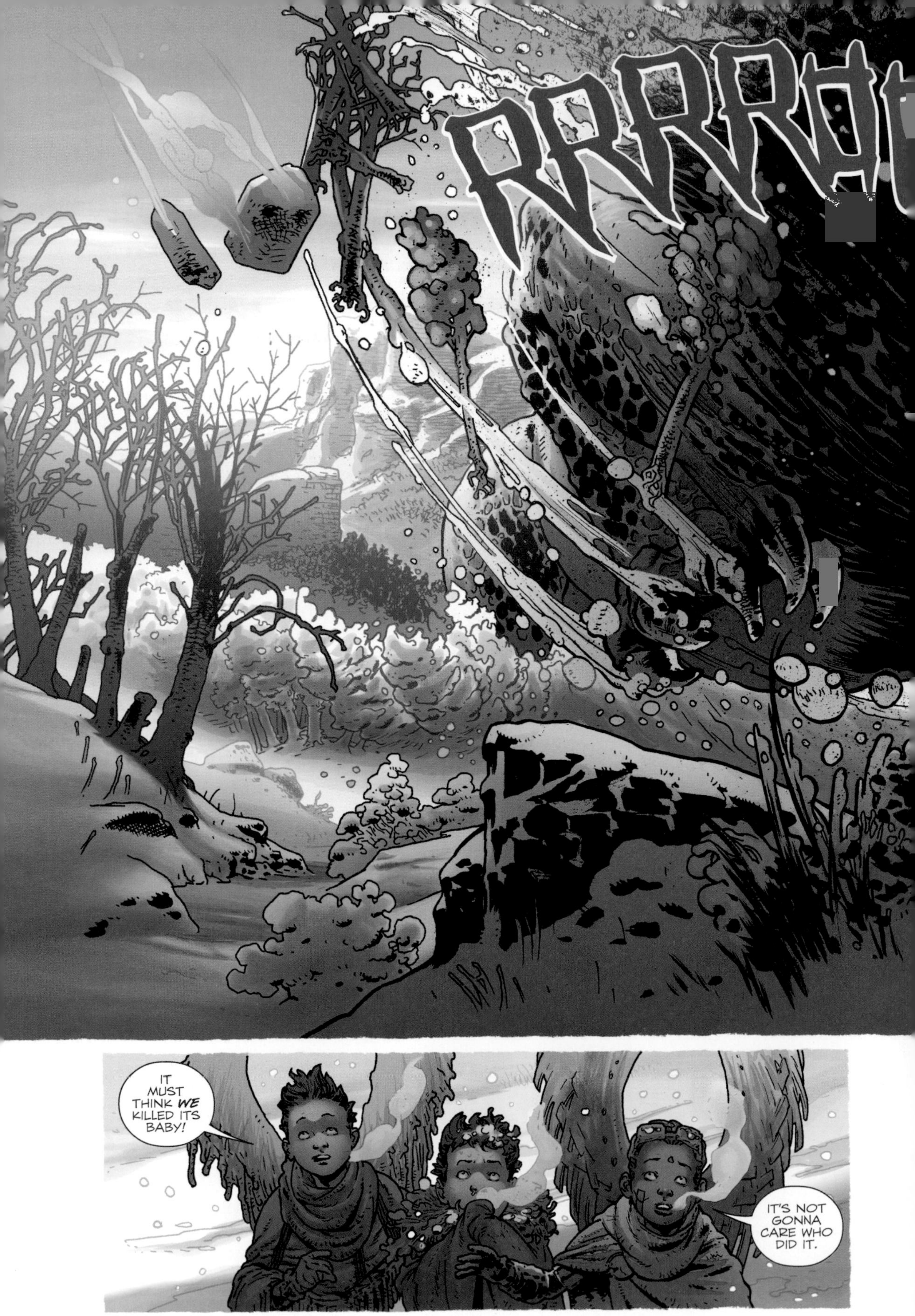
RRRRO
IT MUST THINK WE KILLED ITS BABY!
IT'S NOT GONNA CARE WHO DID IT.

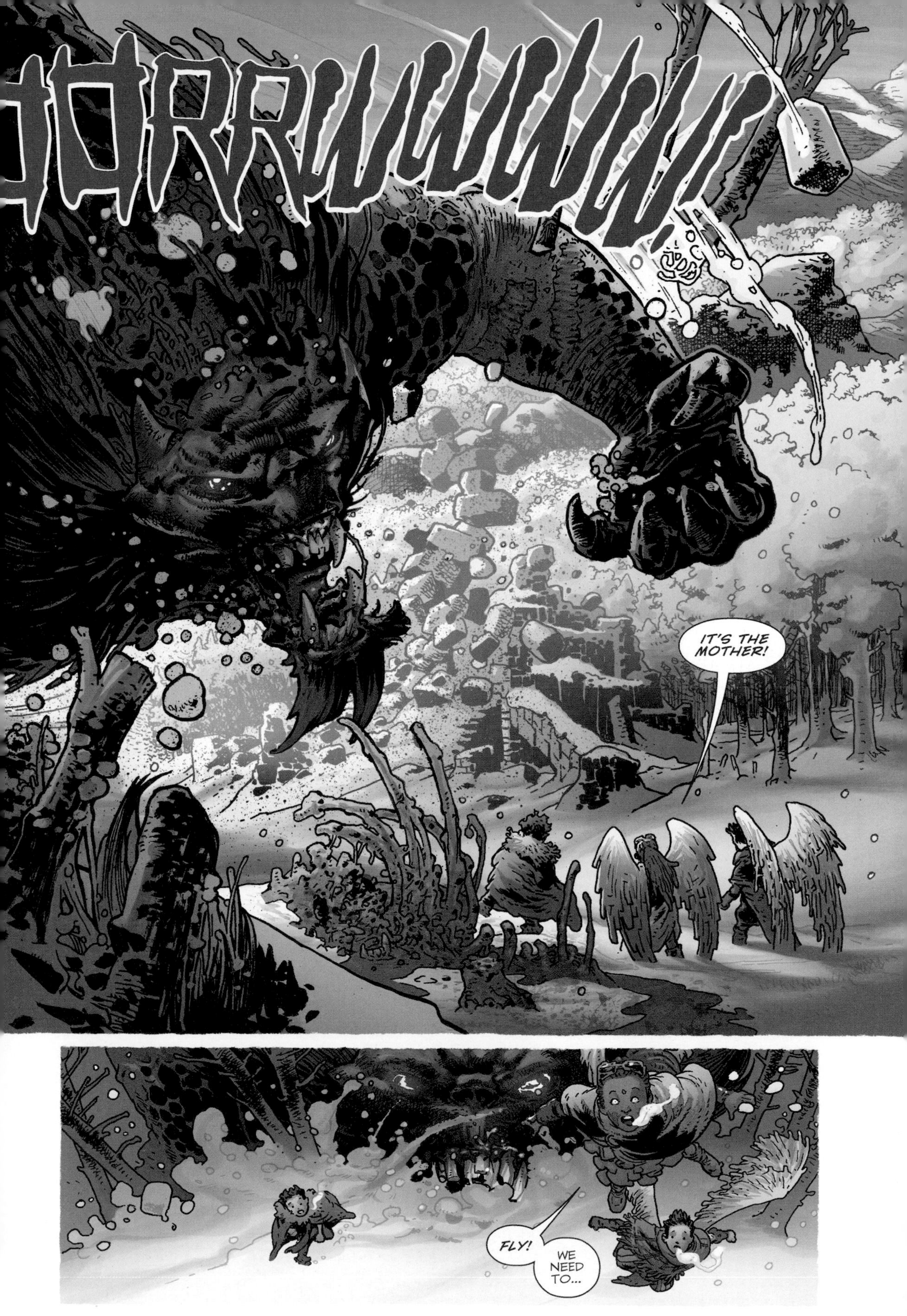
HURRUUUUUUU!
IT'S THE MOTHER!
FLY!
WE NEED TO...

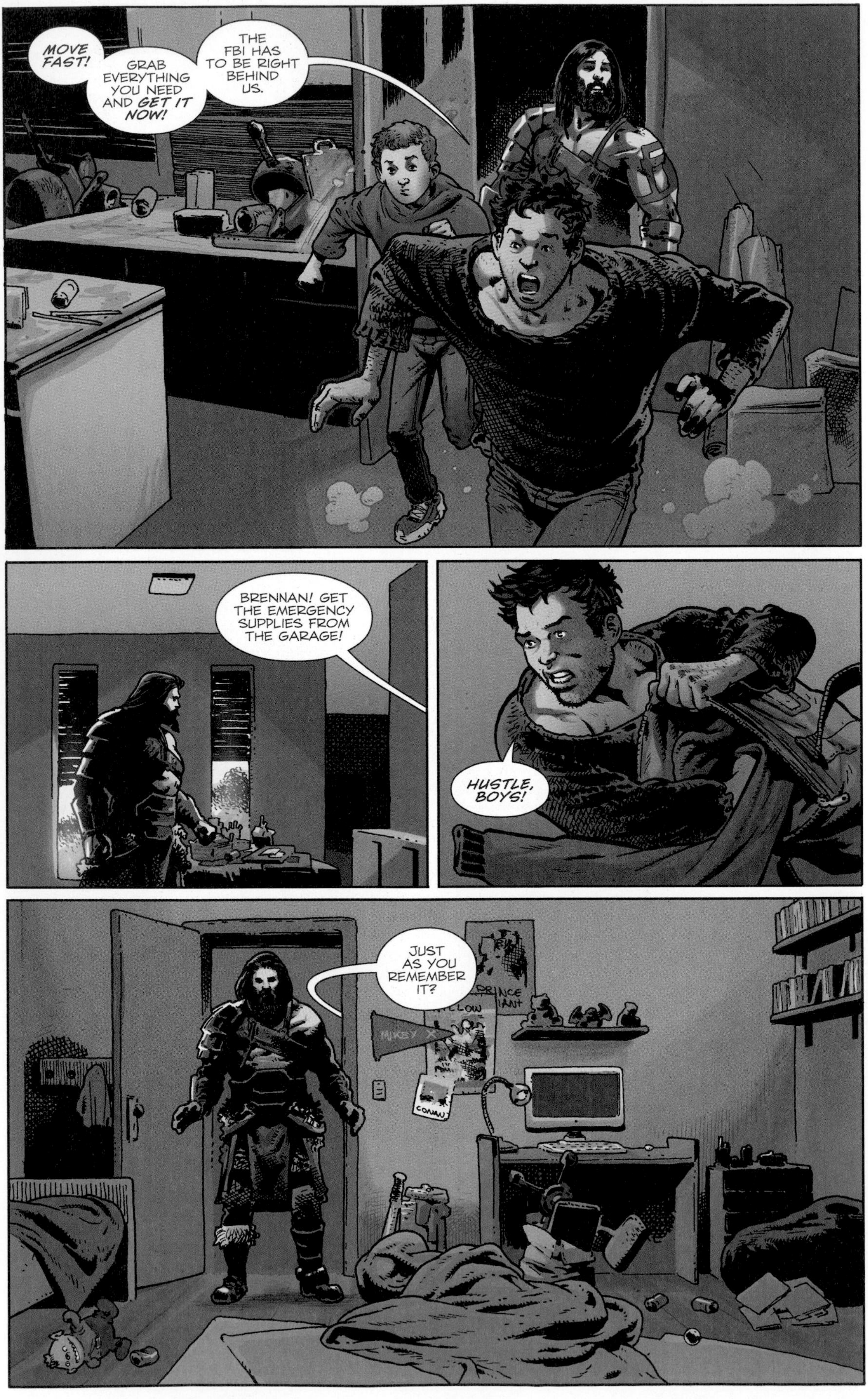
MOVE FAST!
GRAB EVERYTHING YOU NEED AND GET IT NOW!
THE FBI HAS TO BE RIGHT BEHIND US.
BRENNAN! GET THE EMERGENCY SUPPLIES FROM THE GARAGE!
HUSTLE, BOYS!
JUST AS YOU REMEMBER IT?
MIKEY
CONAN

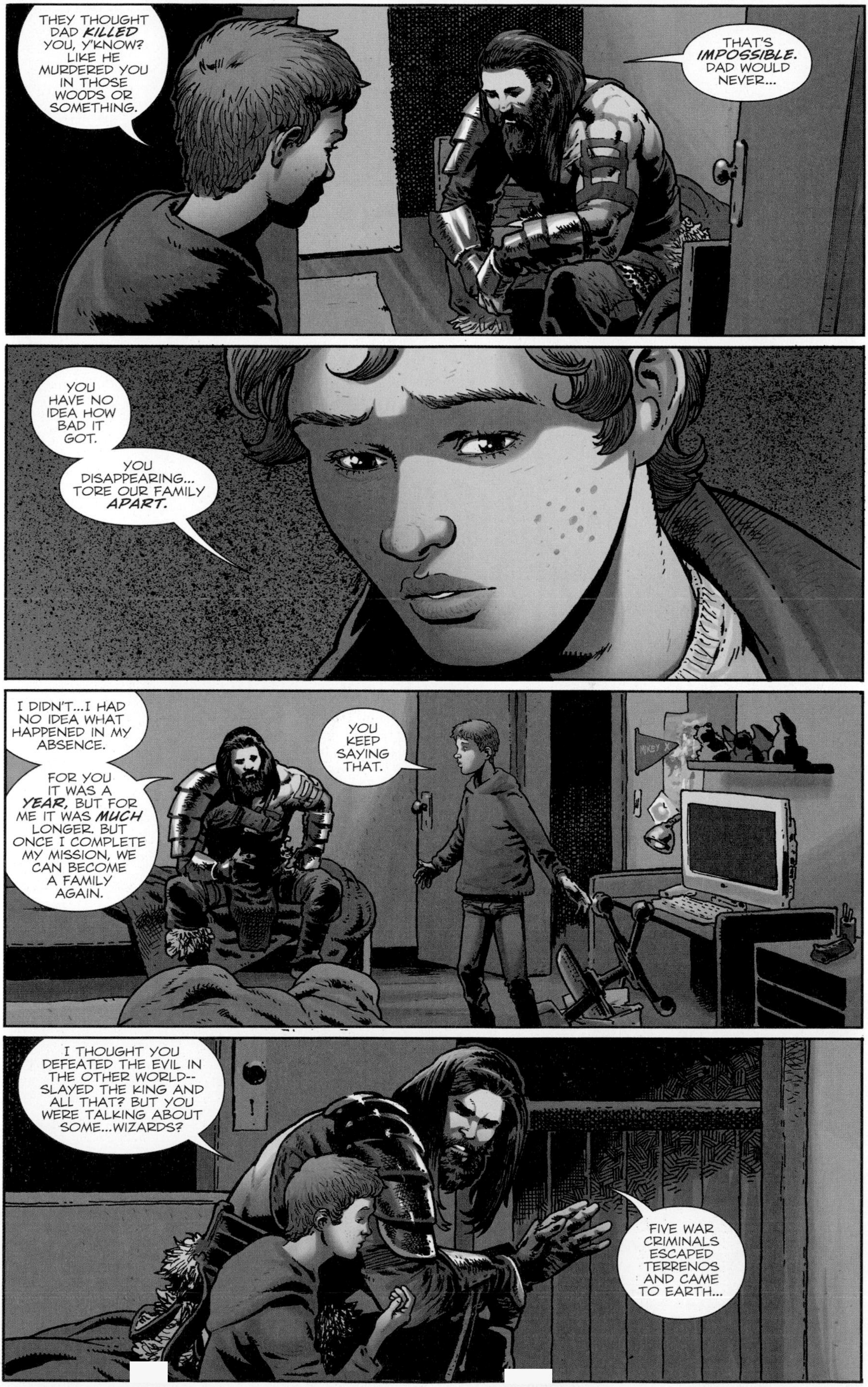
THEY THOUGHT DAD KILLED YOU, Y'KNOW? LIKE HE MURDERED YOU IN THOSE WOODS OR SOMETHING.
THAT'S IMPOSSIBLE. DAD WOULD NEVER...
YOU HAVE NO IDEA HOW BAD IT GOT.
YOU DISAPPEARING... TORE OUR FAMILY APART.
I DIDN'T...I HAD NO IDEA WHAT HAPPENED IN MY ABSENCE.
FOR YOU IT WAS A YEAR, BUT FOR ME IT WAS MUCH LONGER. BUT ONCE I COMPLETE MY MISSION, WE CAN BECOME A FAMILY AGAIN.
YOU KEEP SAYING THAT.
MIKEY
I THOUGHT YOU DEFEATED THE EVIL IN THE OTHER WORLD-- SLAYED THE KING AND ALL THAT? BUT YOU WERE TALKING ABOUT SOME...WIZARDS?
FIVE WAR CRIMINALS ESCAPED TERRENOS AND CAME TO EARTH...

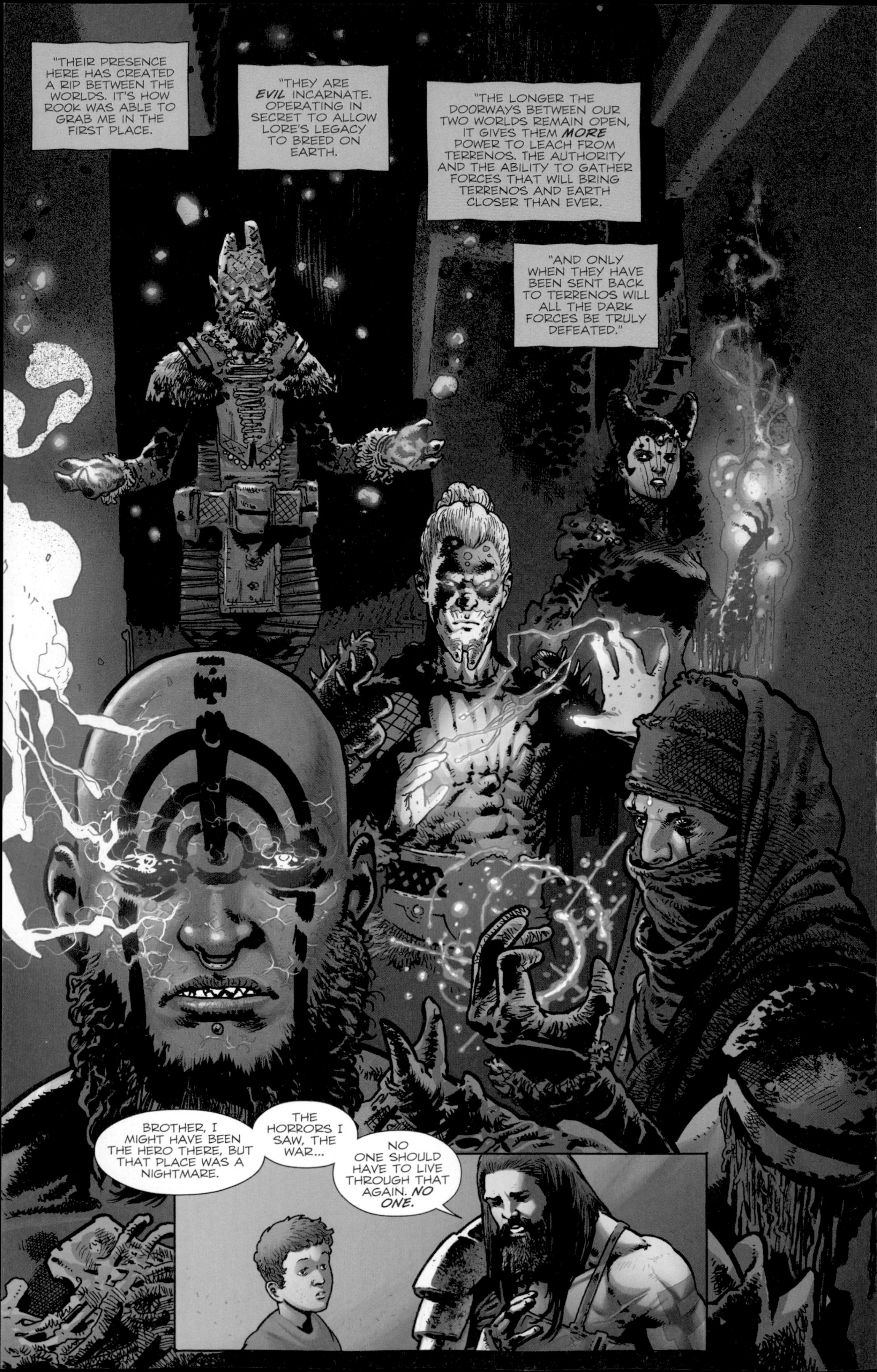
"THEIR PRESENCE HERE HAS CREATED A RIP BETWEEN THE WORLDS. IT'S HOW ROOK WAS ABLE TO GRAB ME IN THE FIRST PLACE.
"THEY ARE EVIL INCARNATE. OPERATING IN SECRET TO ALLOW LORE'S LEGACY TO BREED ON EARTH.
"THE LONGER THE DOORWAYS BETWEEN OUR TWO WORLDS REMAIN OPEN, IT GIVES THEM MORE POWER TO LEACH FROM TERRENOS. THE AUTHORITY AND THE ABILITY TO GATHER FORCES THAT WILL BRING TERRENOS AND EARTH CLOSER THAN EVER.
"AND ONLY WHEN THEY HAVE BEEN SENT BACK TO TERRENOS WILL ALL THE DARK FORCES BE TRULY DEFEATED."
BROTHER, I MIGHT HAVE BEEN THE HERO THERE, BUT THAT PLACE WAS A NIGHTMARE.
THE HORRORS I SAW, THE WAR...
NO ONE SHOULD HAVE TO LIVE THROUGH THAT AGAIN. NO ONE.

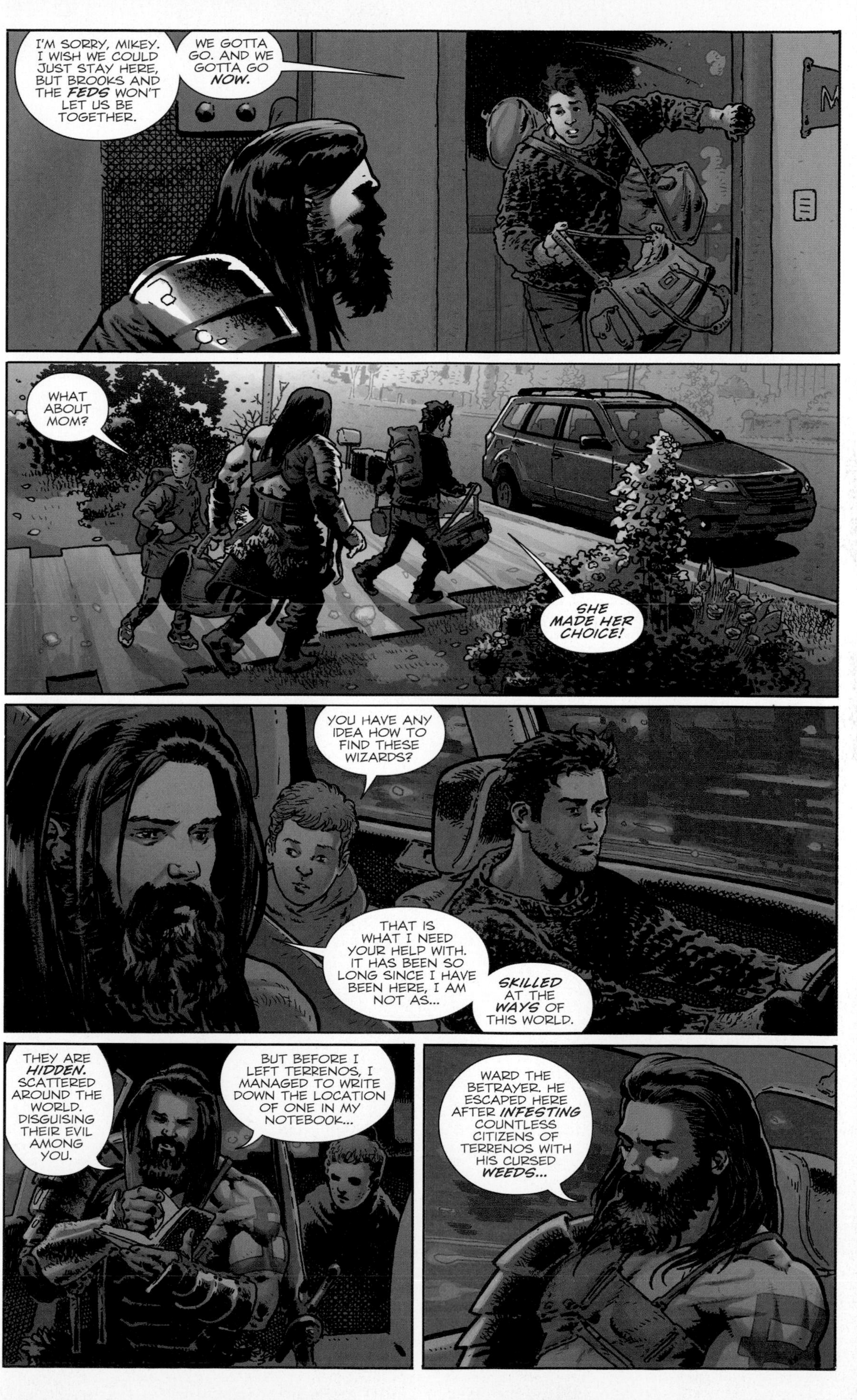
I'M SORRY, MIKEY. I WISH WE COULD JUST STAY HERE, BUT BROOKS AND THE FEDS WON'T LET US BE TOGETHER.
WE GOTTA GO. AND WE GOTTA GO NOW.
WHAT ABOUT MOM?
SHE MADE HER CHOICE!
YOU HAVE ANY IDEA HOW TO FIND THESE WIZARDS?
THAT IS WHAT I NEED YOUR HELP WITH. IT HAS BEEN SO LONG SINCE I HAVE BEEN HERE, I AM NOT AS...
SKILLED AT THE WAYS OF THIS WORLD.
THEY ARE HIDDEN. SCATTERED AROUND THE WORLD. DISGUISING THEIR EVIL AMONG YOU.
BUT BEFORE I LEFT TERRENOS, I MANAGED TO WRITE DOWN THE LOCATION OF ONE IN MY NOTEBOOK...
WARD THE BETRAYER. HE ESCAPED HERE AFTER INFESTING COUNTLESS CITIZENS OF TERRENOS WITH HIS CURSED WEEDS...

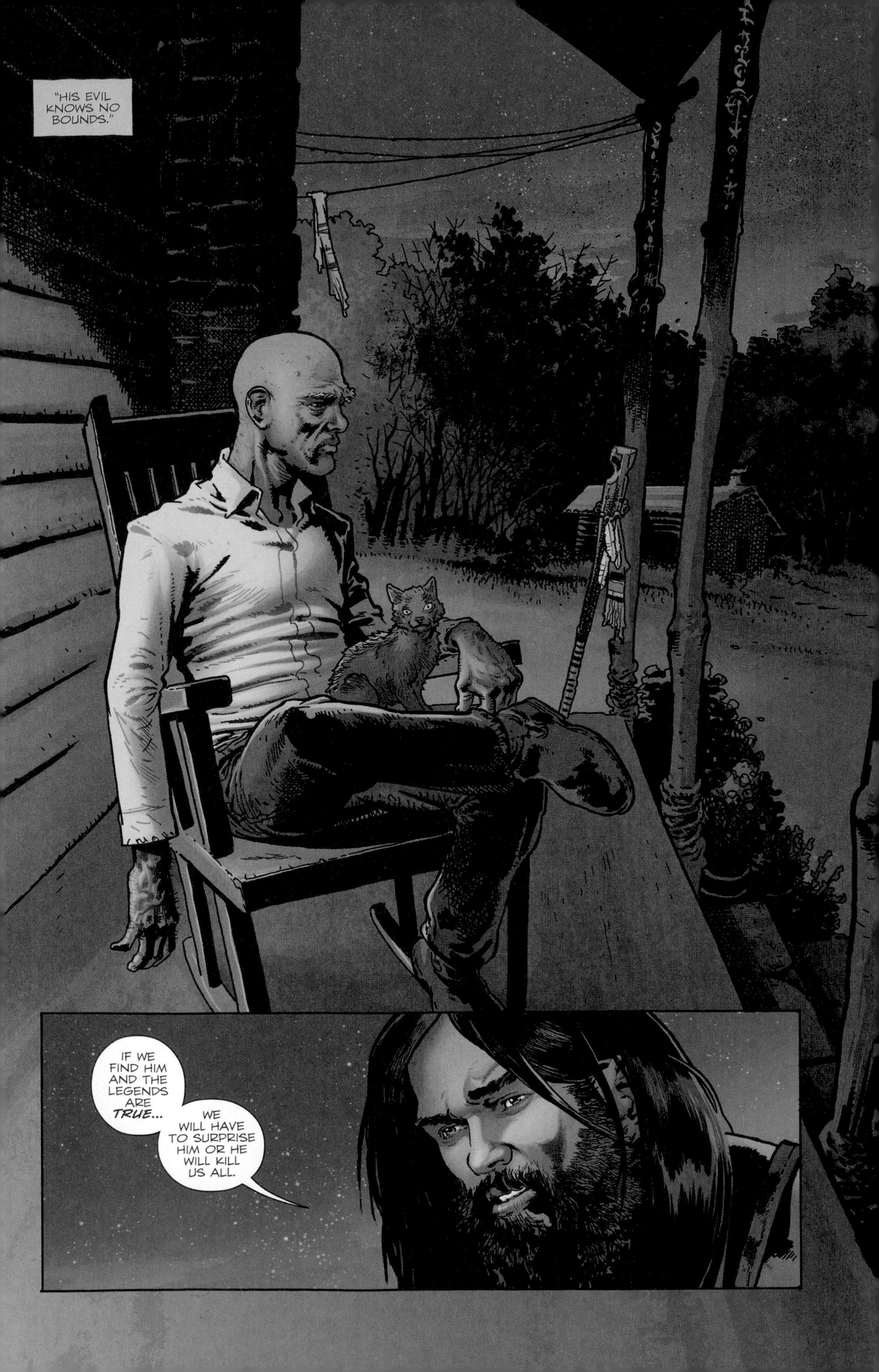
"HIS EVIL KNOWS NO BOUNDS."
IF WE FIND HIM AND THE LEGENDS ARE *TRUE*...
WE WILL HAVE TO SURPRISE HIM OR HE WILL KILL US ALL.

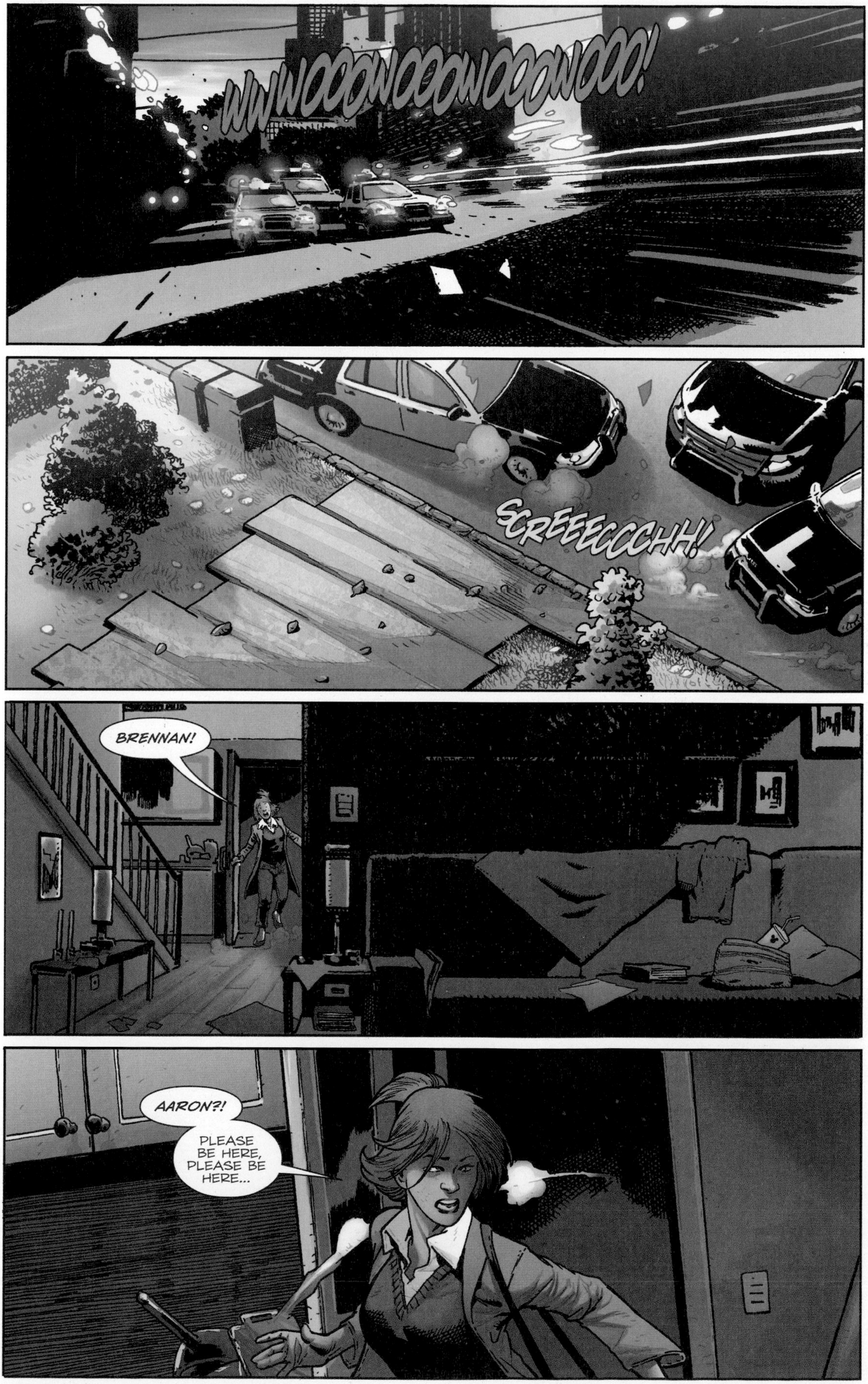
WWWOOOWOOOWOOOWOOO!
SCREEEECCCHH!
BRENNAN!
AARON?!
PLEASE BE HERE, PLEASE BE HERE...

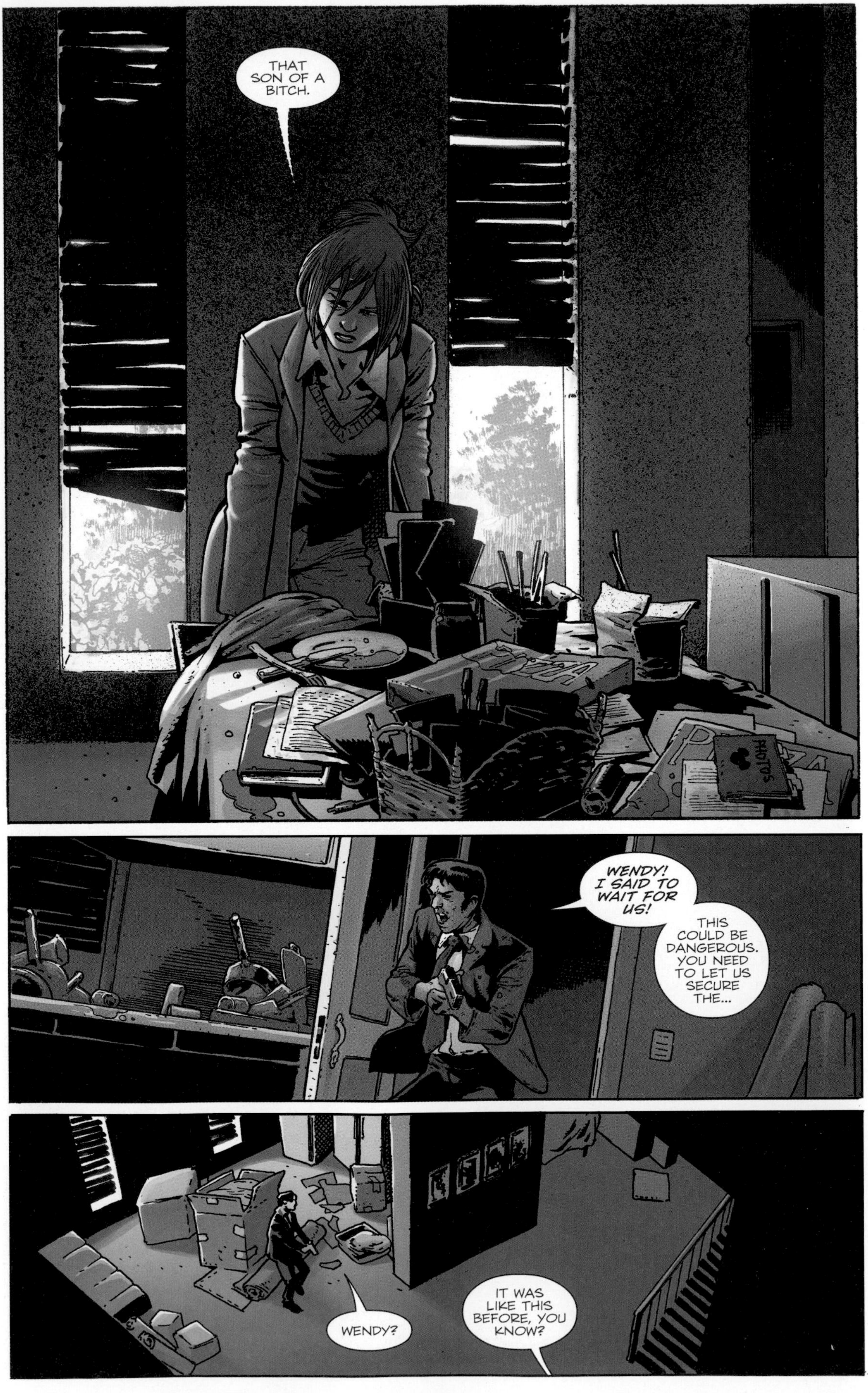
THAT SON OF A BITCH.
WENDY! I SAID TO WAIT FOR US!
THIS COULD BE DANGEROUS. YOU NEED TO LET US SECURE THE...
WENDY?
IT WAS LIKE THIS BEFORE, YOU KNOW?

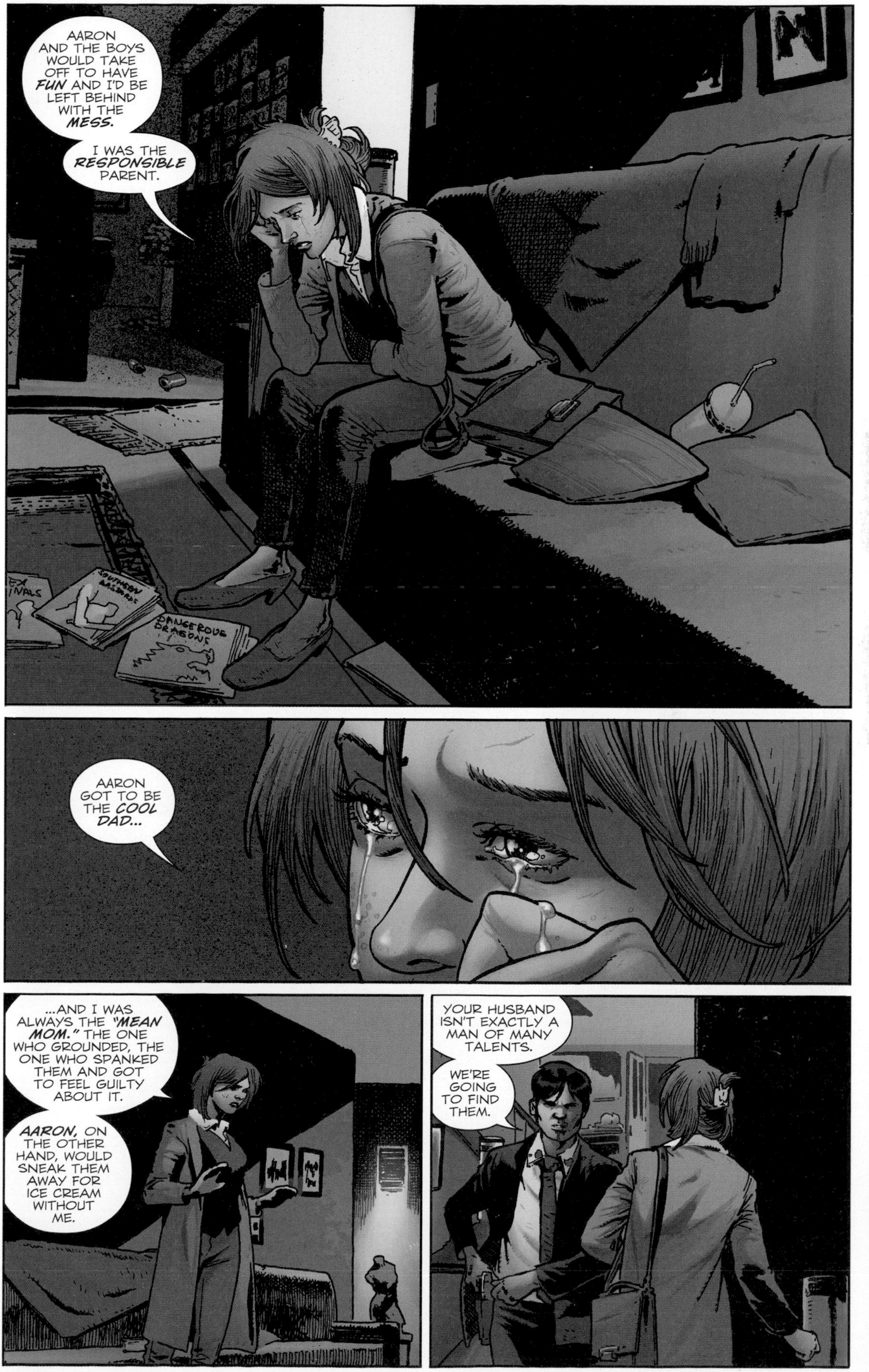
AARON AND THE BOYS WOULD TAKE OFF TO HAVE FUN AND I'D BE LEFT BEHIND WITH THE MESS.
I WAS THE RESPONSIBLE PARENT.
AARON GOT TO BE THE COOL DAD...
...AND I WAS ALWAYS THE "MEAN MOM." THE ONE WHO GROUNDED, THE ONE WHO SPANKED THEM AND GOT TO FEEL GUILTY ABOUT IT.
AARON, ON THE OTHER HAND, WOULD SNEAK THEM AWAY FOR ICE CREAM WITHOUT ME.
YOUR HUSBAND ISN'T EXACTLY A MAN OF MANY TALENTS.
WE'RE GOING TO FIND THEM.

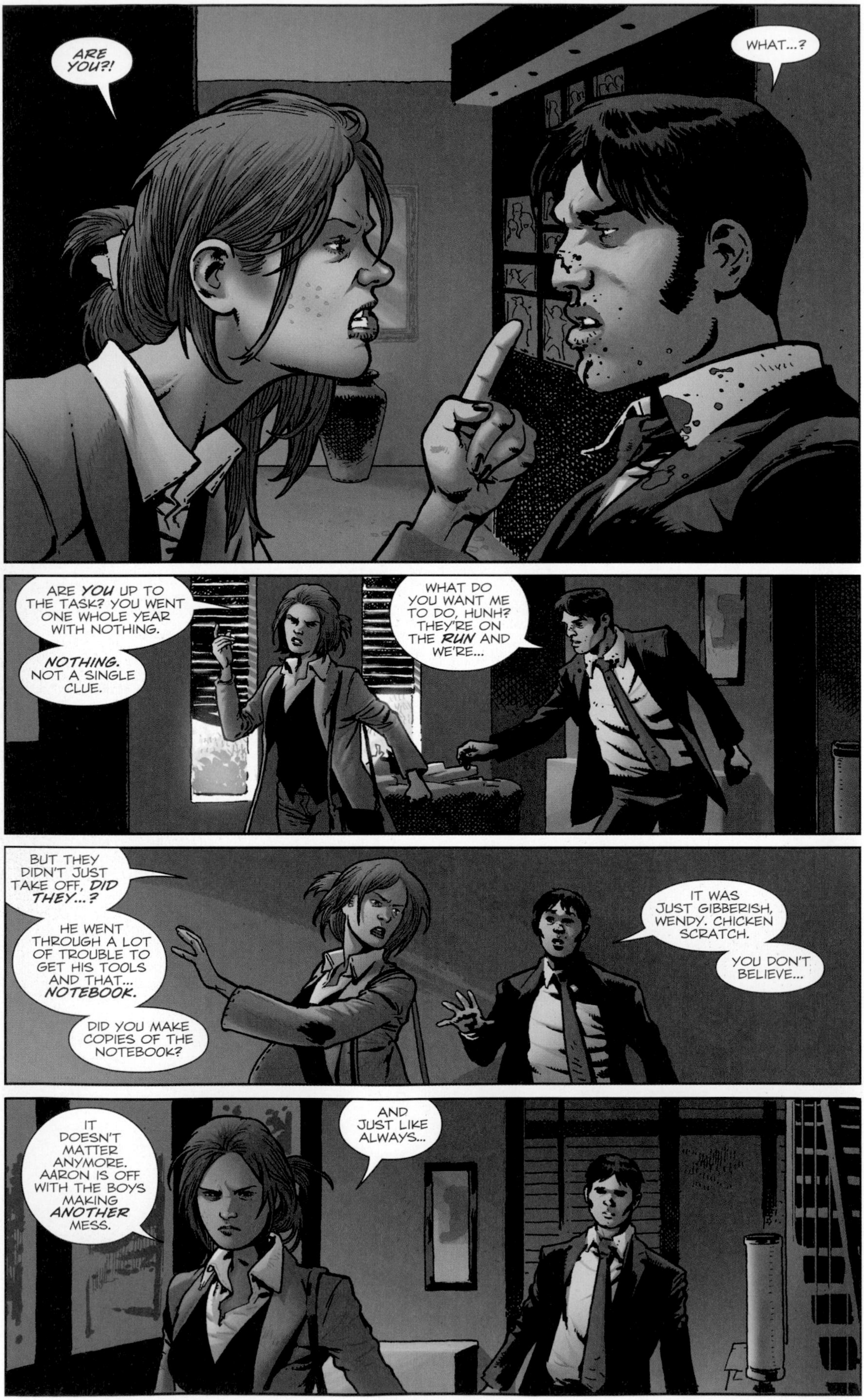
ARE YOU?!
WHAT...?
ARE YOU UP TO THE TASK? YOU WENT ONE WHOLE YEAR WITH NOTHING.
NOTHING. NOT A SINGLE CLUE.
WHAT DO YOU WANT ME TO DO, HUNH? THEY'RE ON THE RUN AND WE'RE...
BUT THEY DIDN'T JUST TAKE OFF, DID THEY...?
HE WENT THROUGH A LOT OF TROUBLE TO GET HIS TOOLS AND THAT... NOTEBOOK.
DID YOU MAKE COPIES OF THE NOTEBOOK?
IT WAS JUST GIBBERISH, WENDY. CHICKEN SCRATCH.
YOU DON'T BELIEVE...
IT DOESN'T MATTER ANYMORE. AARON IS OFF WITH THE BOYS MAKING ANOTHER MESS.
AND JUST LIKE ALWAYS...

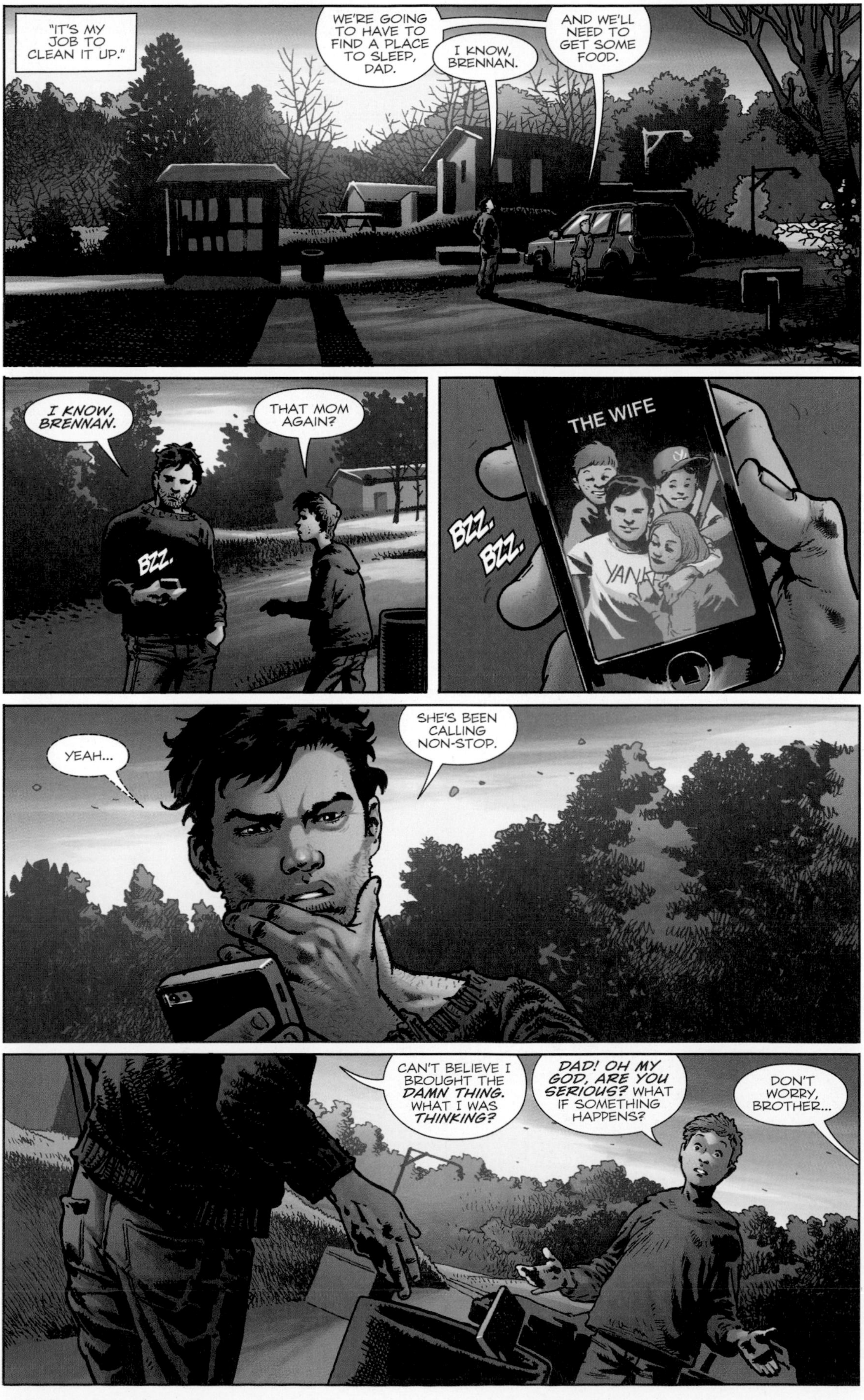
"IT'S MY JOB TO CLEAN IT UP."
WE'RE GOING TO HAVE TO FIND A PLACE TO SLEEP, DAD.
I KNOW, BRENNAN.
AND WE'LL NEED TO GET SOME FOOD.
I KNOW, BRENNAN.
THAT MOM AGAIN?
BZZ.
THE WIFE
BZZ. BZZ.
YEAH...
SHE'S BEEN CALLING NON-STOP.
CAN'T BELIEVE I BROUGHT THE DAMN THING. WHAT I WAS THINKING?
DAD! OH MY GOD, ARE YOU SERIOUS? WHAT IF SOMETHING HAPPENS?
DON'T WORRY, BROTHER...

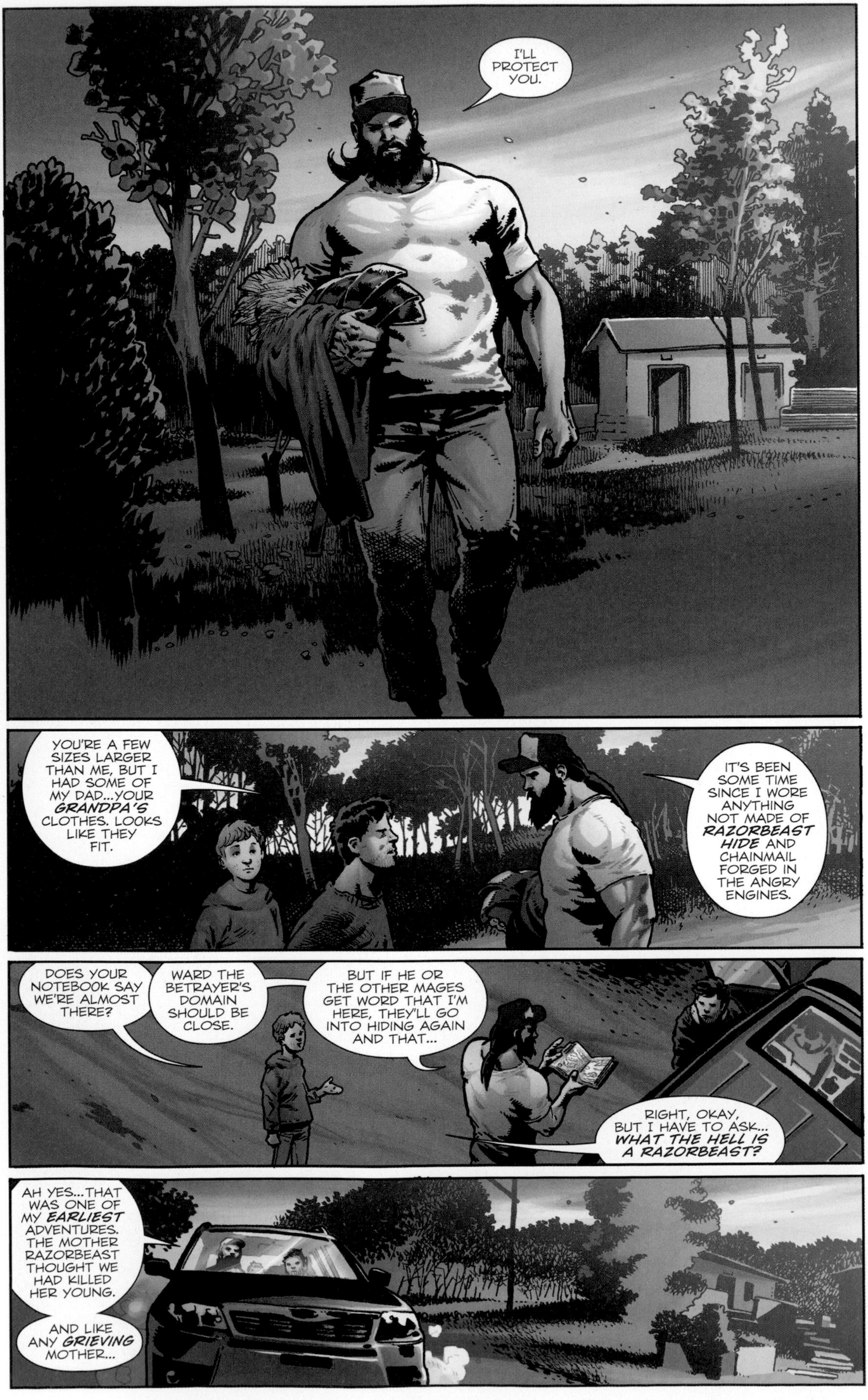
I'LL PROTECT YOU.
YOU'RE A FEW SIZES LARGER THAN ME, BUT I HAD SOME OF MY DAD...YOUR GRANDPA'S CLOTHES. LOOKS LIKE THEY FIT.
IT'S BEEN SOME TIME SINCE I WORE ANYTHING NOT MADE OF RAZORBEAST HIDE AND CHAINMAIL FORGED IN THE ANGRY ENGINES.
DOES YOUR NOTEBOOK SAY WE'RE ALMOST THERE?
WARD THE BETRAYER'S DOMAIN SHOULD BE CLOSE.
BUT IF HE OR THE OTHER MAGES GET WORD THAT I'M HERE, THEY'LL GO INTO HIDING AGAIN AND THAT...
RIGHT, OKAY, BUT I HAVE TO ASK... WHAT THE HELL IS A RAZORBEAST?
AH YES...THAT WAS ONE OF MY EARLIEST ADVENTURES. THE MOTHER RAZORBEAST THOUGHT WE HAD KILLED HER YOUNG.
AND LIKE ANY GRIEVING MOTHER...

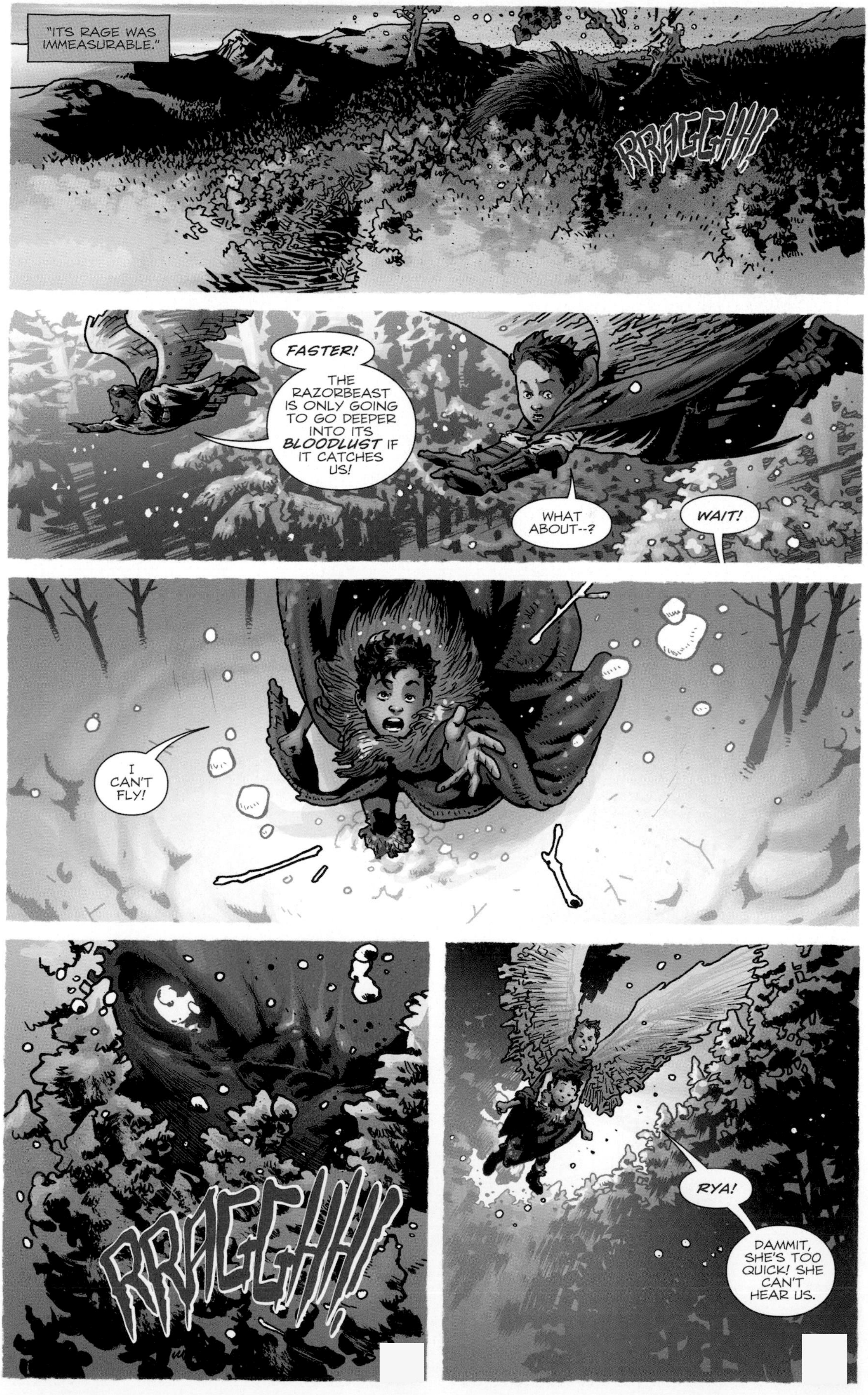
"ITS RAGE WAS IMMEASURABLE."
RRAGGHH!
FASTER!
THE RAZORBEAST IS ONLY GOING TO GO DEEPER INTO ITS BLOODLUST IF IT CATCHES US!
WHAT ABOUT--?
WAIT!
I CAN'T FLY!
RRAGGHH!
RYA!
DAMMIT, SHE'S TOO QUICK! SHE CAN'T HEAR US.

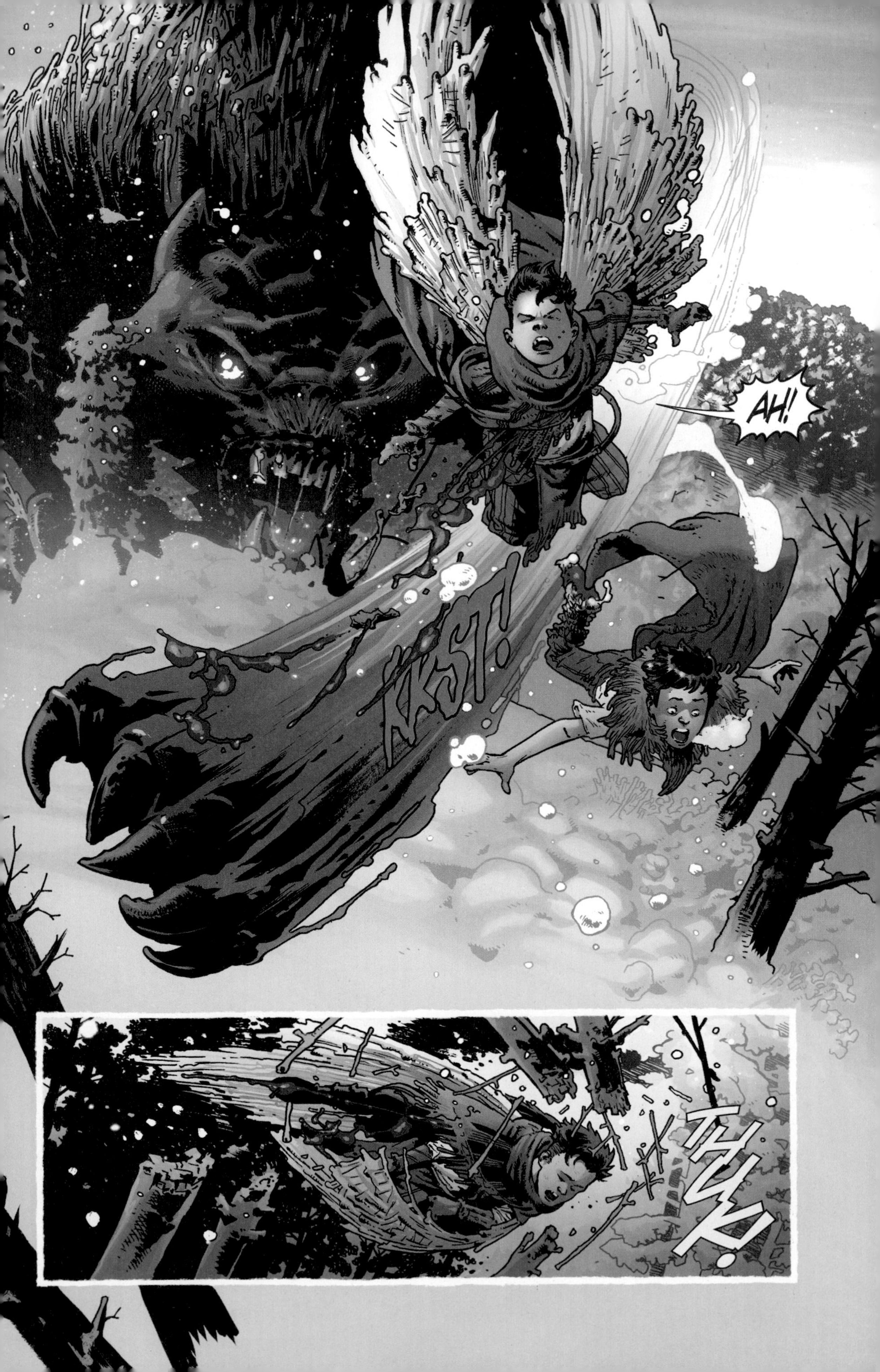
AH!
KKST!
THUK!

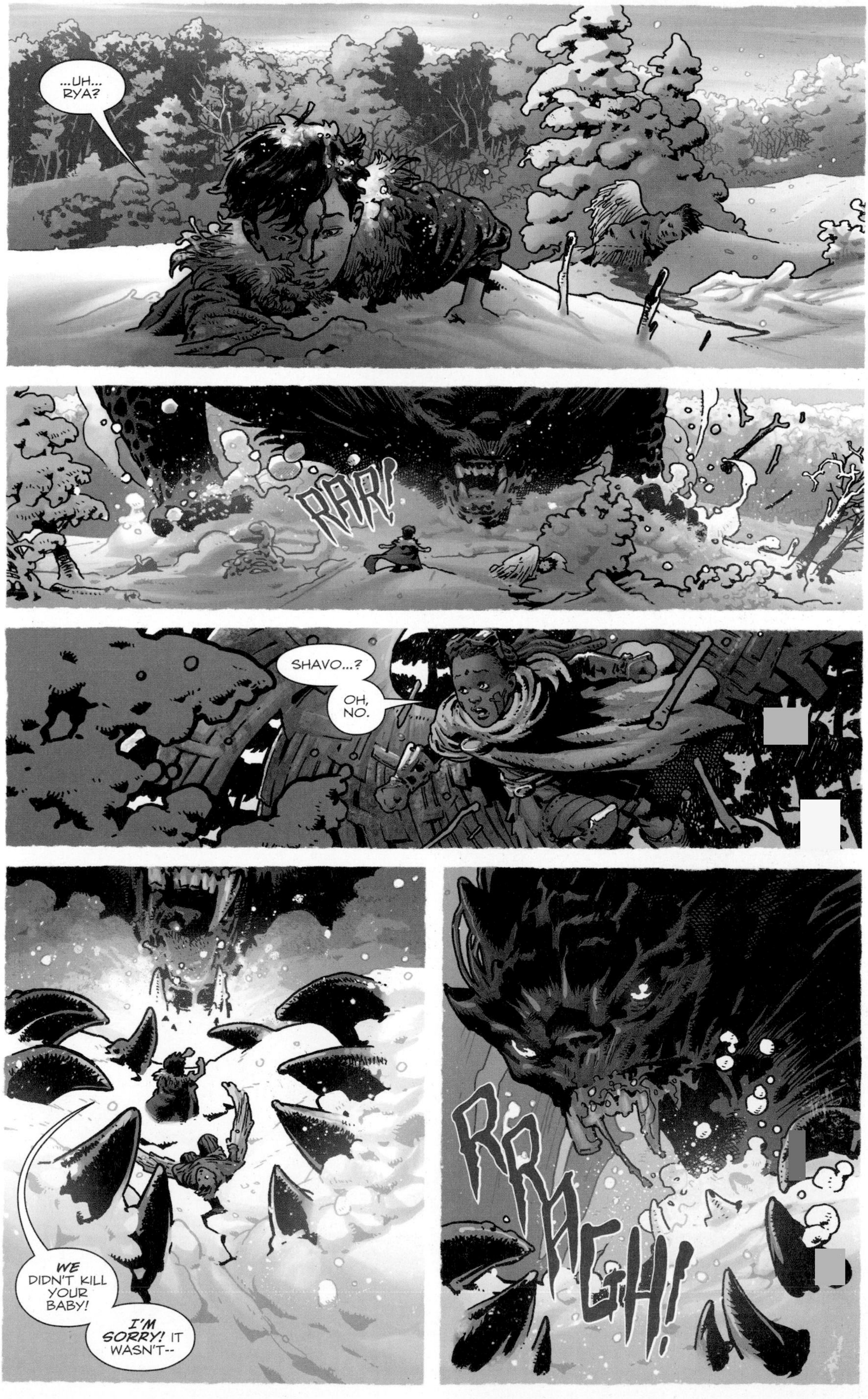
...UH... RYA?
RAR!
SHAVO...?
OH, NO.
WE DIDN'T KILL YOUR BABY!
I'M SORRY! IT WASN'T--
RRAAGH!

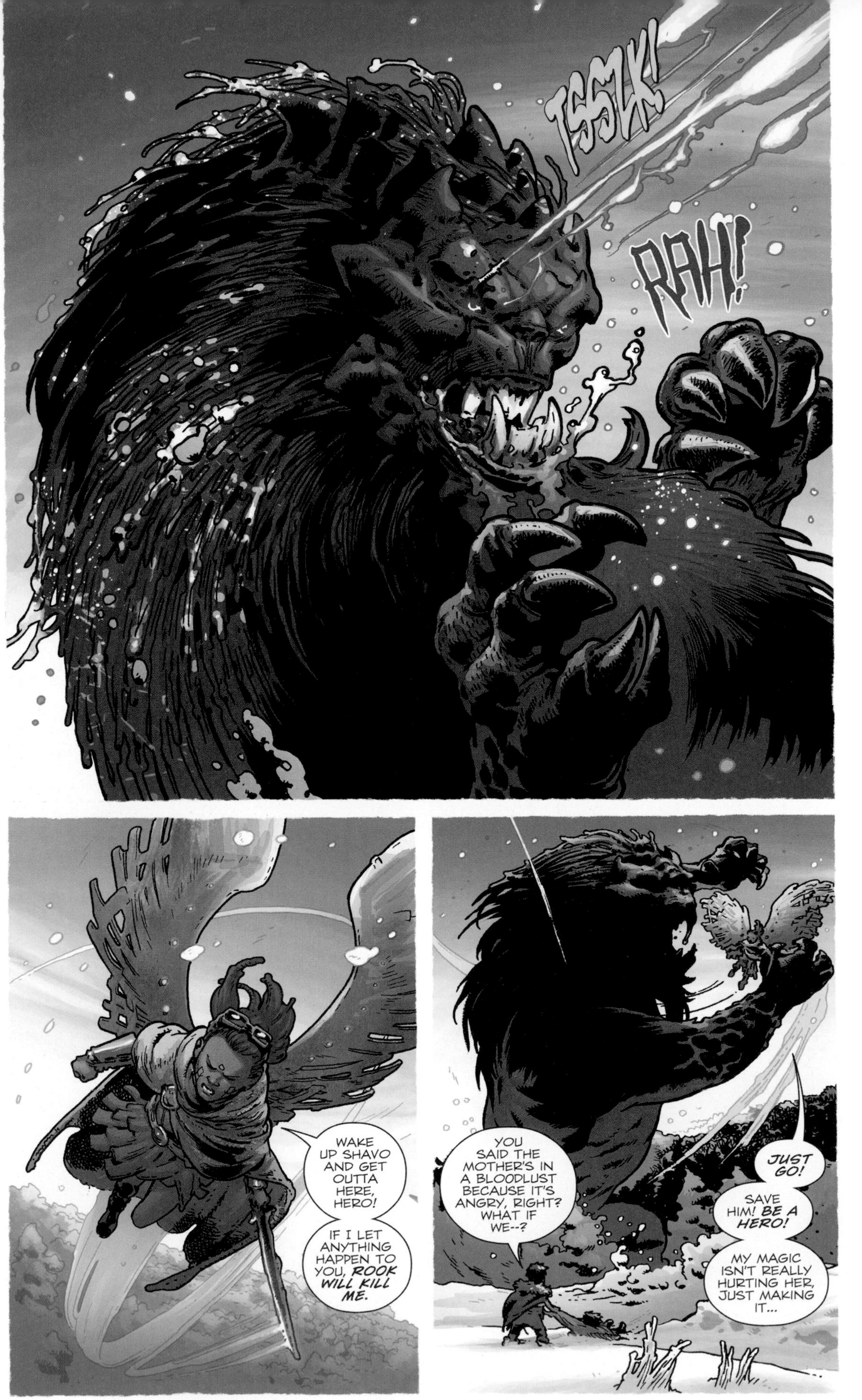
TSSZK!
RAH!
WAKE UP SHAVO AND GET OUTTA HERE, HERO!
IF I LET ANYTHING HAPPEN TO YOU, ROOK WILL KILL ME.
YOU SAID THE MOTHER'S IN A BLOODLUST BECAUSE IT'S ANGRY, RIGHT? WHAT IF WE--?
JUST GO!
SAVE HIM! BE A HERO!
MY MAGIC ISN'T REALLY HURTING HER, JUST MAKING IT...

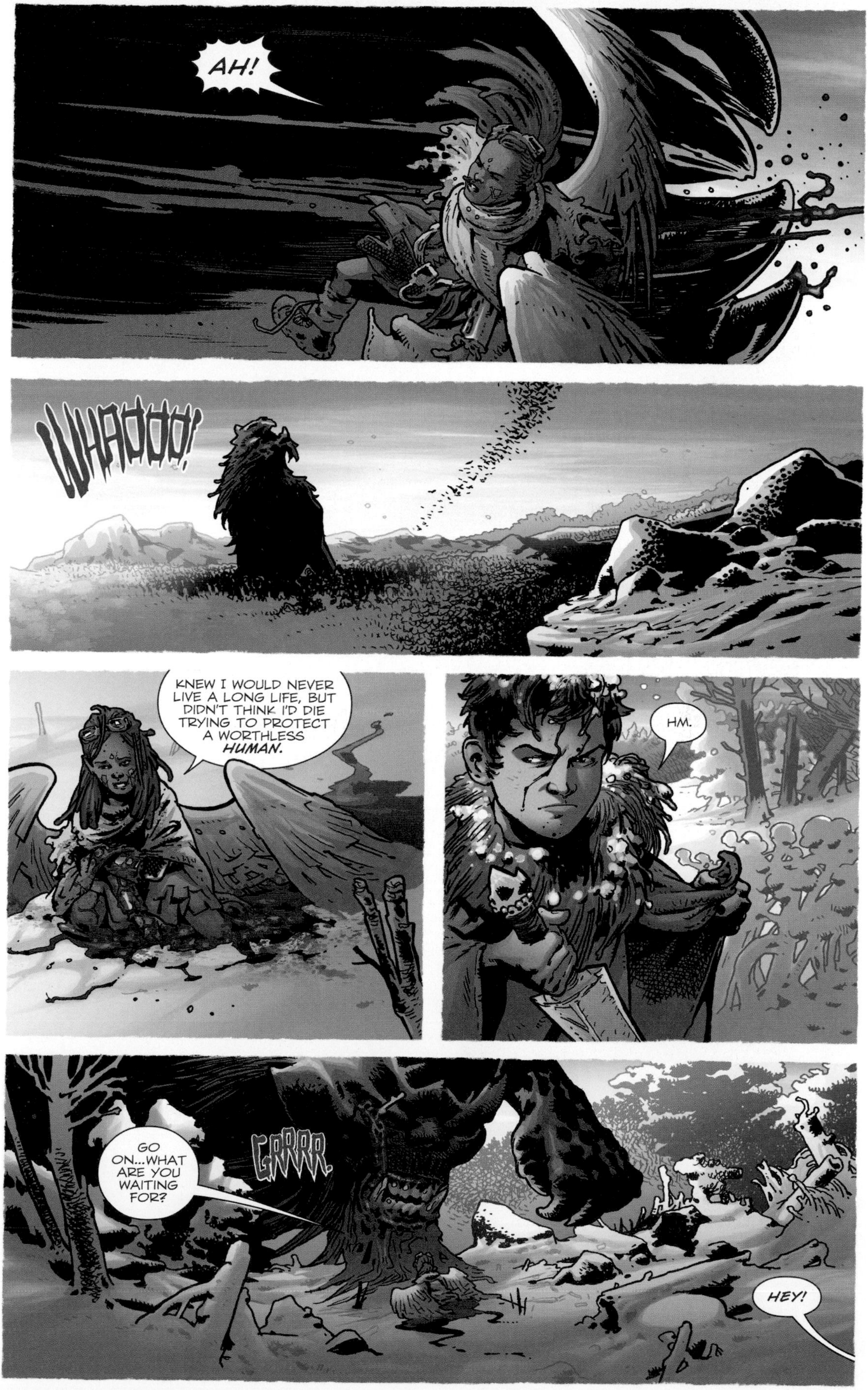
AH!
WHADOO!
KNEW I WOULD NEVER LIVE A LONG LIFE, BUT DIDN'T THINK I'D DIE TRYING TO PROTECT A WORTHLESS *HUMAN*.
HM.
GO ON...WHAT ARE YOU WAITING FOR?
GRRRR.
HEY!

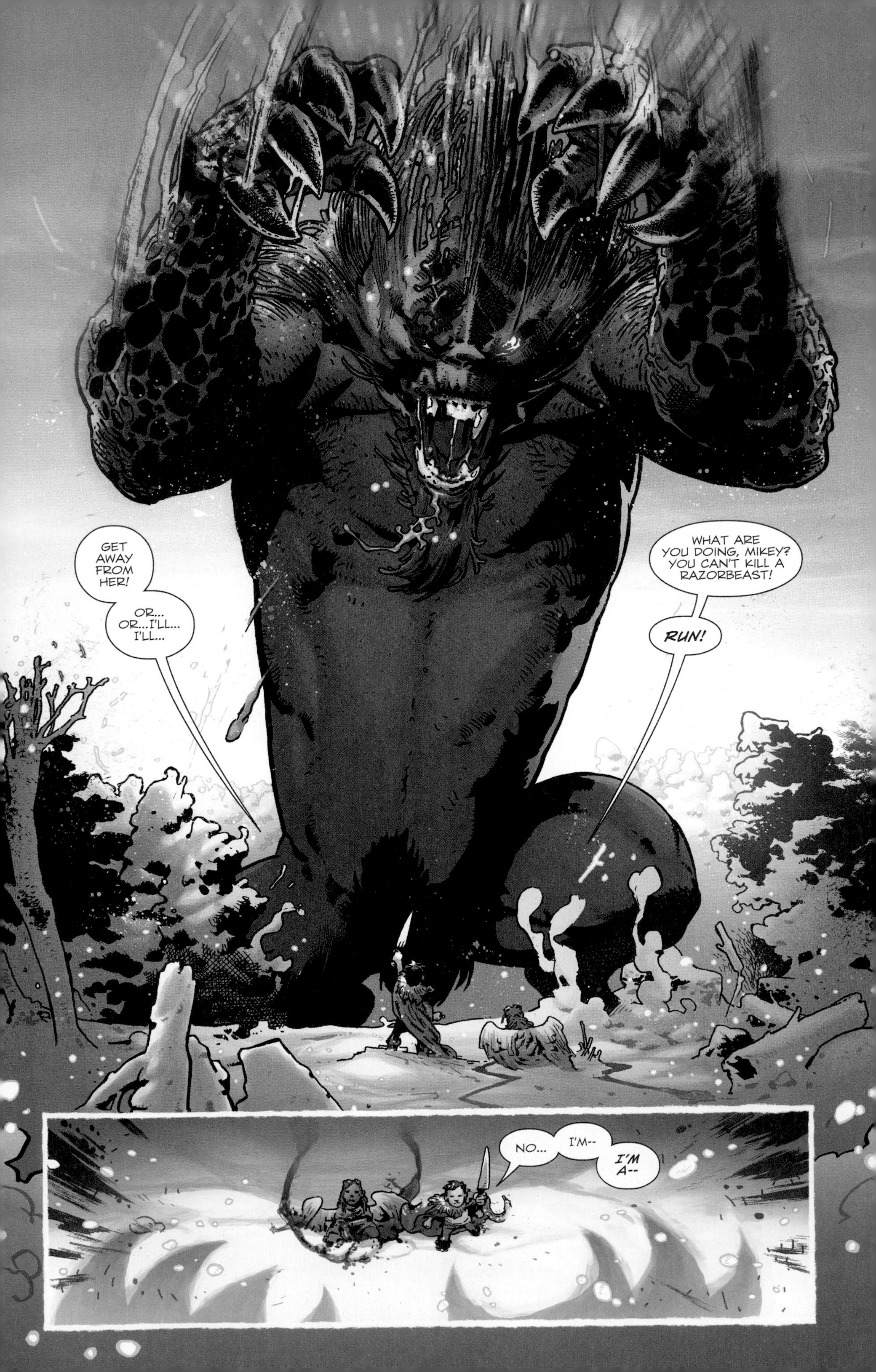
GET AWAY FROM HER!
OR... OR...I'LL... I'LL...
WHAT ARE YOU DOING, MIKEY? YOU CAN'T KILL A RAZORBEAST!
RUN!
NO...
I'M--
I'M A--

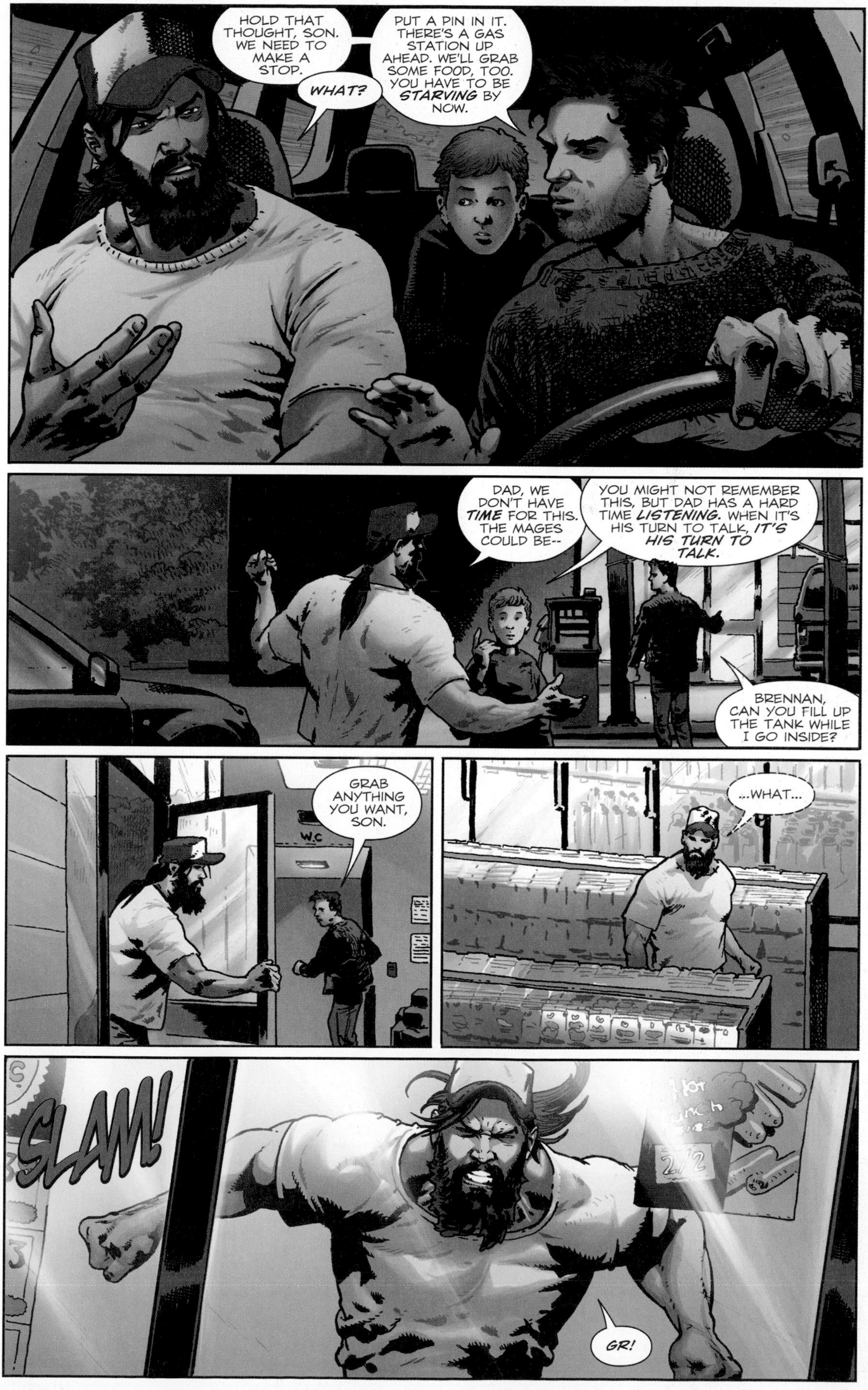
HOLD THAT THOUGHT, SON. WE NEED TO MAKE A STOP.
WHAT?
PUT A PIN IN IT. THERE'S A GAS STATION UP AHEAD. WE'LL GRAB SOME FOOD, TOO. YOU HAVE TO BE STARVING BY NOW.
DAD, WE DON'T HAVE TIME FOR THIS. THE MAGES COULD BE--
YOU MIGHT NOT REMEMBER THIS, BUT DAD HAS A HARD TIME LISTENING. WHEN IT'S HIS TURN TO TALK, IT'S HIS TURN TO TALK.
BRENNAN, CAN YOU FILL UP THE TANK WHILE I GO INSIDE?
GRAB ANYTHING YOU WANT, SON.
W.C
...WHAT...
SLAM!
GR!

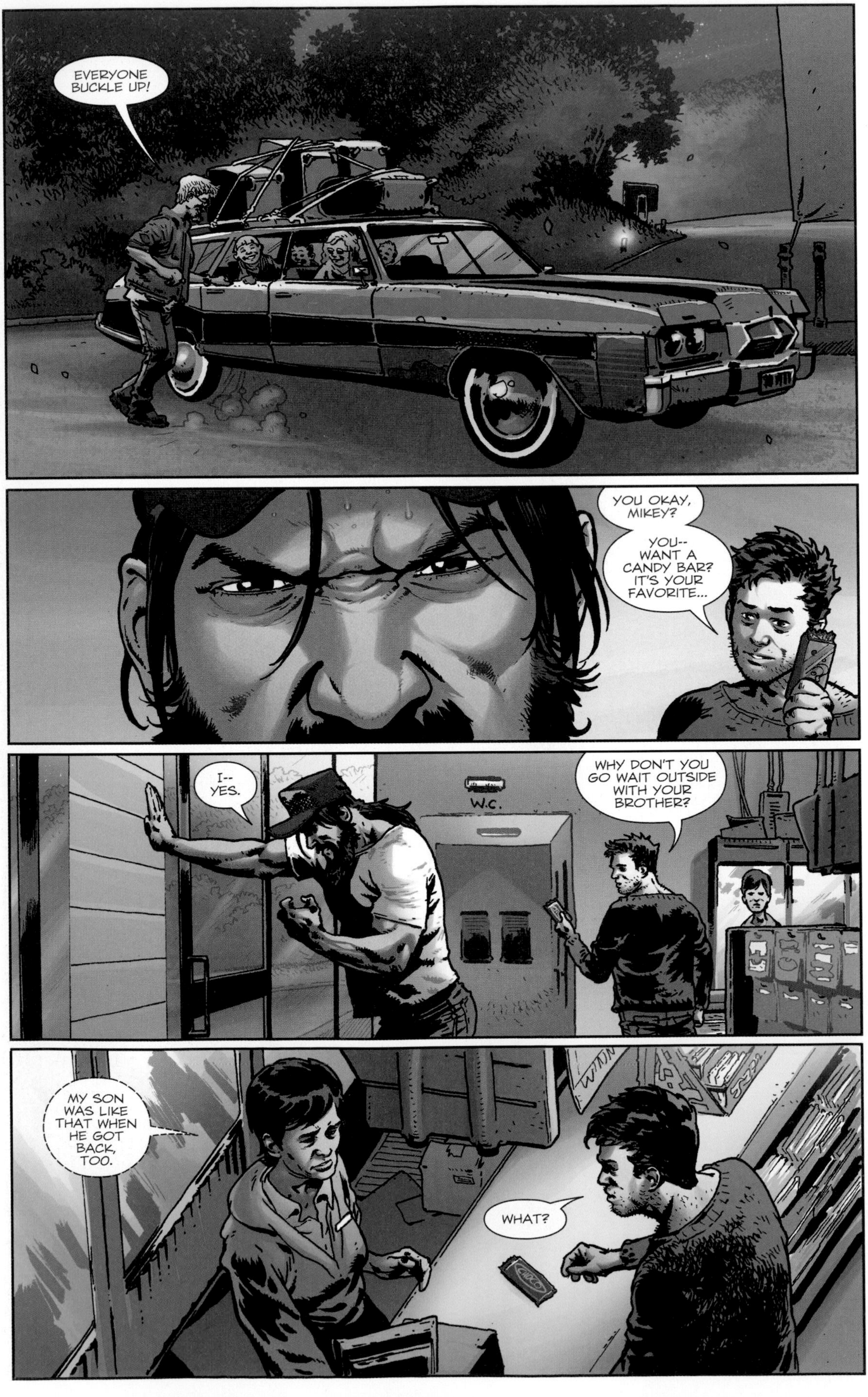
EVERYONE BUCKLE UP!
YOU OKAY, MIKEY?
YOU-- WANT A CANDY BAR? IT'S YOUR FAVORITE...
I-- YES.
WHY DON'T YOU GO WAIT OUTSIDE WITH YOUR BROTHER?
W.C.
MY SON WAS LIKE THAT WHEN HE GOT BACK, TOO.
WHAT?

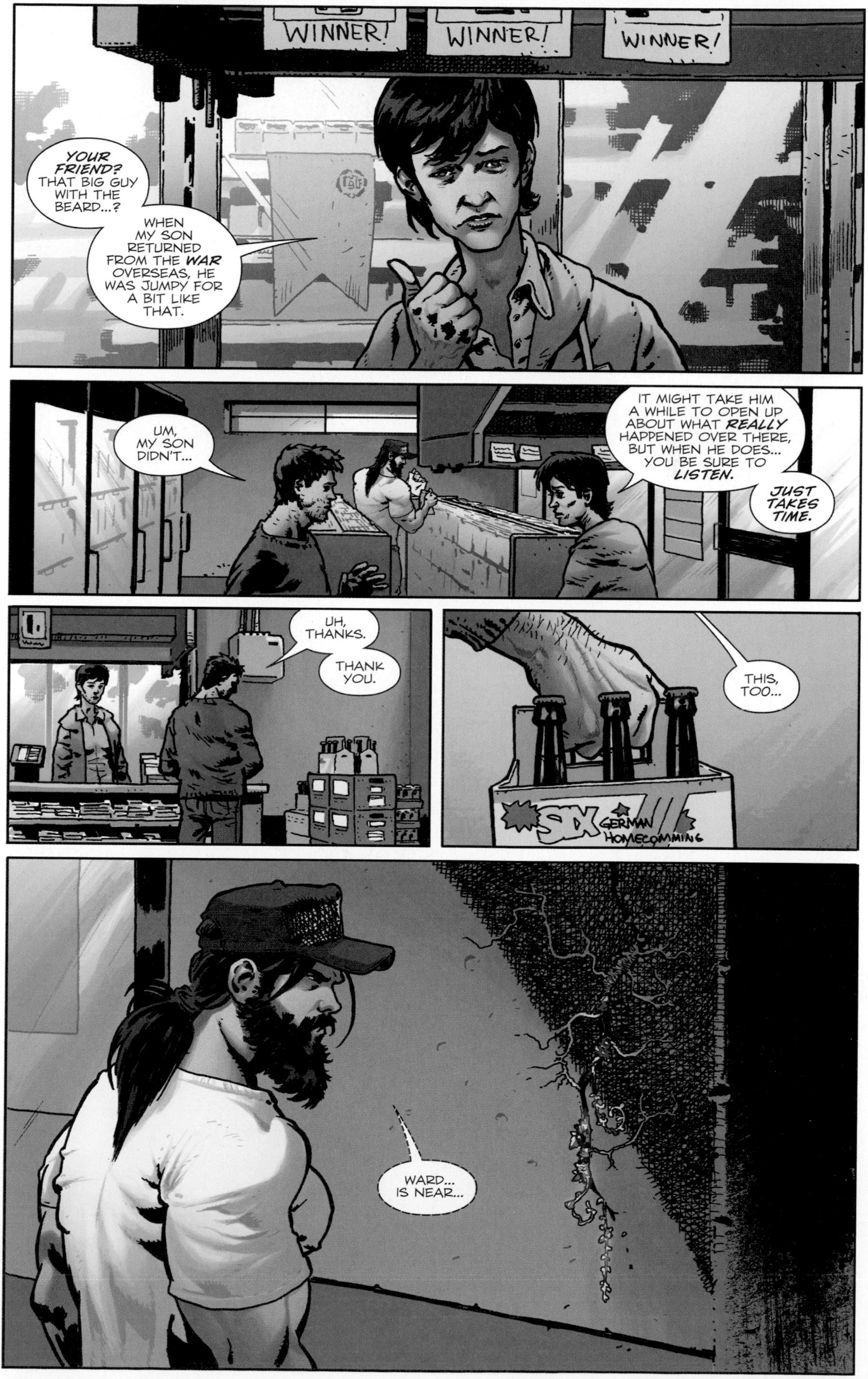
WINNER!
WINNER!
WINNER!
YOUR FRIEND? THAT BIG GUY WITH THE BEARD...?
WHEN MY SON RETURNED FROM THE WAR OVERSEAS, HE WAS JUMPY FOR A BIT LIKE THAT.
UM, MY SON DIDN'T...
IT MIGHT TAKE HIM A WHILE TO OPEN UP ABOUT WHAT REALLY HAPPENED OVER THERE, BUT WHEN HE DOES... YOU BE SURE TO LISTEN.
JUST TAKES TIME.
UH, THANKS.
THANK YOU.
THIS, TOO...
SIX GERMAN
HOMECOMMING
WARD... IS NEAR...

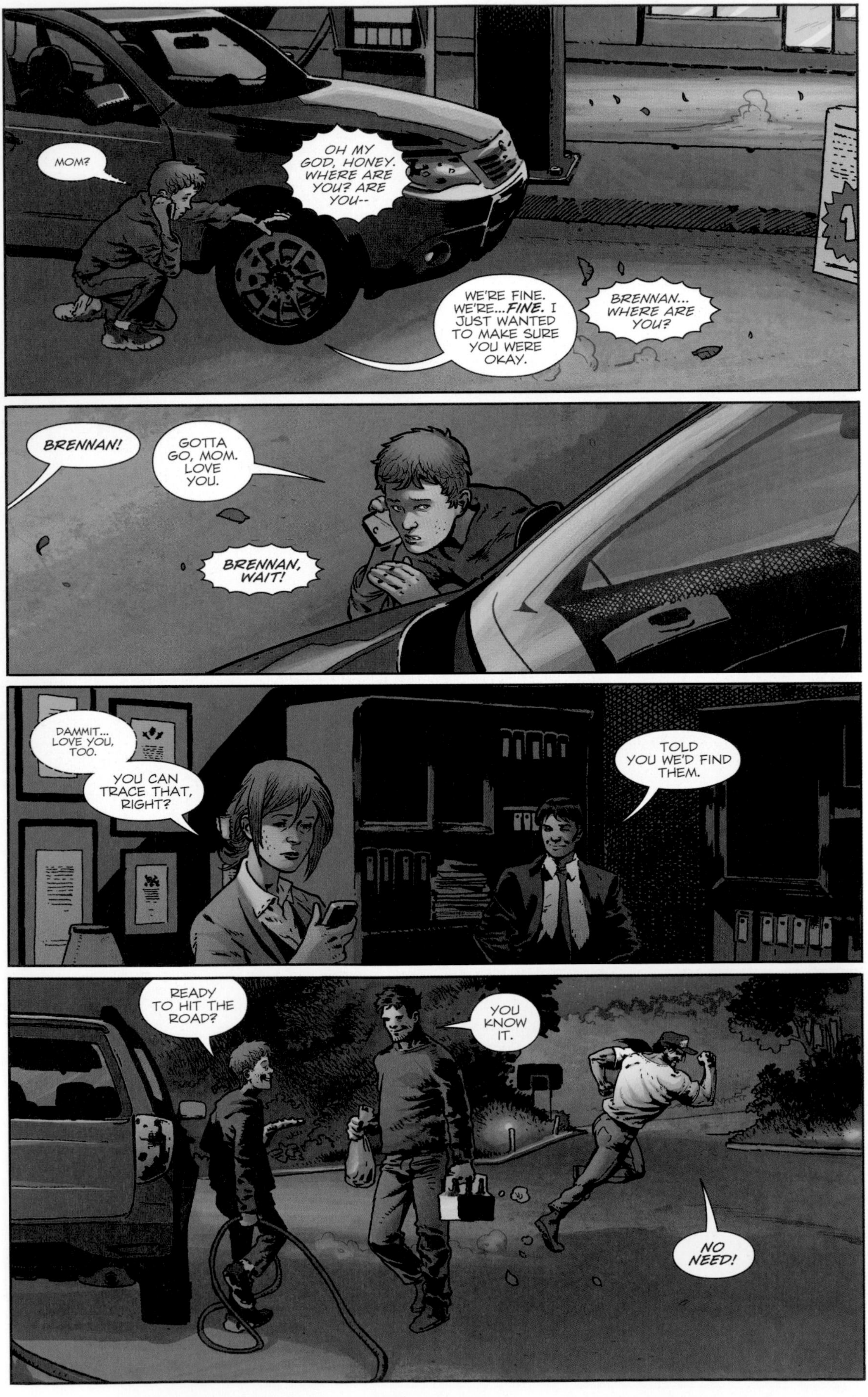
MOM?
OH MY GOD, HONEY. WHERE ARE YOU? ARE YOU--
WE'RE FINE. WE'RE...FINE. I JUST WANTED TO MAKE SURE YOU WERE OKAY.
BRENNAN... WHERE ARE YOU?
BRENNAN!
GOTTA GO, MOM. LOVE YOU.
BRENNAN, WAIT!
DAMMIT... LOVE YOU, TOO.
YOU CAN TRACE THAT, RIGHT?
TOLD YOU WE'D FIND THEM.
READY TO HIT THE ROAD?
YOU KNOW IT.
NO NEED!

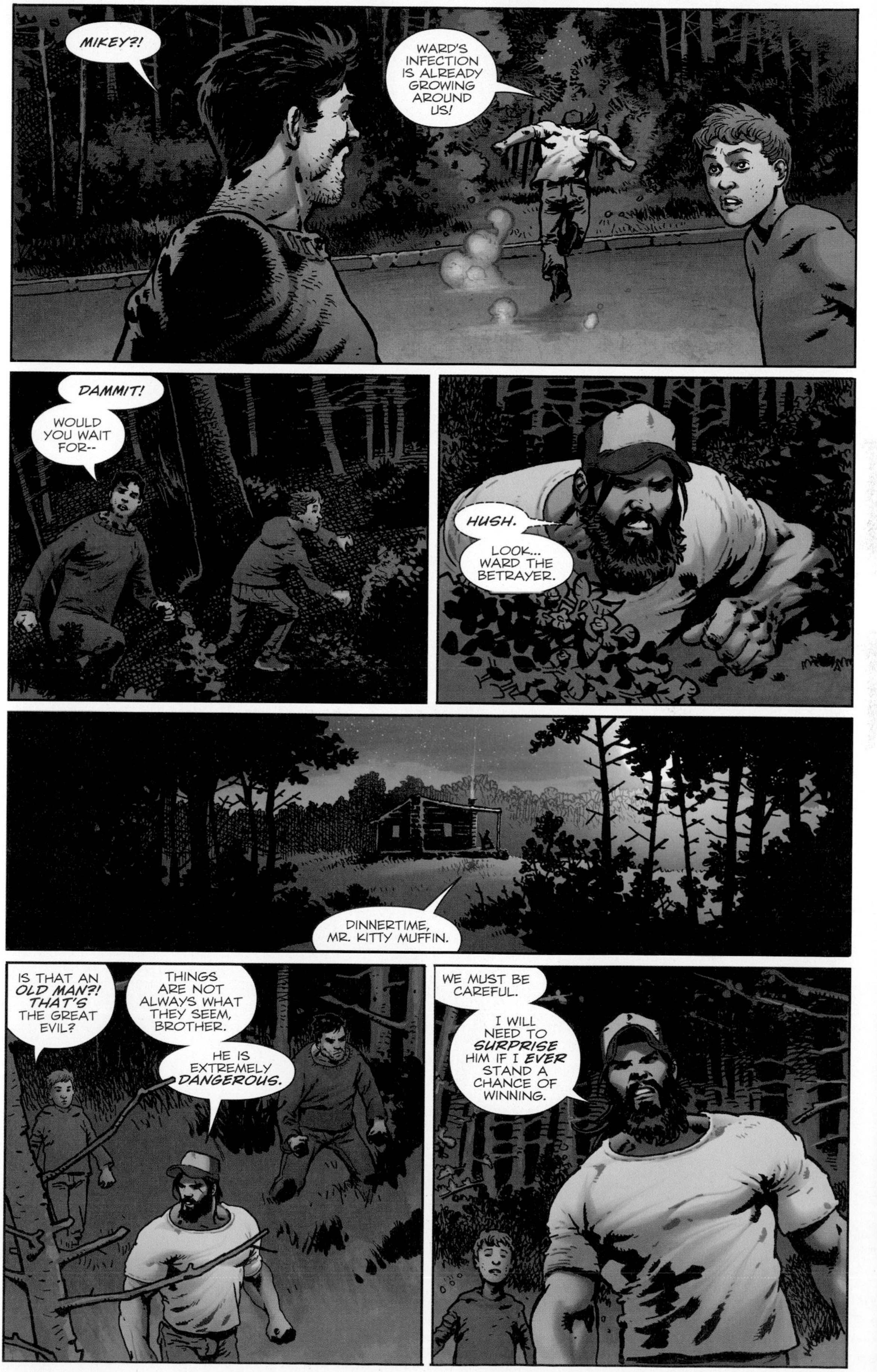
MIKEY?!
WARD'S INFECTION IS ALREADY GROWING AROUND US!
DAMMIT!
WOULD YOU WAIT FOR--
HUSH.
LOOK... WARD THE BETRAYER.
DINNERTIME, MR. KITTY MUFFIN.
IS THAT AN OLD MAN?! THAT'S THE GREAT EVIL?
THINGS ARE NOT ALWAYS WHAT THEY SEEM, BROTHER.
HE IS EXTREMELY DANGEROUS.
WE MUST BE CAREFUL.
I WILL NEED TO SURPRISE HIM IF I EVER STAND A CHANCE OF WINNING.

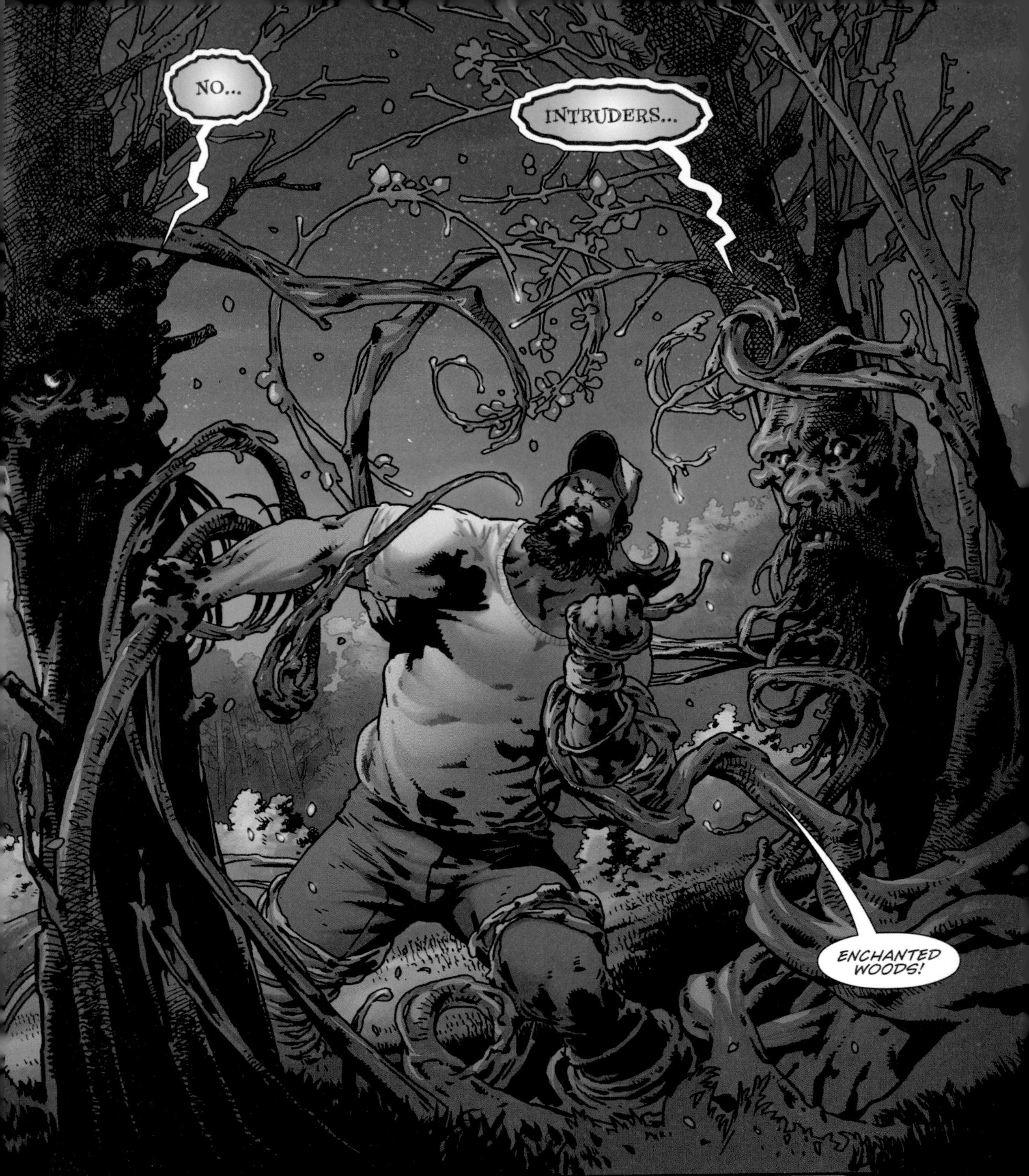
NO...
INTRUDERS...
ENCHANTED WOODS!
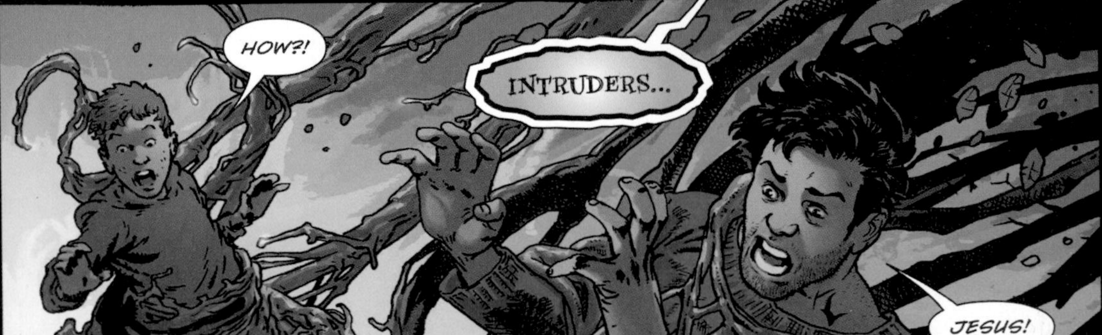
HOW?!
INTRUDERS...
JESUS!

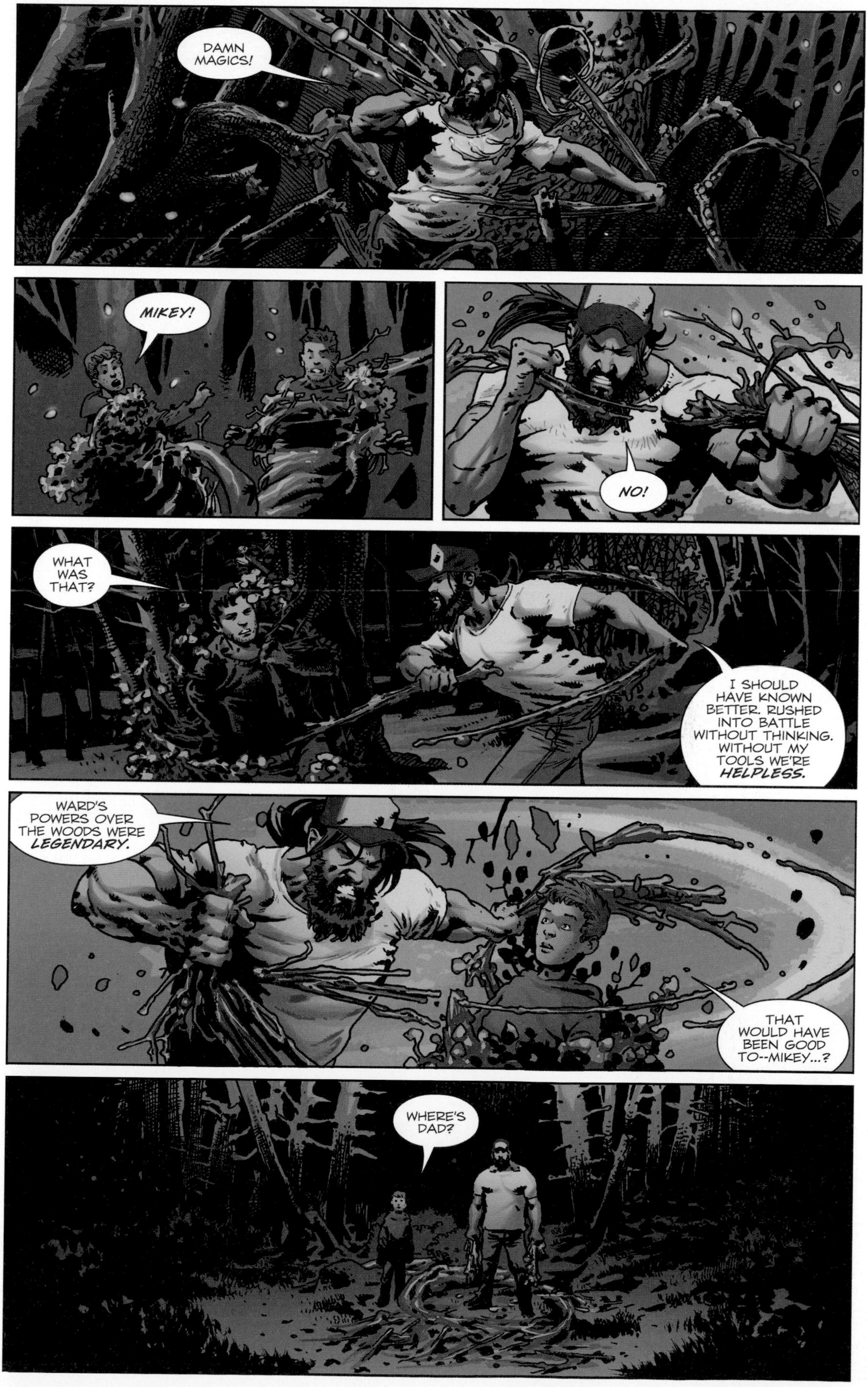
DAMN MAGICS!
MIKEY!
NO!
WHAT WAS THAT?
I SHOULD HAVE KNOWN BETTER. RUSHED INTO BATTLE WITHOUT THINKING. WITHOUT MY TOOLS WE'RE **HELPLESS.**
WARD'S POWERS OVER THE WOODS WERE **LEGENDARY.**
THAT WOULD HAVE BEEN GOOD TO--MIKEY...?
WHERE'S DAD?

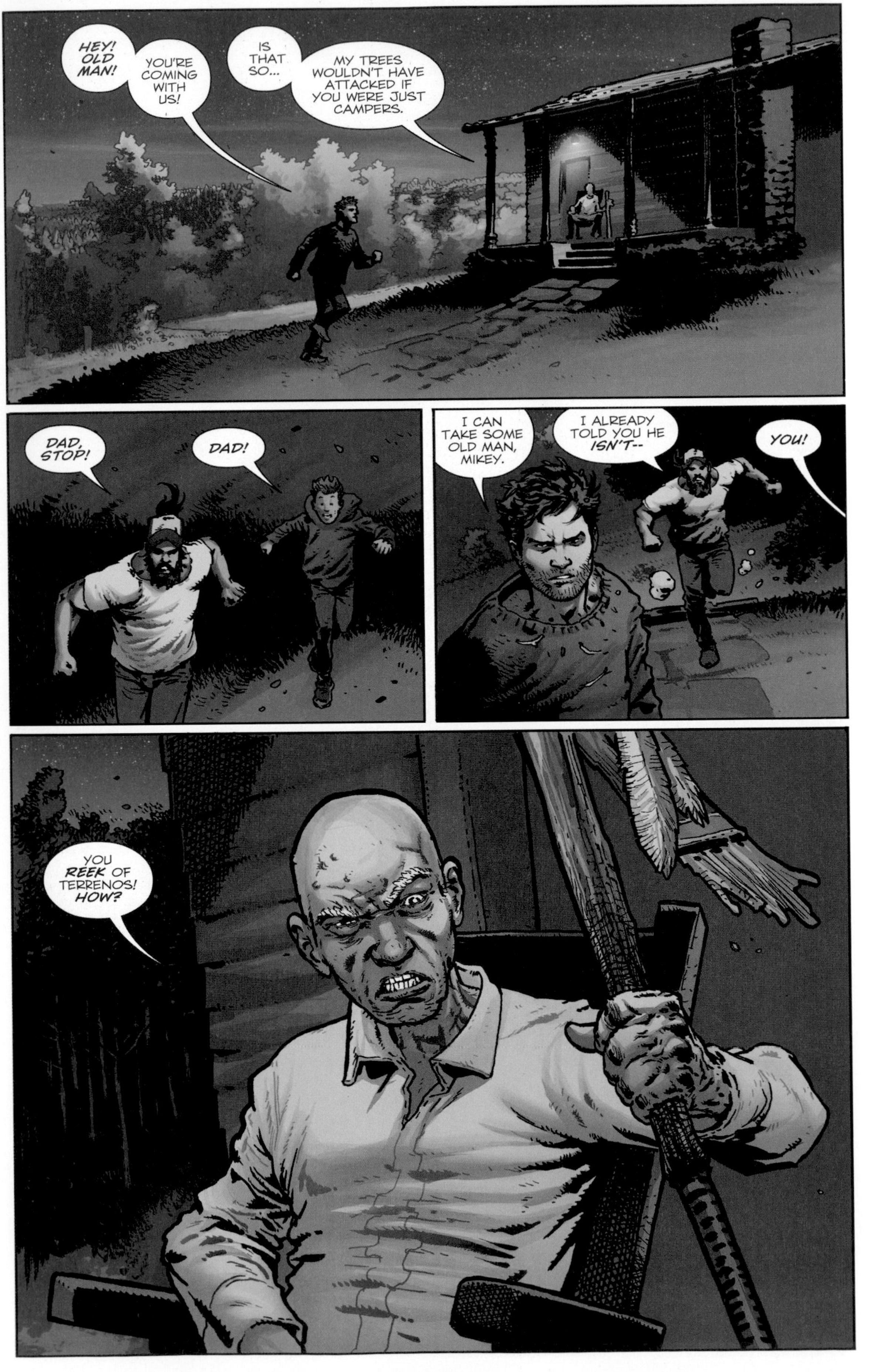
HEY! OLD MAN!
YOU'RE COMING WITH US!
IS THAT SO...
MY TREES WOULDN'T HAVE ATTACKED IF YOU WERE JUST CAMPERS.
DAD, STOP!
DAD!
I CAN TAKE SOME OLD MAN, MIKEY.
I ALREADY TOLD YOU HE ISN'T--
YOU!
YOU REEK OF TERRENOS! HOW?

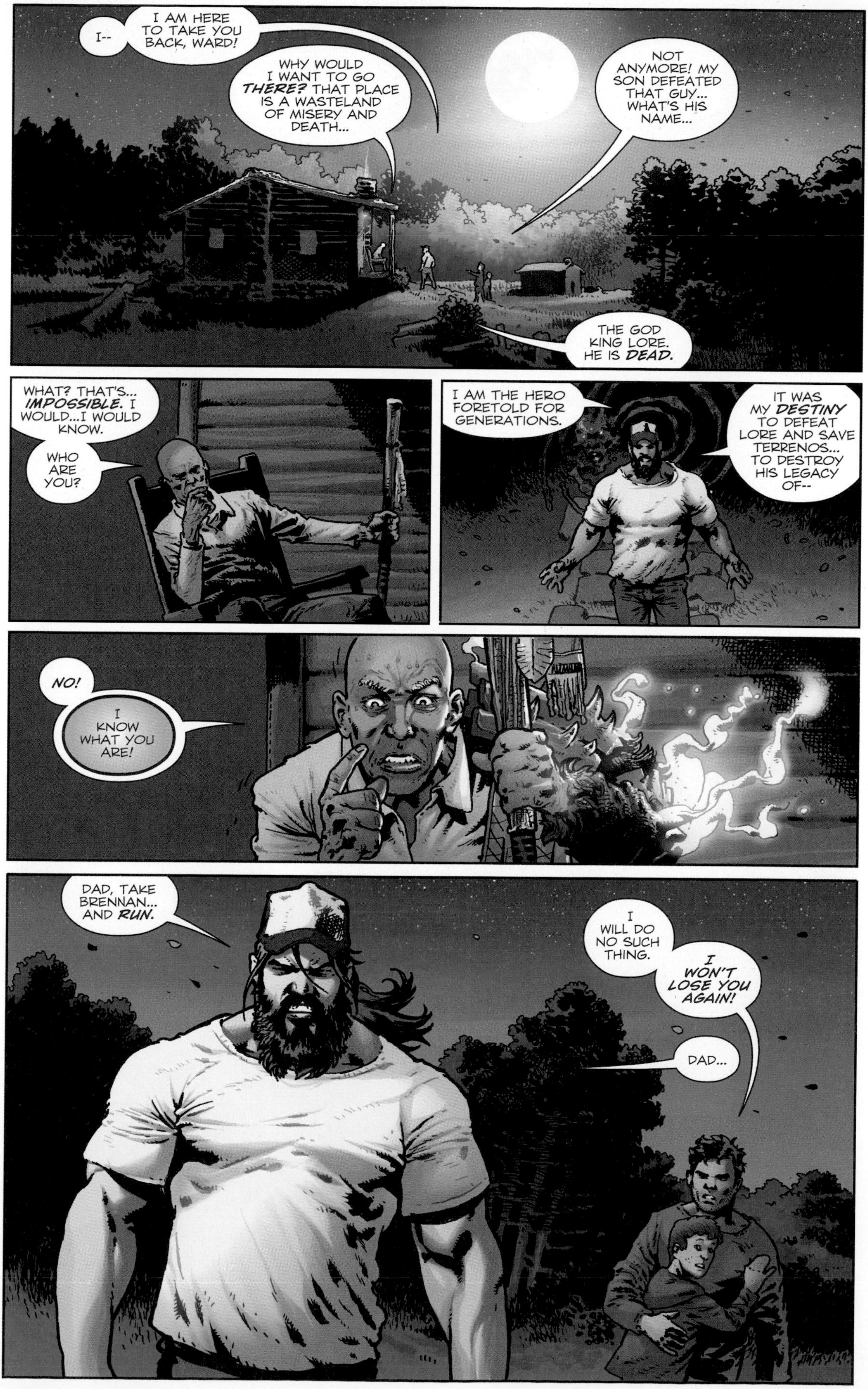
I--
I AM HERE TO TAKE YOU BACK, WARD!
WHY WOULD I WANT TO GO *THERE?* THAT PLACE IS A WASTELAND OF MISERY AND DEATH...
NOT ANYMORE! MY SON DEFEATED THAT GUY... WHAT'S HIS NAME...
THE GOD KING LORE. HE IS *DEAD.*
WHAT? THAT'S... *IMPOSSIBLE.* I WOULD...I WOULD KNOW.
WHO ARE YOU?
I AM THE HERO FORETOLD FOR GENERATIONS.
IT WAS MY *DESTINY* TO DEFEAT LORE AND SAVE TERRENOS... TO DESTROY HIS LEGACY OF--
NO!
I KNOW WHAT YOU ARE!
DAD, TAKE BRENNAN... AND *RUN.*
I WILL DO NO SUCH THING.
I WON'T LOSE YOU AGAIN!
DAD...

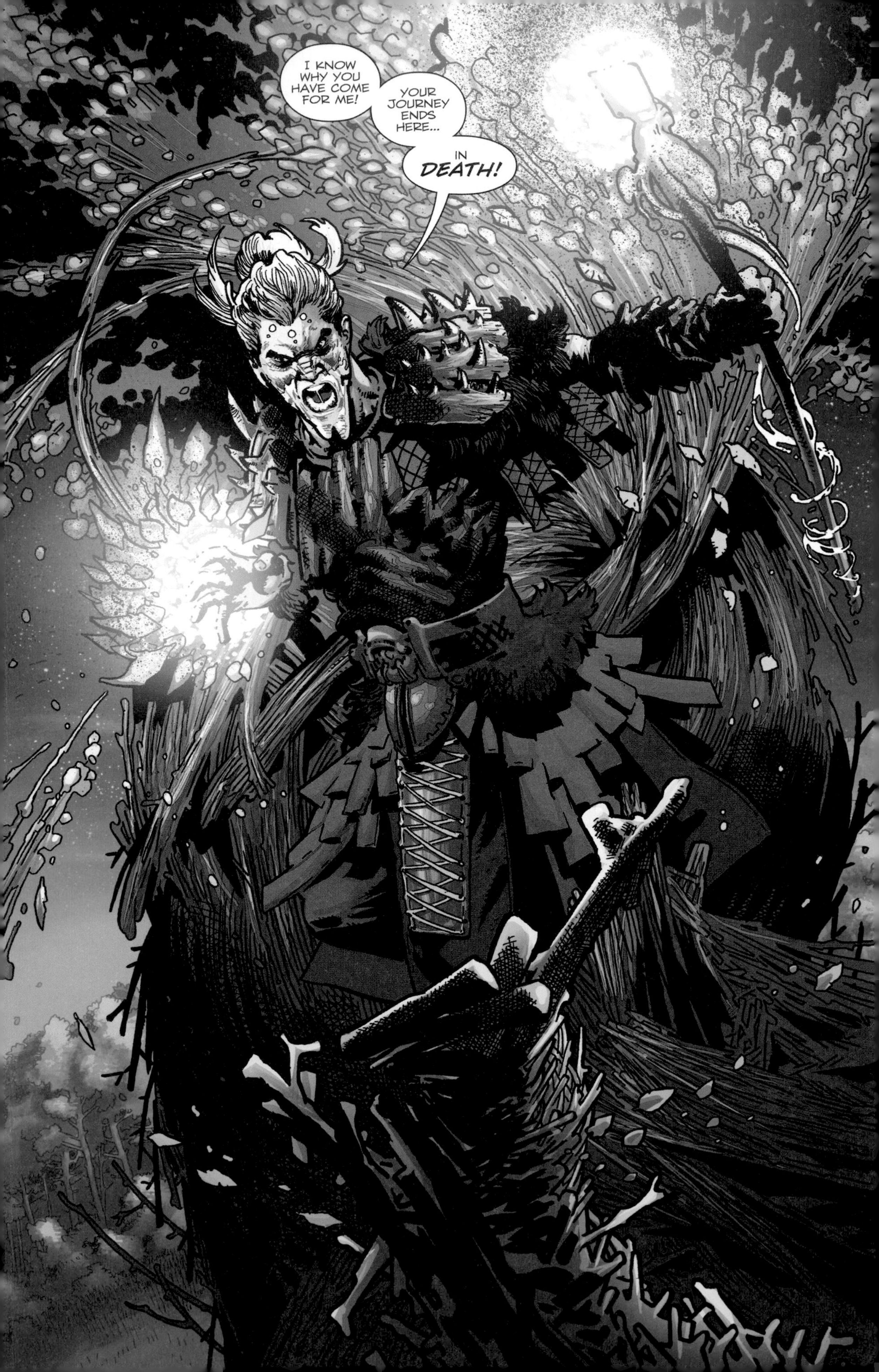
I KNOW WHY YOU HAVE COME FOR ME!
YOUR JOURNEY ENDS HERE...
IN DEATH!

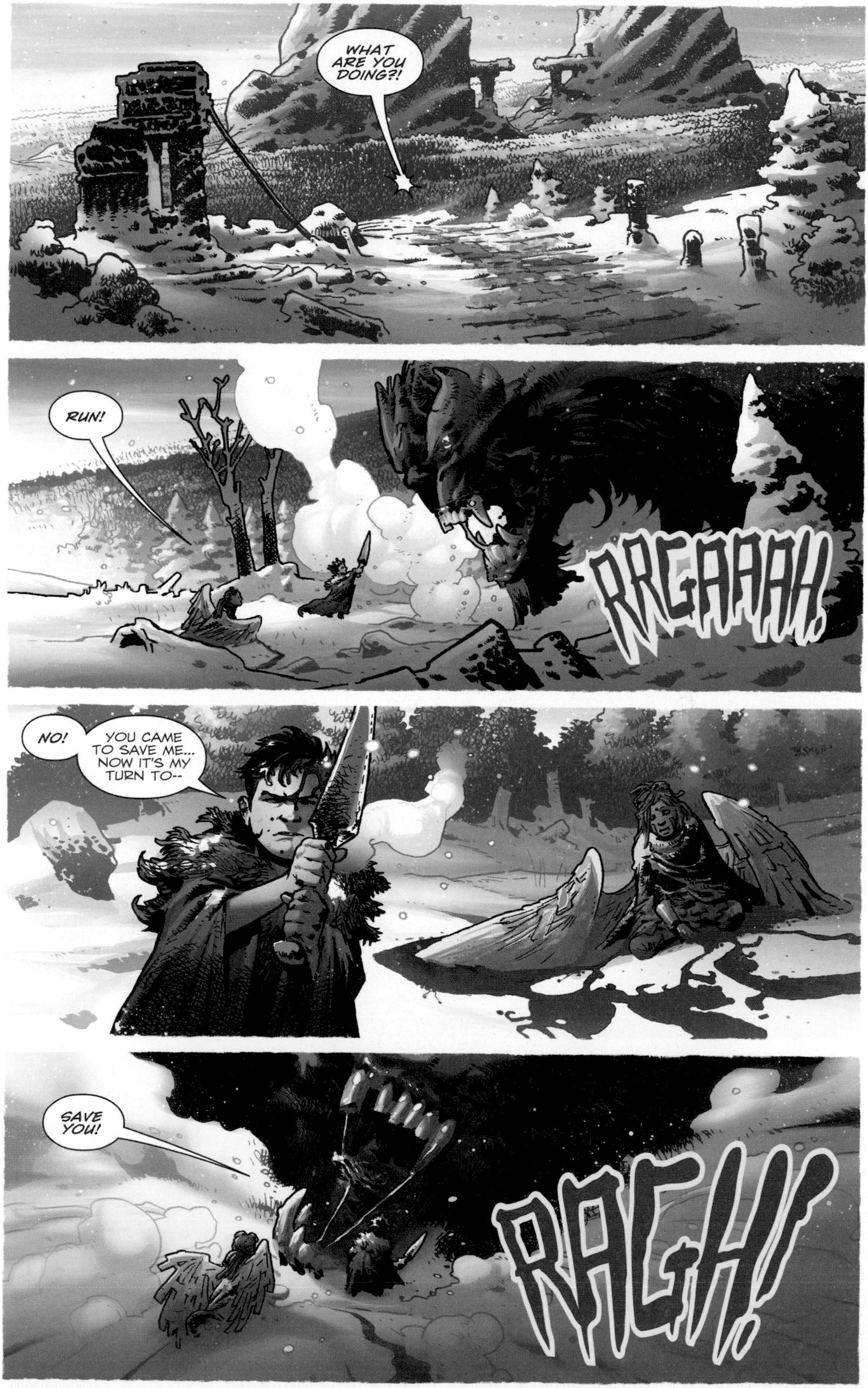
WHAT ARE YOU DOING?!
RUN!
RRGAAAH!
NO!
YOU CAME TO SAVE ME... NOW IT'S MY TURN TO--
SAVE YOU!
RAGH!

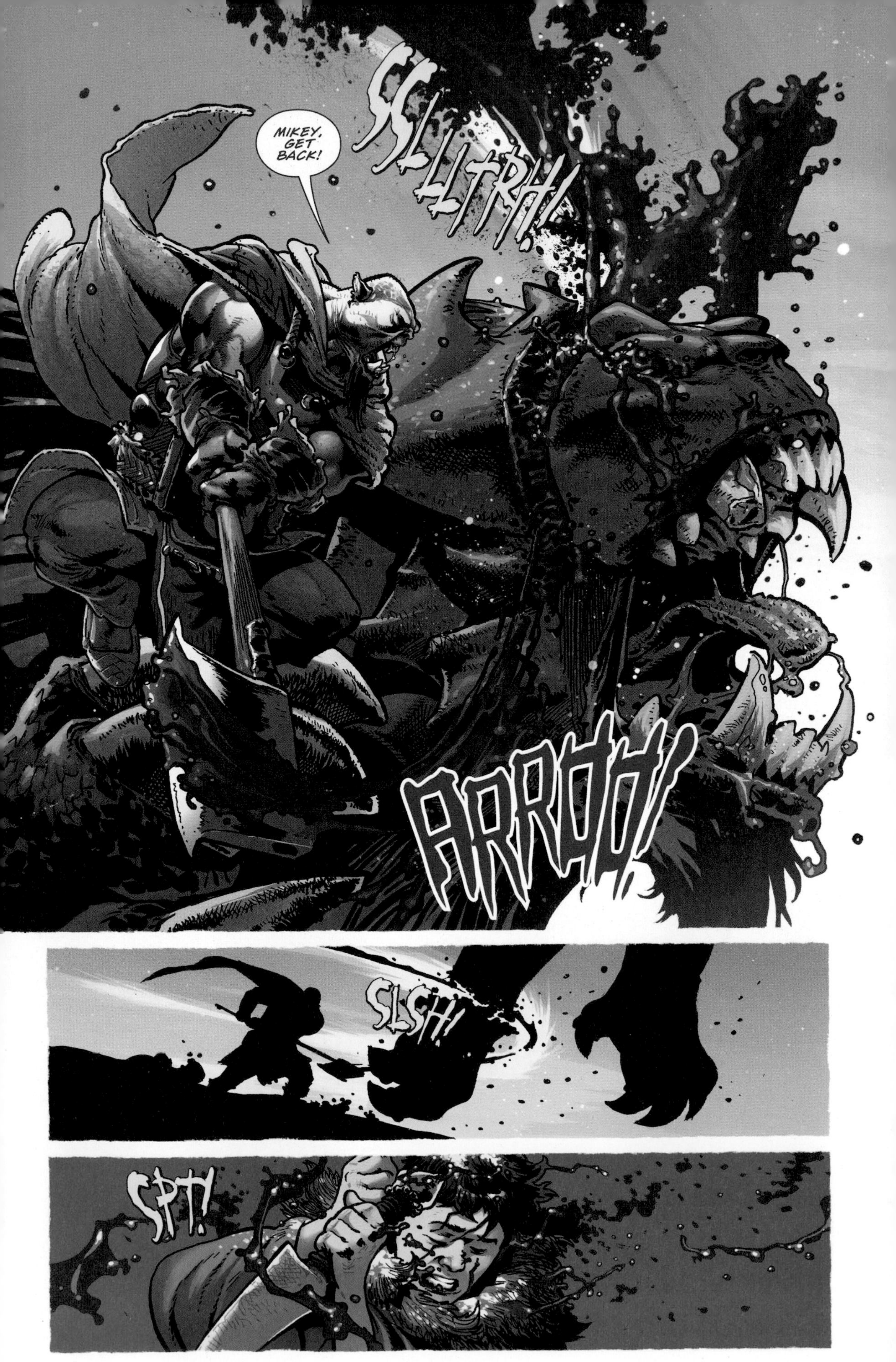
MIKEY, GET BACK!
SSLLLRRH!
ARROO!
SLSH!
SPT!

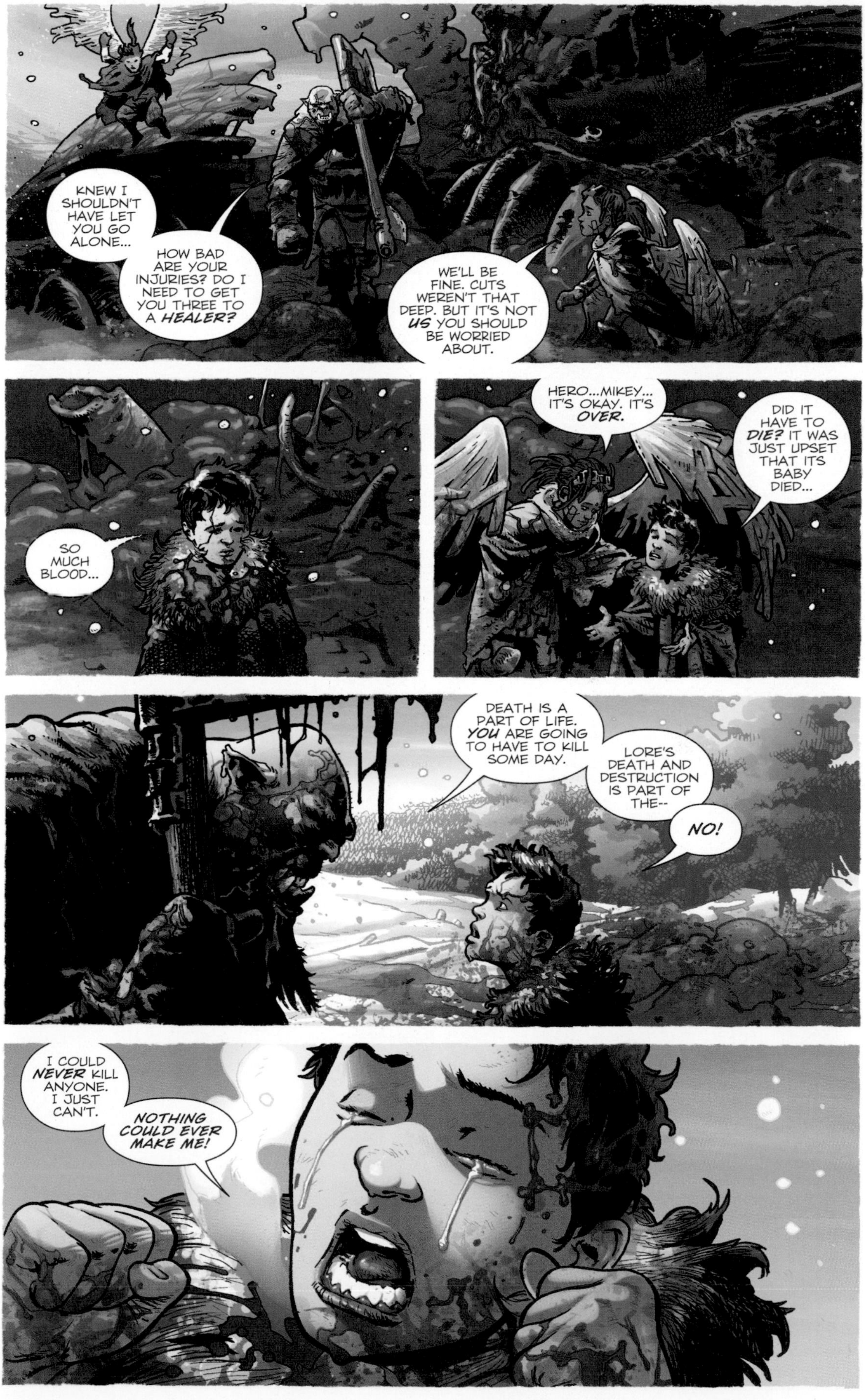
KNEW I SHOULDN'T HAVE LET YOU GO ALONE...
HOW BAD ARE YOUR INJURIES? DO I NEED TO GET YOU THREE TO A *HEALER?*
WE'LL BE FINE. CUTS WEREN'T THAT DEEP. BUT IT'S NOT *US* YOU SHOULD BE WORRIED ABOUT.
SO MUCH BLOOD...
HERO...MIKEY... IT'S OKAY. IT'S *OVER.*
DID IT HAVE TO *DIE?* IT WAS JUST UPSET THAT ITS BABY DIED...
DEATH IS A PART OF LIFE. *YOU* ARE GOING TO HAVE TO KILL SOME DAY.
LORE'S DEATH AND DESTRUCTION IS PART OF THE--
NO!
I COULD *NEVER* KILL ANYONE. I JUST CAN'T.
NOTHING COULD EVER MAKE ME!

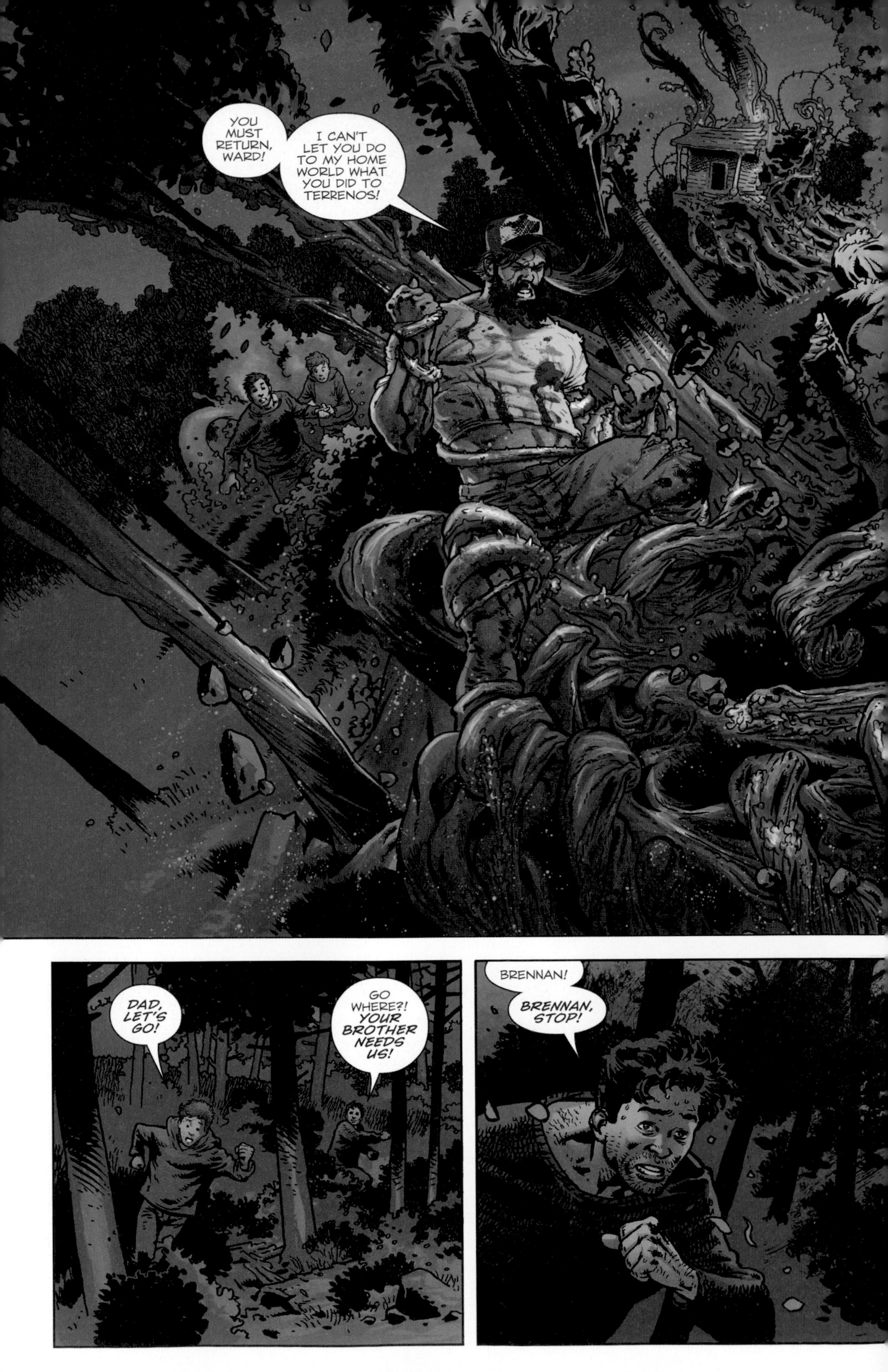
YOU MUST RETURN, WARD!
I CAN'T LET YOU DO TO MY HOME WORLD WHAT YOU DID TO TERRENOS!
DAD, LET'S GO!
GO WHERE?! YOUR BROTHER NEEDS US!
BRENNAN!
BRENNAN, STOP!

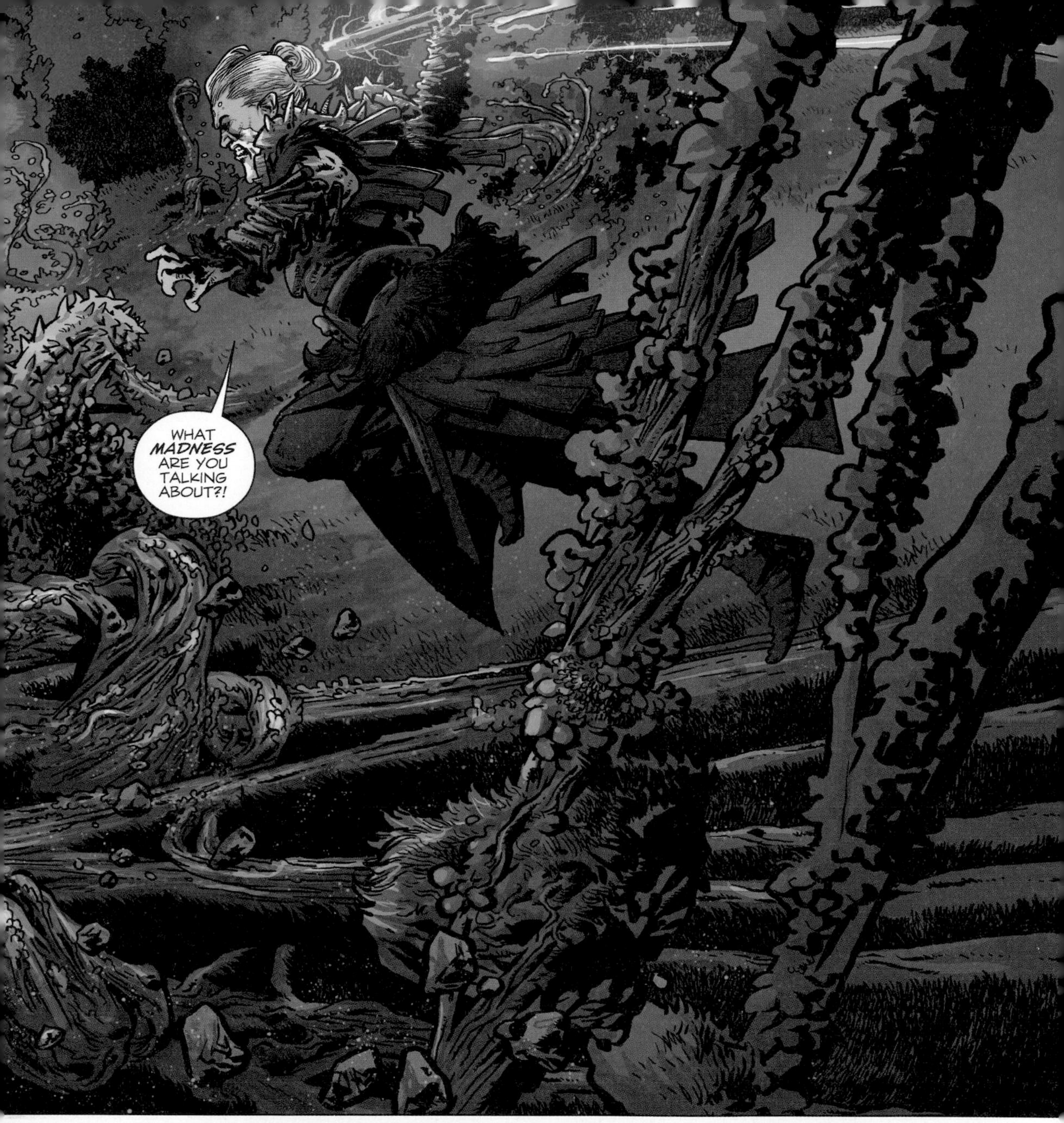
WHAT MADNESS ARE YOU TALKING ABOUT?!
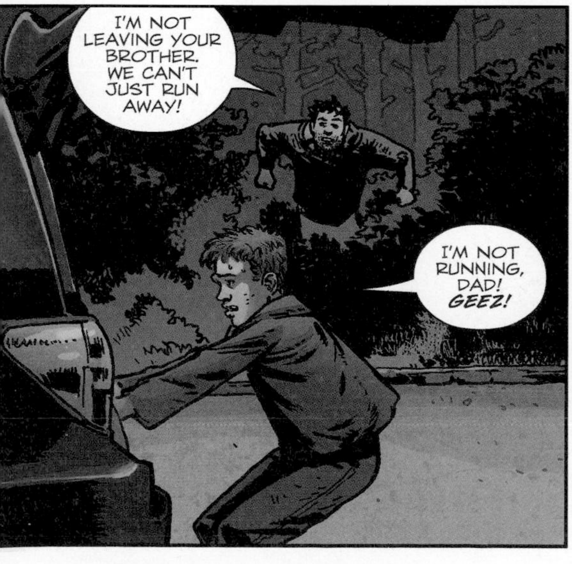
I'M NOT LEAVING YOUR BROTHER. WE CAN'T JUST RUN AWAY!
I'M NOT RUNNING, DAD! GEEZ!
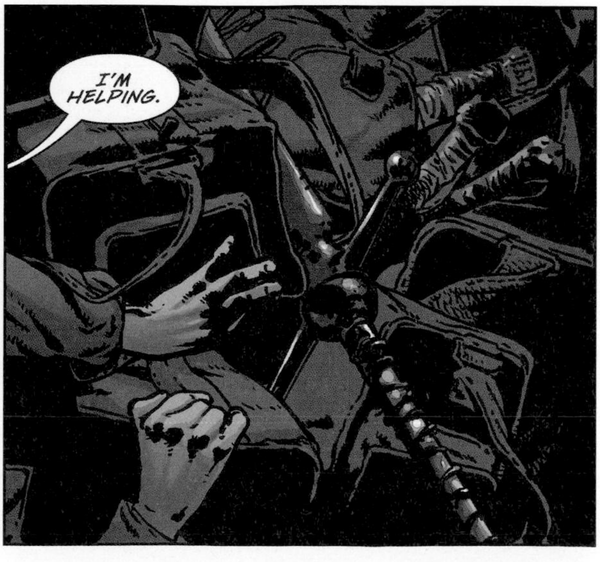
I'M HELPING.

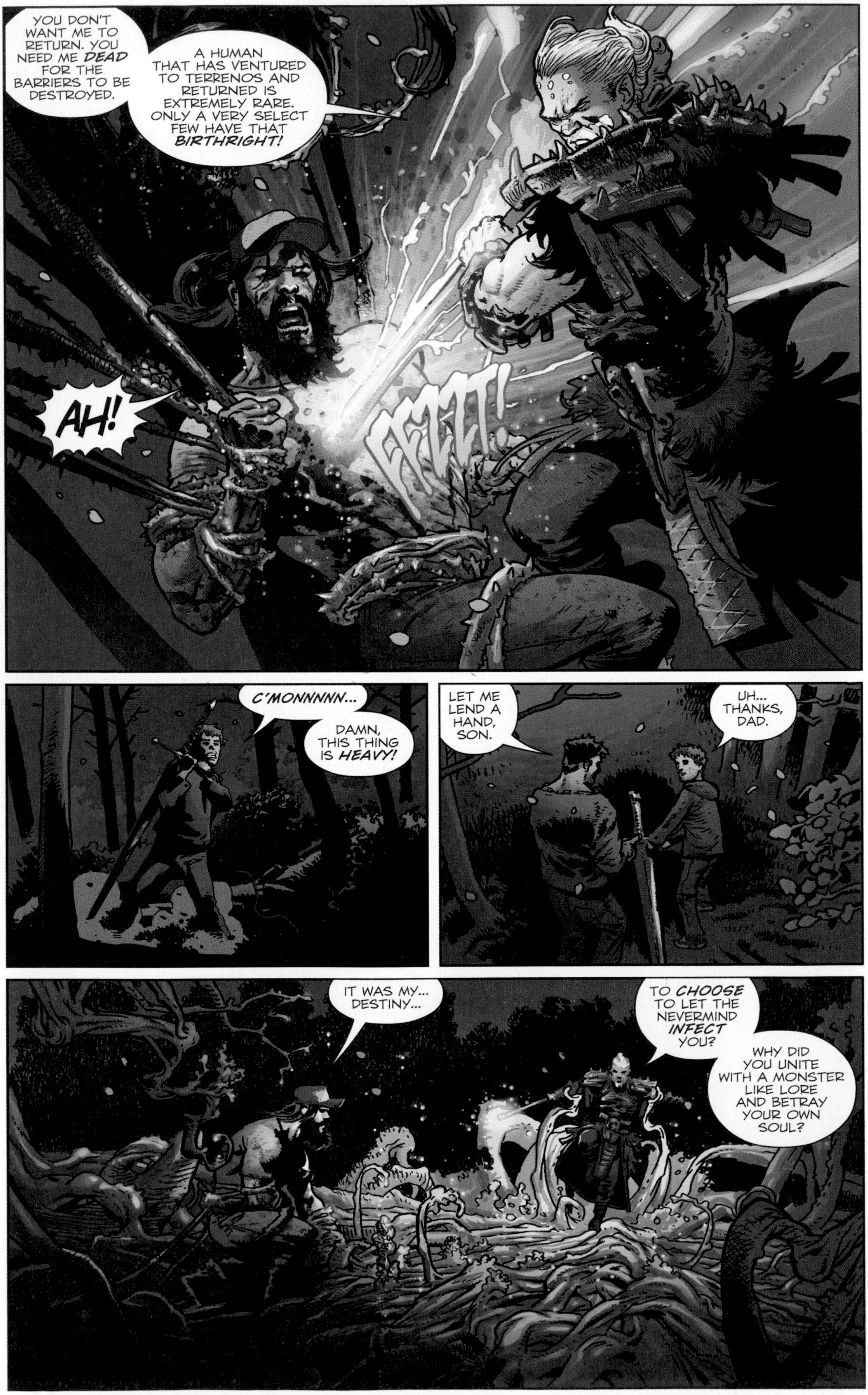
YOU DON'T WANT ME TO RETURN. YOU NEED ME *DEAD* FOR THE BARRIERS TO BE DESTROYED.
A HUMAN THAT HAS VENTURED TO TERRENOS AND RETURNED IS EXTREMELY RARE. ONLY A VERY SELECT FEW HAVE THAT *BIRTHRIGHT!*
AH!
C'MONNNNN...
DAMN, THIS THING IS *HEAVY!*
LET ME LEND A HAND, SON.
UH... THANKS, DAD.
IT WAS MY... DESTINY...
TO *CHOOSE* TO LET THE NEVERMIND *INFECT* YOU?
WHY DID YOU UNITE WITH A MONSTER LIKE LORE AND BETRAY YOUR OWN SOUL?

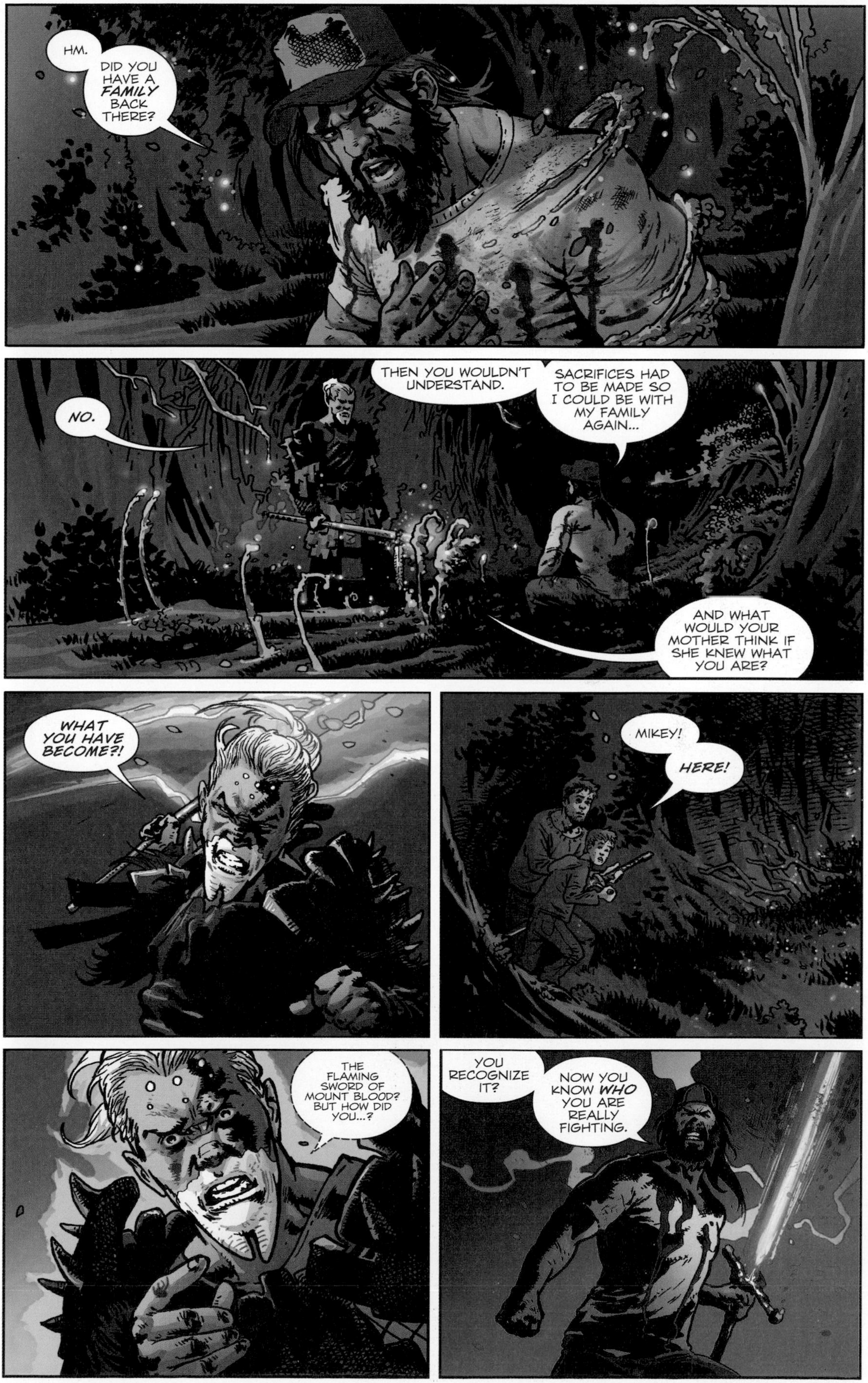
HM.
DID YOU HAVE A *FAMILY* BACK THERE?
NO.
THEN YOU WOULDN'T UNDERSTAND.
SACRIFICES HAD TO BE MADE SO I COULD BE WITH MY FAMILY AGAIN...
AND WHAT WOULD YOUR MOTHER THINK IF SHE KNEW WHAT YOU ARE?
WHAT YOU HAVE BECOME?!
MIKEY!
HERE!
THE FLAMING SWORD OF MOUNT BLOOD? BUT HOW DID YOU...?
YOU RECOGNIZE IT?
NOW YOU KNOW *WHO* YOU ARE REALLY FIGHTING.

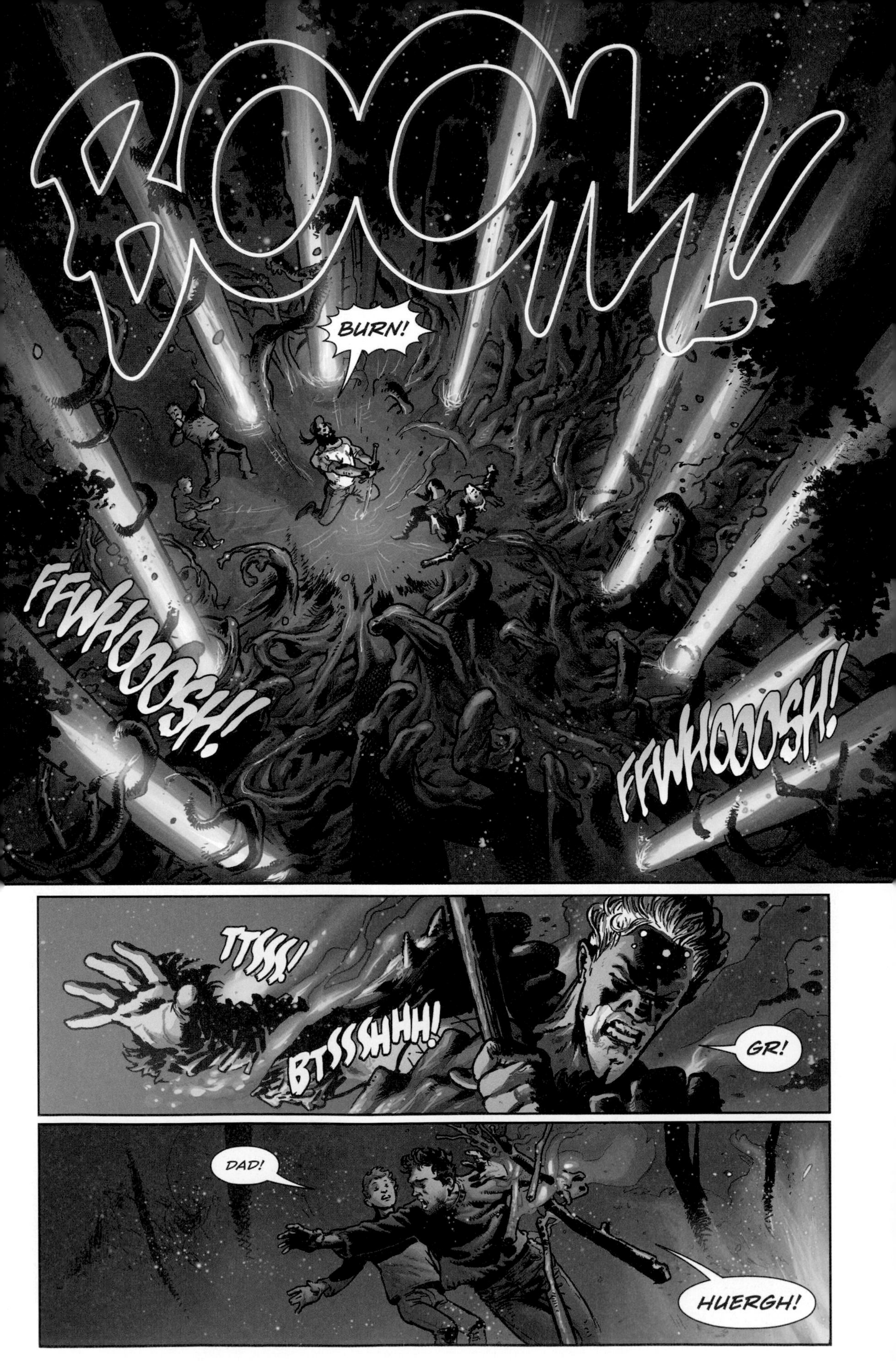
BOOM!
BURN!
FFWHOOOSH!
FFWHOOOSH!
TTSSS!
BTSSSHHH!
GR!
DAD!
HUERGH!

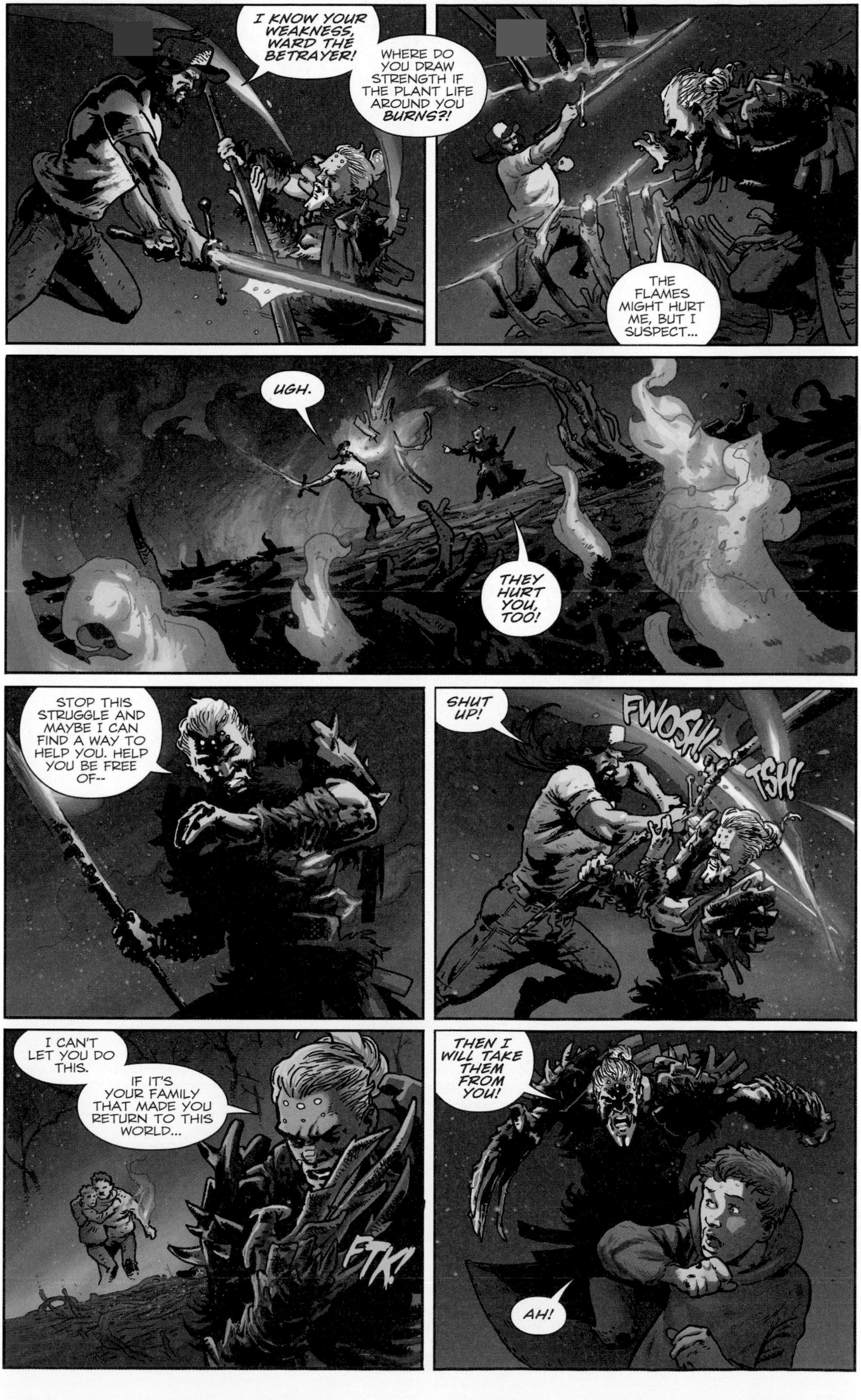
I KNOW YOUR WEAKNESS, WARD THE BETRAYER!
WHERE DO YOU DRAW STRENGTH IF THE PLANT LIFE AROUND YOU BURNS?!
THE FLAMES MIGHT HURT ME, BUT I SUSPECT...
UGH.
THEY HURT YOU, TOO!
STOP THIS STRUGGLE AND MAYBE I CAN FIND A WAY TO HELP YOU. HELP YOU BE FREE OF--
SHUT UP!
FWOSH!
TSH!
I CAN'T LET YOU DO THIS.
IF IT'S YOUR FAMILY THAT MADE YOU RETURN TO THIS WORLD...
FTK!
THEN I WILL TAKE THEM FROM YOU!
AH!

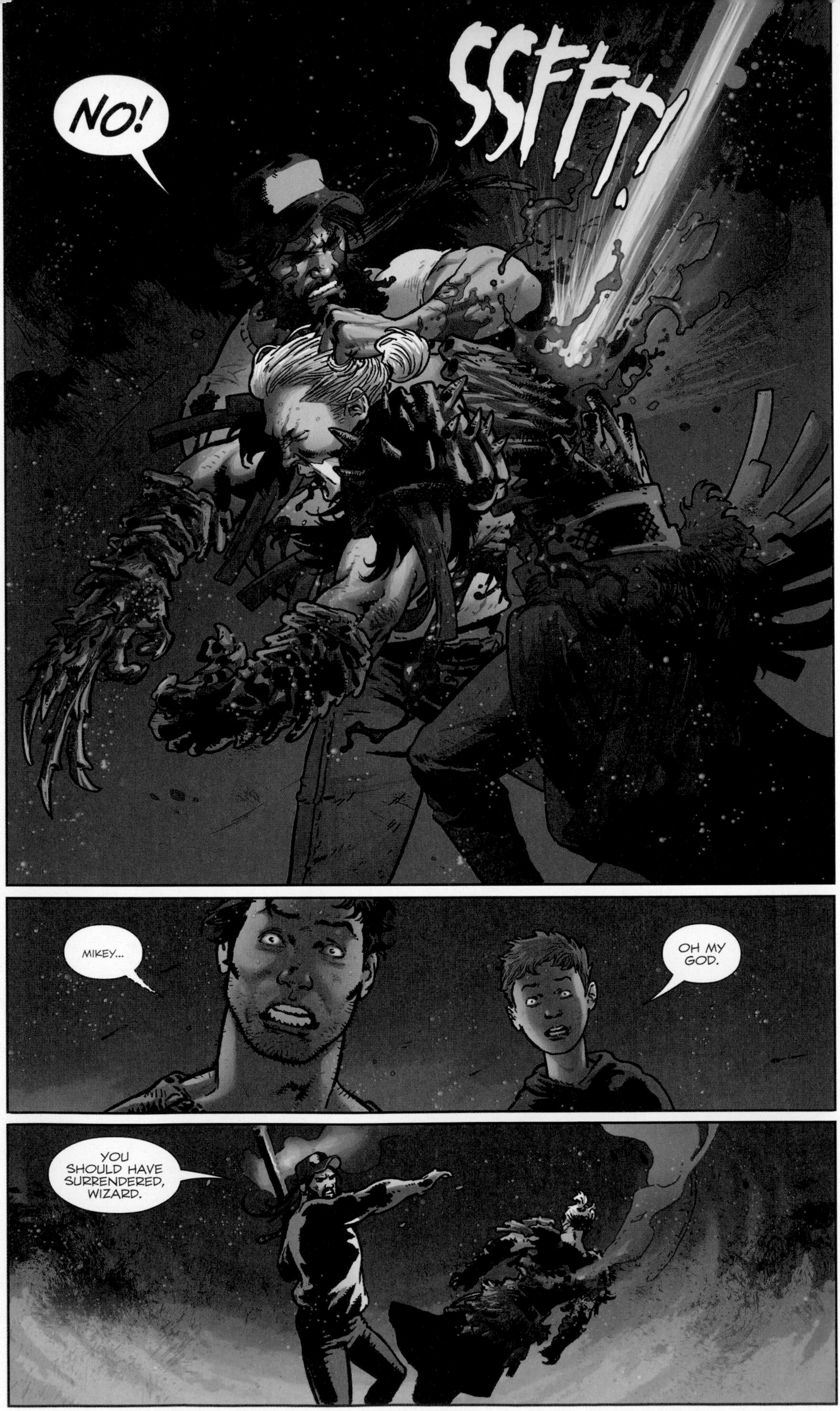
NO!
SSFFT!
MIKEY...
OH MY GOD.
YOU SHOULD HAVE SURRENDERED, WIZARD.

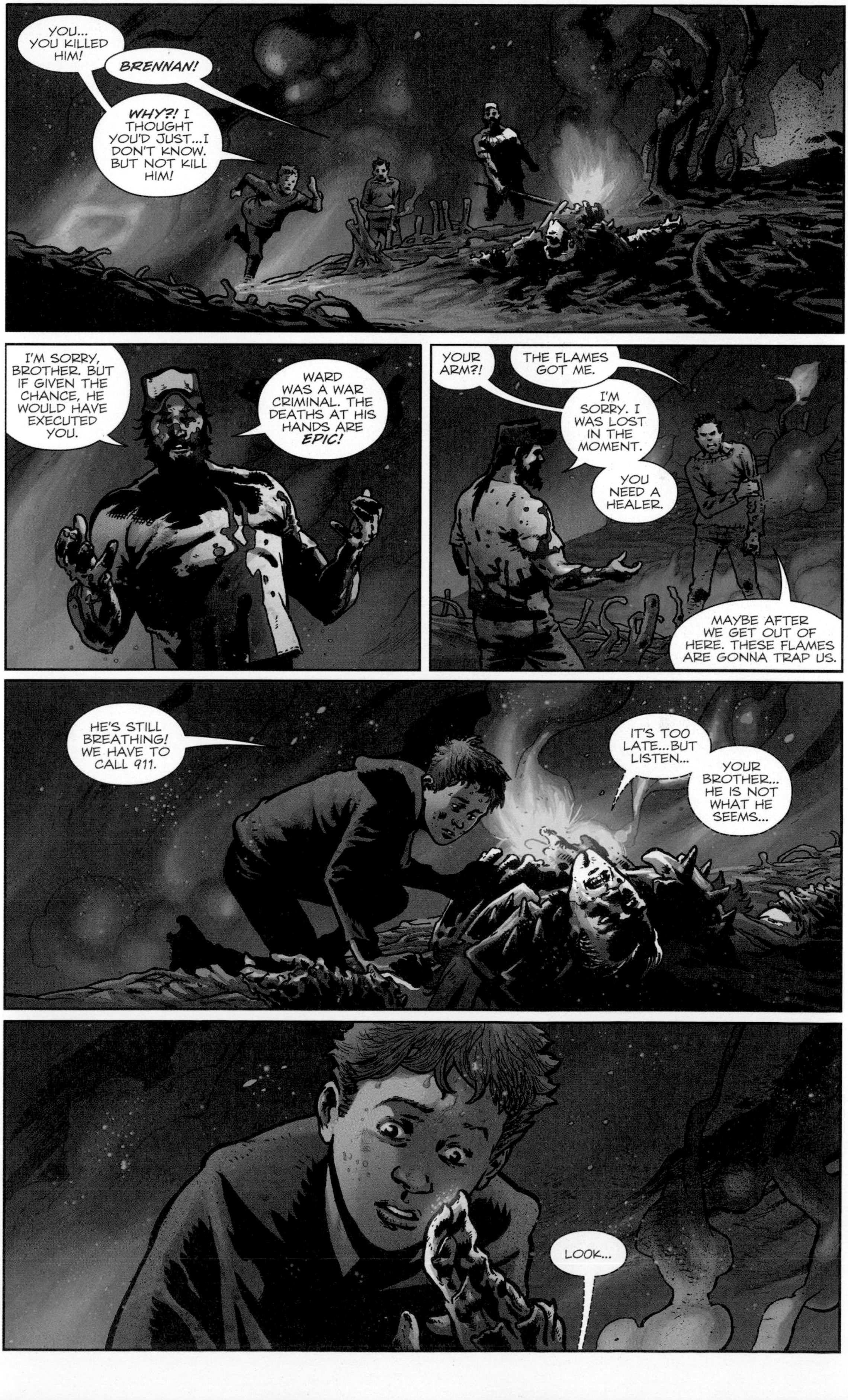

YOU... YOU KILLED HIM!
BRENNAN!
WHY?! I THOUGHT YOU'D JUST...I DON'T KNOW. BUT NOT KILL HIM!
I'M SORRY, BROTHER. BUT IF GIVEN THE CHANCE, HE WOULD HAVE EXECUTED YOU.
WARD WAS A WAR CRIMINAL. THE DEATHS AT HIS HANDS ARE EPIC!
YOUR ARM?!
THE FLAMES GOT ME.
I'M SORRY. I WAS LOST IN THE MOMENT.
YOU NEED A HEALER.
MAYBE AFTER WE GET OUT OF HERE. THESE FLAMES ARE GONNA TRAP US.
HE'S STILL BREATHING! WE HAVE TO CALL 911.
IT'S TOO LATE...BUT LISTEN...
YOUR BROTHER... HE IS NOT WHAT HE SEEMS...
LOOK...

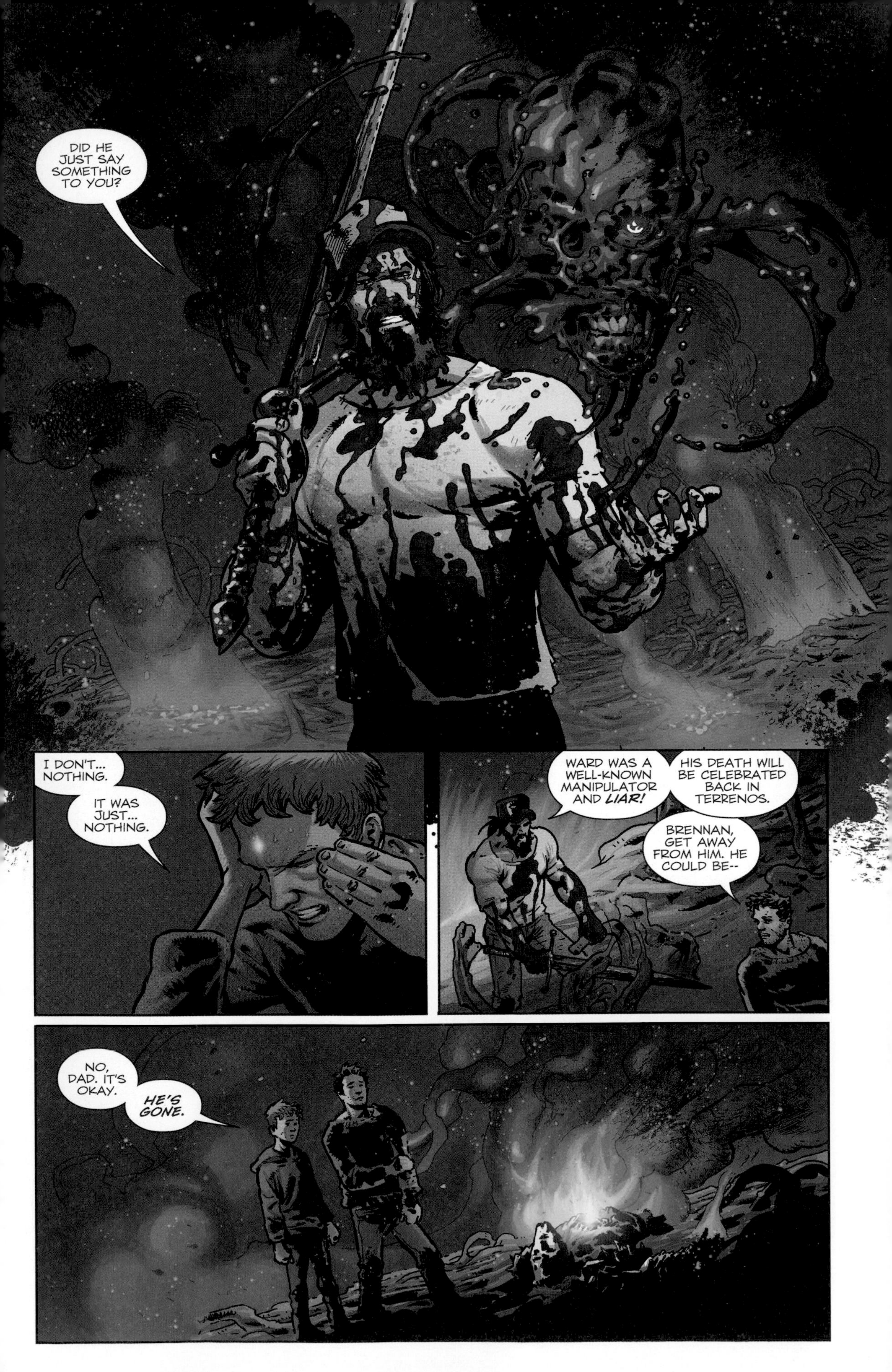
DID HE JUST SAY SOMETHING TO YOU?
I DON'T... NOTHING.
IT WAS JUST... NOTHING.
WARD WAS A WELL-KNOWN MANIPULATOR AND *LIAR!*
HIS DEATH WILL BE CELEBRATED BACK IN TERRENOS.
BRENNAN, GET AWAY FROM HIM. HE COULD BE--
NO, DAD. IT'S OKAY.
HE'S GONE.

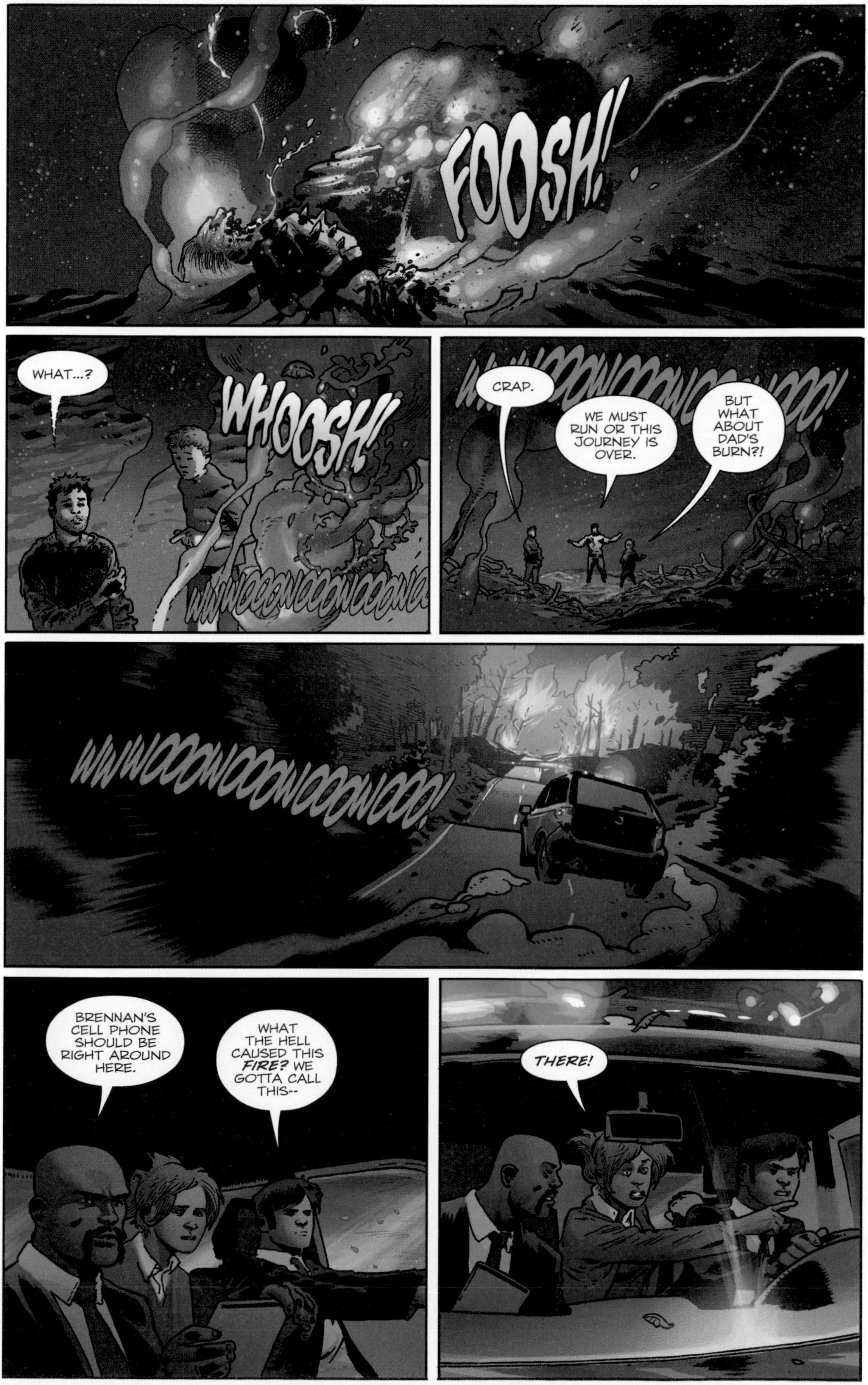
FOOSH!
WHAT...?
WHOOSH!
WWWOOOWOOOWOOOWO
WWWOOOWOOOWOOOWOOO!
CRAP.
WE MUST RUN OR THIS JOURNEY IS OVER.
BUT WHAT ABOUT DAD'S BURN?!
WWWOOOWOOOWOOOWOOO!
BRENNAN'S CELL PHONE SHOULD BE RIGHT AROUND HERE.
WHAT THE HELL CAUSED THIS FIRE? WE GOTTA CALL THIS--
THERE!

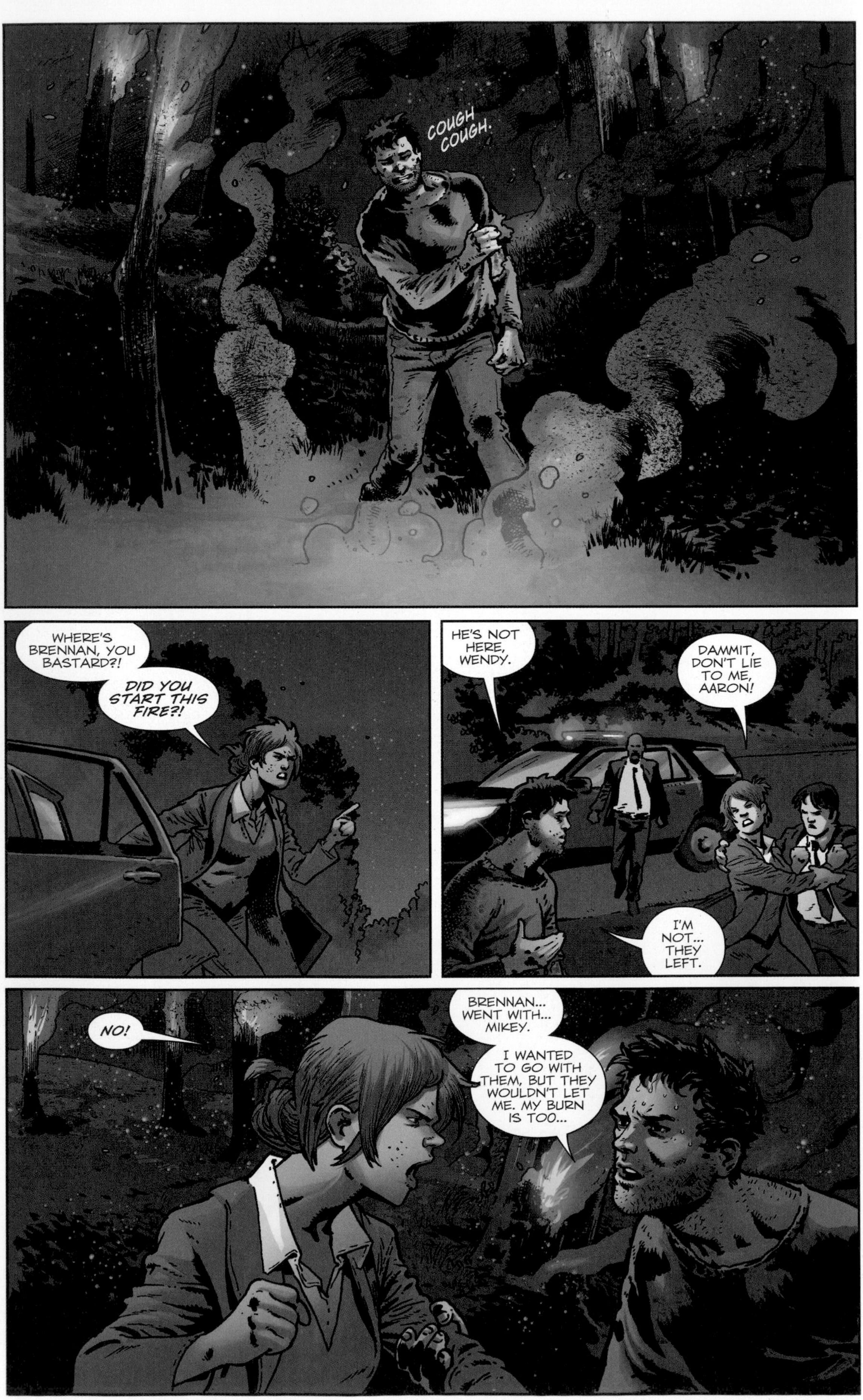
COUGH COUGH.
WHERE'S BRENNAN, YOU BASTARD?!
DID YOU START THIS FIRE?!
HE'S NOT HERE, WENDY.
DAMMIT, DON'T LIE TO ME, AARON!
I'M NOT... THEY LEFT.
NO!
BRENNAN... WENT WITH... MIKEY.
I WANTED TO GO WITH THEM, BUT THEY WOULDN'T LET ME. MY BURN IS TOO...

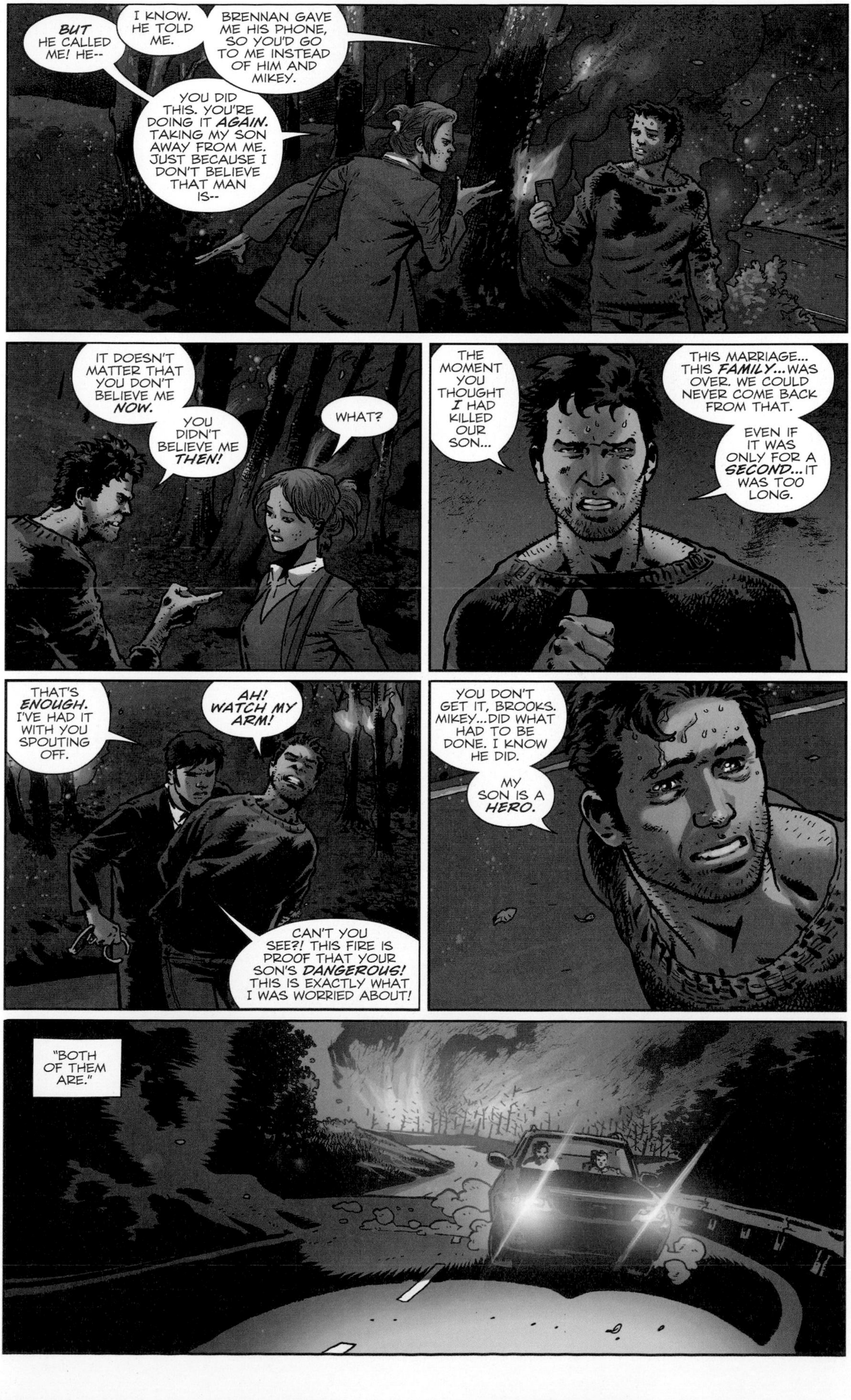
BUT HE CALLED ME! HE--
I KNOW. HE TOLD ME.
BRENNAN GAVE ME HIS PHONE, SO YOU'D GO TO ME INSTEAD OF HIM AND MIKEY.
YOU DID THIS. YOU'RE DOING IT AGAIN. TAKING MY SON AWAY FROM ME. JUST BECAUSE I DON'T BELIEVE THAT MAN IS--
IT DOESN'T MATTER THAT YOU DON'T BELIEVE ME NOW.
YOU DIDN'T BELIEVE ME THEN!
WHAT?
THE MOMENT YOU THOUGHT I HAD KILLED OUR SON...
THIS MARRIAGE... THIS FAMILY...WAS OVER. WE COULD NEVER COME BACK FROM THAT.
EVEN IF IT WAS ONLY FOR A SECOND...IT WAS TOO LONG.
THAT'S ENOUGH. I'VE HAD IT WITH YOU SPOUTING OFF.
AH! WATCH MY ARM!
CAN'T YOU SEE?! THIS FIRE IS PROOF THAT YOUR SON'S DANGEROUS! THIS IS EXACTLY WHAT I WAS WORRIED ABOUT!
YOU DON'T GET IT, BROOKS. MIKEY...DID WHAT HAD TO BE DONE. I KNOW HE DID.
MY SON IS A HERO.
"BOTH OF THEM ARE."

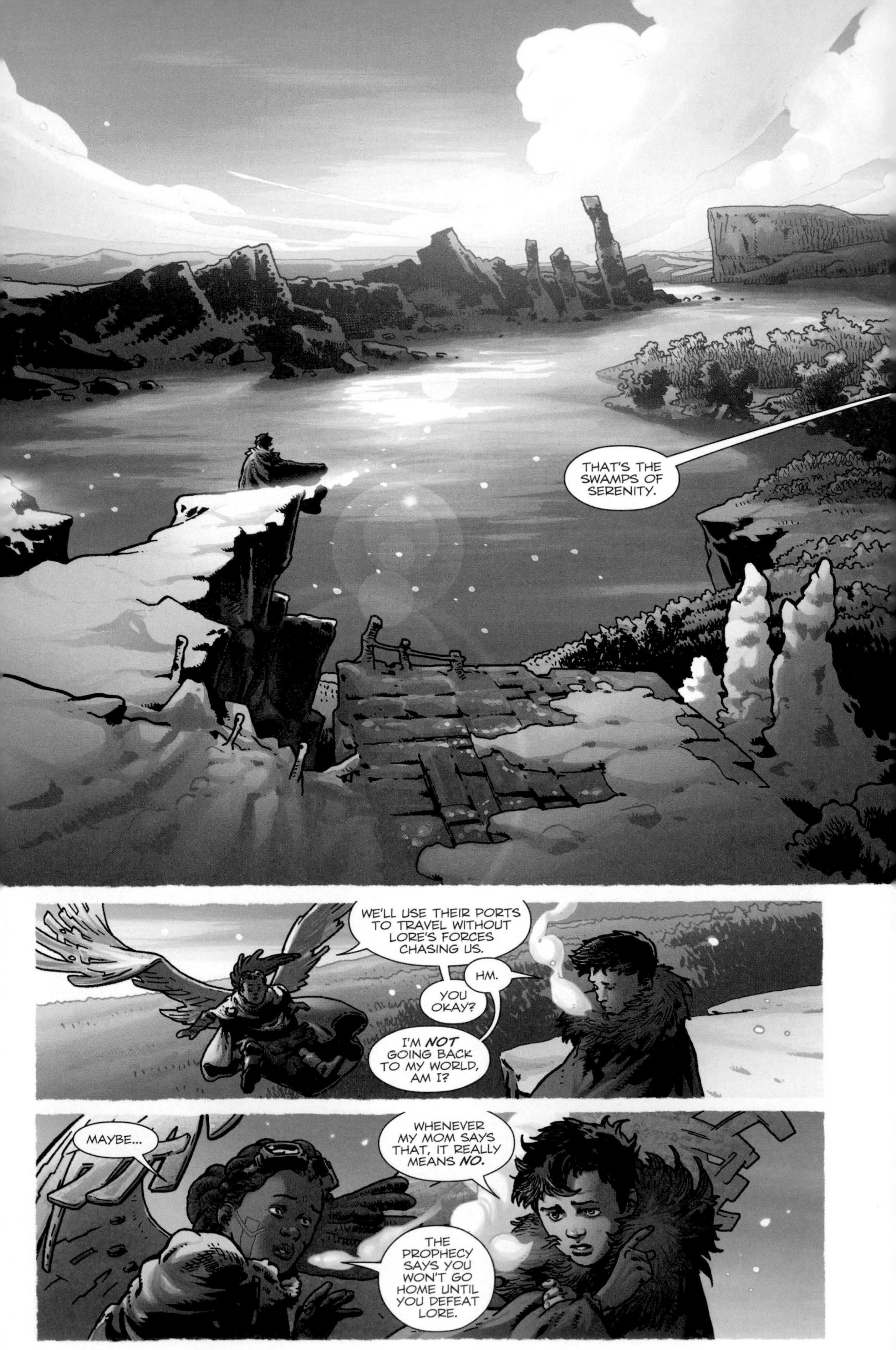
THAT'S THE SWAMPS OF SERENITY.
WE'LL USE THEIR PORTS TO TRAVEL WITHOUT LORE'S FORCES CHASING US.
HM.
YOU OKAY?
I'M **NOT** GOING BACK TO MY WORLD, AM I?
MAYBE...
WHENEVER MY MOM SAYS THAT, IT REALLY MEANS **NO.**
THE PROPHECY SAYS YOU WON'T GO HOME UNTIL YOU DEFEAT LORE.

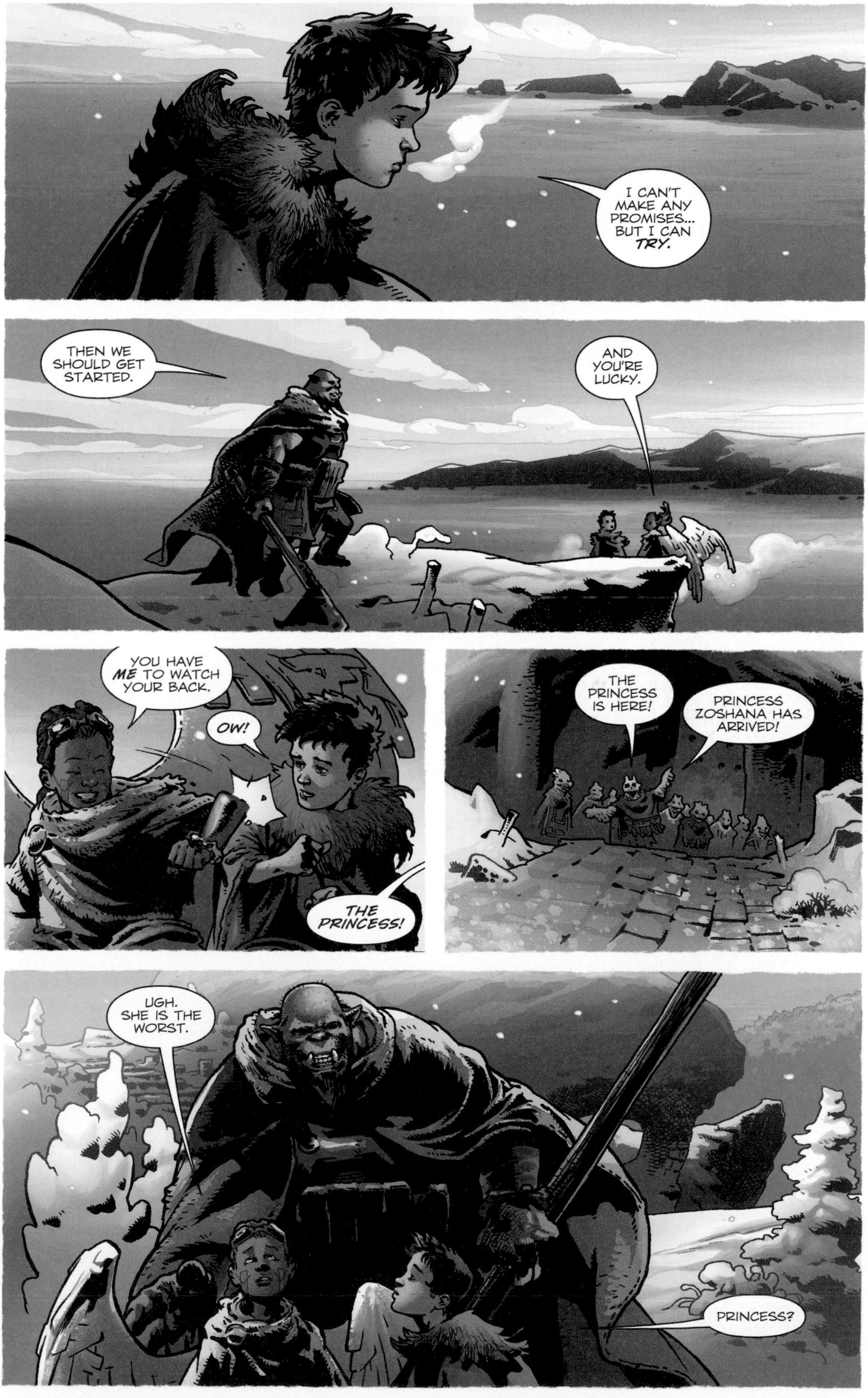
I CAN'T MAKE ANY PROMISES... BUT I CAN *TRY.*
THEN WE SHOULD GET STARTED.
AND YOU'RE LUCKY.
YOU HAVE *ME* TO WATCH YOUR BACK.
OW!
THE PRINCESS!
THE PRINCESS IS HERE!
PRINCESS ZOSHANA HAS ARRIVED!
UGH. SHE IS THE WORST.
PRINCESS?

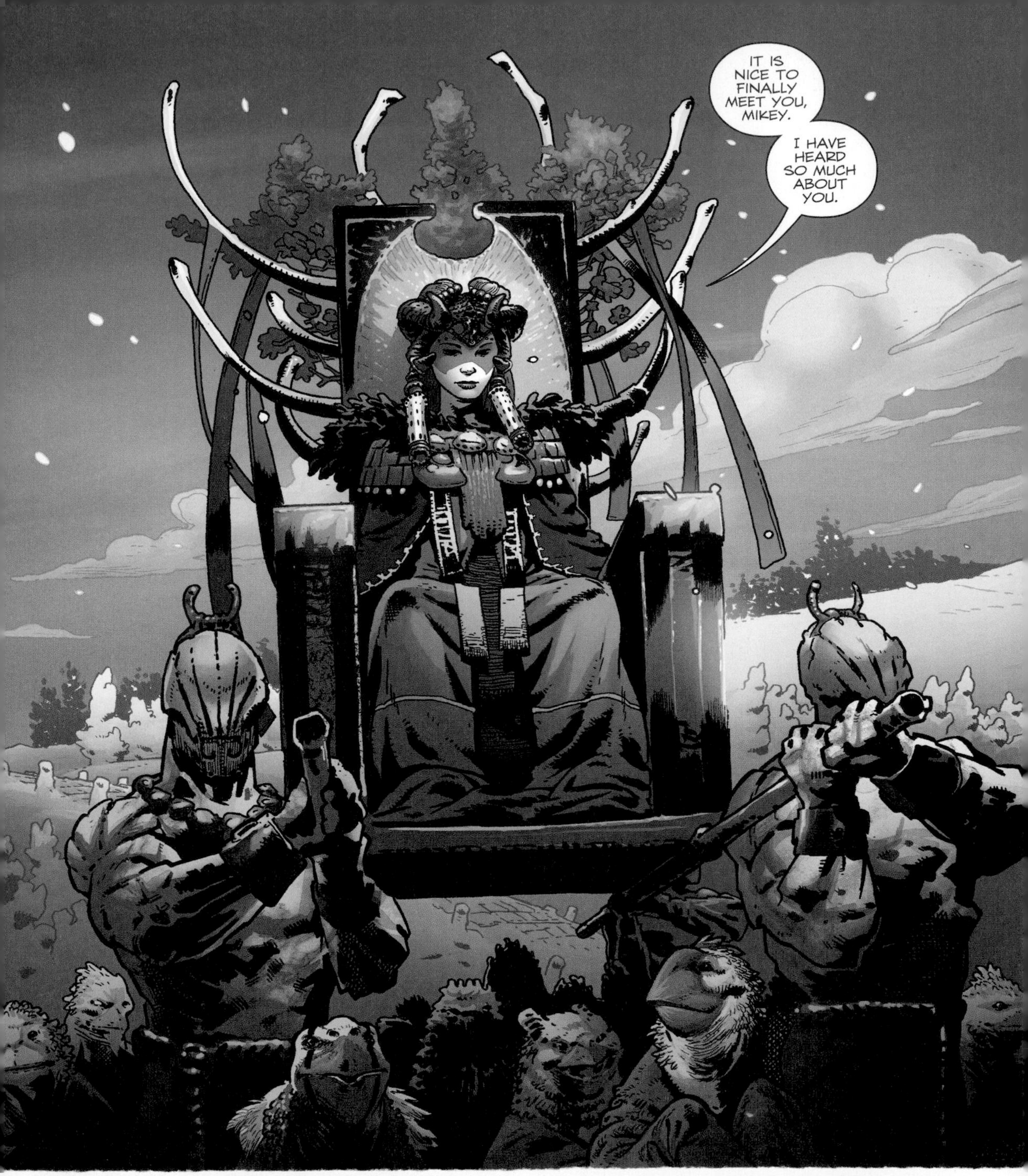
IT IS NICE TO FINALLY MEET YOU, MIKEY.
I HAVE HEARD SO MUCH ABOUT YOU.

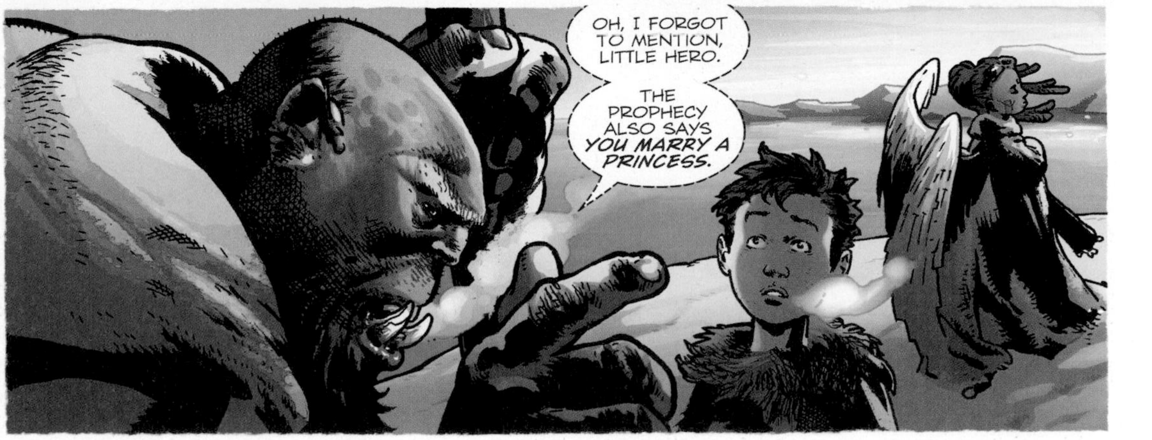
OH, I FORGOT TO MENTION, LITTLE HERO.
THE PROPHECY ALSO SAYS ***YOU MARRY A PRINCESS.***

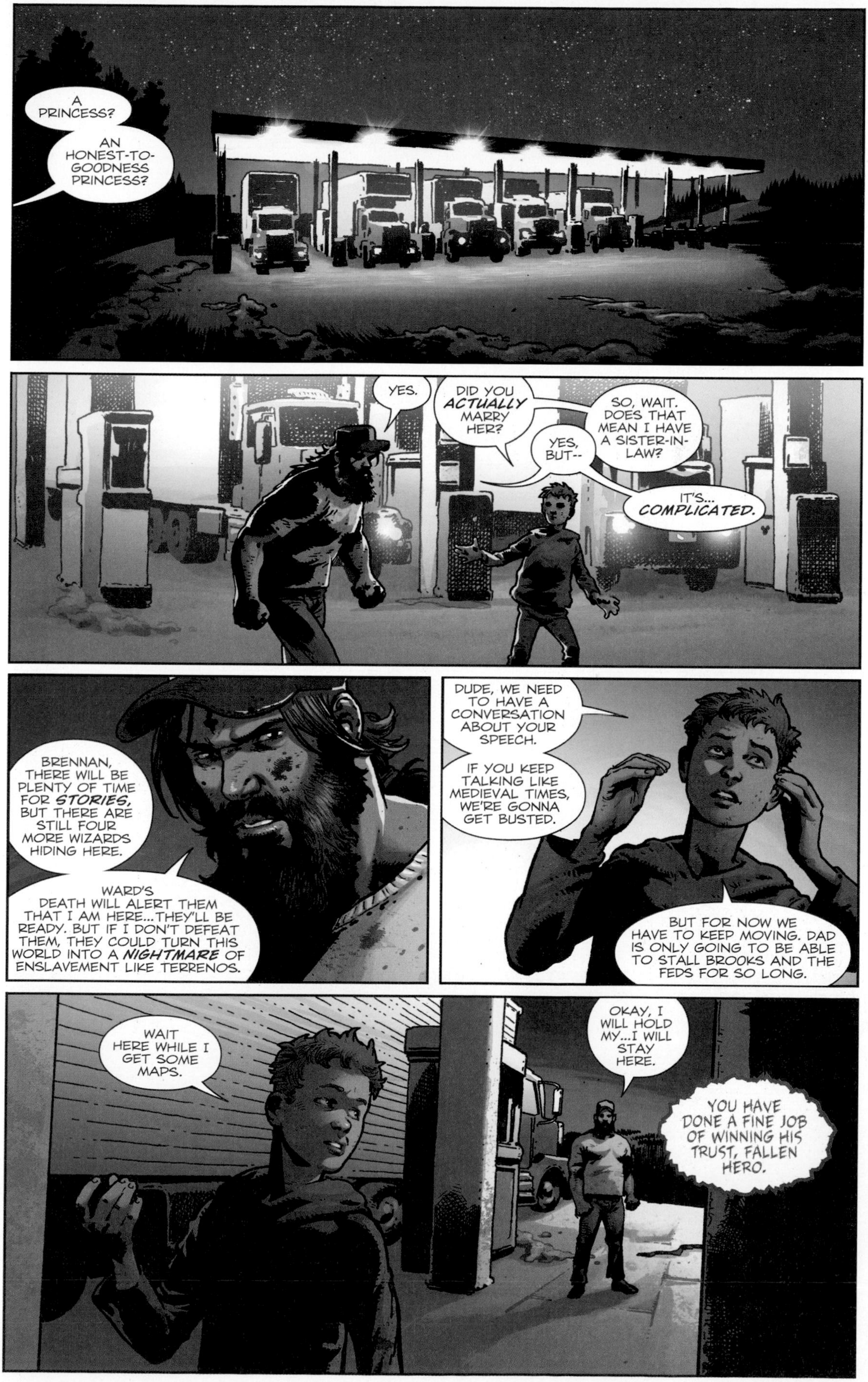
A PRINCESS?
AN HONEST-TO-GOODNESS PRINCESS?
YES.
DID YOU ACTUALLY MARRY HER?
YES, BUT--
SO, WAIT. DOES THAT MEAN I HAVE A SISTER-IN-LAW?
IT'S... COMPLICATED.
BRENNAN, THERE WILL BE PLENTY OF TIME FOR STORIES, BUT THERE ARE STILL FOUR MORE WIZARDS HIDING HERE.
WARD'S DEATH WILL ALERT THEM THAT I AM HERE...THEY'LL BE READY. BUT IF I DON'T DEFEAT THEM, THEY COULD TURN THIS WORLD INTO A NIGHTMARE OF ENSLAVEMENT LIKE TERRENOS.
DUDE, WE NEED TO HAVE A CONVERSATION ABOUT YOUR SPEECH.
IF YOU KEEP TALKING LIKE MEDIEVAL TIMES, WE'RE GONNA GET BUSTED.
BUT FOR NOW WE HAVE TO KEEP MOVING. DAD IS ONLY GOING TO BE ABLE TO STALL BROOKS AND THE FEDS FOR SO LONG.
WAIT HERE WHILE I GET SOME MAPS.
OKAY, I WILL HOLD MY...I WILL STAY HERE.
YOU HAVE DONE A FINE JOB OF WINNING HIS TRUST, FALLEN HERO.

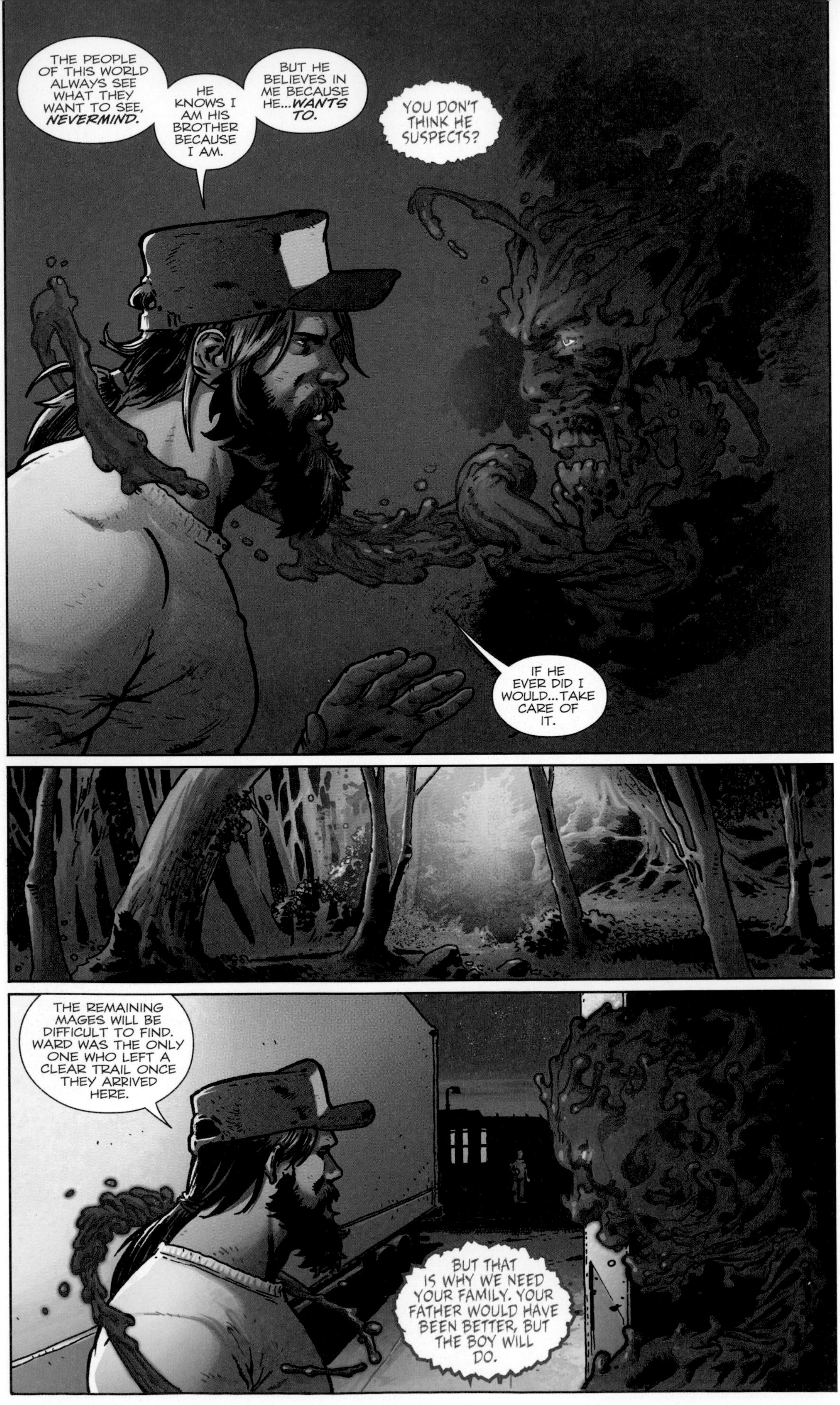
THE PEOPLE OF THIS WORLD ALWAYS SEE WHAT THEY WANT TO SEE, *NEVERMIND.*
HE KNOWS I AM HIS BROTHER BECAUSE I AM.
BUT HE BELIEVES IN ME BECAUSE HE...*WANTS TO.*
YOU DON'T THINK HE SUSPECTS?
IF HE EVER DID I WOULD...TAKE CARE OF IT.
THE REMAINING MAGES WILL BE DIFFICULT TO FIND. WARD WAS THE ONLY ONE WHO LEFT A CLEAR TRAIL ONCE THEY ARRIVED HERE.
BUT THAT IS WHY WE NEED YOUR FAMILY. YOUR FATHER WOULD HAVE BEEN BETTER, BUT THE BOY WILL DO.

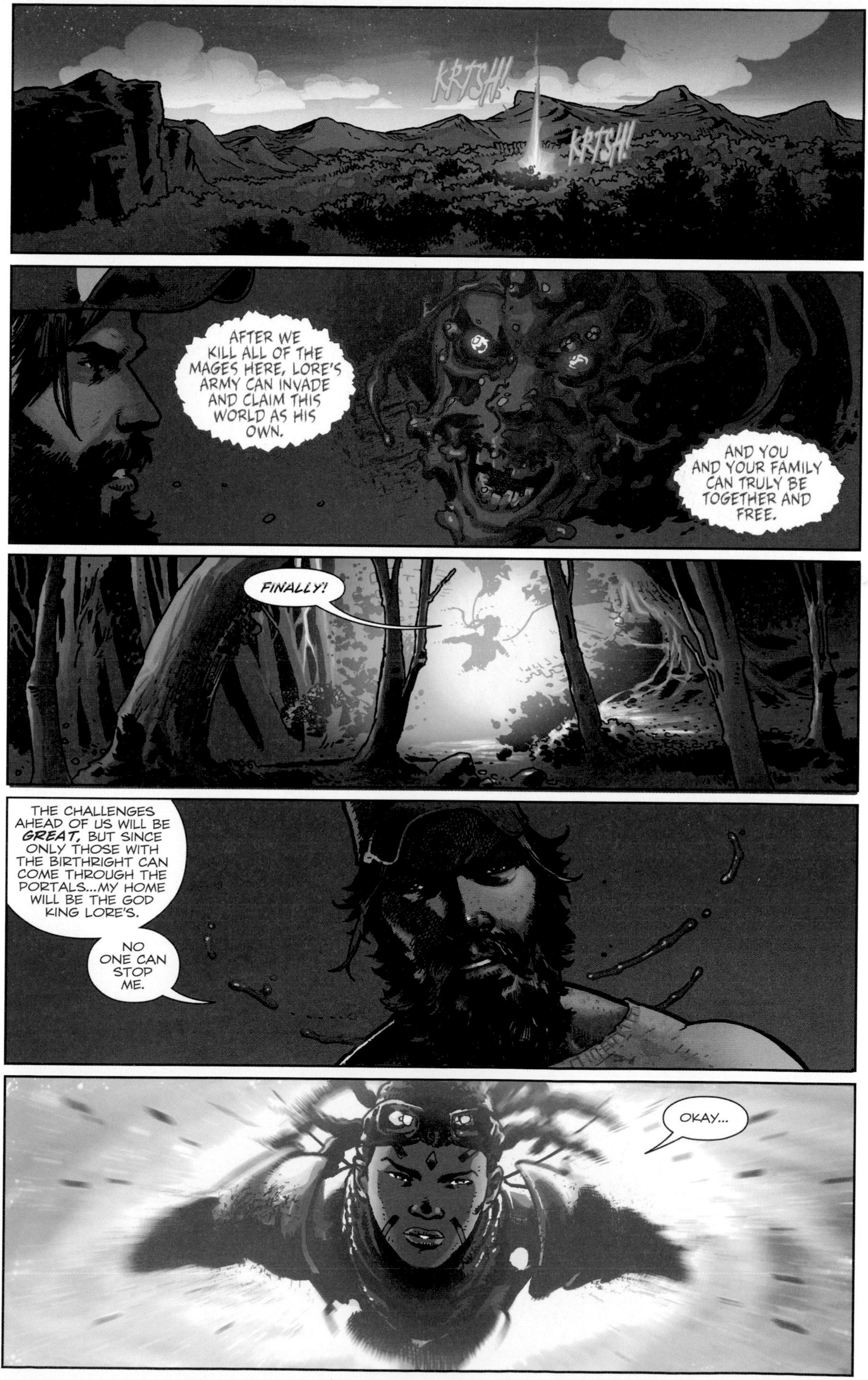
KRTSH!
KRTSH!
AFTER WE KILL ALL OF THE MAGES HERE, LORE'S ARMY CAN INVADE AND CLAIM THIS WORLD AS HIS OWN.
AND YOU AND YOUR FAMILY CAN TRULY BE TOGETHER AND FREE.
FINALLY!
THE CHALLENGES AHEAD OF US WILL BE GREAT, BUT SINCE ONLY THOSE WITH THE BIRTHRIGHT CAN COME THROUGH THE PORTALS...MY HOME WILL BE THE GOD KING LORE'S.
NO ONE CAN STOP ME.
OKAY...

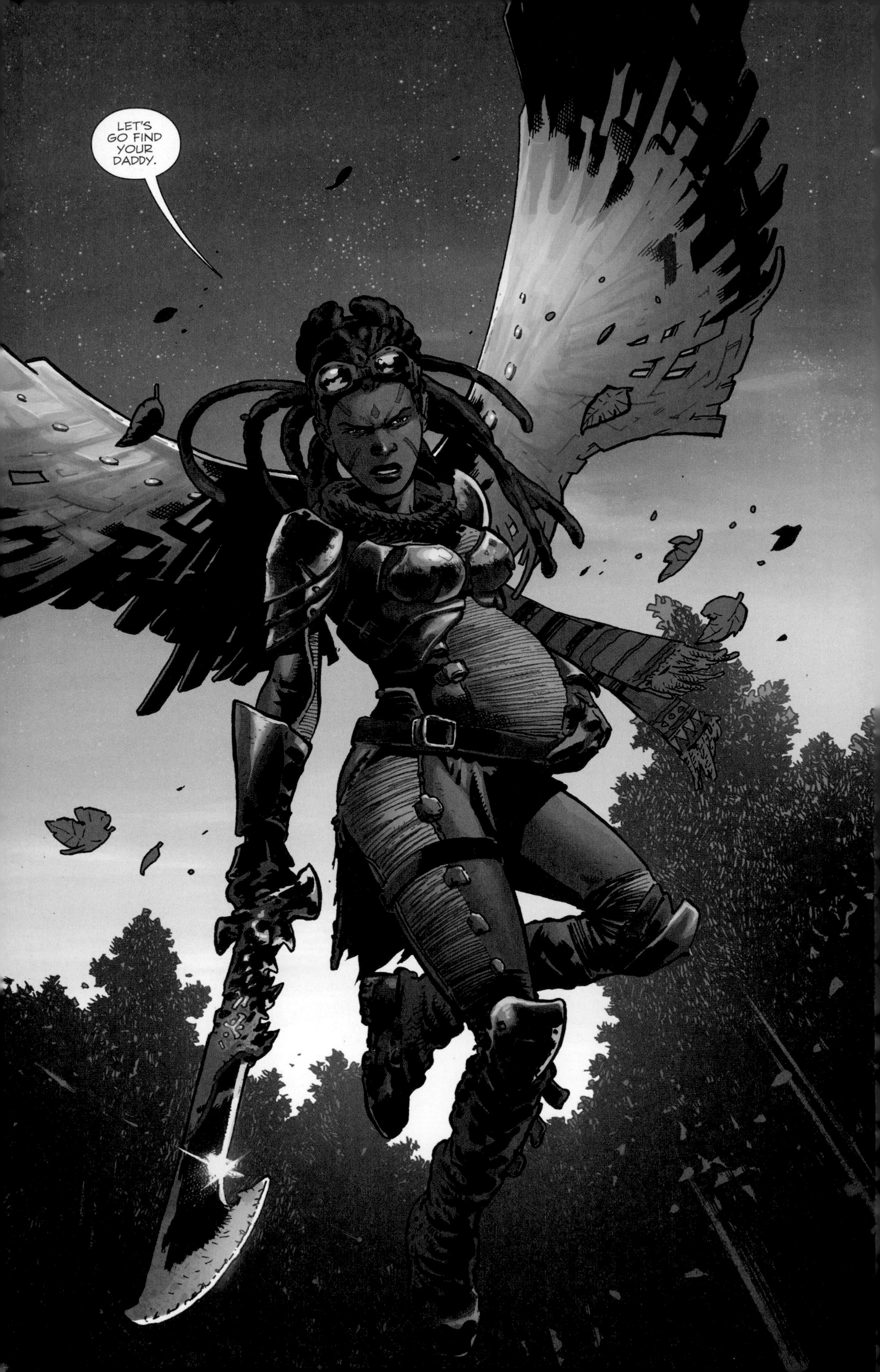
LET'S GO FIND YOUR DADDY.

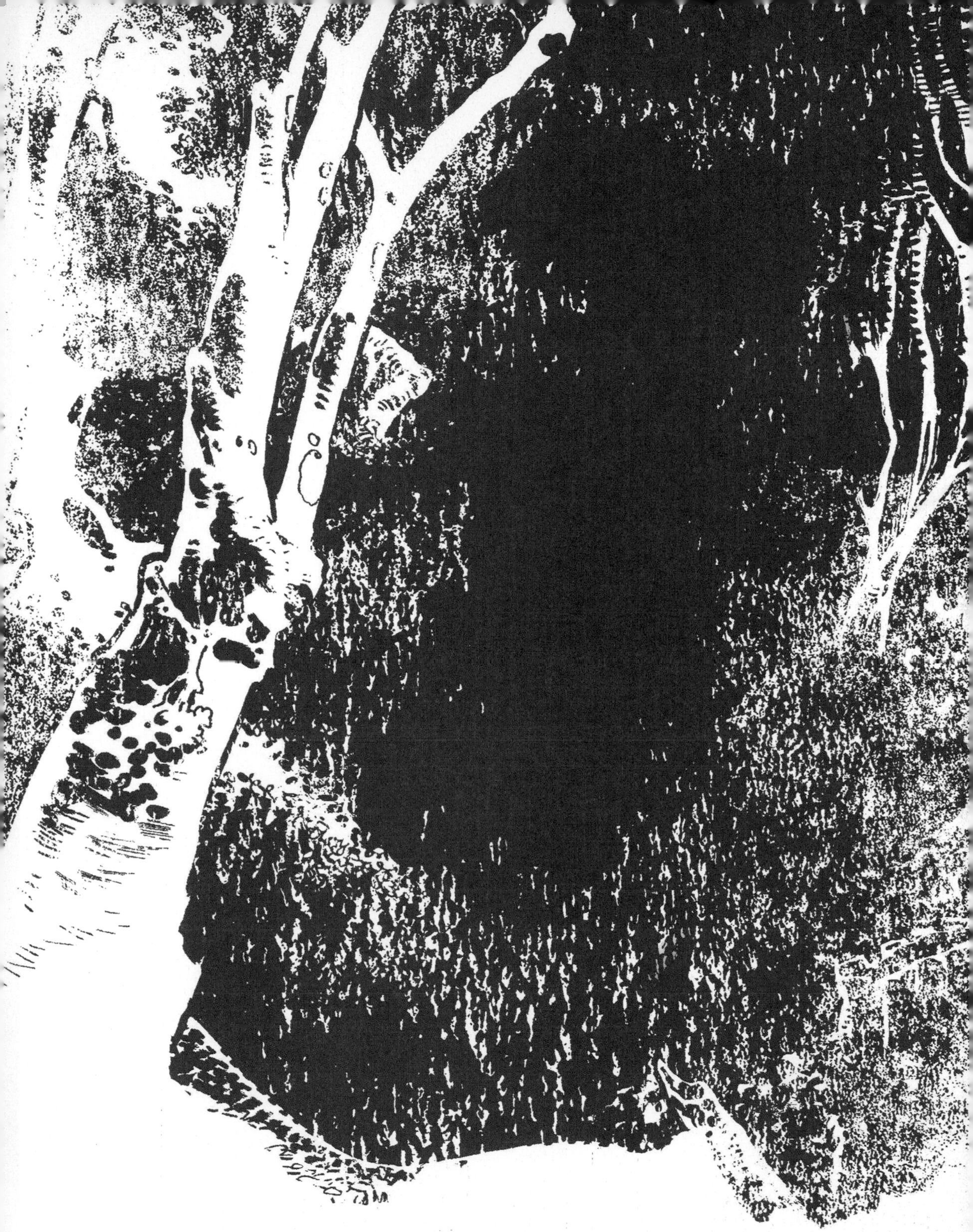

To be continued...

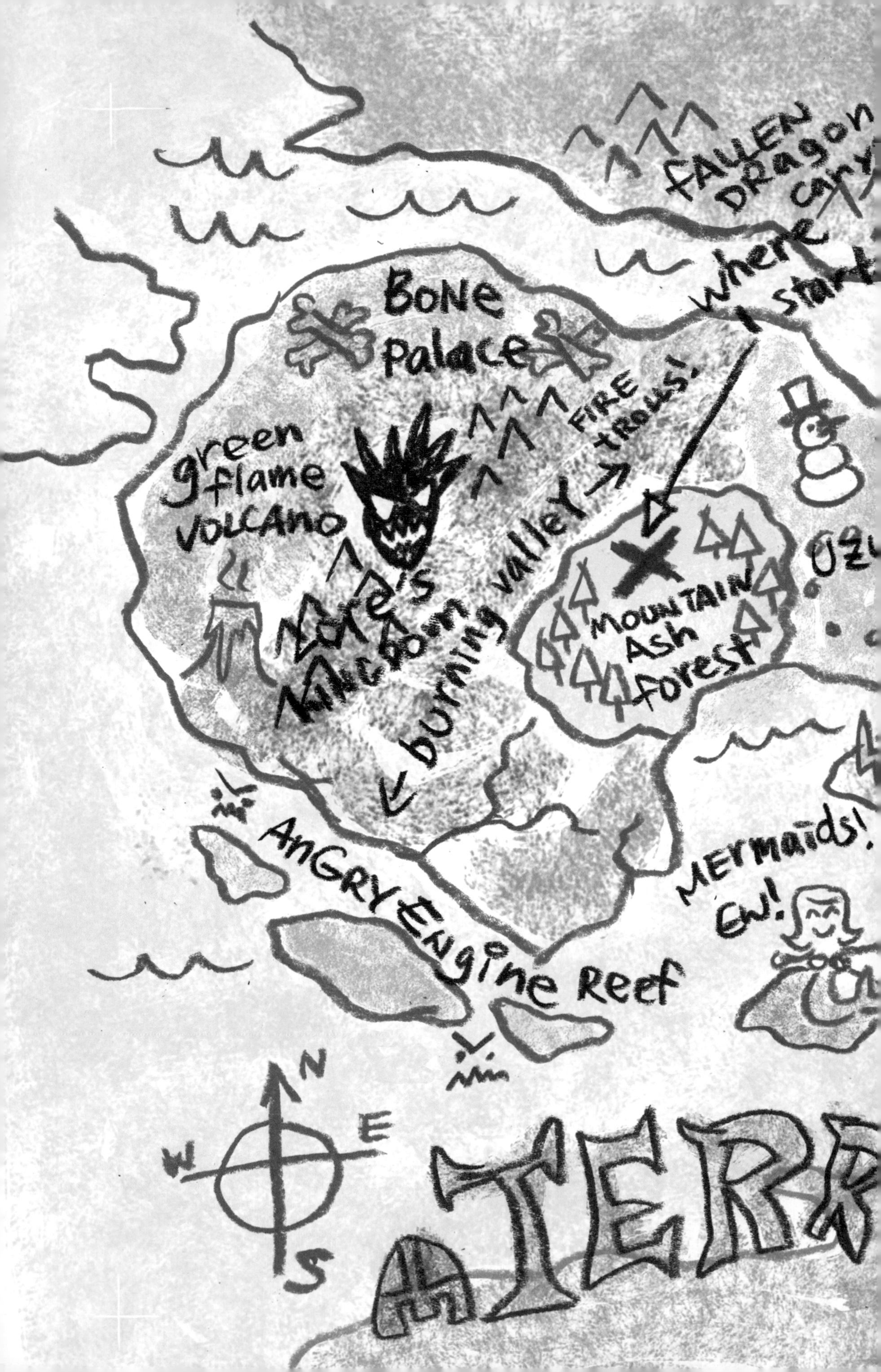

FALLEN DRAGON
where I start
BONE Palace
FIRE TROLLS!
green flame VOLCANO
Ogre's kingdom
burning valley
MOUNTAIN Ash forest
AnGRY Engine Reef
MERmaids! Ew!
N
E
W
S
TERR

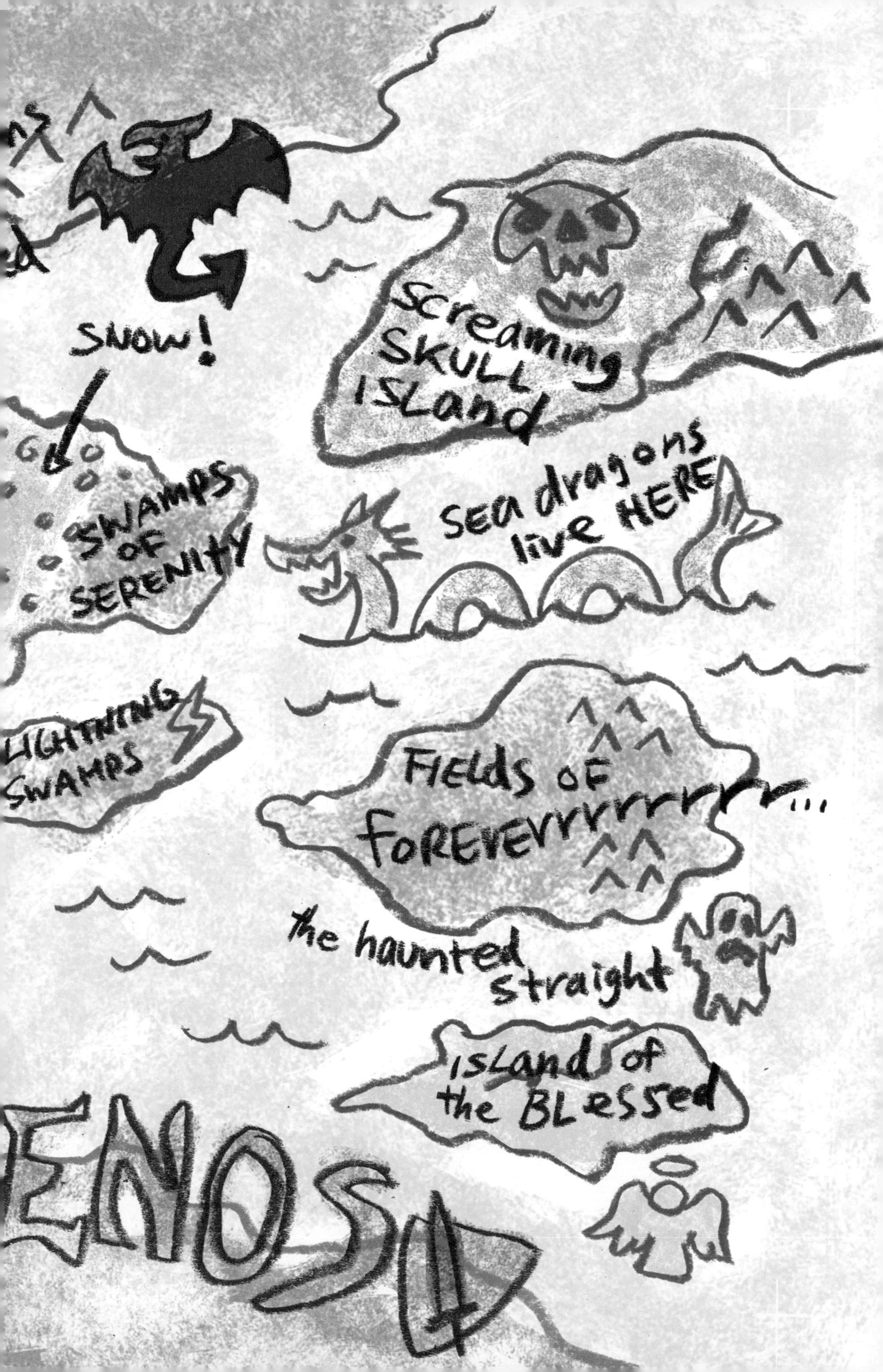
SNOW!
Screaming SKULL ISLand
SWAMPS OF SERENITY
Sea dragons live HERE
LIGHTNING SWAMPS
FIELDS OF FOREVERRRRRRRR...
the haunted straight
ISLand of the BLessed

"*Your fate awaits.*"

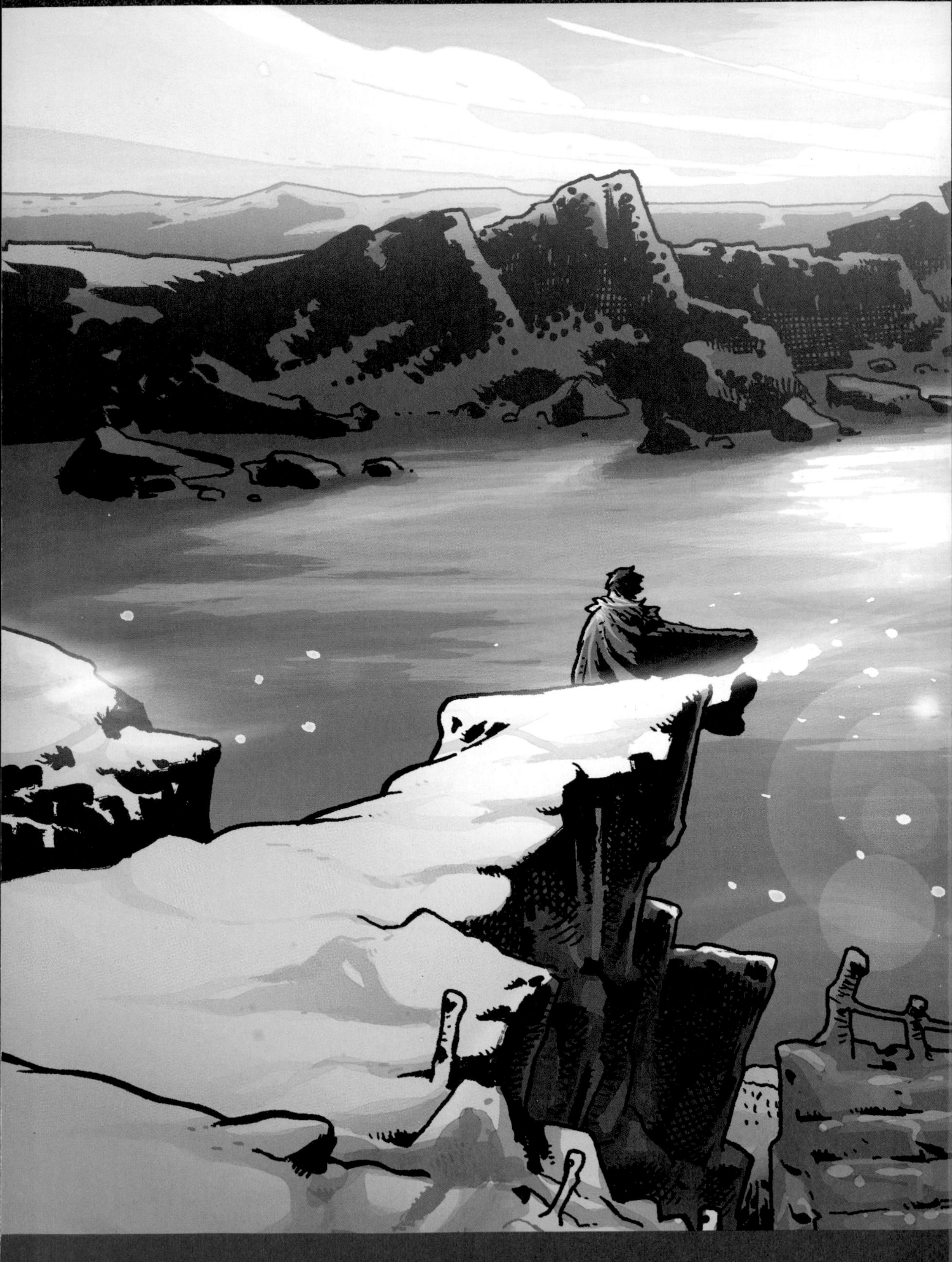

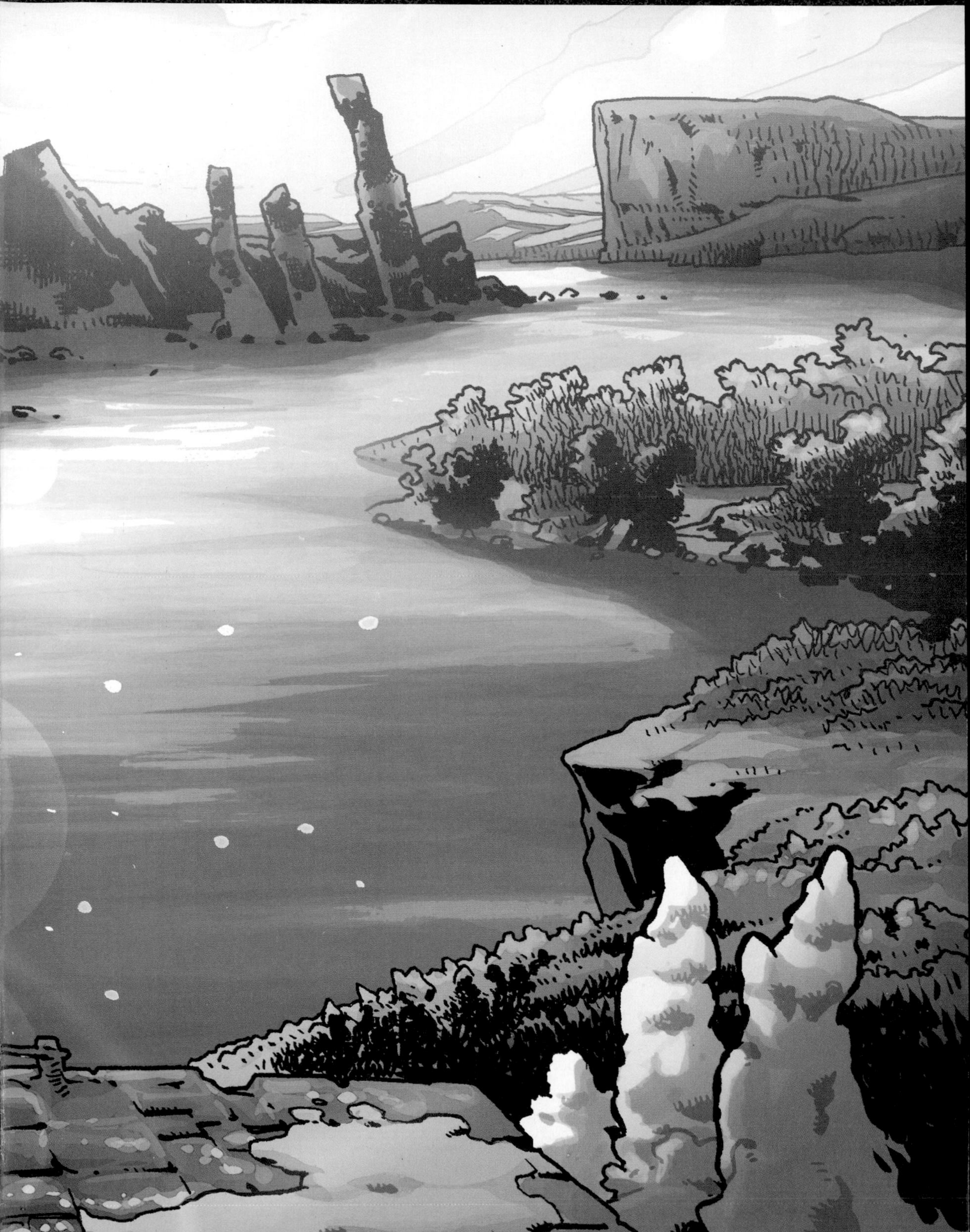

FOR MORE TALES FROM **ROBERT KIRKMAN** AND **SKYBOUND**

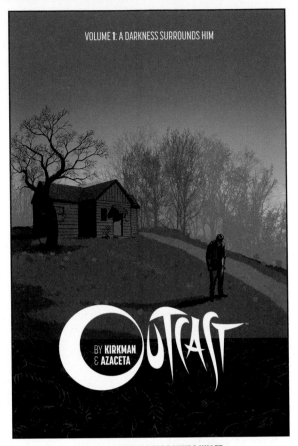

VOLUME 1: A DARKNESS SURROUNDS HIM
OUTCAST
BY KIRKMAN
& AZACETA

VOL. 1: A DARKNESS SURROUNDS HIM TP
ISBN: 978-1-63215-053-0
$9.99

CLONE
VOLUME 4
FOURTH GENERATION

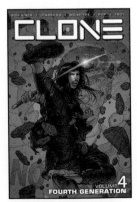

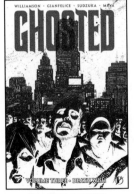

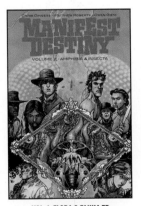

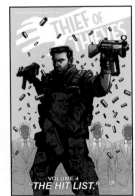

VOL. 1: FIRST GENERATION TP
ISBN: 978-1-60706-683-5
$12.99

VOL. 2: SECOND GENERATION TP
ISBN: 978-1-60706-830-3
$12.99

VOL. 3: THIRD GENERATION TP
ISBN: 978-1-60706-939-3
$12.99

VOL. 4: FOURTH GENERATION TP
ISBN: 978-1-63215-036-3
$12.99

GHOSTED
VOLUME THREE • DEATH WISH

VOL. 1: HAUNTED HEIST TP
ISBN: 978-1-60706-836-5
$9.99

VOL. 2: BOOKS OF THE DEAD TP
ISBN: 978-1-63215-046-2
$12.99

VOL. 3: DEATH WISH TP
ISBN: 978-1-63215-051-6
$12.99

MANIFEST DESTINY
VOLUME 2: AMPHIBIA & INSECTA

VOL. 1: FLORA & FAUNA TP
ISBN: 978-1-60706-982-9
$9.99

VOL. 2: AMPHIBIA & INSECTA TP
ISBN: 978-1-63215-052-3
$14.99

THIEF OF THIEVES
VOLUME 4
"THE HIT LIST."

VOL. 1: "I QUIT."
ISBN: 978-1-60706-592-0
$14.99

VOL. 2: "HELP ME."
ISBN: 978-1-60706-676-7
$14.99

VOL. 3: "VENICE."
ISBN: 978-1-60706-844-0
$14.99

VOL. 4: "THE HIT LIST."
ISBN: 978-1-63215-037-0
$14.99